ANGELS FOUND

THE Z-TECH CHRONICLES
BOOK FOUR

RYAN SOUTHWICK

ACKNOWLEDGEMENTS

The first (unpublished) edition of this book was three times the size it is now. I broke it into three different books, and will separate the acknowledgements appropriately.

Thanks as always to my mom — an avid reader and the first alpha reader for all my books. You're a trooper!

Huge appreciation to Ray, who has read each book in the series enough times to make anyone sick, but still comes back with valuable feedback.

To Keri, for your amazing feedback and support.

Shout out to Steven, for suggesting I break the book into smaller ones. I wasn't sure I could, but with your help, I not only managed to break it down into digestible chunks, but each book shines brighter because of it.

To José, who knocked it out of the park with the cover art yet again, and to April, who pulled it together with a great design.

And to Jiné and Laura, who continue to cheer me along, and without whom few would know my books even exist.

1

FRIGID DISCOVERY

CALUM MACLEAN BRUSHED THE SNOW from his faded map and swore. He looked around the mountain landscape one more time to make sure he hadn't missed anything, then cursed again.

None of the landmarks matched. That everything was buried under a dozen feet of snow didn't help.

He resisted the urge to tear the ancient parchment to pieces. Instead, Calum carefully slid it back into his bag. Obtaining this map had cost him more than anything else on his fruitless search for the mysterious Entity's origin — and that was saying something.

Four months had passed since he'd said goodbye to Don and the scant remains of their society — since he'd left the vampire Anne in Z-Tech's factory-fortress in San Francisco.

Since I had wrongly imprisoned the poor lass.

It still pained him to think of the torture he'd inflicted on Anne, when the real enemy had been standing by his side — the android, Zane, who'd murdered his crew almost to a man. Who'd been sent by Alvin Orwing to collect vampires for his insane army of super mercenaries, and, in doing so, had hastened the vampire apocalypse Calum's society had been trying to prevent.

He pounded his backpack with a growl, then uncurled his fists and took a deep breath.

What happened, happened. Getting upset won't help anyone.

But following the map might.

During the four months following the senseless slaughter of his men, Calum had scoured the farthest reaches of northeast Asia, braving blizzards, floods, starvation, bandits, and titanic language barriers with the intent of tracing the vampire scourge back through song and whispered lore, gleaned from remote villages untouched by modern man. Most of the local legends had proven false. But this one, which had led him to the map and ultimately here to this barren tundra, had rung true enough to risk cold and starvation.

And for all that, it seems I've hit a bloody dead-end.

Calum sat down in the snow and rummaged through his pack.

Seven trail rations left. More than enough to make it back to the nearest encampment.

Calling the leather-like strips of dried meat "rations" was a stretch even by his standards, which had significantly lowered in recent months.

But they were all he had, and his starved body knew it.

His mouth watered in anticipation of the first teeth-wrenching bite. While his aching jaw worked to masticate the dried strips, Calum let his eyes wander the featureless snowscape.

He stopped mid-chew. Sitting on the ground had changed his perspective just enough to pick out gentle rises and crests in the snow.

The remaining ration fell from his frozen lips in his haste to pull the map from his pack. Gloved fingers traced the faded rings, drawn close to one another.

One, two, three ...

There was definitely a correlation between the snow rises and the markings on the map.

Calum could think of only one way to discover if this was the site he had sacrificed so much to find.

He shed his pack, untied a small shovel, and started digging.

The sun had dipped behind the trees by the time he'd moved enough snow to safely reach the bottom of its depths. His back-breaking effort paid off when his shovel struck not stone, but metal. With renewed vigor, Calum cleared a space around the mysterious object.

Just as local legend had indicated, a four-foot, cylindrical metallic column protruded from the rocky floor, miraculously unblemished by time or the harsh elements.

Calum carefully climbed out of his icy trench. Snow covered his scraggly black beard, a condition he'd become accustomed to. He removed his fur-lined hat, letting long strands of curled, salt-and-pepper hair spill onto his shoulders, then unfastened the rolled-up tent from his backpack and set camp. Two more metal columns were likely nearby. He would need to verify their locations before his final excavation could begin, but working at night was dangerous, and not worth the risk. Not when he was so close.

These pillars have probably sat for thousands of years. One more night while I rest won't make a difference to them.

Calum felt the same mix of excitement and foreboding the engineers of the atom bomb must have experienced before testing their horrific invention. His journey was nearly over. Long-sought answers lay buried here. But would the knowledge be helpful? Or would it put the final seal on mankind's fate?

Such worries haunted his broken sleep in his wind-battered tent. Calum's mind jumped from one depressing scenario to the next. The worst by far would be not finding anything at all, and returning to the United States empty-handed. What would he do then? How could Calum — one old man caught in a world of technology that had long ago left him behind — fight a battle where global powers sought to exploit a plague that threatened their very existence? It was an absurd notion, yet hardly unprecedented, as clearly demonstrated by the nuclear powers during the Cold War.

Calum was already up and several feet into his next snow hole when the first rays of sun peeked over the distant mountaintops. By the end of that day, he had made three more gargantuan pits, but he had uncovered only one additional metallic column. The third pit had led only to an old tree stump.

High elevation, sore muscles, and old bones left him barely able to crawl into his tent. Calum slept better that night, however

— well enough that he was already knee-deep in a new excavation site by the time the sun had risen.

A discovery mid-day was cause for celebration. Calum pulled a small silver flask from his pack and allowed himself an entire mouthful. The scotch pleasantly burned its way down his throat and warmed his stomach.

He had found the third column.

Just as the map indicated, the three columns formed an equilateral triangle. The next hole, right in the center of the three, should be his last, though what he would find at the bottom was up for speculation.

Two hours and a small mountain of snow later, Calum found his answer.

Rocks.

A mound of them, each the size of his fist, placed roughly in the shape of a grave. Calum shivered. The significance wasn't lost on him. With grim determination, he began moving the rocks aside.

Several layers down, he noticed drawings etched into the surface of the less-weathered stones, each depicting a crude human skull baring elongated upper canines.

For better or worse, he was on the right track.

The sky turned orange, then purple. Calum stood waist-deep in the ancient grave, surrounded by walls of snow, and still he hadn't found an end to the skull-marked rocks. The stone walls of the grave looked abnormally smooth, as if cut by the finest modern machinery, yet a thick crust of orange and green lichen suggested it was many hundreds of years old.

Calum stopped working when the light became too dim to see by. He had few batteries for his flashlight and preferred to save them for emergencies. Even the hard-packed snow under his bedroll felt comfortable after spending the entire afternoon stooped in a pit, granting him a much-needed night of rest.

He met the morning head-on, ate his leathery rations, washed them down with a mouthful of snow, and was back in the hole before he had wiped the last of the sleep from his eyes.

By mid-day, the hole was over six feet deep. Every inch down was now a fight. The grave was eight feet long and five feet wide, which was large enough to work in, but meant he had to shuttle all the rocks to the surface to prevent rockslides while he worked. The only exceptions were some flatter stones he used to construct a rickety staircase. Each trip up the makeshift stairs to deposit an armful of rocks on the snow was a daring adventure.

Angry blisters on his hands and feet at the end of the day reiterated why Calum had never pursued archaeology. He treated his open sores with antibiotic ointment and wrapped them with clean strips of cloth. To have come this close to uncovering the mystery that had plagued his entire life, only to die at its door from a careless infection, would be intolerable.

The following morning was even harder work. The deeper his pit, the higher his makeshift steps had to be, and the worse his chances became of injuring himself from a fall. It was a three-day hike to the nearest settlement, longer if he sprained his ankle, so he took extra care, which meant lighter loads and slower climbing.

The smooth walls of the ancient grave towered far above him by the time the sky darkened.

I can make three more trips.

After that, Calum had two problems: a lack of light, and climbing out safely. The pit was almost twice his height. The wobbly stairs barely tolerated his weight as it was. Any deeper and he would need a ladder, be it tied rope or cobbled wood scavenged from beneath the snow. Neither was appealing, but he would have little choice if he wished to continue without falling and breaking his neck. His mind already toying with solutions, he started piling rocks into his pack for the next trip.

Calum froze. Beneath this last layer of rocks was a flat, smooth surface. He set his pack aside and brushed a thick layer of dirt away. Shiny metal glinted back.

It was all he could do to keep his measured pace while he continued the arduous rock-moving exercise.

Won't do the world any good if I kill myself because of a stupid mistake, he thought.

Yet twice he nearly tumbled because he was rushing like an overexcited twenty-year-old instead of the experienced sixty-year-old he was.

One more trip, then I'll call it for the evening.

He had made that same promise six trips ago. The dark purple sky challenged his meager night vision, but even in the dim light he could see that the metal surface extended all the way out to the pit walls. Calum carefully climbed down his teetering stairs —

The deafening squeal of rock-against-steel echoed from the grave walls. Before Calum knew what was happening, the stone steps disappeared from beneath him, and he fell. He twisted to brace for impact only to find the metal surface had vanished as well, leaving a black void that swallowed him and the unexcavated rocks whole.

•   •   •

Consciousness returned slowly. At first, Calum mistook the faint luminescence for pre-dawn light sneaking between the loose flaps of his tent. But once the haze finally lifted from his mind, he remembered the fall and sat up with a start.

Pain stabbed his right leg.

Calum screamed. His voice should have echoed from the walls, yet only eerie silence reported, as if he were in a room padded with acoustic tile.

When the stars eventually cleared from his vision, Calum looked around, taking care to keep his injured leg still. The small pile of fallen rocks he sat against was the only natural feature in the modest-sized room. The ceiling, walls, and floor were all crafted from a spongy black material. Although it was bright enough for Calum to see, he couldn't tell where the light originated, for he cast no shadow. It was as if the light came from the air itself. The only other features in the room were a narrow hallway before him, and the shiny metallic hatch above through which he had fallen, now sealed tight.

Fucking lovely, he thought. *A fly caught in the spider's web.*

His pack, which had fallen with him, contained only the bare essentials he'd needed while excavating. His food and trusty pistol were topside in his tent. If the proverbial spider didn't kill him, he would dehydrate or starve if he couldn't find a way out. Calum shifted again and grunted at a shooting pain.

Even if I do get out, I won't make it to a settlement in this condition.

But he had to try, which meant picking himself up.

Three times, the pain in his leg crumpled him back to the floor. On his fourth attempt, he managed to keep his balance long enough to examine the closed hatch. He found no obvious handles or controls.

He threw a rock at the hatch. The rock bounced from the metal surface with a *clang*, then landed on the spongy floor with maddening silence.

The hatch loomed a dozen feet above him. He had nothing to climb on, nor any sticks to pry it open with. The only items at his disposal were rocks, so he gathered a few and slowly limped toward the only exit.

Two steps into the narrow hall, a slight movement of air behind him caused Calum to turn.

A black wall made of the same spongy material now blocked his retreat. Calum inspected its edges, but could find no seams, as if the wall had been there all along.

Marvelous. Either I'm going crazy, or I've just fallen into a bloody magical labyrinth.

Progress down the hall was slow and excruciating. He leaned heavily on the spongy wall, taking each step with care to minimize the weight on his wounded leg. It was definitely broken. With every movement, jagged pieces of his fractured femur ground against each other. The vibrations shot up his spine and set his teeth on edge, but, as Calum saw it, he had little choice. He had no suitable materials to make a splint, his painkillers were aboveground with his pistol, and sitting in a corner waiting to die simply wasn't an option.

Calum stifled another cry when his weight settled on his injured leg, then continued on.

The eerie black corridor curved left, gently but steadily, giving the impression of a large, circular complex — easily a half-mile in diameter, if he had to guess. No offshoots had presented themselves. Given the mysterious closing wall from earlier, he suspected none would until he reached whatever destination the leprechauns who ran this place intended.

Step after painful step, his anxiety rose. The legends he'd uncovered during his research diverged on many points, but they all agreed this was a place to avoid, hence the thousands of skull-carved rocks barring the entrance. Despite months of searching for vampirism's unholy birthplace, without even his pistol for protection, Calum wished he were anywhere else.

A wall slid into place in front of him. Calum stumbled back onto his bad leg.

The pressure sent a shock of pain right up his spine. He crumpled in a heap, cradling his leg with both hands and swearing loudly. A wave of nausea nearly cost him his meager lunch.

When the pain had finally subsided, Calum opened his eyes and saw that a new opening had formed to his left, leading toward the inside of the circle.

"Stop fucking around!" he yelled.

There probably are *leprechauns running the place, the mischievous little gits.*

Using the wall as a brace, Calum struggled to his feet and limped deeper into the labyrinth.

Five turns later, Calum couldn't have said which direction he was facing if his life had depended on it. Worse than the disorientation, however, was the absolute silence. Even his footfalls were absorbed by the spongy surroundings. Calum hummed a tune to reassure himself that he hadn't somehow gone deaf.

The next turn revealed the first abnormality he had seen since leaving the entryway. A mound of shale had long ago poured in from a large crack along the ceiling and wall, blocking the lower half of the hallway. Calum carefully crawled over the loose pile, only to find another pile farther on, then yet another. Sweat dappled his brow from the pain of his broken leg by the time he reached the next turn.

Calum peered around the corner and softly swore. Where the previous hallways had been featureless, the expansive room before him was anything but. Like something out of a classic science fiction movie, vast consoles stretched the length of one curved wall, flashing faint lights of red and blue in seemingly random patterns. A window ran above it, giving a clear view of another room beyond. Calum stumbled over to stand between two consoles and pressed his hands to the glass.

His mouth fell open.

Hundreds … no, *thousands* of metallic capsules lay inside, each approximately nine feet tall and four feet in diameter. Most sat in organized rows, but several were scattered on the ground, as if a giant had shaken the entire room. Ceiling cracks abounded, burying many capsules in dirt and rock. A small information console sat at the base of each capsule. Many were lit with the same soft, seemingly random patterns as the large consoles in this room, though some were dark — notably the capsules that had shaken loose from their moorings, and those that had been damaged by the cave-ins.

Each capsule also had a window near the top, but Calum was too far away to see inside. Farther down, a capsule in the opposite room had fallen close to the window, but the capsule's viewport wasn't visible. Calum hobbled along the consoles to the far side of the room. Not daring to breathe, he leaned over a console and pressed his nose to the glass ...

He covered his mouth and quickly turned away. The hideous face inside that capsule would haunt however many dreams he had left in this world. Large bald head, purple leathery skin, huge eyes, grotesque fangs ... whatever lay inside that casket was not — nor ever had been — human.

An image flashed on the console beneath him, hovering in the air like a statue made of pure light.

Calum gasped.

Anne?

It couldn't be. Yet he had seen her nearly every day for over a month, chained spread-eagle to the wall in his prison. The hourglass figure of the female hovering on the console, made up of thousands of dim red lines of light, was definitely Anne's. A small blue dot sat just above her right breast. He leaned in for a closer look and was surprised to find it wasn't just a dot, but a fine mesh of even smaller lines.

Curious, Calum poked his finger through the floating image. The image zoomed in on the blue mesh above her breast to reveal what looked like an intricate circuit, rendered with the detail of an engineering schematic.

Everything about this set Calum on edge. According to Don, Anne and the rest of the Z-Tech staff had died during the assault on their factory, which he assumed had included the master vampire, Almos.

William had also perished, killed along with several of his lackeys, a few blocks away from the factory. They had all borne the signature burn wounds of the Dark Angel, suggesting the Z-Tech crew may not be as dead as everyone assumed.

The image before him, as surreal as it was, seemed proof that at least Anne had survived. The wireframe tissue around the implant pulsed as if it were alive, like he was watching her insides through some incredible remote x-ray machine. But if this place was the source of Almos' apocalyptic visions of the future — and Calum had every reason to believe it was — then why did this thing have direct access to Anne?

The first reason that came to mind was that Almos hadn't survived. Almos had once said that, upon a master vampire's death, the new master vampire would be selected from any of the previous master's sirelings. With Almos and William dead, the master vampire role could have passed down to Anne.

Calum stared at the intricate blue device embedded below her collar bone.

Is that why Anne was chosen?

As much as Calum admired the spirited lass, she hardly struck him as a fierce commander who could lead the dark army to victory.

But this device ...

He looked again at the panel. He couldn't decipher any of the symbols, but he wouldn't get anywhere gaping like a dullard, either. Calum removed a glove and touched a symbol at random, praying to whichever saint watched over him this day that it wouldn't trigger a doomsday explosion.

Too late, he realized the stupidity of touching his bare flesh to the machinery that may have created the entire vampire race. His finger sank into the seemingly hard surface like water, but the surface hardened when he tried to pull his finger free.

Oh, bloody hell ...

Calum tugged and tugged until he thought his finger would pop from the socket, but it was no use. The console had him, and it wasn't letting go.

A humanoid image appeared next to Anne's, composed of the same red lines, but lacking the blue dot on its chest. What began as a vague outline rapidly filled in with details. Before long, Calum was staring at another x-ray-like moving picture. This one was much more active than Anne's: its stomach churned steady and insistent, its heart beat rapidly, and its lungs expanded and contracted with quick breaths.

All in perfect timing with his own.

Oh no you fucking don't!

Calum fumbled for a rock in his pocket with his free hand and poised it over his trapped finger. The console may already have infected him with the vampire virus, but if there was even a sliver of a chance that it hadn't, he would gladly lose a digit or end his own life than become a thrall to some unknown being. Alien, machine, or whatever the hell it was, Calum MacLean would not become the winning pawn for the wrong player.

Two new images appeared, one next to each of his and Anne's projections, halting his downward blow. Blurry pictures flashed in rapid succession. Most passed by too quickly to see, but a few next to his own projection lingered long enough for Calum's breath to catch. His parents, his deceased wife, their dearly departed child ...

It was sifting through his and Anne's memories. On his side were things both familiar and long forgotten, and in no particular order. The murder of his family was followed by the loss of his first tooth, then his second dog, Toolie, from his teenage years. Anne's progressed in similar, disorderly fashion — flashes of what must have been her family, old, then young, then somewhere in between. A few images he recognized: Doris, Hal's Diner, Charlie, Don, Almos, and even himself.

The rapid slideshow stopped on his image, which appeared to be Anne's memory of him while she had been chained to the wall, when she'd first awoken in his prison.

How she must have hated me then.

Calum couldn't imagine being shot, kidnapped, tortured, locked in a dark room for a week, seeing the person he loved be mutilated during a daring rescue, and yet still risk life and limb to make sure his captors were taken to safety.

Anne had done all that and more. His life, and those of his crew she and Zima had been able to rescue, was a debt that Calum could never repay. This suicide mission, in a way, had been an attempt to atone for his mistake, paying it forward to the world in the form of salvation from the threat of extinction.

It's a pity my quest has to end here.

He raised the stone high.

The memory slideshow next to his own projection paused. It was an image of Anne, taken from the same moment she had awoke in his dungeon, but from Calum's perspective. Both of the slideshows began to advance in tandem, like watching the same movie from two different cameras. Faster and faster they went. Calum relived shooting her to save Almos, the interrogation sessions, the showdown with Zane, their hasty, but amicable, parting —

The slideshows disappeared, leaving Calum momentarily disoriented.

What he saw next, he liked not at all. Both projections zoomed in to the areas above their right breasts. Anne's view once again showed the interwoven mesh of blue circuitry. Calum's began as only red outlines of muscle, but blue lines rapidly filled the space, tracing similar shapes and patterns to Anne's.

In a panic, Calum dropped the rock and felt his chest for a lump.

Nothing.

Yet, he realized with growing horror.

Lines appeared, then changed, then reappeared in different configurations, all so quickly that it made his head spin.

It's sizing me up, tailoring the design for me, or for its own purposes.

Calum took another rock from his pocket. He stared at his finger, gathering the courage to do what needed to be done. Changes to the blue-lined device in his projection were slowing, showing a complex device similar to Anne's, yet notably different in places.

The design was almost finished.

Muttering a quick prayer to the saints for strength, Calum brought the rock down on his trapped finger with all his might.

Pain blinded him, brought him to his knees. Calum shook his head and gave an experimental tug. The agony of moving his broken digit made him gag, but the console still held him tight. Calum forced himself to his feet.

He had a job to do.

He attempted to raise the rock for another blow, but quickly discovered that his other hand was now trapped in the console as well. It had swallowed his hand up to his wrist when he had accidentally fallen against the console.

"No, no, *no!*"

Calum pulled furiously, wrenching this way and that. He spat. He snarled. He swore. He growled like a cornered mongrel. The demonic console weathered it all in stolid silence.

The blue lines on his projection settled, then stopped. A soft hum came from the section of console before him. The black material parted, and a silver object rose from its depths. It was thin and metallic, about one-inch square, with fine filament wires protruding everywhere.

Calum bared his teeth, ready to bite the infernal contraption in half.

Electricity jolted his arms, causing his muscles to contract. He slammed down onto the surface, which put the silver device a few inches below his right clavicle. Searing pain erupted from his chest. Calum screamed, his face inches from the projection of himself. The blue lines overlaid with a purple copy, merging until they were indistinguishable from one another.

His last conscious thought, oddly, was wondering if the agony he felt was anything close to the torture he'd inflicted on Anne when he'd thrice shot her with silver.

2

EDEN

ANNE WOKE WITH A START and sat bolt upright. Unlike her usual nightmares, Calum's screams refused to fade. She pulled her knees up to her chest and clutched two fistfuls of hair.

It seemed so real ...

Charlie sat up with her and turned on the light, which, even on the lowest setting, made her squint.

"What is it?"

"Hopefully nothing." Anne smiled warmly and kissed his cheek. "Go back to sleep."

Charlie glanced at the clock, his thick, dark hair sticking out at all angles, and shook his head. "The alarm will be going off soon anyway." He took her hand. Lines of concern etched his forehead and his thick eyebrows. "Tell me about it?"

Anne caressed his chest and pushed him back down. "I'd rather take advantage of the early wakeup call."

He frowned, but his hazel-green eyes eventually softened. "You know, I almost miss the days before your sexual awakening."

Anne rolled on top of him and pressed her bare chest to his, then nuzzled his neck with a soft brush of her lips. His human scent was intoxicating. She purred softly and began to nibble, careful to keep her rapidly extending fangs from breaking his skin.

Charlie had allowed her to bite him once, and that was when they'd discovered the hard way that sex and her vampire thirst were a terrible combination. Potent by themselves, together they had overwhelmed Anne's senses and driven her into an uncontrollable frenzy. She still couldn't remember exactly what had happened that night. In his cyborg body, their intense lovemaking session wouldn't have been an issue, but as a fragile human, she had left Charlie with scratches, bite marks, and three broken ribs. They'd agreed to keep feeding and romance separate after that.

Anne pushed the unpleasant memory aside and slid her hand down his washboard stomach.

"All right," Charlie said with a laugh. "Have it your way, Miss Insatiable. Let me at least brush my teeth."

"Fine." Anne rolled aside to let him out of bed. "But hurry back. I only get you every third night, and I don't want to waste a single minute."

She watched his naked, toned form retreat to the restroom, enjoying the show every step of the way.

Her smile faded once the door closed. Anne hated dodging his questions like that, but she had an uneasy feeling that her nightmare of Calum hadn't been a dream at all. The Entity's thoughts were normally sporadic and muted, so much so that Anne had learned to tune them out over the last several months.

Ever since the Z-Tech factory's destruction and their escape here to Montana, however, Mark, Zima, Cappa, and especially Charlie had become jumpy and inquisitive whenever she mentioned anything Entity-related. That often led to long, uncomfortable, and ultimately unhelpful conversations. So, right or wrong, Anne had stopped bringing it up months ago.

This morning was different. The only person the Entity had ever projected through their mental bond, other than Anne, was Almos. She hadn't heard from or about Calum since Don's visit to Z-Tech with his niece, Rose. The Scottish vampire hunter was supposedly scouring the world for clues to the origins of vampirism — a quest Anne hadn't put much stock into until just now.

She shuddered. Calum may have actually found what he was looking for: The Entity itself. Judging by his screams, the meeting hadn't gone in his favor.

Anne flopped onto her pillow and closed her eyes. Despite their rocky start, she liked Calum, and respected his commitment to the cause. For his sake, she hoped she was wrong, and that his misery was just the tail end of some post-traumatic nightmare from her incarceration in Calum's dungeon.

There was only one way to know, however. Reluctantly, Anne tuned into the Entity's stream of consciousness. She searched for hints of Calum among its constant insistence for Anne to shut down her implant's defensive program, which ran twenty-four-seven, that prevented the Entity from exerting its will over her. It wanted her to embrace her role as the new master vampire and aid its mission to expand their numbers.

Anne also sensed its frustration. The defensive program not only protected her from the Entity's influence, but it blocked her and the Entity's access to the rest of the vampires by scrambling the part of her brain connecting her to the hierarchy.

Anne didn't know how many vampires there were now — and neither did the Entity, for that was the number-one question in its thoughts. She and the others from Z-Tech had cut all ties with their previous lives. What Anne didn't know, she couldn't share with the Entity, and she intended to keep it that way.

The other vampires knew Anne was alive, of that she was certain. Tim — her sireling and direct descendant — was likely safe from the debilitating effects of her defensive program, since she had all but severed their mental bond early on.

Not so for William's bloodline. Anne couldn't imagine how they had organized themselves after William's death. All of his direct descendants' bonds would have transferred to her, making Anne their new sire and master.

As far as she knew, her defensive program affected everyone in the hierarchy with a direct or indirect connection to Anne. Every vampire of William's bloodline who had been aboveground when she'd assumed control would have suffered a debilitating headache until those directly connected to Anne were properly shielded to break the chain. At best, that meant Tim and the rest of the Resistance had had an easy time picking off the incapacitated vampires. At worst, William's Firsts had quickly been moved underground and now had even more reason to hate Anne.

Except they don't hate me.

They couldn't hate her, no matter what Anne did. She was their sire, their reason for being. They would do anything she asked with a smile, eager to please their master.

Wouldn't that be a cruel irony? Forced to love the very reason you're stuck in a pit for the rest of eternity.

Fortunately, vampires who were descended from her own mutated bloodline, such as Tim and his sirelings, felt no such adoration for their sires, which left them with their own free will — and, most importantly, their compassion for humanity.

The truth was that Anne had no idea what had happened to William's vampires, nor at this moment did she care. The Entity's thoughts were devoid of Calum now. She let its ramblings settle back into the recesses of her mind.

The bathroom door opened, blinding her with bright light until Charlie hastily turned it off.

"Sorry," he said, climbing in beside her.

Anne wrapped herself around him, enjoying the return of his warmth, but her passion had fled. He must have sensed her change in mood, for he simply held her close. The sound of his breathing was a comfort; the steady beat of his heart a sad reminder of what she had lost, yet a joyous celebration of the biological body Charlie had reclaimed.

A shiver ran through him. Charlie was cold, and her chill body wrapped around him only made things worse.

"Sorry," she mumbled into his chest, but couldn't bring herself to disentangle from his reassuring embrace.

And his delicious scent.

"Don't be sorry. That's why we have this."

Charlie clicked the switch on the electric blanket controls. Warmth soon flowed through the filaments, and his shivering subsided.

"See? All better." Charlie rubbed her back. "Ready to talk?"

Anne sighed. Although it would prematurely end their enjoyable morning, her dream of Calum wasn't something she should keep to herself.

She reluctantly filled him in on what she remembered of her disturbing vision. Charlie listened in silence, although his heart rate increased, and his muscles tensed.

"You're sure it was Calum?" Charlie said when she'd finished.

"Positive. I could feel him, like …" Anne settled into him, unable to finish her thought.

"Like another vampire."

"No, this was different. I-it's hard to explain. It was Calum, but his thoughts were … constricted, like the transmission was being run through a bad connection."

"But why were you able to feel his presence at all? Your implant is supposed to prevent that."

And there it is.

Charlie's voice was steady, but it held an accusatory tone that made Anne feel guilty.

"I … I don't know," she said. "I wish I could tell you more."

"Do you know his location?"

"No. Like I said, it was a fuzzy connection."

"How about —"

"Charlie, please! I've told you everything. If I remember anything else, you'll be the first to know, okay?" Anne kissed his cheek to take some of the sting from her words. The romantic mood was shot, but the morning might yet be salvageable. "How about some breakfast? I'll make you something extra special before the others get up."

Charlie brightened.

Bingo.

Ever since his jump back into his human body, Charlie had been unable to resist the offer of a home-cooked meal. Especially Anne's.

She hopped out of bed and grabbed her fluffy robe from the closet. Even with the lights off, to Anne's abnormally large, black eyes, the room was bright as day. Her deathly pale skin, webbed with faint blue veins, reflected in the closet mirror door like a specter in the night. Auburn hair fell almost to her shoulders. She hadn't cut it since it had burned off in the fire, which, even after months of growth, had left the fringes downy-soft and feathered in a way that Zima and Charlie claimed was attractive. She donned her robe and cinched it around her narrow waist, accentuating her hourglass curve between her ample breasts and full hips, then tossed Charlie's striped pajamas over to him.

"Come on, mister," Anne said. "You're in for a treat, but only if we beat the crowd."

"True. If Mark shows up, I'll be lucky to get a bite."

Anne watched him dress with unabashed appreciation, even waggled her eyebrows, which made him smile. When he finished, Charlie slipped his arms around her waist.

"I'm sorry for the interrogation," he said, his warm breath pleasant on her ear.

Anne draped her arms around his neck. "It's all right, I just ... I thought we'd put that behind us. But every time I bring something up —"

"I jump down your throat, I know. Old habits die hard, I guess." Charlie kissed her tenderly. "I don't want you to feel like you have to hide anything from me. From now on, I'll try to keep my curiosity in check. If I get aggressive, you have my permission to bite me to calm me down. Deal?"

"That depends," Anne said with a toothy grin. "Is your offer retroactive? A snack would be nice before making your breakfast."

"Sadly, I can't afford to be high today. This morning is our first round of negotiations with Big Sky Foods, the supermarket chain. I need my wits intact."

"That's wonderful! So they liked your chocolate samples?"

"Yes, but they're high-end retailers, so they want a tour of our factory to make sure our quality process is up-to-snuff, and that we can keep up with demand for their twenty-eight stores across the state."

"Well, no matter how it turns out, I'm proud of you. I know it's not weapons or global electronics manufacturing, but the art of making quality chocolate is still a noble profession."

"A little too noble, maybe. I keep eating the merchandise."

Anne slid her hands down his firm back. "If it's any consolation, it doesn't show."

"You can thank Mark for that. Training with him is like an Olympic event, but the guy never breaks a sweat."

"And you wonder why I used to just watch you practice when I was human."

"Not anymore," Charlie said.

A stomach gurgle made them both look down.

Charlie raised an eyebrow. "Was that you or me?"

"Hopefully you, for your sake." Anne took him by the hand and opened the door. "Let's go fix that, tiger."

Faint light from behind the hallway's closed drapes announced dawn's approach. Unlike their dearly departed Z-Tech factory, their country mansion had many windows, each with thick curtains and several layers of tinting to prevent Anne's sensitive skin from burning when she passed by.

Also unlike Z-Tech, the mansion's décor was suited more toward living than working. Plush floral carpet runners lined beautiful hardwood floors. Serene landscape paintings decorated the walls, softly lit by brass sconces that flickered as if alive with real flame. Living rooms were comfortable and spacious. The library was enormous and smelled of ancient knowledge. The dining room was large enough to host a full banquet.

In fact, Anne's only complaint about their new home was so nit-picky that it hardly counted as a strike. Z-Tech's kitchen had been large enough for three chefs to work full-tilt without bumping elbows. While the mansion's kitchen certainly had more character, it lacked function. Tight corners and narrow pathways caused her and Cappa to collide frequently during their tandem cooking sessions, sometimes at the expense of the entire meal. They had since reduced the number of incidents by slowing their pace, but Anne still missed the factory kitchen's brilliant design.

Despite their ambition to be first for breakfast, Anne wasn't surprised to find Cappa and Zima already sitting at the island counter.

"Morning, sunshines," Cappa said with her trademark radiant smile. Her long, dark hair shimmered as if freshly brushed, pulled back with a yellow hairband and a beautiful bow that complimented her vintage white sundress perfectly. "I trust you slept well? Or better yet, not at all?"

Charlie laughed. "Between the two of you, it's a miracle I can even walk."

"Consider us the most pleasant part of your workout program," Cappa said with an impish grin.

"Without a doubt."

Zima rose from her stool, showing tantalizing cleavage from beneath her white V-neck shirt, and a streak of teal where it wasn't quite long enough to cover her underwear. The display of porcelain skin and shapely legs made Anne want to skip breakfast and whisk Zima away for dessert.

Zima wrapped Anne in a warm embrace, which Anne returned with a kiss to her cheek. Although Zima never complained, Anne knew these nights with Charlie were harder on her than on Cappa. Anne hated it, but when she and Charlie had offered to forego their own relationship, Cappa and Zima had refused.

"Hey, honey." Anne gently ran her fingers through Zima's platinum-blonde hair, which was cut in a laser-perfect bob. "How was your patrol?"

Zima's beautiful, ice-blue eyes met hers. "We escorted an intoxicated local to his residence, but there were no other events of note."

"Hat Manson again?"

"Yes. His spouse was even less pleased at our arrival than last time. I do not understand why he persists with behavior that antagonizes her so."

"Well," Charlie said, "if I were married to Coral, I'd probably drink, too." He kissed Cappa, which she eagerly accepted. "Morning, hon."

"That is what puzzles me," Zima said, taking Anne's hand. "If they are so displeased with each other, why do they not divorce and seek happiness elsewhere?"

"I don't think it's that simple," Cappa said. "They might still love each other, but have forgotten how to show it."

"Or they're together out of habit," Charlie said. "Sometimes it's easier to keep doing the wrong thing because it's familiar."

"I'd like to think they're madly in love, and their public arguments are really just for show," Anne said. "When they're alone, I bet they can't keep their hands off each other."

"You would think that, wouldn't you?" Cappa said with a laugh. "You're such a hopeless romantic."

"Until the day I die." Anne went behind the counter with Zima still attached to her. "I was thinking Eggs Benedict for breakfast. Want to help?"

"Yes," Zima said. "I shall poach the eggs."

"Aw, you don't trust me after last time? There were only a little overcooked."

Zima handed her an apron, then pulled a pot from the cupboard. "It is not a question of trust. Properly poaching an egg requires precision. My measurements of time and temperature are simply more acute than yours."

"And they were very overcooked," Cappa said, grinning. "I could have played hockey with my egg."

Anne shook a paring knife at Charlie. "This is your fault, you know. They were perfectly delightful breakfast companions until last month, when you gave them taste buds."

"I was inspired," Charlie said, holding up his hands. "Besides, your culinary talent deserves a bigger audience."

"If I'd wanted a bigger audience, I would have taken the Chef position at Mama Belle's when she offered it to me." Anne turned to Cappa. "I'm surprised you didn't jump on that one, come to think of it."

"It was tempting, but I'm too used to running the show, and would probably have driven everyone else crazy. I'd rather open my own restaurant."

Anne's knife slipped at the thought, slicing a shallow gash in her finger. She checked the blade for signs of blood. It was clean, but, rather than risk infecting anyone with her vampire taint, she put the knife in the dishwasher and retrieved a new one from the drawer.

Better safe than sorry.

"Would you really?" Anne said. Running her own restaurant was something Anne had always dreamed of, but she lacked the business skills to make it happen.

But with Cappa as a partner ...

"I've thought about it," Cappa said. "Compared to Z-Tech, running the chocolate factory is easy. My other selves have the entire process covered, so I'm open to taking on a new challenge."

"Speaking of ..." Anne bit her lip. It was a sensitive topic, but she had to ask, if only to show that she cared and understood. "How are you doing with ... with Rose's re-integration?"

Cappa sighed. "Better than yesterday. I only cried for a few minutes last night."

Charlie stood behind her and put his hands on her shoulders. "I'm sorry."

Cappa took his hand and nodded, but the pain on her face was both distressing and familiar.

As Cappa had predicted, her factory self, Rose, had taken the news of Almos' death poorly, but no one had been prepared for just how poorly. The pixie-like automation had moped the mansion halls for days until they eventually discovered her as a puddle of nano-goo in a box next to her bed. She had refused to activate her body after that.

Eventually, the little black box containing Rose's consciousness stopped communicating altogether. Dela, who had been her biggest supporter, and one of the few people she would talk to, had threatened to crack into the box with a crowbar if Charlie and Mark couldn't find a means to get through to her. They had, fortunately, which had paved the way to the last conversation anyone had with the person known as Rose.

She had lost her reason for living. Rose had allowed her relationship with Almos to define her, which had set her apart from Cappa's other selves. With Almos and the factory gone, her purpose in life had vanished, and she had fallen too far down the hole of depression to climb out.

Rose had wanted to be turned off. Permanently.

Again, Cappa had offered to re-synchronize Rose with her other selves. Rose had refused at first, but eventually they'd all convinced her that trying and failing was preferable to oblivion, and a far better way to immortalize her fond memories of the former master vampire.

The integration process had taken over two weeks of concerted effort on Cappa's part — which had meant absorbing everything Rose had experienced since Cappa's departure to China: loneliness, isolation, Anne's disappearance, her conflicting friendship with Dela, falling in love with someone who wasn't Charlie, and the loss of her home and lover the same night they had fled San Francisco. Anne hadn't known how or if Cappa would succeed, but she had.

That was when the real challenges had begun.

The day after Rose's conscience had been merged into her, Cappa had done nothing but cry. Everyone flocked to her side, intent on succeeding where they had failed with Rose. Charlie had held and comforted her. Dela had regaled her with jokes. Doris had taken her shopping. Anne had reminisced fond memories of Almos with her. Mark had brought small projects for the two of them to tinker on. All of that, combined with meditation exercises she had learned from Master Wung, had eventually turned Cappa around, but Anne still occasionally heard her sobbing when she thought no one else was around.

"The eggs are almost ready," Zima said. "Would you like me to finish slicing the ham?"

Anne blinked and looked down at the untouched ham hock. "Sorry, I was daydreaming. Can you please stir the Hollandaise sauce?"

Minutes later, their masterpiece was ready. Charlie, Cappa, and Zima watched Anne serve them up with starving-dog focus.

Anne pulled a stool up and sat with her hands folded over her own empty plate. "Dig in!"

They didn't need to be told twice. Cappa took small bites of her single portion, closing her eyes with every mouthful. Charlie was so intent on his meal that Anne thought he might take it into the next room for a little private time.

Watching Zima eat, however, had become the most entertaining spectator sport in the house. Despite having no digestive tract, nor any need for nourishment, Zima had just as much food stacked on her plate as Charlie, but where he ate with a series of happy grunts, Zima's face lit in ecstasy with every bite. The look was so similar to the one she wore in the heights of passion that Anne suspected she had somehow hooked her new taste buds up to her Desire routine.

Far be it from me to criticize. The lucky girl ...

Floorboards squeaked overhead. Mark and Dela were awake, but Anne seemed to be the only one who cared.

Sure enough, the pair soon strolled into the kitchen wearing matching silk pajamas.

"Is that what I think it is?" Mark said, sniffing the air. He scratched his short, sandy-blond hair, his gray eyes fixed on Charlie and Zima's rapidly disappearing meals.

Dela's mouth fell open. "Oh man, Eggs Benedict! Why didn't you wake us? Is there more?"

"There will be," Anne said, chuckling. "Have a seat."

Mark sat his tall frame at the end of the breakfast bar and rested his muscled arms on the counter in eager anticipation. Dela grabbed an elastic band from the counter and tied her frizzy red hair back into a ponytail. With her arms up, her large breasts, which already looked gigantic on her otherwise boyish figure, stood out from her chest like mighty titans, straining her sheer nightgown to its limits. She sat between Mark and Cappa, then lightly bumped Cappa's shoulder.

"How are you doing?" Dela said.

Cappa greeted her with a warm smile, as she had every morning since she'd merged personalities with Rose. Rose's friendship with Dela was one of the few positive memories that had carried over, and made for a welcome change from their usual bickering.

Cappa slid her half-eaten portion over. "I'm stuffed. Care to finish it off?"

"First," Dela said, cutting off a small portion, "it's a kind offer, but you only ate a few bites, so I don't buy this 'stuffed' malarkey." She raised her fork to Cappa's mouth and waited.

Cappa laughed and obligingly opened up, where Dela deposited the tender morsel.

"Second, you didn't answer my question."

"I'm doing better. Thank you for asking, Mrs. Suther."

Dela beamed, her sparkling teeth outshone only by the diamond ring on her finger. She sighed contentedly and leaned into Mark. "I never get tired of hearing that. Too bad I can't say my real surname outside of this house."

"Someday." Mark kissed her forehead. "We won't have to use our aliases forever, just until things stabilize."

Dela shrugged. "Could be worse, I guess. At least I got to pick my alias."

"Veronica Slayer," Anne said with a sideways grin. "Or V. Slayer for short. You might as well carry wooden stakes in your jacket, while you're at it."

"Like stakes would be any help against a vampire. No, I commissioned a pair of swank silver knives from this master weaponsmith I know." She smiled at Mark. "He gave me a really good deal."

"You made a very persuasive offer," Mark said. "In a red satin negligee, if I remember."

"You'd better remember! I froze my butt off strip teasing for you with those frigid power tools against my —"

Cappa stuffed a bite of Eggs Benedict in Dela's mouth, making her gag. "Manners, child! Not everybody wants to hear about your machine fetish."

"Oh, that's rich," Dela said when she could speak again, "considering present company."

Cappa jabbed another forkful at her, which Dela bit with exaggerated ferocity.

"Hopeless," Cappa said, chuckling.

"You know it."

Anne cleared her throat. "Assuming anybody still has an appetite left after that little exchange, Mark and Dela's breakfast is on the stove. Anyone else care for seconds while I'm at it?"

Cappa shook her head, but Charlie and Zima raised their hands.

Anne arched an eyebrow at her girlfriend. "Seriously? You've already eaten three servings!"

"Yes." Zima headed for the exit. "I shall return as soon as I have made room for a fourth."

"Talk about lost appetites ..." Dela's face soured.

"Think of it as baby food," Mark said. "Since she can't digest, the masticated materials come out as —"

Dela's sharp elbow to his ribs silenced him. "The Dark Angel's inner workings are not for casual discussion! It diminishes her air of mystery, which is a crucial edge in her fight against evil. Plus it's gross."

"As you wish, my desert flower," Mark said.

Rough as she could be, Dela's adoration for him was unmistakable when her freckled dimples shone, just as they had on their wedding day. Their departure from San Francisco may have turned their lives upside-down, but everyone had agreed that Mark and Dela's wedding should continue as planned.

Almost as planned, anyway, Anne thought.

Instead of a grand ocean-side venue with three hundred guests and a full band, as Dela had originally wanted, the ceremony had been held under cover of night in their beautiful estate garden. The only attendee outside of their close circle had been the local justice of the peace.

Cappa and Anne had spared nothing for the reception: everything from simple mashed potatoes and roast beef to duck confit with blueberry wine reduction sauce had graced the tables around a seven-tiered wedding cake that had sparkled like edible diamonds. Fortunately for the others, that had been before Cappa and Zima had received their senses of taste, which had left Mark and Charlie many a happy morning of gourmet leftovers for breakfast.

"The eggs are seven seconds overdone," Zima said when she returned to the kitchen.

Anne snapped from her memories of the lovely wedding and hastily fished the eggs from the boiling water. "Sorry. They should still be edible."

She must have been right, for soon there wasn't a scrap left on anyone's plate. Everyone helped clean up, which was a welcome change from the Z-Tech days where she and Cappa shouldered much of the burden, then they left to ready themselves for their busy days.

Charlie caught Anne on her way out of the kitchen and gave her an unusually passionate goodbye kiss. "See you at home this evening?"

"Of course," Anne said, puzzled by his wistful tone. "Where else would I go?"

"Just checking. Have a great day at the hospital."

"Thanks, and knock 'em dead on the tour. I expect to see your Graven Chocolates in every supermarket by Halloween."

"I'll see what I can do," Charlie said with a smile.

He and Cappa left for the bedroom they shared on their nights together to get ready. Anne and Zima soon returned to theirs to prepare for their undoubtedly busy workday at the hospital.

Just another, typical day.

Anne flashed a broad smile. She couldn't wait.

3

PASTRIES

B Y THE TIME ANNE had chosen her work outfit, Zima was already dressed and waiting by their bedroom beauty station.

"Ready?" Zima said.

"Ready."

Anne laid her clothes out on the bed, then sat next to Zima. Foundations and blushes lined the tabletop in organized rows — all the ingredients necessary to make Anne look like a warm-blooded human instead of the cold, walking corpse that she was. Zima opened the nearest jar of UV-protective foundation, Anne grabbed another, and the two of them set to work.

Thirty minutes later, the ashen, sharp-toothed vampire in the mirror was gone. The reflection revealed someone Anne recognized from long ago: the face she had grown up with — the woman she had been before William had turned her into a pulseless, blood-sucking monster.

Anne sighed. Where her daily makeover had once given her comfort, allowing Anne to pretend that she was still human, it was becoming harder and harder to fool herself. Blush gave her the appearance of a healthy complexion, but it didn't give her a pulse.

Her false porcelain caps looked like oversized canines, yet razor-sharp teeth designed for piercing human flesh still hid beneath them. Colored contact lenses restored the dark brown color of her eyes, disguising her abnormally large, alien-like black pupils that could see in the darkest night as if it were day.

"How do I look?" Anne said out of habit.

"Human."

It was the response Anne had expected, but Zima surprised her this morning by following up with a light kiss on her lips.

"Though it makes no difference to me," Zima said. "I love you no matter your appearance."

"Thanks, I needed that."

Zima cocked her head.

Rather than answer, Anne gave her a lingering kiss. She then put on her own outfit, consisting of a white full-length dress with blackout material sewn inside to protect her from the sun, a wide-brimmed hat, and comfortable sneakers.

A quick mirror check confirmed that everything was in place: Anne looked as human as she was going to get. Zima also wore a white dress — without the sun-protective material, of course. Combined with her fair skin and platinum hair, she looked like an angel.

"You're beautiful," Anne said with a smile.

"Thank you."

"Does wearing a dress still make you ... uncomfortable?"

"Yes, but less so than being unarmed."

"Oh come now. When is the Dark Angel ever truly unarmed?"

"That depends upon the threat."

"Say ... playful kids in a hospital who've missed their Auntie Zima?"

"Especially then." Zima took her by the hand. "Speaking of which, we should depart, or we shall be late for our shift. Do not forget that you promised to bring pastries today."

Anne glanced at her bedside clock. "Damnit! Breakfast took longer than I thought. You want to drive today?"

"No. We shall be fine as long as you do not receive a moving violation again."

"Once! I got a speeding ticket one freakin' time, and I'll never live it down. You're a harsh master."

Zima brow-knit and started to respond, but Anne put a finger over her lips.

"I'm just teasing. You're a wonderful, patient driving coach."

"Oh. Thank you."

Zima took her hand, and together they went downstairs. Charlie's car was already gone when they reached the garage.

Anne climbed into the white sedan, put on her wrap-around sunglasses, and opened the garage door. Morning sunlight glared from the concrete, a pool of liquid gold too brilliant for Anne to stare at for long, even with the tinted windows and the aid of her reactive contacts and shades. She pulled out slowly, allowing time for the bright world around her to come into focus.

The drive from the garage to the street was Anne's favorite part of the trip. Their long gravel driveway wound through the gentle valley, hiding their mansion from casual eyes. Autumn's kiss had painted the estate's green trees with hints of amber and russet. The car crossed over a white bridge spanning the river that cut through their property, sunlight sparkling from its rippled surface like a thousand tiny goldfish.

The drive to town wasn't quite as breathtaking, but still picturesque. Cows dotted the spacious green pastures running from the small country road to the distant foothills. The peace and simplicity reminded Anne of her childhood in Indiana, where a trip to the grocery store was a ten-mile drive, and a shopping mall outing merited its own holiday.

The colorful buildings of Graven, Montana soon came into view. Like many small towns, a strip of shops and other businesses sat at its heart. Their chocolate factory occupied a large lot just inside the township. The once-abandoned lumber mill had undergone a startling transformation shortly after Mark and Charlie had purchased it from the township. Once-dirty, broken windows now glinted in the sunlight like fine crystal. The derelict machinery that had littered the grounds was now artwork, complements of a talented local welder with an eye for turning junk into aesthetic masterpieces.

And that's just the outside.

Anne fought a twinge of longing as their vehicle passed by. Charlie, Mark, and Cappa were likely already hard at work. As much as she would have liked to stop in, she and Zima had other obligations — the first of which was buying pastries.

Anne turned the radio on.

"— more gang violence in San Francisco yesterday," a serious-sounding newswoman was saying, "making this the third month in a row where reports of gang violence have risen over thirty percent from the previous month. Shots were heard north of China Town, though, as usual, there were no eyewitnesses, no bodies, and no arrests, leaving this reporter wondering how seriously the nation-wide increase in gang activity is being taken by authorities. Now over to Joe for the ..."

Anne stopped listening with a sigh. "Gangs, huh?"

Zima glanced at her, but remained silent, which Anne had expected. William had extensively infiltrated the government and media when he was alive to hide the existence of vampires from the public, which, by the sound of it, was becoming harder by the day.

The opposing force, Anne assumed, was Timothy Chen and Nick Orwing's Resistance — a secret volunteer society predicated on synergistic existence between humans and vampires of Anne's bloodline, established to combat William's rising scourge by fighting fire with fire. How many there were, and how they were faring, Anne didn't know.

And she didn't want to. The less she knew, the less the Entity knew. So Anne swallowed her curiosity, accepted Zima's silence, and changed the radio to a music station.

•　　•　　•

Jessie's Bakery Café was bustling when Anne parked out front, which was no surprise for a weekday morning. Unlike San Francisco, where every city block held a vast selection of restaurants of every type, choices for quality baked goods in Graven were few indeed. However, Jessie Hornbrook's incredible family recipes were at the top. Anne had lost her appreciation for food along with her pulse, unfortunately, but everyone else swore Jessie's were the most flaky, buttery, heavenly pastries in the state.

Anne squeezed Zima's hand. "Ready?"

"Yes," Zima said, though her blue eyes remained fixed on the bakery's window.

"Zima?"

She turned suddenly, as if snapping out of a daydream. "I am ready."

Anne gave Zima's hand another squeeze, but kept silent. Zima had been distracted since they moved to Graven. Anne had asked several times if anything was bothering her. Zima insisted she was simply acclimating to their new environment, which involved the generation of millions of new tactical and social simulations. Anne had believed her at first, but here they were, almost four months later, and Zima was still acting just as spacey.

Who am I to question her? I can only imagine how hard this adjustment has been. I should just be grateful that she has.

Morning sun basked the front of the bakery. Anne put her hat on and secured it with a bow under her chin, having learned the hard way that a gust of wind was all it took to whisk it away and scorch the top of her head. She made sure her white gloves safely overlapped her sleeves, and that her high-neck dress was buttoned all the way up to her chin.

Fighting her instincts to the contrary, Anne stepped into the blazing sunlight.

Pinpricks gouged every inch of her body, as if she were suddenly clothed in nettles. Anne ground her teeth against the discomfort and kept her pace steady. She wanted nothing more than to take Zima's hand for comfort, but they had learned early on that Graven wasn't as accepting of same-sex relationships as the city she had grown to love. By the time they had realized their mistake, the damage was already done. She and Zima were dykes in most people's eyes. The best they could do now, unfortunately, was keep their hands to themselves in public and maintain a friendly distance to prevent others from feeling uncomfortable. It sucked, as evinced by Zima's lonely, flexing fingers. But in the grand scheme of things, separating in public was a small sacrifice to maintain their cover and avoid suspicion.

Anne sighed in relief when they finally entered the shelter of the store. Every table in the tiny dining area was filled. Jessie Hornbrook, a heavy-set, energetic woman about Anne's age, wearing a blue checkered apron, peeked around the queue of waiting customers and waved.

"Morning, Sue," she said to Anne. Then to Zima, "Morning, Jayne. Don't mind the line. I'll have you back on the road in no time."

"The starving medical staff of Saddle Ranch Children's Hospital appreciates it," Anne said.

She and Zima took their places at the end of the line, but Anne's good mood faltered when she saw who waited ahead of them.

Billy Connup and Wade McIntire. Perfect ...

"Good morning," Zima said to them before Anne could stop her.

Billy turned with a contemptuous sneer on his freckled face. "What a shock to see you two together. Again."

Zima head-cocked. "We drive to work together every weekday. Why is this morning a surprise to you?"

"Jayne, let it go," Anne said under her breath.

"Oh," Zima said, undeterred, "that was an abstract suggestion of a sexual relationship between us." She turned back to them and cocked her head again. "The two of you are frequently in each other's company. Should I infer the same?"

Wade's flat nose flushed red. "W-what? No! We've been friends since we were kids, you stupid dyke!"

"That was unflattering," Zima said, her tone and expression unreadable.

"No shit," Wade said. Both of them stood a full head taller than either Anne or Zima. Wade stalked forward, towering over Zima with barely contained fury. "You called us fags, bitch!"

Anne watched her carefully, but Zima stood as still as a statue.

"That was also unflattering," Zima said. "And I did nothing but apply your own logic to illustrate the flaw in your grossly generalized assessment."

For a frightening moment, Anne thought Wade was going to make the last mistake of his life and hit her, but he reined himself in with visible effort and raised a warning finger. "This isn't over. We'll see you at shooting practice. Tonight."

With that, they turned their backs to Zima.

"Maybe we should skip pastries this morning," Anne whispered to Zima. "I'll bake something this evening to make up for it. The hospital staff will understand."

"No. I have a strong desire for Jessie's blackberry turnovers, and there are several remaining in the display. We shall wait in line and hope they are still available when we reach the counter."

"Yes, ma'am."

Anne wanted to hug her wonderful girlfriend and congratulate her on a decisive, if unintentional, victory against the young bullies, but now wasn't the time. Their quiet spat with the boys had drawn the attention of everyone around them. Any hint of public affection could easily spark another incident — if not from Billy and Wade, then from any of the other homophobes who might be watching. As much as she hated it, Anne tucked her hands under her arms and kept her distance from Zima.

True to her word, Jessie Hornbrook kept the line moving, and soon Billy and Wade were up.

"What can I get you boys?" Jessie said.

Wade leaned on the counter and smiled. "Your delicious blackberry turnovers, Jess."

"You got it. How many?"

"How many you got?"

She peered behind the counter. "Looks like five."

"We'll take them all," Wade said, shooting a cruel glance at Zima.

Son of a bitch!

"Guys, come on," Anne said. "You're not going to eat all five of those."

Billy leaned on his elbow and smiled as if he owned the place. "Says who? We're extra hungry this morning."

"That'll be seven fifty," Jessie said.

Anne seethed while they settled the bill. Wade had the gall to take a huge bite from his turnover when he passed Zima. Her beautiful, impassive blue eyes followed it the entire way.

"I don't suppose you have any more of those in the back?" Anne said to Jessie.

"Just what's in the display, sorry."

"That is unfortunate," Zima said.

Anne settled a frigid stare on Wade's retreating back. "Don't worry, you'll have your blackberry turnover. Just get our order started."

Anne marched after him. She wished it were nighttime in a secluded alley so she could beat the ever-loving snot out of the spiteful brats and ram the stupid turnovers down their throats.

But it wasn't night, and this wasn't an alley. She was in the middle of a café with a dozen witnesses in a town where they needed to fit in, and who already disliked them for who they were. Violence wasn't the answer.

That was fine, however, since Anne had a better idea.

"Guys, wait," she called when they reached the door. Anne fished her wallet from her purse and pulled out a twenty-dollar bill. "I'll buy one of the uneaten ones from you."

"Love your girlfriend that much, do you?" Wade's sneer said it wasn't a compliment.

"No." Anne took the rest of the cash from her wallet and held it out to him in a folded wad. "I love her this much. My entire paycheck for one lousy pastry. Do we have a deal?"

A hush fell over the café. Every eye was on them.

Anne could see Wade weighing his options. His earlier bullying had been quiet, but Anne had just made it very public. To refuse her now would prove beyond a doubt that he and Billy were nothing but brutes picking on a pair of innocent women.

Likewise, if he took her up on her full offer, which his greedy eyes said he wanted to do, they would be taking obvious advantage of someone who was just trying to make her loved one happy. Everyone knew Zima. She was a respected member of the militia who many also considered simple due to her social naïveté. Extorting her would be like taking candy from a well-liked child.

Wade glanced at the crowd. His face hardened. Anne was surprised when he snatched the entire wad of cash from her hand, dropped the pastry bag in its place, then pushed Billy out the door.

Anne returned to the counter and slid the costly prize over to Zima. "As promised. Enjoy."

Zima clutched it to her chest as if it were a precious treasure, then wrapped her arms around Anne.

"Thank you," Zima said, her voice barely a whisper.

"My pleasure, honey."

So much for no public displays of affection.

Thankfully, no derogatory homosexual mumblings came from the crowd.

"That was … something else," Jessie said with a smile. "I'll be sure to put one aside for you from now on."

"That would be appreciated," Zima said into the crook of Anne's neck.

Once the baked goods were packed, Anne secured her hat and ventured back into the morning sun. Her spirits fell once again when she saw Billy and Wade standing in front of their car, which was parked right next to Anne's.

Good God, what now?

She froze when she spotted Billy's gun.

No, no, no!

Even though his militia-issued pistol contained silver bullets, which would paralyze a vampire like Anne in an instant, she wasn't worried about her own safety.

If Zima sees them …

Zima did see them. She unceremoniously handed the box of pastries and her prized bag of turnovers to Anne. The hum in her chest built to a low whine, too soft for humans to hear, but Anne knew she was readying for action.

Billy didn't raise his gun, however. He was fiddling with it.

Zima brow-knit, then walked over to Billy with her hand outstretched.

He eyed her suspiciously, but eventually pressed it into her palm.

Zima quickly dismantled it into a dozen pieces on the hood of his car. She examined each part, then drew her combat knife and shaved a thin layer from one of the smaller pieces. She re-assembled the gun nearly as fast as she had taken it apart, tested the slide, the magazine, and the hammer with expert precision, then handed it back to him.

Billy tested it himself and nodded. "Thanks," he said, not meeting her eyes. "If rumor's true, I'll need a working gun if I'm gonna have a prayer of taking a vampire down."

"Rumor does not do them justice," Zima said. "If you ever encounter one, and I hope for your sake that you do not, then you shall need every advantage at your disposal."

"You've fought one before?" Wade said, crossing his arms.

"Not personally," Anne said for her. She knew how difficult it was for Zima to lie, and how easy it would be to reveal something they wished to keep secret. Taking over the conversation now meant less cleanup later, and certainly less stress on Zima. "But we did get to watch them tear our friends apart," Anne lied. "That's why we moved here from Chicago. We hoped a remote place with plenty of sunshine like Graven would be low on their priority list."

Speaking of which ... Anne's skin prickled incessantly under the bright morning sun, becoming more uncomfortable by the second. She forced herself to stay still. *I hope we can wrap this up soon.*

"Oh." Billy ran his fingers through his brown curls. "I ... I'm sorry to hear about your friends."

"What was it like?" Wade said. "We've never met anyone who saw a vampire attack firsthand. Even the government hasn't acknowledged them."

Billy rolled his eyes. "That's because they've already infiltrated the government, dumbass."

"I wasn't talking to you!"

Anne held her hand up. "Boys, boys! Billy's probably right. Evidence of vampires is all around, yet troops were recalled after the terrorist strikes around the country a few months ago. The only way that makes sense is if someone's pulling the strings from higher up."

"Indeed," Zima said. "The lack of federal military support is the reason local militias have gained popularity nationwide."

"To answer your question," Anne said, leaning against the car, "the vampire attack was frightening. They were so fast, so strong, that our friends never stood a chance. One of our friends had a gun, but the vampires moved so quickly that he could never land a shot. Our friends were dead before we could even scream, so Jayne and I ran for our lives and never looked back." The scenario was fabricated, of course, but Anne felt it answered the essence of his question truthfully.

"You're lucky," Wade said. "I heard vampires like it when you run. They like to chase."

"True on both counts."

Especially the latter.

Anne had to fight the urge to hunt each and every time she saw something scurry away, be it animal or human.

"We didn't wait for them to come find us, either," Anne said. "We packed up that very night and drove west." The pinpricks now felt like tiny flames erupting on her skin. Any longer in the sun and she would start to smoke. "Sorry to cut this short, but we have to get to the hospital. The kids are counting on us."

"Wait." Wade hung his head and handed over the wad of bills he had taken from Anne. "I ... I wasn't going to keep it."

"Thanks." Anne mustered her friendliest smile, but the constant burning made it difficult. Even the Entity was urging her to seek shelter. "Do you mind driving?" she said to Zima. "I'm not feeling so well."

"Of course."

"See you tonight," Anne said to Billy and Wayde, then ducked into the car's protective interior. As soon as the engine started, Anne cranked the air conditioning and turned all the vents toward her. "Oh my God, I thought I was going to die out there. Sorry for making you drive again, I ..."

She trailed off when she noticed Zima sitting in the driver's seat, staring at the bag in her hands containing her hard-earned blackberry turnovers.

"You okay?"

"No."

Zima gently set the bag in her lap and backed out of the parking spot. It wasn't until they were back on the road that she spoke again. Her fingers caressed the paper packaging of her prize.

"I do not deserve these."

Anne laughed. "Oh, honey, you've earned so much more than a bag of pastries. Tonight is our night together. Wait until we're alone, and I'll show you just how much —"

"There is something I have not told you," Zima said, not taking her eyes from the road. "About the night we left San Francisco, when the tanks appeared."

"I heard about that on the news. One of the tank barrels melted and fused to the body. Your handiwork, I assume?"

"Yes, but there was a cost. The enemy terminated three civilian hostages in retaliation, and a fourth when it appeared I might attack the second tank."

"Oh."

The article had glossed over that fact, citing only that several were killed during the unprecedented assault. Anne had never asked for details of what had led up to their retreat from Z-Tech because, well ... there were *tanks.* No one seemed eager to relive that night either, so she had set her curiosity aside and moved on. She gently brushed Zima's hair back with a finger.

"You feel responsible for their deaths?"

"Yes."

"Zima, you couldn't have known —"

"I did. The consequences of my actions were all but assured, yet I proceeded anyway with the small hope that our way of life would be preserved. It was a selfish action. Their deaths are my responsibility."

Anne let that sink in.

Those civilians had not been the only casualties that night. Explosions across the country had claimed hundreds of lives. Some communities were still picking up the pieces, despite both Federal and international support, but the families who had lost someone dear had a much longer road ahead of them. Their stories, their struggles, and their sorrow would continue long after the rest of the world had forgotten the atrocities of that night.

Four of those tragic stories were now on Zima's head.

As sorry as Anne felt for their families, sympathy for her aching girlfriend rattled her more. "Were ... were you afraid I would hate you when I found out?"

Beautiful blue eyes met hers, glistening in the sunlight. "Yes."

"Pull over. Behind those trees, if you don't mind."

Zima brow-knit, but did as instructed. When the vehicle stopped behind the copse of trees, Anne unfastened both of their seat belts, reclined Zima's seat as far as it would go, then straddled her lap. Zima started to speak, but Anne kissed her, and didn't stop until they were both flustered and breathless.

"I could never hate you," Anne said. "And I will never abandon you. Whatever Hell holds for you, it holds for both of us. That's a promise."

Zima fell silent. Anne searched her face, but, as usual, found no hint of how she was feeling.

"I ... fear we have squashed the blackberry turnovers," Zima said.

Anne pulled the now-flat paper bag out from under her rear and plopped it in the passenger seat. "Oh well," she said with a mischievous grin. "I guess I'll just have to make it up to you."

"What about our shift?"

"They'll survive if we're a few minutes late. Right now, my baby needs some tender loving care, and that's exactly what she's going to get. Into the back seat with you so we can take advantage of the rear window tinting."

Zima gently stroked her cheek, sending a pleasant tingle through Anne's body. "As you command, I shall happily obey, my love."

And so she did, with a gusto that nearly flattened the tires.

4

HER CALLING

S ADDLE RANCH CHILDREN'S HOSPITAL looked more like a school than a medical institution. The facility was a collection of single-story buildings sprawled across acres of green lawns and parking lots, surrounded by clear pastures running all the way to the distant mountains.

Zima parked in their usual spot alongside the playground. Children's laughter floated over the fence, expanding Anne's already satisfied grin into an ear-to-ear smile.

They hurried into the changing room and were happy to find it empty. She and Zima changed and freshened up with inhuman speed, then headed for the children's ward.

Dr. Carol Toben caught them in the hallway and waved them over.

"Ready for your daily briefing?" she said cheerfully.

Anne's stomach rumbled in answer, which she covered with a bashful smile. "Lead the way, Doc."

She was salivating by the time Carol locked the door to her office.

Carol took one look at her and laughed. "You haven't eaten since the last time you were here two days ago, have you?"

"I'm trying to be good."

Anne shifted impatiently while the doctor rolled up her sleeve. She removed the caps from her canines, which were rapidly pushing down from her gums. Tart venom from their hollow tips filled her mouth.

Come on, come on, come on ...

"Admirable," Carol said, settling her stocky frame into one of the chairs. "Too bad Jayne is too squeamish to let you drink from her."

Anne pulled up a chair, eyes fixed on the throbbing veins under Carol's silky white skin. "She's working on it," Anne said, supporting their cover story, "but until then ... you're a real saint, Doc."

"The occasional high is a small price to pay for the miracle you give these kids. Now, don't just sit there drooling on the carpet, you poor thing. Dig in."

Anne didn't need to be told twice. Her sharp upper canines punctured the crook of Carol's arm.

She shuddered when the first heavenly drops hit her tongue. Drinking was much easier from the larger veins in the neck. Carol would probably have allowed it, except even the rapid healing from Anne's venom would leave visible marks and raise questions from the staff.

An arm, however, was easily covered. The doctor's extra weight also worked in her favor. She had a larger blood volume than normal, which meant that not only could Anne drink more, but the heroin-like effects of Anne's venom were diluted. The results were a fully satiated Anne and a mostly functional Carol, who usually spent the following hour working on reports until her head cleared enough to not be a hazard to her patients.

Not that her patients require much work anymore.

That alone was the reason why Dr. Toben allowed herself to be compromised on the job.

As if on cue, Carol fumbled in her lab coat pocket and set a pair of vials on the desk. "If you please ..."

Anne felt so good after the hearty meal that she would have kissed the doctor's shoes if she asked. She punctured each rubber cap with a canine. In no time, her crystal-clear venom shimmered nearly to the tops.

Carol held them before her. "The sheer volume never ceases to amaze me. How I'd love to take an MRI and see where in your head you store all that good stuff. Or how you function without a heartbeat, for that matter."

"That makes two of us," Anne said.

It wasn't the first time the topic had come up, but they'd all agreed that satisfying the doctor's curiosity didn't outweigh the risk of someone else stumbling on the MRI images and asking the wrong questions. Carol was the only person in the hospital who knew what Anne really was, and they intended to keep it that way. Parents and staff alike seemed willing to turn a blind eye to the inexplicable miracles, but they could only ignore so much before calling a formal investigation.

Meanwhile, Saddle Ranch's reputation as a healing institution had soared. Parents from around the state came with their ailing children, many with terminal diseases, to watch their rapid recovery with joyous celebration. Anne lived for the moments when the children first stepped from their beds and were able to run, often for the first time, into their parents' tearful embrace.

Such things weren't just worth the risk of being discovered; they gave meaning to Anne's blighted existence, and offset the hazard her tainted blood presented to the rest of humanity.

At least, I hope they do.

Anne stood and stretched her arms. She felt invigorated. "Well, we should probably hop to it. Is there anyone you'd like us to visit?"

Carol shook her head, eyes drooping. "There will be in an hour, though. A transport is inbound from Billings. One or both of these vials will go to her."

"How old?"

"Four. Rapid health decline. Staff doesn't know what to make of it, so the parents are bringing her here because of our reputation for miracle cures. Until then, I suppose, you're both free to play."

"Thanks, boss," Anne said with a sharp salute.

"As you were, you little gremlin. And don't forget your caps unless you want to start a panic."

Anne almost had. She grabbed the porcelain fittings from the desk and fastened them over her fangs. "How do they look?" she said to Zima.

"Passable, except …" Zima dabbed a tissue on the corner of Anne's mouth. It came away red. "There. Now you are presentable."

"What would I do without you?"

"Frighten the children, I suspect."

"Very funny. Let's go."

The ward erupted in happy squeals on their arrival. Anne knelt and caught as many flying hugs as she could handle before she finally toppled over, laughing all the way down.

Zima caught several children as well and carried them under her arms to the library like bundles of sticks.

"What shall we read today?" Zima said over their giggles.

Little hands stretched in all directions, pulling a variety of colorful books from the shelves. When everybody had one, Zima lowered the kids to the carpet, where they settled into a circle.

"Tony, shall we read yours first?"

A little boy with thick glasses triumphantly fist-pumped and handed his book over.

"Lafcadio, the Lion Who Shot Back, by Shel Silverstein."

The kids quieted when Zima started to read, completely transfixed, and Anne couldn't blame them. What expression Zima lacked in normal conversation, she more than made up for in storytelling — partially thanks to her practice sessions with Anne, but mostly due to her precision vocal cords. Lions roared with chilling authority, hunters gruffed in threatening voices, rifles fired with such realism that twice the staff had come running to save the children from the mad gunman.

In the early days, Anne had feared Zima's performance would invite uncomfortable questions, but once again people seemed content to leave well enough alone as long as the children were safe and happy.

"Hi, Susan," a familiar adolescent voice said.

Anne turned to find her blushing fifteen-year-old admirer rocking on his heels near the window.

"Morning, Kurt," Anne said with a smile. "You look well today."

He shoved his hands in his jean pockets. "Yeah. Dr. Toben says I'll be released by the end of the week, at this rate." His frown said he wasn't happy about it. Anne had a pretty good idea why.

"Well, don't think that gets you off the hook with me, mister." She waggled a finger at him. "I expect an update every week on how you're doing, or I'll be sad. You hear?"

"Really? You'll ... miss me?"

"Very much. Who's going to kick my butt at card games when you're not around?"

It wasn't the answer he wanted to hear, she could tell by his slump, but Anne wasn't about to play Mrs. Robinson, either. Kurt was a handsome young man with broad shoulders and short spiky hair that she could have played with for hours, but he was also half her age, and had a heartbeat besides. She needed to find a way to let him down easy ...

The solution hit her so suddenly that she coughed to cover her laugh. Anne motioned him away from the others and drew him close.

"I'd like your help with something," she said softly. "It's a little sensitive, so ... can you keep a secret?"

Kurt rallied, as she'd hoped he would, his adolescent face comically serious. "Of course I can. What is it?"

"This isn't public knowledge, but ... I sort of have the hots for this girl ..."

"Girl? You mean, you're ..."

"Yes. I told you it was sensitive." *Out here in the country, that is.*

"Is it someone I know?"

"Actually, yes." She nodded toward Zima, then grabbed a pen and pad from a bedside table and began scribbling a note. "What I'd like your help with is slipping this to her without getting caught. I'd like to stay anonymous for now, and that'll be much easier if I have an accomplice." She tore the note from the pad, folded it into quarters, then held it out to him. "Are you up to the task?"

A smile brought out his adorable dimples. "Leave it to me."

"Thanks, Kurt." She risked a quick kiss on his cheek, hoping he wouldn't notice how cold her lips were. "I knew I could count on you."

The teen walked away with a spring in his step. His eyes fixed on Zima, no doubt already plotting his plan of attack. Anne gave herself a mental pat on the back and returned her attention to the few children who had too much energy to sit still, even to listen to Zima's masterful storytelling.

"Come on," Anne said, "last one to the playground gets tickle fingers!"

She caught Zima's eye and winked, then chased the giggling troupe of children through the halls. The urge to hunt was strong. Anne surrendered to her instinct for once and pounced on little April, whose deformed foot even Anne's venom couldn't cure, and carried her out with the pack, tickling her all the way.

•　　•　　•

Anne heard the medical transport approaching long before she was summoned to prepare for the new arrival. She helped Jimmy put the finishing touch on his sandcastle under the shaded refuge of the play structure, herded the rest of the kids back inside, then met Zima in the washroom to clean up.

"That was a thoughtful note," Zima said while they stood together at the sink. "Thank you."

"Don't mention it. I'm just glad my secret agent came through. How'd he manage to slip it to you?"

"He convinced Sally to deliver it to me along with a chocolate chip cookie. The cookie went to the messenger, unfortunately, but the note was intact."

"Good," Anne said. "Hopefully that'll take his mind off of me for a while."

"I have furthered the cause by giving him a counter mission."

Anne grinned and bumped her shoulder, pleasantly surprised that Zima had continued their little charade. "Oh? Like what?"

"You will find out soon."

Anne was dying to know, but kept her mouth shut. Zima would surely tell if she asked again, and she didn't want to spoil the surprise.

They watched the medical transport pull into the emergency room entrance under the shade of the awning, far from the fierce rays of the noonday sun. Medical personnel unloaded a portable stretcher which, even from this distance, Anne could see contained a very small passenger strapped tightly beneath a mound of blankets.

She swallowed a lump in her throat, but refused to let the rising grief consume her. This was the hardest part: watching the sick and poorly children, and their parents' barely contained anguish while they try to be brave for the dearest part of their lives who lay dying before them.

Tomorrow would be a different matter, however, and that was why Anne kept coming back to the hospital, even with the ever-increasing chance of someone discovering her true nature.

Let's hope tomorrow brings another miracle.

Her hopes died when she saw the cadaverous little face come through the emergency entrance.

Oh God, no!

"Her body temperature is extremely low," Zima whispered, "as is her pulse and respiration. She should not be conscious."

Yet she was. Her little ashen face turned this way and that, her eyes seeking a salvation that Anne knew would never come. Not now, not ever.

The child was turning.

"Who would do such a thing?" Anne said under her breath. The thought made her ill. This little bundle of blond curls, who was just beginning to explore the world, was about to have the most horrific night of her life, assuming ...

Oh no.

"Dr. Toben!" Anne called over the bustle.

Carol must have read the urgency on Anne's face, because she hastily excused herself from the procession and joined Anne and Zima.

"Looks like Becky arrived just in time," Carol said. "Her condition worsened during the drive. I was going to administer her, ah ... special treatment through an IV, but I'm going to skip the pretense this time and give her an injection as soon as — hey!"

Dr. Toben tried to shake her arm loose, but Anne's grip was absolute. She practically dragged the larger woman into an exam room, with Zima close behind them, and closed the door.

"Susan! What the hell do you think you're —"

"She's infected," Anne said sharply. "Becky's turning into a vampire."

Carol's angry flush drained in an instant. "Are you sure?"

"As sure as I can be."

Carol sat heavily on a stool, looking as though the world was about to end. She took the vials of Anne's venom from her lab coat and rolled them in her hand. "Will these help?"

"No. The pathogen is very aggressive. Judging by her condition, she's been infected for at least twelve hours, which means it's infiltrated just about every cell in her body." Anne knelt beside Carol and took her hand to make sure she had the doctor's full attention. "She doesn't have long. The cycle completes approximately twenty-four hours after infection. The question is what she will be at the end."

Carol's brow furrowed. "I thought … Won't she be like you?"

"She must consume human blood to trigger the transformation," Zima said. "If she does not, she may die."

Carol jumped to her feet and paced the small room. "This is insane! Y-you're asking me to condone feeding blood to a child so —"

"I'm asking no such thing," Anne said, trying and failing to keep her voice down. "If Becky hasn't already bitten someone, the urge to do so is going to get stronger, and chances are that she'll sink her teeth into someone before the timer's up. Carol, you can't imagine how strong that little girl will be if she makes it through. She's going to be ravenous for blood, and not you or her parents will be able to stop her from taking it."

"Then what do you suggest?" Carol said, throwing her hands in the air. "Lock her in a room? Let her die?"

"Discharge her."

"Susan! You're not making any s—"

"Becky needs to be on the first flight to San Francisco," Anne said over her. "We can't cure her, but we can make sure that she and her family are in an environment where they aren't a danger to each other."

"And exactly what environment is that?"

Anne pursed her lips and fiddled with her uniform. "I … can't say."

The doctor drew herself up like a rising storm. "You want me to discharge a deathly ill pediatric patient — an act that at best gets me arrested and at worst gets her killed! — and you won't goddamned tell me why?"

"Y-yeah."

Anne felt stupid saying it, but it was the truth. She had told Dr. Toben just enough about herself to establish trust, made a hundred times easier when Carol had first seen the effects of the venom, but it was a mere scratch of the surface. Zima's true nature, their affiliation with Z-Tech, Tim's rebellion, Anne being the master vampire … none of that information was necessary for Carol to heal sick kids.

And it still isn't.

"Carol, please believe that if there were a happier way to resolve this, I would tell you. There's a lot going on out there that most people don't know — much that I've lost track of myself. But the further I bring you in, the more dangerous it becomes for both you and some very good people who are trying to make a difference in other ways. I-I know taking me at my word is a lot to ask, but discharging Becky and sending her and her entire family to San Francisco is our only option. And the longer we deliberate, the slimmer her chances become."

Carol's internal struggle played out in a series of frowns and groans.

Anne couldn't blame her. If some creature of darkness had asked Anne to trust her with a child's life, consent would come grudgingly, if ever. Zima must have come to the same conclusion, for neither of them spoke while the good doctor worked things through in her head.

Minutes ticked by. Anne was afraid they had lost when Carol's hands fell to her lap and she shook her head, but the valiant woman surprised her.

"I … I can drum up an excuse to discharge her that may let me keep my medical license, but I have no idea how to get them to San Francisco. Even if I manage to convince her parents, Becky's in no condition for another road trip."

"We shall arrange air transportation from here to SFO," Zima said, "including a helicopter pickup from this facility. We will also ensure that someone meets them at the airport to take them to their final destination."

Anne was both surprised and relieved to hear Zima speak. Anne hadn't a clue how to arrange transportation for someone who needed critical medical support — not that EMTs would be able to help Becky anyway — but Zima's offer hopefully meant she did.

As for the promised safe haven, neither Tim nor Nick knew of their whereabouts, to Anne's knowledge, nor had they communicated at all since they had moved up here. Following through could mean breaking radio silence, and making that decision on her own wasn't fair to her other friends. She would discuss that with Zima as soon as they were alone.

Carol stared as if she didn't recognize them, then shook her head. "I've trusted you this far, and you've worked miracles. It would be foolish to question you now. You do your magic; I'll do mine." She opened her mouth to say more, but clamped it shut and left Anne and Zima alone in the exam room.

"Thank you," Anne said, grabbing Zima in a hug. "I'm sorry, I-I should have spoken to you before making a promise like that, but ..."

"There is no need to apologize. You were correct in your assessment. It would be selfish not to assist, since the solutions are well within our means to deliver."

"They are?"

"Yes. I have already reached out to Mark, who is now speaking with a transport company about a medical helicopter. They should arrive within the hour. They will fly her to the nearest airport, where an air ambulance is standing by. Assuming Dr. Toben releases her by the time the helicopter arrives, Becky and her family should be in San Francisco before nightfall."

"That's ... amazing," Anne said, her voice thick with emotion. "When we get home, I'm going to make you both the best dinner of your lives."

"It is our pleasure, though someone else has already made plans to cook dinner tonight."

"They have? Fine, another night, then. I guess that just leaves contacting Nick and Tim to make sure they're ready to receive the family. Should I call them, or —"

"That, too, has already been taken care of. They have been forwarded Becky's contact information, and shall be awaiting her arrival at the airport."

"But how —"

"Please do not ask for details," Zima said. "Just trust that it has been done."

Anne nodded with a sigh. Although she understood Zima's reasons for keeping information from her — or from the Entity, rather — she couldn't help sharing Carol's frustration at being kept in the dark.

Had the message been sent anonymously? Or had her friends re-established contact with the Resistance? If the latter, how were they faring without Zima as their general? How many Resistance members were there now? Was their social theory about peaceful coexistence between humans and Anne's bloodline of vampires proving correct?

The questions burned Anne's tongue, but she let them smolder in silence. There was no telling what the Entity would or could do with the information. Anne would simply have to be content to wonder.

In the privacy of the exam room, Anne stole a kiss from Zima and smiled. "Come on, let's see if we can lend Carol some emotional support. That can't be an easy conversation she's having with Becky's parents."

They found Dr. Toben in the critical care wing. She was locked in an empty hospital room with the parents, however, so they visited Becky a few doors down instead. Although paler than before, her eyes were wilder. Twice she snapped her teeth at the surrounding nurses with a growl more suited to a panther cub than a four-year-old child.

Anne stifled a sob. It was heartbreaking. It was wrong.

And it was all-too familiar.

The hunger, the need ... Much of Anne's own transformation was a blur, but those two things she remembered with utter clarity. *Becky won't know what she wants, or why she's snapping, until she gets her first taste of blood. Then she'll never stop wanting it.*

An hour of interminable waiting later, raised voices from Dr. Toben's room drew most of the staff's attention. Anne waited until the nurse had injected a sedative into Becky's IV, and her little eyes had drooped, before joining the others in the hall. She'd only caught a few words when the door burst open. A red-faced Carol stormed over to the nursing station.

"Becky's being discharged," Carol said in a tight voice. "Ready her for helo transport."

The station nurse gulped, her eyes as wide as everyone else's. "B-but Dr. Toben —"

Carol's clipboard smacked to the floor in a flurry of papers. "Just do it, Joan!"

The staff fell silent at her uncharacteristic outburst. Carol looked around at the wide eyes focused on her, and she deflated.

"I'm ... I'm sorry. The patient is being transferred to a private facility in San Francisco, better suited for her care. Her parents" — she bit the word like a sour grape — "agree it's her best hope for survival."

"Transportation has been arranged," Zima said evenly, the only person in the ward unflustered by the doctor's anger. "The helicopter will arrive in approximately three minutes."

Carol retrieved her clipboard and took a shuddering breath. "You heard her," she said to everyone else. "Hop to it. The chopper's coming."

Within a few minutes, Becky was on her way out again. Anne found the sheepish looks on her parents' faces almost as odd as Dr. Toben's refusal to acknowledge their existence.

Once the chopper was safely away, Carol turned on her heel and marched inside without her usual words of comfort to the staff. Anne followed her back to her office, and was pleasantly surprised the door wasn't slammed in her face.

"Carol?" Anne said, peeking inside.

The doctor ignored her. She stripped her lab coat, then grabbed her jacket.

I can't blame her for being upset, Anne thought dismally. *I just hope she comes back to work tomorrow.*

Anne and Zima stepped aside to let her pass, but Carol stopped in front of them with a grimace.

"Drinks are on me. The bus leaves in five minutes."

"I'll drive," Anne said. "I can't drink alcohol anyway."

"More for Jayne and me, then. Meet you in the parking lot."

She and Zima quickly changed out of their white uniforms. A rustle of paper in Anne's jacket made her frown. She didn't recall leaving any receipts in her pockets, but she was in such a hurry to leave that the mysterious noise was soon forgotten.

Carol was waiting by their car when they reached the parking lot, leaning against the door with a faraway look. She climbed in the back, gave Zima an address, then fell silent for the rest of the trip, leaving Anne more worried about the doctor than ever.

5

DANCERS

C AROL'S MYSTERY DESTINATION turned out to be a cheery bar in a nearby town that Anne had never visited. Skylights brought unusual brightness to the expected dinge. Combined with soft colors and a nice country décor, the atmosphere was closer to a comfortable living room than a place for beer swilling.

The smell of hops and other spirits overpowered Anne's sensitive nose. She stopped breathing for a few seconds to allow her olfactory senses time to adjust, then followed them inside.

Carol went straight to the bar and flagged the bartender, who was the only other person in the empty establishment. The bartender was a striking young man with strong features, sharp eyes, and just enough stubble to make Anne want to stare for hours, dreaming of the adventures his rugged look suggested he'd seen.

"The usual, Sam," Carol said, sitting her girth on a padded stool.

Sam nodded and retrieved a glass from behind the counter. "Surprised to see you so early," he said in a tenor voice every bit as dreamy as his face. "You off today, Doc?"

"I am now. And I have a driver this time, so do an exhausted girl a favor and keep them coming." A cold lager slid toward her shortly after, which Carol drained in a single pull.

"Anything for you two?" Sam said.

"Nothing for me," Anne said, watching Carol polish off her first pint with incredible speed.

Zima cocked her head at him. "What do you recommend?"

"Depends. What sort of drinks do you like?"

"I am unsure. I have never consumed an alcoholic beverage before."

"For real?"

"Yes."

Sam's grin was so adorable that it should have been illegal. "Then let's start with something basic, Miss ...?"

"Morrison. Jayne."

"Jayne." His grin went from illegal to Geneva Convention-grade irresistible. "You're in for a treat. I have everything here from cheap tequila to four-hundred-dollar-a-glass scotch. This evening, I'd love to be your guide through as much as you'd like to try."

Anne had to close her mouth to keep from drooling.

This guy's a charisma dynamo, and he isn't even trying. I see why Carol comes here.

The good doctor was oblivious, however, focused instead on her empty glass. "I'm ready for another, Sam," she said in a hollow voice. A full pint appeared seconds later, which she attacked with the same ferocity as the first.

"Very well," Zima said when Sam returned to her. She pulled a thick stack of hundred-dollar bills from her wallet and placed them flat on the bar. "Will this suffice?"

"Jeez, that'll buy half of our stock. How much do you intend to try?"

"All of it."

Crap.

Anne started to intervene, afraid Zima was going to prove beyond a doubt that she wasn't human, but, thankfully, Sam saved her the trouble.

"Tell you what," he said, sliding the money back to her. "Hold onto that for now. The first few are on me."

"Thank you. That is very kind."

"It's self-serving. I want your first experience to be a good one so you'll come back." The twinkle in his eye made his lecherous meaning clear.

At least, it did to Anne. She'd seen it time and again over her long waitress career, usually directed at her — confident studs plying their wiles on the serving girl in the hope of a one-night stand.

Sam's smile had irrecoverably lost its charm.

Let him waste his money, Anne thought. *He won't get far with Zima anyway, and she'll get a free education on spirits.*

Anne's self-consolation lasted about three seconds. Sam laid his hand next to Zima's, brushing their knuckles in a casual yet surely calculated maneuver. Anne gripped the bar so hard that the wood cracked. Anger drove her fangs down from her gums and dislodged her false caps.

Suddenly, Anne was very, very hungry.

And only the blood of a lecherous bartender would do.

Carol looked pointedly at Sam and tapped her second empty glass. "Whenever you're done corrupting the alcohol virgin ..."

"Right-o," Sam said.

A tension lifted from Anne's shoulders when Sam's hand stopped touching Zima, and he went to serve Carol another lager.

Anne shook herself.

What's wrong with me? A cute guy talks to my girl and I turn into a rage monster. Zima can take care of herself.

Her anger was totally unreasonable.

And if he touches Zima again, I swear I'll rip his head off.

By the time Anne had finished stewing, Carol was setting down another empty glass. This time, Anne left Sam alone, who had poured Zima her first sample and resumed his predatory perch. Carol's unfocused eyes were on the wooden counter. Her fingers idly stroked lines in the condensation of her glass.

"They did it on purpose," Carol said, her voice distant.

"They?"

"Becky's parents. The little girl's ... *condition* wasn't an accident. It was part of a vampire-worshiper cult ritual. But they changed their minds after she drank the blood, and rushed her to the hospital."

Anne's mouth fell open. There were so many things wrong with that sentence that she didn't know where to start. "Jesus Christ."

"Yeah." Carol waved down the bar, where Zima was sipping the second in a line of colorful shot glasses. "Sam! Another, please."

He grabbed a pint glass and stuck it under the tap. "Going for a record tonight, Doc?"

"Several."

A glass of amber liquid slid down the counter and stopped neatly before Carol.

"Thanks." She turned to Anne when Sam was once again out of earshot. "What's going to happen to Becky?"

Anne fiddled with a napkin. "Are you sure you want to know?"

"It's the reason I got liquored up."

Fair enough.

Anne tried to think of a gentle way to explain the horrors of the transformation to Carol. There wasn't one.

"Pain," Anne said softly. "More than you can imagine, like every cell in your body is breaking and reforming. The transformation only takes a few hours, but it ... it feels like a lot longer."

"I'm sorry," Carol said, her eyes glistening.

"Yeah, me too. The good news, if there is any, is that when Becky wakes up, she'll feel better than she ever did in her life. The bad news is that she'll be hungry, her new diet will be very restricted, and she'll never get to play in the sun again."

"Will she grow up?"

Anne stared at her hands. "I don't know. But if I had to guess ... probably not. The pathogen seems to freeze the body in whatever state it's in at the time of transformation. Including fat cells," she said with a grim chuckle. "You're looking at the only figure I'll ever have."

"You could certainly have done worse." Carol tipped back half her beer in a long series of gulps. "Do me a favor and give me plenty of warning if you ever decide to turn me. I want to hit the gym so I can look my best."

The off-handed joke struck Anne like a jab to the stomach. "I'd never do that, Carol," she said with more heat than she intended. "Not even if you asked."

Carol stared at her before returning to her beer. "Just as well, I guess. This is the only liquid diet I've ever fancied."

"Is this a regular thing for you?" Anne said, eager to change the subject.

"Yep. Sam and I are pals. He keeps the beer flowing, and I keep his cash register full. We're a match made in heaven." She looked down the bar and yelled, "Isn't that right, Sammie?"

"Whatever you say, Doc."

Carol leaned against Anne with an inebriated sway. "Plus he's easy on the eyes," she said, grinning.

Mr. Easy, it turned out, had his eyes glued on Zima, though, fortunately for him, he kept his hands to himself. He was attempting to dazzle her with his vast knowledge of whiskey. For her part, Zima listened attentively, drank when instructed, and described the flavors of each to him as best she could.

Anne smiled despite a pang of jealousy. Seeing Zima interact so naturally with a complete stranger was heartening — even a scumbag like Sam, who was just trying to get her drunk so he could score.

Good luck with that, pal.

"Here it comes," Carol whispered, nodding surreptitiously down the bar. "Watch."

Right on cue, Sam knocked a bottle of whiskey over, spraying golden-brown liquid all over Zima.

That was probably his intention, anyway.

Zima jumped from the stool with characteristic speed and precision, escaping the so-called accident without a drop on her white dress.

Carol stifled a laugh. "That's a first. Usually he gets top and bottom, then it's upstairs to throw the clothes in the wash while he prepares a steamy shower for two."

Anne wasn't amused. Zima even helped him clean up the mess, which only made Anne angrier.

The next thing Anne knew, she was standing behind Zima. Her fangs were at-the-ready — a dangerous position given the world's rising vampire fears — but she couldn't help herself.

"Dance with me?" Anne said through tight lips to keep her canines hidden. It was an absurd request. Neither of them knew how to dance, and even Carol didn't know they were an item.

It doesn't matter.

The music was mellow, and Anne had the fierce need to hold her love. Slow dancing was the excuse she needed.

Zima spared her lecherous host a glance and nodded. Anne led her out to a clear spot between tables, feeling better with every step away from the interloper, and pulled Zima into a comfortable embrace. The music's lull soon had them gently swaying with the rhythm. Anne closed her eyes, nestled her head on Zima's shoulder, and breathed in that earthy scent she loved.

The world fell away. It was just the two of them in all creation, and Anne was happy.

"I did not know you enjoyed dancing," Zima said, snuggling against her.

"Only in the right mood," Anne said softly. "And with the right person."

"That is flattering. Thank you."

They swayed in silence through that song and the next. Anne felt content right down to her toes. She would have stayed like that for the rest of the evening, but Zima cast a pebble into her tranquil pond.

"Is your 'right mood' related to Sam's advances on me?"

Anne nestled deeper into the crook of her neck to hide her embarrassment. "Maybe a little ..."

Zima stopped swaying. When Anne looked up to see what was wrong, Zima kissed her with a tenderness and passion usually reserved for the bedroom. She stopped all too soon, leaving Anne breathless, then touched their foreheads together.

"Thank you," Zima said. "Your jealousy is also flattering."

"No problem," Anne said with a smile. "But just so you know, there are easier ways to get my attention."

"True, though none so far have provoked public exposure of our relationship."

"Is ... is that why you did it? To bring us into the open?"

"No, I merely wished an education in alcoholic beverages from an experienced tutor, and Sam met those requirements. I have learned much."

"Such as?"

"There is a vast price and taste difference between aged and non-aged whiskeys, and I do not like either."

"It's important to know your liquors," Anne said, laughing.

She was about to fall back into their slow-dance embrace when she noticed Carol staring at them. Anne sighed and guided Zima back to the bar. She didn't know where the doctor stood on same-sex relationships, but she had a feeling they were about to find out.

"Not many people dance in this bar," Carol said. She took a long pull from her beer glass. "I think it's nice. Lightens up the place."

Thank God.

"It's good to hear you say that, Carol."

She nodded. "Not everyone likes to dance, of course. I happen to love it. In fact, you may not have guessed, but I'm quite a good dancer myself."

"No, I ... I hadn't guessed." *Not by a long shot.*

"Figures," Sam said, setting another beer in front of Carol. "All the good ones are dancers."

Anne shot him a look, ready to leap over the counter and satisfy her thirst for bartender at the snarky comment, but his smile seemed genuine. As much as she despised his attempted seduction of her girl, not only had he received the message that Zima was off-limits, but he didn't appear to hold a grudge, either.

Sam will live to serve another beer, Anne decided.

"A euphemism," Zima said, sitting up straight. "You are using the word 'dance' as a veiled reference to same-sex relationships."

"You got it," Anne said, happy that Zima had clued into the abstract reference so quickly.

She never would have caught that when we first met. She really has come a long way.

"A clever subterfuge. I shall remember it for future conversations." Zima pulled a hundred-dollar bill from her wallet. "Come," she said to Sam, "I understand rum is made from fermented sugar, which sounds intriguing. I wish to sample your selection."

Sam glanced at her long line of empty shot glasses. "After all that? I don't know how you're even standing, let alone ready for more. Sure you're not really a vampire here to suck all my alcohol away?"

Anne nearly fell from her stool at the casual joke, while Carol sputtered into her glass. Zima simply shook her head and peeled her lips back to show her completely normal canines to him.

"All right." Sam grabbed two clean shot glasses from a shelf. "Round two, coming up."

Once they had settled again at the other end of the bar, Anne leaned close to Carol, who teetered precariously on her stool.

"Are you okay?" Anne said.

"Hmm? Oh, sure. I'm just getting started."

"I mean ... with Becky."

Carol gave her beer an appraising look, then heaved a long sigh. "I don't know. Ask me again in the morning."

Anne nodded. *That's about the best I could hope for.*

The rest of the afternoon was less dramatic. She and Carol chatted about the children, and shared ideas for making the ward more conducive to active patients. Zima's tasting commentary came in a steady stream, often making Anne laugh out loud.

The establishment filled up quickly after five o'clock, turning the quiet bar into a raucous maelstrom of conversation and laughter that hurt Anne's sensitive ears. Carol noticed her discomfort, so they pulled Zima away from her vast collection of empty shot glasses, which she had stacked into a large, perfectly symmetrical pyramid, and Anne drove the doctor to her house a few miles away.

While it wasn't how Anne imagined her first bar experience with Zima would be, it certainly could have gone worse.

6

FAIRYTALE ENDING

T HEIR COUNTRY MANSION was uncharacteristically dark when Anne and Zima finally pulled in the driveway. The paranoid side of Anne immediately suspected trouble. Zima reassured her everything was fine, however, and led her straight inside.

"Charlie and Cappa are in the dining room," Zima said. "We should not keep them waiting."

When Anne saw the dining room, she understood why. The full-length table was set with flickering candles, fine bone china, genuine silver utensils, and wine glasses already filled to the brim. The exception was her own setting, of course, where vampire-paralyzing silverware had been replaced with a lone crystal drinking glass, containing a delicious-smelling liquid. Even from across the room, Anne could tell it was Charlie's blood. For the others, platters of food occupied the center, including mashed potatoes, ham, steamed vegetables, and gravy.

"Wow," Anne said with a laugh. "What's the occasion?"

"You and Cappa always cook for us," Charlie said. "I thought I'd return the favor. Your meal was definitely the easiest." He rounded the table and gave her a warm kiss. "Welcome home."

Anne went to her spot to find Zima waiting attentively behind her chair.

"Why, thank you, madam," Anne said, allowing herself to be seated. "Keep this up and you're going to spoil me."

Zima took the seat next to her, leaving Anne between her and Charlie, as usual.

That was as far as the ceremony went, however. The moment Zima sat down, platters began to make the rounds until the others' plates were piled high. Anne forced herself to sip her delectable meal. Every instinct told her to gulp it down, but she preferred to pace herself so she didn't end up twiddling her thumbs while everyone else ate.

After several minutes, Charlie set his utensils down and raised his wine glass.

"I'd like to make a toast," he said in an uncharacteristically shaky voice. He lowered his head, as if searching for the right words, his wine glass trembling. "The last decade has held so many impossible surprises that I can hardly name them all. One that stands out tonight, however, is Cappa."

Cappa lit up at the compliment, but her frown said she was just as confused as Anne.

"While she was designed with artificial intelligence as the goal," Charlie said, "I would have been happy if she could perform searches for me on the internet, pay the bills, and maybe play a rousing game of chess.

"Cappa exceeded my expectations in every regard. Before I knew it, she was laughing, crying, telling jokes, and evolving at an exponential rate. Only once in all those years did she ask for anything — a body of her own, which I was more than happy to give. I spent over a year getting every detail just right because I wanted it to do justice to the incredible person it would host."

"Charlie ..." Cappa covered her mouth, her eyes misting.

He stood behind her. "She soon became an indispensable research assistant, then an irreplaceable component of lab operations.

"But above all, she was my partner and my friend. When I was working through the night, she was there to correct my sleep-deprived mistakes. When my research hit a wall, she kept me motivated and wouldn't let me give up. When the business became a success, she was there to share the joy and cheered the loudest. When tragedy struck, and I walled myself away, she was my lifeline to the world, my beacon of hope, and my reason for continuing. Even when I found someone else" — he smiled at Anne — "Cappa put her own feelings aside in favor of my happiness. Not only did she support the relationship, she nurtured it, and welcomed the new woman as a sister.

"Cappa has a beautiful soul, which we now know for a fact," Charlie said with a wink, "and it grows more radiant every day. It wasn't until our trip to China, where she expressed her true feelings to me, that I realized it was only a matter of time before some lucky guy snatched her up."

He took Cappa's hand, held her gaze with a tenderness that caught Anne's breath.

"That's a risk I'm no longer willing to take."

Anne's wonder turned to shock.

He isn't, she thought, even as Charlie bent to one knee. *He can't! I mean ...*

Charlie pulled a small black box from his pocket and opened the lid, revealing an elegant golden ring set with a large diamond.

"Cappa, will you marry me?"

The world lurched. Anne grabbed the chair to keep from falling over.

He did. Charlie made his choice.

I've lost him.

She gripped the chair tighter. The wood cracked in her fingers.

No, this is a joke. It has to be, because Charlie would never do something like this without discussing it with me first.

Would he?

If it was a joke, the person hit hardest would be Cappa. Her lips trembled. Tears spilled down over her widening smile. She stretched her fingers out, but seemed afraid to touch it, as if the ring were a skittish animal that would run away at the slightest provocation.

All at once, Cappa's hands fell to her lap. She turned to Anne, her happiness from a moment ago replaced with concern. She, too, knew what this meant for Anne and Charlie's relationship.

Anne clenched her jaw.

There were two things she knew for certain. First, this was Cappa's moment. No one deserved a happy ending more than her soul sister did, and Anne was damned if she would ruin it. Second, Charlie rarely did anything without thinking it through.

She trusted him. They all did. Anne had little reason to question him now.

Setting her misgivings aside, Anne focused on the positive. Two people, whom she loved dearly, were about to be engaged. Anne had the honor of bearing witness to the momentous occasion. It was her privilege to support them, as they had supported her in so many ways. Her rigid jaw relaxed into a genuine smile.

"I can't imagine a better couple," Anne said sincerely. "You were made for each other — and I mean that in more than just the figurative sense."

Charlie had the good grace to look abashed, but Anne waved it off with a grin.

"Well, in that case ..." Cappa turned back to him and held his outstretched hand, her lips trembling with excitement. "Yes! Charlie, I want to spend whatever time we have left on this world as your wife."

The last word stung like a dart in Anne's stomach, but she hid it well, watched Charlie place the ring on Cappa's finger, and the flying hug and kiss that nearly tackled him to the floor. Anne was still reeling when Charlie cleared his throat and pointed behind her.

Anne's breath caught. There on bended knee, with a small white box in her hand, was Zima.

"I —"

"*Yes!*"

Joy flooded Anne like a tidal wave and swept her from the chair, where she landed on her knees before Zima.

"A thousand times yes! I don't know if same-sex marriage is legal in this state, and I don't care. I'll marry you, Zima, even if it's just reciting our vows in front of Mark. I'm sure he can get ordained from one of those online ..." She stopped when Zima's eyes fell to the floor. "What's wrong, honey?"

"You accepted before I recited my proposal speech."

Anne cupped her chin and lifted her gaze. "I can't think of a single thing you could say out loud that you haven't already said in deed. You're my partner at work, my support when I'm in need, and the first person I want to share my joys and sorrows with. You always have my back, even when I'm being stupid, and you seem to understand me when I don't understand myself. You manage to point out my shortcomings without ever making me feel less than wonderful. You're the reason I look forward to the day, and my last thought at night. You've stormed the gates of Hell to rescue me so often that they've given you a named parking spot, and you've asked for nothing in return except my company." Anne kissed her soundly, drawing an eager moan. "My life is yours, Zima, now and forever."

Zima brow-knit. "I ... did not think that you had read it."

"Read what?"

She reached into Anne's jacket hanging on the back of her chair, causing a rustle that Anne suddenly remembered hearing in the locker room at the hospital, and pulled out a folded piece of paper.

"The boy, Kurt, succeeded in his last assignment by delivering my note to you undetected," Zima said, "though it appears you have not read it."

"He snuck into the girls' locker room?"

"Apparently so."

"That little rascal," Anne said with a laugh.

She unfolded the note and frowned. Each letter was precisely crafted and spaced, leaving little doubt in Anne's mind as to the author. What struck her, however, was that apart from the occasional signature, this was the first sample of her girlfriend's — her *fiancée's* — handwriting Anne had ever seen. Zima had so many other efficient means of communication that traditional notes had never been necessary.

This is a limited-edition collector's item, in a way. Dela would probably pay real money for ...

Anne forgot all about that once she started reading. By the end of the short page, her mouth was hanging open. Although the wording was different, Zima's note summarized Anne's speech from a moment ago almost point-for-point. She read and re-read the note until the letters blurred and she had to hold it safely away to keep her tears from staining the precious artifact.

"I ... I guess this means we really are meant for each other," Anne said, wiping her eyes.

"Of that I am certain."

Zima opened the white box, revealing an unadorned, wavy band, the same shade of gray as Zima's preferred outfits. While not a traditional engagement ring, the metallic surface sparkled as if coated with microscopic diamonds.

"It's gorgeous," Anne whispered, not trusting her voice. "Is it made of nanites?"

"No, but they aided in its construction. The base material is pure tungsten, which is four times more durable than titanium, but the optical effect is from approximately two hundred and eighty-seven thousand pieces of embedded wurtzite boron nitride crystals, a mineral reputed to be stronger than diamond, and so rarely occurs in nature that it is difficult to obtain for anything other than research."

Cappa peered over Anne's shoulder and whistled low. "That's beautiful! You don't do anything by halves, do you, Zima?"

Zima shrugged. "I wished it to be durable, yet aesthetically pleasing. These were the best materials to achieve the desired goals."

Zima took the ring from its cradle and held it up expectantly. Anne proffered her trembling ring finger, which Zima placed it on. It fit perfectly, of course, sliding comfortably over her knuckle, yet it stayed firmly in place when Anne experimentally shook her hand.

"Thank you," Anne said, her voice thick. She wrapped her arms around her blue-eyed beauty. "Thank you, thank you, thank you. We'll have fun picking yours out soon, I promise."

"I look forward to it."

Charlie, if anything, looked even more nervous than before. He cleared his throat and stuffed a hand in his pocket.

"There's, ah ... one other matter we need to resolve this evening." He placed a third ring box on the table, then stepped back. "I'd like to propose to Anne, but, as of a few minutes ago, tradition holds that my love belongs to Cappa, just as Anne's now belongs to Zima. We're hardly a traditional family," he said with a grin, "but that doesn't mean we have to break all the rules. Zima and I have already discussed it, and we both agree the decision really lies between Zima and Cappa." His eyes found Anne's. "Please speak out if you don't agree. I know this whole thing was a surprise to you."

Understatement of the century, bucko.

Anne felt like she might drown from the whirlpool of emotions swirling around her head. She took a deep breath to collect herself.

"N-no, I agree. Cappa, Zima, we've made this offer to you before, and it still stands. If … if Charlie and my relationship compromises either of your happiness, especially in marriage, then …" Anne swallowed a lump in her throat, but she knew her offer would carry little weight if she couldn't even finish her sentence. "Then we'll end it."

Charlie looked at Cappa and Zima in turn. "I understand if you'd like to talk it over in private."

"We would," Cappa said, her gaze locked with Zima's.

"Right. Well, then …"

Cappa and Zima didn't take their eyes from each other, even when Charlie and Anne left the room.

They wandered in silence through the halls and into the back garden, where a dusky orange hung over the western sky. Overhead, the night was just starting to take form. Anne fished a container from her pocket, removed her photosensitive contact lenses from her eyes, and placed them inside it.

The black eastern sky exploded into a full canvas of stars. Dark hills in the distance became sharp, every leaf on every tree clear and distinct.

It was beautiful.

Charlie gazed out with her, though she knew his human eyes could never experience the night like she did.

At least, I hope he never does.

He stood close, but Anne sighed when she realized he was deliberately keeping his hands in his pockets.

Instead of around me, as they should be.

"So this is really happening."

"Hard to believe, isn't it?" Charlie shoved his hands further into his pockets. His eyes fell to the grass at his feet. "I'm sorry we didn't get to talk about this beforehand. Zima desperately wanted to surprise you, which meant radio silence until tonight."

"I get it." At the risk of making it harder on both of them, Anne sidled closer and leaned against his pleasantly warm arm. "I'd do just about anything to make her happy."

"I know."

Wind rustled the apple trees, knocking some of the riper fruit to the ground. Anne saw each fall, heard every thump with utter clarity.

"In case this is the end," Anne said softly, "I want you to know that I treasure every moment we've shared."

"M-me too."

The break in his voice made Anne look up. Charlie had already turned away, but his arm snaked around her shoulders. She selfishly pretended that dinner had never happened — that neither of them had just pledged themselves to someone else — and wrapped herself around him as she had so many nights before. She felt his will falter, then eventually break when he returned her embrace, holding her with a strength that bespoke his feelings for her more than words ever could.

"Just for a little while," Anne said, "until —"

OUR DISCUSSION HAS CONCLUDED, Zima sent, the message relayed through Anne's implant into her thought stream. PLEASE RETURN.

"Until they've decided."

Anne's words were a whisper carried away with the breeze. She waited several selfish minutes in his embrace before relaying the message to Charlie. They reluctantly parted, then walked the halls to the dining room like a death row procession.

Their executioners — or saviors — were standing by the table. Zima's face betrayed nothing, as usual, but Cappa wore a frown and looked as if she might regurgitate Charlie's fine cooking.

"First," Cappa said, wringing her hands, "although I appreciate you leaving the decision to us, I really feel it should have been a group discussion. But you did leave it with us, and ..."

Anne watched Cappa's fingers walk toward the box on the table with the apprehension of a spider crawling for her arm. Cappa carried it over to them, biting her lip the whole way.

A piece of Anne shattered when Cappa delicately put the box containing Anne's would-be engagement ring from Charlie back into his pocket.

Cappa, if anything, looked even more pained. "Hold on to that, j-just for now. Zima and I … we love you both, and we love that you love each other, but …" She gripped her dress so tightly that Anne thought she was going to tear it. "Damn! It seems so selfish now that I have to say it out loud."

Cappa took a deep breath and relinquished the death grip on her hapless clothes.

"I-I know that marriage is just a formality, in a way, but it's also a symbol of a new phase of our relationships, where we build our lives together. The problem — and this is the really selfish part — is that I don't know what it's like to have Charlie all to myself. Not since we've been dating, anyway, and if we really are going to build a life together … I feel that if we don't at least try to do it on our own, just for a little while, that our marriage would somehow be a sham."

On our own …

"Wait," Anne said, her mouth so dry she could barely move her tongue. "You're talking about … moving away?"

"No!" Cappa yanked her dress again, then lowered her voice. "Well … yes. B-but just down the block or something. We're still family, after all, and I couldn't stand the idea of being too far from any of you. Even Dela," she said with a lop-sided grin. "The thing is, I've never had a normal life. I didn't grow up in a house with a mom and a dad and a dog named Buddy. My earliest memory was crunching data for a simulated biological tissue experiment. Part of me — a stupid part, maybe — will always feel incomplete until I've at least had a taste of living like a normal human." She stood before Charlie and hesitantly took his hand. "With another normal human — one who understands me like no one else could."

For some reason, the endearing sentiment made Charlie pale. His condition worsened to the point that Cappa and Anne rushed to his side for fear that he might faint.

"I'm fine," Charlie said in a shaky voice. "I just …" He grabbed Anne's arm as if she were his only tether to the world. "Can we talk outside for a minute?"

Without waiting for an answer, he dragged her down the hall and back outside. His long strides didn't stop until they were at the back of their vast property, where he finally released her and began pacing.

"Idiot!" Charlie yelled into the hills. "I'm such a moron! It was obvious. Right there in front of me. But I was so eager to make her happy that ..." He gripped his hair and continued pacing with a series of frustrated grunts.

"What the hell are you talking about?"

"Cappa! I-I shouldn't have done it. It was a mis—"

"Charlie fucking Z!" Anne fought the urge to shake his head from his shoulders. "She's just starting to cope with Almos' loss. You *proposed* to her, for God's sake! With a ring and a flowery speech and everything. If you go back on that now, you'll destroy her!"

Charlie rounded on Anne with such ferocity that she stepped back despite herself.

"I'm not what she needs!" he yelled with fingers clawed. "Didn't you hear her?"

"I heard every goddamned word! Cappa wants a normal life with a normal human who understands her. And last I checked, Mr. Warm-And-Tasty, you fit that description perfectly."

"That's what she wants, not what she needs!"

His anger bled so quickly that Anne wasn't sure it had been there to begin with. Charlie plopped down on the grassy hillside and hunched over his knees.

"You heard her," he said softly, his voice rough. "Cappa didn't have a real childhood. All she ever had was work — thanks to me. It wasn't exactly a nurturing environment, especially in the early days. I gave her life, but I didn't handle it responsibly. She deserves the chance at normalcy that I didn't provide."

Anne sat down next to him and hugged her knees. "So don't shy away from her. Make it right." She nudged him with an elbow. "That's what you do, isn't it? Fix things?"

"Not this time," Charlie said into his arms. "In fact, I may be the only person on the planet who can't."

"You're not making any sense. You love her. She loves you. What more —"

"She wants a normal life. I can't give that to her for the very reason she said she wants me." When Charlie turned to her, tears ran freely down his stubbled cheeks. "I know Cappa too well. Her ins, her outs, how her mind works, what it's made of, the algorithms that make her tick, how to optimize her body functions, power outputs ...

"To have a normal life, she needs someone who sees her as a normal person, and I'll never be able to do that. To me, she's the most wonderful woman I could ever hope to meet, but she'll always be my creation." Charlie's head sank lower. "She deserves more. Cappa needs a fresh start if ..."

Anne was so caught up in the conversation that she hadn't heard the approaching footsteps until they were almost upon them. Cappa and Zima strode into view and sat before them without a word.

"How much did you hear?" Charlie said to Cappa.

"From the time you started talking crazy, so most of it." She took his hand, not a trace of anger on her round face. "Believe it or not, I agree with your logic. Falling in love with Joe Normal and settling down with some adopted kids would be the ideal.

"But here's a harsh truth I don't think you've considered: You're human now, for better or worse, and that means I'll probably outlive you by decades, if not centuries. When you pass away — and I'm not looking forward to that day — I can take as much time as I need to find the right guy and get my fill of the good life, but ..." She grabbed his shirt and drew him in for a tender kiss. "You're here now, Charlie, and I don't want to miss a single minute of it. Can you understand that?"

Charlie gave a weak smile. "No, I ... I think you should explain it again. Especially that last part."

Cappa happily obliged. Minutes later, when they finally parted, her expression grew serious. "So we're okay now? No more talk of backing out because I'm too good for you?"

"Too good for me?" Charlie crossed his arms. "The wind must have confused your audio sensors, because what I said was —"

Cappa silenced him with another kiss. "Quit while you're ahead, buster."

"I guess we know who's going to be in charge of that household," Anne said with a grin.

Zima brow-knit. "In charge? Is not marriage a partnership where each member holds equal —"

"Kidding, honey. You're right. They're equal partners, just like we are."

"Oh." Zima looked back at the house. "We should return to dinner if we are to finish before militia training tonight."

"That's my girl," Anne said, rising gracefully to her feet. "Always thinking with her stomach."

Zima opened her mouth to respond, then snapped it shut and brow-knit. "An expression which insinuates that I irrationally prioritize food above all else?"

"Bingo!" Anne laughed. "First a food connoisseur, now expressions. You'll be ready for a trip to the comedy club before we know it."

"If that is your recommendation."

Anne hooked an arm around her shoulders. "There's no doubt in my mind that you'll enjoy it someday, sweetheart, and it'll be my pleasure to help you get there."

Anne slowed their pace, allowing the others to walk ahead. When Charlie and Cappa had disappeared into the house, Anne stopped and turned to her fiancée.

"So, the decision for Charlie and me to stop seeing each other ... Was the feeling ... *mutual*, between you and Cappa?"

"Yes. I hope that does not upset you. As she stated: it is a selfish request, but I, too, wish for an opportunity to build and explore my relationship with you in a more isolated manner. It is not that I oppose your relationship with Charlie, rather I am curious how our own might differ without him as a factor, and I can think of no practical way to uncover the answer short of doing it."

"Hang on ... You want us to move out, too?"

Zima blinked. "Yes. Is that not how marriage works?"

"Well, yeah, but ..." Anne sighed in frustration. She felt as if the ground were sliding out from under her, and she was clawing at the grass to keep from tumbling into the abyss.

This isn't how an engagement is supposed to feel! We're supposed to be happy and dousing each other in champagne and shoving strawberries down each other's throats.

So why do I feel so miserable?

The answer was simple, of course.

Change.

After losing the factory, they had quickly built a new life here in Montana, and it was a good one. Anne had finally found her groove, both at work and at home. But this joyous thing called marriage threatened to derail her.

As for Charlie ... They had known for a while that this day was coming, but that hadn't stopped them from making the most of the time they were allowed. She didn't regret a single moment of it.

Besides, it's not like we're moving across the country.

They would still see each other at what she hoped would be frequent gatherings, though whether their encounters would be bitter or sweet remained to be seen.

Probably both.

She realized Zima was staring at her, patiently awaiting a response. Anne took a deep breath. When she exhaled, she tried to push all her misgivings out with it.

Her new engagement ring caught the moonlight. Its gray surface sparkled, bringing a tear to her eye.

Change isn't bad, Anne told herself. *I have to let go of the past and embrace the future.*

She wrapped an arm around her fiancée, gave her a reassuring kiss, and walked them both inside.

It sounded like good advice. Anne just hoped she could follow it.

7

HEADQUARTERS

G ENTLE RUBBING ON HIS CHEST stirred Charlie awake. His groggy brain told him he hadn't slept long, but once his mind cleared, he remembered he wasn't supposed to have slept at all. His eyes opened under protest to find Cappa smiling at him from the neighboring pillow.

"Morning, sleepyhead," Cappa said.

Morning? Crap!

Charlie sat bolt upright, but flopped back down when he saw the time on the alarm clock, which read just past midnight.

"Don't scare me like that. I thought you were serious."

"Nope."

"Sorry for dozing off again."

"That's all right." Cappa ran a sultry finger down his bare chest. "I got what I wanted from you first. Besides, I like watching you sleep."

"There must be more interesting ways to pass the time."

Cappa shrugged. "After spending so long inside your cyborg body, regulating your breathing and such, seeing your biological body operate on its own is still novel." She leaned over and pressed her ear against his stomach. "All the little gurgles and wheezes are mesmerizing. Mysterious. It's a wonder human bodies even function with all that chaos inside."

"Now you understand why I made the cyborg." Charlie glanced at the clock and sighed. Another hour or three of rest would have been nice. "Anne's asleep?"

"Yep. She went to bed when they returned from militia training about an hour ago. Zima says she's already in deep slumber."

"Without any help?"

"A little. Making a vampire sleep at night is like putting a toddler to bed in the middle of a birthday party. But with her implant's help, and Zima's clever programming, Anne's adjusting. If nothing else, she does seem peppier during the day."

"That's good, at least," Charlie said, though he felt guilty.

Using her implant to help her sleep had been Anne's idea, mostly so she could work at the hospital during the day without feeling groggy.

What Anne didn't know was that he and the others had actively encouraged the behavior not because she needed it, but to make sure she stayed unconscious until morning.

"You okay?" Cappa said. "You're wearing frowny face again."

"Yes, I just … I hate lying to her."

"Me too," Cappa said with a sigh. "On the bright side, Zima has almost figured out a way to block the Entity entirely. Another few weeks of data and she should be ready to implement a solution."

"That's great news."

Charlie slid from under the sheets and headed for the dresser, but stopped when he saw a full set of clothes already laid out on the chair. He raised an eyebrow at Cappa.

She shrugged. "Picking your clothes out gives me something to do while you sleep besides listening to your tummy gurgles. It also means I get to choose which boxers you wear."

"Silk ones, I see. What a surprise."

"They're comfy," Cappa said, pouting. "I even ordered some for myself."

"I didn't know they made boxers for women."

"They don't. I wanted a fly so I could give you easier access to the good stuff."

"How thoughtful," Charlie said, chuckling. "So when are you going to let me pick out your clothes?"

"When you learn to appreciate fashion." Cappa swept back the sheets with a flourish and strolled naked to the closet, then plucked a blue dress out from her vast collection. "In other words, never."

"I don't know, I think you'd look hot in a flannel shirt and jeans."

Her smug expression faltered. "Really?"

"Really. Women in men's clothes are a turn-on."

Cappa stared off for a second. "I hope you're serious, because I just ordered five full outfits and two pairs of hiking boots."

"I guess you'll find out when they arrive," Charlie said with a smirk.

She threw a wadded pair of panties at him. "I really hate you sometimes."

"Now where have I heard that before?"

"From anyone who knows you. Get dressed, smartass. Everyone's waiting for us in the garage."

Everyone except Anne, Charlie thought bitterly.

Smiles greeted them all around when they finally reached the garage for their nightly work *soirée.*

"Congrats on your engagement," Mark said, clasping his shoulder. "Zima told us the good news."

"How's Anne doing with it?" Doris said.

"Fine," Charlie lied. He looked at Zima for confirmation, who shrugged.

Thanks for nothing.

"We all agreed it was time to move on, so ..." Charlie tried to play it cool, but Doris' scowl said she didn't buy it.

"Later," Doris mouthed.

For once, Charlie was grateful. Doris understood Anne like no one else, and, although she could be brash, he found her relationship opinions insightful.

Not to mention she's the only one among us who's been married before.

He accepted a hug from Dela, too, before they all piled into their cars.

•　　　•　　　•

The drive to their chocolate factory was a short one. They parked around back, as they always did for these nightly sessions. Charlie led the way inside, through the manufacturing floor, past his office, and into the middle of the loading dock.

Dela pressed her palm to the wall, a spot that looked like any other, then bounded over with a grin to stand with the others.

Seconds later, a large section of floor lurched downward, carrying them two stories underground to the real manufacturing floor.

When they had bought the factory, the basement had been littered with aged boxes and crates. Now, rows of nano-manufacturing units churned out a steady stream of parts, which robot arms assembled into the reason for the company's existence.

Zima pulled a submachine gun from the nearest rack. She examined it from every angle, cocked it, triggered the firing pin a few times, then repeated the process with several others at random.

"Quality is improved over yesterday's batch," Zima said. "The slides no longer stick."

"Good thing, too," Cappa said. "The delivery truck will be here in three hours. I was afraid they might have to leave with only the leftover pistols from last week."

"I'll start the live-fire testing," Dela said. "It'll be a stretch, but I should be able to finish in time."

"Might as well bring a few of the new vests," Doris said. "Ain't no sense shipping this fancy stuff if it won't actually stop a bullet."

"I'm sure Nick and the rest of the resistance agree," Mark said. "Thanks, Doris."

"You betcha. I ain't good at tech stuff like you boys, but I'm a great hole checker."

Dela wheeled a full gun rack out of the way with a groan and put a new one in place, where robot arms began filling it from the bottom.

"Speaking of Nick," Dela said to Zima, "what's the sitrep since last night, General?"

Zima grabbed another full rack and rolled it away with enviable ease. "No new incidents from Houston, Nashville, San Diego, or Atlanta. Chicago reports two skirmishes resulting in four allied deaths and seven confirmed enemy kills. No skirmishes reported from New York, although analysis of recent crime activity indicates a sixty-two percent chance that a major assault is imminent. I have transferred seventy-four combat units from Philadelphia and Buffalo in anticipation. They shall require additional supplies, which I have already itemized for Cappa. Vampire activity in Los Angeles has increased by one hundred and thirteen percent over the last eight days."

"Christ!" Mark plopped down at his workbench. "Seriously?"

Zima brow-knit. "Yes. Why would I lie?"

"It's ... never mind. Please continue."

"As you wish. We do not have armed units to spare in Southern California, so I have authorized the conversion of three hundred and sixty-four Resistance members to vampires to fill the anticipated need."

Charlie's mouth went dry. "Three *hundred?* Is that necessary?"

"Yes. I have run extensive simulations, and the crime patterns depict not only disperse enemy activity, but advanced tactical execution. Los Angeles extends over a large geographic area. The extra units are necessary to ensure adequate coverage. I have also ordered three senior officers from San Francisco to assist with training, and shall devote more of my simulation time to ensure optimal strategies are being employed."

"I don't know how you do it," Doris said. "Calling the shots for the entire country is one hell of a feat."

"Especially at that level of detail," Cappa said. "Are you holding up all right, Zima?"

"It is ... taxing, but the greatest difficulty is excusing myself to Anne. She has asked four times about my inattentive behavior while I am running intensive strategic planning, and I am beginning to struggle for excuses."

"Leave that one to me, doll cakes," Doris said. "I'll spin a yarn for her tomorrow and fill you in on the details. Anne won't ask again."

"What does yarn have to do with —"

"It means she'll lie for you," Dela said, smiling.

"Oh. Thank you, Doris."

While the others carted the day's batch of weapons and equipment off for testing, Charlie pulled a chair up next to Mark. His friend held one of the prototype gauss rifles. It had no muzzle flash, little recoil, incredible range, and was safer than plasma to the surrounding area. Mark's other hand held a companion prototype: self-guided rounds built especially for the gauss rifle. Together, they were more powerful than a 30 mm gunship cannon and had unerring accuracy — or would be once they worked out the kinks.

But Mark's hands were still, and his eyes unfocused.

"Over three hundred new vampires," Mark said softly. "How many does that make now?"

"Roughly twelve thousand, by my count," Charlie said.

They shared a grim look.

Mark shook his head. "I wish there were another way."

"Me too."

There were other ways, of course, some of which he and Mark were currently working on. But, right now, they agreed Nick Orwing's approach of fighting vampires with vampires was the only viable option which both limited civilian casualties and kept the opposing vampire population in check.

And it had proven effective. Cappa's forecasting models estimated the total vampire population would be twenty to forty times higher without the constant pressure and occasional culling from their strategic strikes. Rebels patrolled likely feeding zones and raided enemy blood supply houses, which restricted enemy vampire population by necessity.

That the government hadn't stepped in was no surprise. The enemy had made several crucial plays early on that were now paying off. Top officers in key government branches were either vampires themselves, had family members held captive by them, or had simply been bought off.

Enemy infiltration ran deep. Very deep. Any serious inquiries that might result in significant action were tied up in bureaucratic knots so tight that it would take a veritable Armageddon to get anything moving.

Meanwhile, Charlie was happy to see that citizens had taken matters into their own hands. What was once whispered by conspiracy theorists was starting to become fact.

Vampires were real. Everyone knew someone who had a friend who had seen one: a dark figure leaping the rooftops with impossible speed, a pale stranger lurking the street corner who moved more like a panther than a person, or someone who had inexplicably estranged themselves from friends and family.

Vampires stole memories, some said, which was why firsthand accounts were so few. They could only be killed by silver, others maintained. Growing witness accounts espoused theories of a secret war fought in the shadows between demonic factions.

These rumors and more continued to build, mostly fed by the rebellion in an effort to spur the populace. People didn't feel safe. The government wasn't helping. Local police were underfunded and overextended. So militias had begun to spring up everywhere.

Gun shops couldn't keep anything on their shelves. Silver prices had skyrocketed. Cracks of firearm practice echoed from every hill and valley.

We will not be caught unprepared, their voices said. *We shall not be taken without a fight,* their actions screamed. *We are afraid, but we are not sheep.*

We are wolves. We have teeth, strength in numbers, and we, too, can hunt.

His cyborg body — or Cappa's Charlie self, as she called it — entered the room carrying a stack of heavy boxes that the real Charlie couldn't even lift.

Soon, Charlie thought.

The damage to its neural matter during their escape from Z-Tech had been beyond repair, but a replacement was almost ready. It would take time for his spirit to bond with the new artificial brain, he knew, but Charlie wasn't worried.

His spirit was strong. Cappa's spirit was even stronger, and she wielded it with unprecedented skill. They wouldn't repeat his mistake from five years ago.

Charlie would inhabit his creation again. His real body would remain safe and strong. They would block the Entity from Anne, and then ...

Charlie grabbed a prototype weapon from the table and, without a word, shot his cyborg body twice. The high-velocity rounds whipped through the air with sharp cracks. Each left a growing red stain in his shirt, but his doppelgänger simply looked over and gave him a thumbs-up.

"No structural damage," Cappa said. "The new armor plating held up great."

Charlie set the pistol down and smiled. His cyborg body smiled back, so like his own that, for a moment, he thought he was looking in a mirror.

Soon, we'll reclaim our home — our San Francisco.

One bloodsucker at a time.

8

UNEXPECTED GUEST

ANNE TWIRLED IN THE MIDDLE of the living room once more. *Our living room,* she thought with giddy delight. *In our house.*

It seemed too good to be true, yet here it was: a vaulted ceiling, a plush couch, reclining chairs, throw rugs, a country-style coffee table, a fireplace, even a chiming grandfather clock. Their house was nicer than anything Anne had ever dreamed of owning.

And the best part was that she and Zima had done it together. Everything from fabric to paint color to the design on the cork coasters had been joint decisions to craft their home into a place they both enjoyed.

Zima emerged from the kitchen holding a bowl and a wooden spoon. Her apron was spotless, as usual, a feat Anne could never manage when making anything with cocoa powder. Yet Zima repeatedly produced brownies with such precision that the counters rarely needed more than a single wipe to be returned to their pristine state.

"What is it, my love?" Anne said. "Can I help with dinner?"

"No. The others are due to arrive in six minutes, which is two-minutes-and-forty-three seconds longer than the casserole needs to finish, and the table is already set. I merely wished to be in the same room as my wife."

Wife.

The word still made Anne tingle, especially when Zima said it. They had been married for a full week now — one week less than Charlie and Cappa — but it still felt like yesterday that she and Zima had recited their vows beneath the white trellis in the manor's estate gardens.

Anne sashayed over, dipped a finger in the brownie mixture, and smeared the tip of Zima's nose. Zima went cross-eyed at the smudge.

"Sorry," Anne said, giggling. "Let me clean that for you." She tilted her head sideways and sucked the mixture off, letting her tongue play before declaring it clean. "Better?"

Bowl forgotten, Zima pulled her into a passionate kiss that made Anne wish dinner guests weren't arriving in a few minutes. Zima ended it sooner than she would have liked and nuzzled her neck.

"Thank you," Zima said.

"For what?"

"Cleaning me. I shall return the favor later, I promise."

They were silent for a moment, happy in each other's embrace, until Zima brow-knit.

"Do you wish to have children? With me?"

Anne gulped. "A-are you serious?"

"Yes. Raising children is a core component of marriage, is it not?"

"Well ... yes, but not for every couple." Anne fidgeted with Zima's apron while her love waited with trademark patience for the answer Anne had hoped she would never have to give.

It was a foolish wish. Like Cappa, Zima wanted to experience every aspect of married life. Children were a natural part of that, which meant the topic had to come up eventually.

"Honey," Anne said softly, feeling a lump form in her throat. "Th-there's something you need to know. Something I should have told you long before the wedding." Her trembling fingers had nearly unraveled the knot at the back of Zima's apron. Her tongue felt like dried parchment, but Anne swallowed and forged ahead. "S-something that happened after I was raped as a teenager."

"Whatever it is, I wish to hear."

She needs to know. My dearest Zima deserves no less.

Even if she hates me for it.

Anne drew a ragged breath, fingers shaking like brittle twigs in a gale. "Zima, soon after I arrived in San Francisco, I dis—"

Footsteps on their wooden porch made Anne pause. She was guiltily relieved for the interruption. She went to answer the door, but a gentle tug pulled her back. Zima was staring at her, seemingly unconcerned with the arrival of their guests.

Anne kissed her lightly and smiled. "Later," she whispered. "I-I'm not ready to tell anyone else, and you know Cappa and Mark are already listening."

Zima's expression was unreadable, as usual, but she eventually nodded and released Anne to admit the others.

Cappa was first in. Her face lit up when she saw their new living room. "It's beautiful! Country décor with a modern edge."

Anne wrapped her soul sister in a hug. "Thanks. Zima was a big help with the color matching."

"I'm surprised it's not all gray," Charlie said from behind Cappa.

Anne matched his grin and wrapped him in a friendly embrace. Their lips instinctively went on a collision course, but they remembered themselves at the last moment and ended with a light peck on each other's cheeks. Neither could hold back a regretful sigh when they parted. Anne quickly plastered a smile on and let her hand rest on his arm, doing her best to ignore how good his firm muscles felt.

I'm so glad I don't blush anymore.

It was too much to hope that Cappa hadn't noticed the awkward exchange, but Anne did her best to pretend it had never happened, and spoke to Charlie as she would any other friend.

"How's your own house coming?"

Charlie glanced across the street at the yellow house facing them and feigned a grimace. "Very teal. It's like living in an aquarium."

"You had every chance to give creative input," Cappa said with a shrug. "You abstained. I was feeling marine. Live with it."

"Can't beat the location, though, can you?" Doris said.

It was true. Selecting a house had been a more arduous process than Anne imagined. She and Zima had visited every available home in town, and several of them two or three times. They'd had long conversations about location, layout, view, and structure before finally agreeing on one that they both liked.

But there had been a problem. No other houses had been available for miles in any direction, and Anne had desperately wanted Cappa and Charlie for neighbors.

Charlie had fixed that by offering the owners across the street a ridiculous amount of money, which they'd accepted with smiling faces. Charlie and Cappa had moved in the same week as Zima and Anne. Dela had been very vocal about wanting to remain at the mansion, to which Mark and Doris heartily agreed. Fortunately, the few miles distance had not diminished how often Anne saw her friends.

Mark and Dela shuffled in last, arm in arm. Anne hugged them both in turn.

"Love the new place," Mark said. "Cheerful and practical, just like the owners."

"It's too bright," Dela said with a scowl. "The master of all vampires should live in a stone castle with gargoyles. And the Dark Angel's dwelling should be foreboding, like a skull cave high on a stormy mountain. This," she said, gesturing around, "is about as intimidating as Donna Reed's kitchen."

Cappa planted a fist on her hip and glared. "One of these days, I'm going to teach you about manners, young lady. And I swear it won't be an easy lesson."

"Bring it on, Mary Poppins. We'll see who breaks first."

Fortunately, Zima chose that moment to emerge from the kitchen, carrying two piping hot dishes with her bare hands, and placed them on the perfectly set table. "Please sit. The other courses will be out shortly."

The domestic scene brought a tear to Anne's eye. Zima had once struggled to hold a conversation without killing everyone in the room. Now she was hosting dinner, and doing it marvelously.

Zima cocked her head, eyes flitting from person to person. "What is wrong?"

Anne looked around. Apparently, she wasn't the only one who had noticed. Mark and Charlie were staring at Zima with open mouths, while Cappa's smile spoke of surprise and delight.

Dela's scowl only deepened. "What's next?" she grumbled. "A quiche?"

"Yes," Zima said. "I shall return with it in a moment."

Dela fell to her knees and clawed Anne's dress. "No, no! You've turned the Dark Angel into a quiche eater! We're all doomed!" She clambered to her feet and grabbed Anne by the shoulders. "Is this the Entity's work? Is its doomsday plan to turn everyone into quiche eaters so it can simply pluck the world from their meek little fingers?"

"No," Anne said with a sigh. "Just the usual. It wants me to bite you, then feed you my blood and turn you into a vampire."

"Thank goodness! That's a plan I can live with." Dela grinned and rolled up her sleeve.

"Don't even joke about that," Cappa said, her face ashen.

"Who says I'm joking?"

"Oh! I'm going to thump you so hard when we spar next that it'll knock those insolent freckles right off your face."

"Not if I'm a vampire, you won't!"

It was Anne's turn to grab Dela by the shoulders. "I'm not turning anyone into a vampire!"

Though I wouldn't mind a little snack ...

Dela smelled delicious, as usual, but Anne forced the tantalizing thought from her head. Feeding on houseguests was undoubtedly a no-no in the Vampire Book of Etiquette. If it wasn't, she was about to write it in.

"Now ... please put your" — *mouthwatering* — "arm away and let's sit down for dinner. Zima insisted on cooking it herself, and has worked very hard on everything — *including* the quiche."

Dela winced, but Anne ignored her and saw everyone to their seats. Zima soon brought out the rest of the food, including a warmed glass of blood for Anne, and, for a time, the only sounds were those of happy eating.

A solitary set of footsteps on the porch made her and Zima pause.

"Solicitor?" Mark said.

Anne shrugged.

Zima rose from her seat, but Anne waved her back down.

"You sit, my kitchen hero. I'm still wearing my makeup, so I may as well make use of it."

Silence followed Anne to the door, where came a knock. She listened for a second, and was satisfied to hear a heartbeat on the other side.

Not a vampire, then.

It was beating rapidly, accompanied by short, shallow breaths, as though the person was very nervous. Movement behind Anne showed Zima retrieving the plasma pistol from the custom holster mounted under the table. She casually concealed it behind her back, then stood just a few paces behind Anne.

Welcome, stranger, Anne thought bitterly.

She wasn't upset with her love for being cautious, rather that they lived in a time that merited such extreme measures. With a sigh, she opened the door, hoping for the new arrival's sake that their intentions were non-hostile.

Anne froze.

A young woman, twenty-years-old at most, stood rocking on her heels. She bit her lip when the inside lights shone upon her fair skin and shimmered from her shoulder-length auburn hair. The girl fidgeted with the button of her jeans rounding her hips and cinching her waist under a full bosom, accentuating her hourglass figure.

Looking into her dark brown eyes was like staring into a mirror of the past, when Anne's own were bright and full of wonder. A large suitcase slipped from the girl's fingers and landed on the porch with a weighty *thunk*.

No, Anne thought, feeling her legs wobble. *S-she can't be ...*

The girl smiled, a gesture of innocence and happiness that Anne knew all too well — felt in her soul.

Then the lovely young woman removed all doubt by uttering the only word in the English language capable of driving Anne speechless to her knees.

"Mom?"

9

REUNION

T HE ONLY SOUND in Anne's new living room was the ticking mantle clock over the fireplace.

Anyone with eyes could see that the lovely girl standing in the doorway was Anne's daughter: her hourglass figure, her uncertain shuffling from foot to foot, her brown eyes, focused on Anne with a mixture of anxiety and hope.

There were differences, of course. A small diamond stud dotted the left side of her nose. Where Anne's hair was pure auburn, the girl had a natural white shock at her right temple. Her clothes, too, were a generation ahead of her mother's. Metal rivets dotted the sleeves and collar of her black leather jacket. A steel chain hung between the belt loops of her jeans, and beneath her pant legs were steel-toed black leather boots.

Anne had never seen anything more beautiful in her life.

"Mom," the girl said, more confident this time. "Are you okay?"

Anne nodded in a stupor. "Just ... p-please say that again."

The girl smiled with misty eyes. "Mom."

Still on her knees, Anne held her trembling arms out. The young woman took a hesitant step inside the house. Her composure broke, and she rushed into Anne's eager embrace.

That did it. The tears Anne had been holding back came forth in a torrent. She laughed, she cried, she held her daughter tight. The baby she remembered — the tiny newborn who had fit comfortably in her palms — was a full-grown woman, the same age Anne had been when she'd given birth.

Anne clutched her daughter tighter, as if doing so would make up for all the years she had missed, the books she had never read to her, the birthday parties she hadn't attended, the scraped knees she hadn't kissed, the homework she hadn't helped with, the advice she hadn't given, the —

"Mom, you should put a jacket on," the girl said. "You're freezing!"

Anne jerked away. The girl released her, but quickly caught Anne's hand, as if she was afraid Anne might run away.

"Right," Anne said, "I'll j-just, ah ..."

Charlie knelt beside Anne and wrapped his coat around her shoulders. "There you go." He turned to the girl with a smile that almost hid his shock. "I don't believe we've been introduced."

"Oh, sorry. I'm Tabitha."

"Tabitha," Anne said dreamily. The name fit her daughter like a tailored dress. "That's beautiful."

"Thanks. You can call me that if you want, but I normally go by Tabby."

"Tabby, then," Charlie said. "I'm Mason Roebuck, and this is my wife —"

"I think we're past aliases," Cappa said, putting a hand on his shoulder. She graced Tabby with a radiant smile. "I'm Cappa, though you can call me Auntie Cappa, if you want, since Anne is practically my sister. And this is Charlie Z."

Tabby's eyes widened. "Charlie Z? As in ... Z-Tech?"

"None other," Charlie said, though his eyes reflected the same doubt as everyone else's. Tabby knew Anne's identity, but not his, begging the question ...

"Tabby," Anne said, "I'm glad you're here, but ... how did you find me?"

Tabby blushed. "Oh, um … it wasn't hard. You can find anything on the internet these days if you know what to search for."

"Not us," Mark said, crossing his arms. "Tabby, listen very carefully. We've gone through great pains to keep our identities and whereabouts hidden, and that includes doing frequent internet searches to make sure we don't accidentally show up somewhere. Few people outside this room know we're even alive, let alone where we are. I can count them on one hand — and I can all but guarantee you don't know any of them. So, let's try this again. How did you find your mother?"

Tabby shrank with every word until she was shaking. "I … um … I sh-shouldn't say."

Mark advanced. No one tried to stop him.

Tabby cowered against Anne, who wrapped her in an embrace. Her protective mother instincts were in full swing, conflicting with the obvious fact that if information had leaked somehow, the lives of her and those she loved — including Tabby, now — might be in danger.

Anne gently leaned away to look her daughter in the eyes. "Tabby, this is important. You need to tell us what you know, or —"

Anne cursed when her phone buzzed in her pocket. She was tempted to ignore it, but Dr. Toben sometimes called with emergencies. She pulled it out and glanced at the screen.

It was her brother, Doug. Anne started to put it away until the realization struck her.

Doug was one of the few people who knew where Anne lived.

And he's the only person outside of the adoption agency who knows I have a child.

With a sigh, Anne accepted the call. "Hi, Dougie," Anne said with exaggerated sweetness.

"Anne! Um … I-I'm not sure how to tell you this, but —"

"You found my daughter, for some reason," Anne said coolly, "and then you gave her my address."

Silence. "I, ah … guess she contacted you, then."

"You could say that. She's in my living room."

"Hi, Uncle Doug," Tabby said. "S-sorry for not telling you I was leaving. I, ah, might have rifled your desk while you were at work and found Mom's address."

Mark leveled a stern glare at Anne.

"He's my brother! I-I couldn't let him think I was dead again. It would have torn him apart!"

"But you could have told *us* that you told him," Mark said.

Anne fiddled with her dress, feeling as embarrassed as her daughter looked. "Yeah. Sorry."

"And *I'm* sorry for not telling you Tabby was living with us," Doug said through her phone. "With you out of the area and in hiding, I just ... I thought you'd want me to keep an eye on her."

"No, it's ... it's fine."

The fault, if anywhere, lay with Anne. Her brother had spent most of his life not knowing whether Anne was alive or dead. They had only just recently reconnected, then Anne had been kidnapped and allegedly died. And then Z-Tech had gone up in a ball of fire, effectively killing her again. When she'd arrived in Montana, she couldn't bear the thought of Doug believing he'd lost his sister again, so she'd reached out to him with strict instructions to not tell anyone.

She had not, however, told him she was a vampire — let alone the master of all vampires with a strange Entity in her head. Nor had she told him any of Z-Tech's secrets, including Zima, that she was married, that anyone else from Z-Tech had survived, or about Orwing and how they were probably still hunting for her. Doug didn't have the full story, so it wasn't his fault if he had inadvertently put Tabby in danger by allowing her to discover Anne was alive and where she lived.

But there's one thing it doesn't excuse.

"Dougie, why didn't you tell me she knew I was alive?"

"She's nineteen, and has a right to know who her biological parents are. But I never told her you were alive, let alone your address, though in retrospect I should have been much more careful about where I kept that information. Look, I assume she just arrived. I don't want to interrupt your reunion. Please call me later. There are some ... things you should know about Tabby, but they can wait."

Things?

"Okay, we'll talk later, then." Anne said goodbye and turned back to her daughter. "Well, regardless of how you found me, I'm glad you did, so let's introduce the rest of the family. This is Mark and Dela Suther."

"Pleased to meet you," Dela said behind a strained smirk.

"Should I call you Auntie, too?" Tabby said.

"That's more Cappa's thing, but if you're interested in learning karate, you can call me *sensei*."

"Oh, I've always wanted to learn! Sign me up, *sensei*."

Dela grinned. "I like her already."

"And this is Doris," Anne said, "without whose wisdom and guidance I wouldn't have survived my twenties."

"It's a pleasure, sugar cakes," Doris said. "Anne's the kid I never had, which makes you instant family. If you need anything, just let me know."

Tabby's smile grew wider. Her eyes sparkled. "I will, Doris. Thank you."

"Last, but not least," Anne said, "this is Zima, my ... my wife."

"Your wife?" Tabby laughed. "That's great! I guess I have two moms now. Pleased to meet you, Zima."

Still holding Anne's hand as if she was afraid she'd lose her, Tabby stood and stepped toward Zima, her other hand extended in greeting.

Her smile faltered when Zima took an equal step back.

"I ... I won't bite, I promise." Tabby took another step forward, dragging Anne with her.

Zima stepped back again, maintaining a fixed distance, as if an invisible pole separated them.

Tabby frowned and looked at Anne.

Anne took a deep breath. "Zima, I know this is a ... a bit of a surprise, but I promise it doesn't change anything between us. I understand if you're angry with me, but can you at least give Tabby a chance?"

Zima didn't answer. She was staring at Anne and Tabby's joined hands, her expression unreadable, as usual.

Tabby released her mother. "Sorry for coming to your house unannounced," Tabby said to Zima. "It looks like I've interrupted dinner. I can come back later, if you like."

Zima remained silent.

Tabby cleared her throat. "Like Mom said, I don't want to replace you. In fact, I'd like to get to know you." She extended her hand again and took another step forward.

Zima stared at the proffered hand for several seconds, stone-still. She eventually reached out, but gasped at the last instant and jerked away. Her eyes darted around the room, as if she'd suddenly remembered everyone was there.

Before Tabby could utter another word, Zima skirted around her, maintaining a wide berth, and hurried out the front door.

Anne rose to follow, but Dela darted past her and grabbed a jacket from the coat hook.

"Don't worry, I'll take care of Zima," Dela said. "You just enjoy your reunion."

"I'm coming, too," Doris said. She joined Dela and grabbed her own jacket. "Don't pout, Red. I know you mean well, but that mouth of yours is likely to do more harm than good, and we both know it. Now get a move on!"

The door had just closed when Mark opened it again and followed them out.

"Damage control, just in case," he said, to which a grateful Anne, Charlie, and Cappa nodded.

Tabby turned back to Anne with tear-filled eyes. "She ... didn't know about me?"

"No," Anne said, feeling two-feet tall. "No one did, except your Uncle Doug. I was going to tell her — tonight, in fact — but ..."

Anne choked on the last word. There was no excuse other than her own cowardice — her shame at being so unstable that she'd had to give up her newborn daughter to complete strangers.

"Well," Cappa said cheerfully, "what's done is done. As far as surprises go, this is a great one." She took Tabby by the shoulders and smiled. "Tell you what ... why don't you stay at our place tonight? That way Anne and Zima can have some space to work things out, and everyone will be fresh for tomorrow."

"Oh, I ... Well, if you're sure it's okay."

"Okay? As your Auntie Cappa, I insist! We'll take your suitcase over right now and set up one of the guest rooms."

Cappa joined Charlie at the door, who grabbed Tabby's suitcase. Tabby started to follow, but Charlie waved her back.

"Stay here with your mom. Zima and the others may not be back for a while, and I'm sure you two have a lot to catch up on."

"Thanks, Mr. Z."

"Call me Charlie," he said with a smile. "Anne is family, which means you are, too."

Tabby brightened. "Thanks, Charlie. That means a lot."

"And it would mean a lot to *me* if you would please keep our identities and locations to yourself. It's very, very important. Okay?"

"Okay," Tabby said, looking less sure of herself. "I promise."

Charlie gave a final nod, then the two of them left Anne alone with her daughter.

"What was that all about?" Tabby said. "Mom, are you in some kind of trouble?"

That's putting it mildly.

But telling her daughter about the Entity in her head and Anne's linchpin role in keeping it from taking over the world would frighten Tabby away before Anne even got a chance to know her. That story could definitely wait.

"Nothing immediate," Anne said truthfully. "More of a precaution is all. It's kind of a long story, best told when the others are around."

"Oh." Tabby's frown indicated she wasn't happy with the answer. She glanced at the table of half-eaten food, then at the door where everyone had just left, and sagged as if a sudden weight had piled onto her shoulders. "I'm sorry for being so disruptive. I had this joyous reunion in my mind. I guess I didn't expect ..."

"That I wouldn't have told anyone." Anne sat back down on the floor. "No, it's my fault. This would have gone a lot smoother if I had. Zima has enough trouble with social situations without having something like this sprung on her."

"'Zima' is a strange name," Tabby said. "Where's she from?"

"Eastern Europe." In fact, Anne had no idea in which country Orwing's cybernetics operations — where Zima had been created — were located, only that it was "over there." She made a mental note to ask Zima later. "Have you traveled much?"

"Oh, sure. After Mom died, Dad took me with him on business trips, usually to Singapore or Hong Kong. My favorite trip was Paris, though, because of the awesome drinking chocolate."

"You mean hot chocolate?"

"No, I mean drinking chocolate. Imagine a chocolate bar melted into an espresso cup, served with a fresh croissant."

"That sounds delicious," Anne said, trying to remember a time when it was actually true. "I'm … I'm sorry to hear about your mom. Your real mom, I mean."

"You are my real mom."

"No," Anne said, fighting a swell of emotions. "I gave up that privilege when I signed the adoption papers."

Tabby fiddled with her jacket zipper — a move so familiar that Anne could have been looking in a mirror.

"If you don't mind me asking … Why did you sign those papers? I won't get upset," Tabby said quickly, "no matter what the answer is. But if I don't ask, I'll always wonder."

Oh boy.

Anne stood and paced the room while she gathered her thoughts.

"F-first, please understand that I didn't want to give you up. Handing you over to the doctor, knowing I may never see you again, was the hardest thing I've ever done."

And, given the insane events of this last year, that's saying something.

"I cried for three weeks straight after leaving the hospital. But if I had to do it over again, I'd make the same decision."

"But … why?" There was no mistaking the hurt in Tabby's voice.

"Because it was the right thing to do." Anne took Tabby's hands into her own, heedless of how frigid they must have felt to her daughter. "I was a mess, Tabby. I could barely take care of myself, let alone raise a child."

"Then why have me at all?"

"How can you even ask that? I mean, look at you! Without any help from me, you've grown into a lovely young woman, just like I knew you would."

Tabby blushed. "So, who's my real dad? The adoption papers didn't say. Is it Charlie?" Her sparkling eyes said she hoped he was.

"N-no, honey, I, ah …" *Mayday, mayday!* "Th-the truth is that I … I don't know."

"You don't know? W-what's that supposed to mean?" Tabby reddened. "How is that even possible? Look, if you don't want to tell me, just say so."

"No! It's not that, I swear. It's …"

God help me.

Anne drew a breath, intent on telling Tabby the awful truth about her conception, but the twinges of a flashback stopped her short. Her post-traumatic stress disorder hadn't triggered even once since her reconciliation with her brother. But for some reason, with her daughter here, the idea of telling her the awful tale threatened to bring a full hallucination with it.

Anne wouldn't put her daughter through that. Not only would it be traumatizing for them both, for Tabby it would be dangerous. Anne sometimes lashed out during her flashbacks. With her vampire strength, the result could be deadly. She needed to change the subject.

"Tabby, would you like to go for a walk?"

"Sure, but first I'd like to know who my d—"

"Tabby, please! We'll talk about that later, I promise."

When the others are around to keep you safe from me.

"Zima and I are active members of the local militia, who train nightly," Anne said. "With any luck, Dela, Mark, and Doris have already tracked her down and are headed there now. It's not the best place to talk, but it would mean a lot to me to be able to share the experience with you. And Zima," she said quickly. "Maybe she'll be open to talking if she interacts with you in a more routine environment."

"If you don't mind me saying, her behavior was a little strange. Is she on the autism spectrum? Asperger's syndrome?"

"Something like that, but she's also the sort of person who'd give you the shirt off her back once you get to know her. And I'd really love it if you did."

"Oh, I-I had no idea." Tabby drew herself up and sighed. "You promise we'll talk more about my father later?"

"I pinky swear it. Deal?" Anne held her little finger out.

Tabby hooked her pinky around Anne's and smiled. "Deal. Let's go, and … you should bring some gloves, Mom. Your hands are still freezing."

"G-good call," Anne said, laughing nervously. "How have I lived without you?"

"Like a walking icicle, I'd guess."

"True enough."

Anne did as suggested, added a scarf for good measure, then followed her daughter outside, fervently hoping that her Zima — her love, her wife — was waiting for them at the training grounds.

10

NEGLECTED

Anne bent a branch back to let Tabby pass. Several small scratches already lined her daughter's once-pristine black leather jacket, which was more a testament to her lack of country exposure, Anne suspected, than the narrow forest path. Once just an animal trail, regular use by Anne, Zima, and other militia members who lived in this part of town had widened it into a comfortable hiking path. Moonlight filtered through the tree canopy to paint a glowing silver lattice all around that shimmered in the gentle night breeze.

Anne was in her element.

A frustrated grunt from Tabby snapped her out of it.

"I don't get it," Tabby said, picking a leaf from her mouth with a sour face. "How can you even see, Mom?"

"I guess my eyes are more accustomed to moonlight than yours," Anne said. In truth, the forest was as bright as day to her vampire senses, but Tabby didn't need to know that just yet. "It also helps that I've walked this trail a lot. Like I said before, you're welcome to use the flashlight."

"No, if you can —" Tabby cursed when another branch brushed her face, then took a deep breath. "If you can do it, so can I."

"That's the spirit. Just follow close behind me and you'll be fine."

Anne felt a tug on her jacket, where Tabby had evidently latched on, and smiled. The small gesture spoke of innocence, vulnerability, and trust. Tabby had accepted Anne as her guide, and Anne had accepted responsibility for her safety.

Just as a mother should.

"So tell me, where do you live? Nowhere with nature trails, I'm guessing."

"You guessed right," Tabby said, spitting out another leaf. "I'm in Chico right now, but I've lived all over the state, including San Diego, Los Angeles, Santa Barbara, and the jewel of California, Fresno!"

"Sounds like your dad moves around a lot."

"He, uh … used to. Before he died."

Anne missed a step and stumbled into a bush. "Your dad died, too?"

"Yeah, a few years after Mom." Tabby cleared her throat. "Is that the militia training ground up ahead?"

Anne wanted to continue the conversation, but the flicker of lights through the trees unfortunately signaled they had arrived. The trail emerged into a large clearing ringed with gas lanterns. In the center were all but a few of their thirty-odd militia members.

Including Zima.

Oh thank God.

Anne was about to call to her love, but Tabby beat her to it.

"Jayne! Over here!"

Tabby bounced and waved, but Zima spared them only a glance before returning her attention to Clem Johnson, who held a snub-nosed pistol, similar to the ones all militia members carried.

"Thanks for trying," Anne said quietly. "And for remembering to use her alias."

"No problem, Susan," Tabby said with a smile. "Which reminds me, is it okay to call you Mom around strangers?"

"Probably best to stick with Susan until we have a chance to get our stories straight."

"Oh, right." Tabby's shoulders sagged, which Anne draped her arm around.

"Hang in there, I'm —"

"As I live and breathe," Marie Halford said, staring at them with wide eyes. "Susan, you never told me you had a daughter! She looks just like you."

Anne kicked herself for forgetting their uncanny likeness to each other. "Ah ... yes, well, I do. Her name is, um ..."

"Tabitha," her daughter said, rolling her eyes. "Call me Tabby."

"Welcome, Tabby. Are you here to train?"

"I guess."

"Ever shot a gun before?"

"Sure have. Mostly handguns."

Marie brushed her salt-and-peppered hair back from her eyes and smiled. "Of course you have. You're Susan's daughter, after all. I won't tell you your business, then. Just suit up and join in wherever you like. Rabbit fire starts in an hour."

"Did she mean 'rapid fire'?" Tabby said after Marie had left.

"No, you heard right. And what's this about you shooting guns before?"

"Oh. Dad used to take me to the range every weekend. He even bought me my own pistol."

"How cavalier. Did you bring it?"

"No, it's ... I lost it a while ago."

"Lost it?"

"Yeah. But before that, I used to sleep with it under my pillow. Dad insisted. He was away on business trips a lot, and after Mom was killed, he hated the idea of me being home alone without —"

"*Killed?* Tabby! W-what happened to your mother?"

"A mugging gone wrong, apparently. I was just a kid. She left me with the nanny at the house to run some errands, but when Dad got home that evening, she hadn't returned. I still ..." Tabby swallowed hard and averted her eyes.

"I'm sorry, honey. You don't have to tell me. I know how difficult talking about traumatic experiences can be."

All too well.

"No, it's okay. If I can't talk about it with you, of all people, that doesn't give our relationship much of a chance. Bonding is about trust and opening up, right?"

"Right," Anne said, feeling guiltier than ever.

Later, Anne promised herself. *Tabby has enough adjusting to do already. She doesn't need the "your mother is a vampire" trauma yet. And Zima ...*

Anne glanced at her wife, who was wholly focused on teaching Clem how to quick-draw, and sighed.

We'll need to sort that out before we drop any more bombshells on the poor girl.

Anne focused on her daughter. "So, what were you saying?"

"Oh, yeah. When Mom was killed. The thing I remember most about that night wasn't my own grief, but Dad's. He was always so confident, so full of life, I honestly believed he could do anything, like fly me to the moon or turn Brussels sprouts into candy.

"But the moment he heard the news, it was like his candle had been snuffed out for good. He didn't laugh anymore, didn't smile. He quit his job, but I didn't get to spend any more time with him. He spent most of his time in his room, leaving me with the nanny. When he finally did come out, he immediately got another job and spent all his time at work."

"That must have been hard for you."

"Yeah. I was a kid, though. I missed my mom, but I had the nanny. Dad had lost his wife. He had it worse than I did by far, but there wasn't anything I could do to help, because I couldn't get close to him."

Anne put a sympathetic hand on Tabby's shoulder. "It's ... it's like you lost both parents the night your mother died."

Tabby nodded, her eyes distant, then shook herself. "Anyway, now I have you."

"Yes you do," Anne said softly. She pulled Tabby into a hug to hide her tears. "Yes you do."

They stayed in the comfort of each other's embrace until Anne felt she could speak without her voice breaking.

"Come on, let's get you suited up so you can have a few practice shots with a snub before rabbit fire starts."

"Um, not to spoil this wonderful bonding exercise, Mom, but I've never shot a living thing, and I don't intend to start now."

Billy Connup chose that moment to waltz up with a broad smile. "Then how do you intend to protect yourself from a vampire? You gonna talk to it? Ask it nicely to not eat your friends and family?"

Perfect …

Billy and his friend, Wade, had been more civil to Anne and Zima since their encounter in the pastry shop last month, but that hadn't changed Anne's opinion that they were both bullies who badly needed the lesson in humility — also known as an ass-whooping — she had talked herself out of giving them.

"Vampires?" Tabby snorted. "Are you serious? I thought militia training was just an excuse to drink beer and shoot guns."

Billy turned his confused gaze to Anne. "Is she really yours? 'cause that don't sound a thing like what you and Jayne have been telling us."

"She's mine, all right, but she just arrived in town this evening. We haven't had The Talk yet."

"The Talk?" Tabby laughed. "My God, you two make it sound like an intervention!"

"Vampires are real," Billy said, crossing his arms. "Believe it."

"Yeah? Have you ever seen one?"

"Well … no, but your mom has!"

Tabby gave Anne a skeptical frown.

"It's true. Jayne and I had trouble with them a while back, and have vowed to fight them ever since."

That, at least, is the truth.

"And the militia is our best chance of survival," Billy said. Unlike earlier, his haughty veneer was gone, his voice calm and steady. "The government has turned a blind eye. If the vampires come here and things go to hell, they ain't going to help us one bit, and I for one ain't going to end up some ghoul's dinner. Not without a fight."

"You're serious?" Tabby said softly. "But … I-I thought vampires were just conspiracy theory."

"That's what they want you to think," Billy said. "Just like the Devil, they've tricked the world into believing they don't exist, so they can just keep eating us like cattle without anyone lifting a finger to stop them."

Anne squeezed her shoulders affectionately. "Look, whether you choose to believe vampires exist or not, I think you'll enjoy militia training tonight. If they're real, you'll be better prepared to kill one if you see it." *I can't believe I just said that.* "And if not, you'll learn a few new tricks, and hopefully make some new friends."

"Like me," Billy said. "I'd be happy to show you the ropes, like how to put your armor on and shoot a snub."

"Nice try," Anne said, pulling her daughter close, "but Tabby's with me tonight."

To her surprise, both Billy and Tabby seemed disappointed, but one glance at her wife, who had switched her focus to Tommy Willup, made Anne stand her ground.

"Jayne and I have her covered," Anne said.

"All right. Well, I'll be around if you change your mind." Billy's gaze lingered on Tabby before he turned to join a group of boys gathered around the firing range, which was just a fallen log with short-range tree stumps for targets.

Anne smiled at Tabby. "Let's get your gear, then we'll see if Jayne's free. She's the best shooting instructor here."

"You're the boss."

Gearing Tabby up was simple. The armored suits were really just overalls with leather patched on the outside, topped by a riot helmet, which Tabby easily slipped into. She also seemed comfortable with the snub — a small handgun with a short, large-bore barrel.

"So, what is this thing?" Tabby turned the snub in her hands and traced her finger around the abnormally wide barrel. "Does it shoot tranquilizer darts or something?"

"Tranquilizers won't stop a vampire. Their physiology is too different."

"Does it shoot rockets, then?"

"No," Anne said, laughing. "A rocket won't help you much, either, unless it's a big one. Vampires have few critical points and heal incredibly fast, so they're hard to take down with conventional weapons. They also have lightning reflexes, so your chances of hitting one with a single projectile are slim."

"I'm believing you less and less, Mom. You make them sound like aliens or supersoldiers."

"They may be a little of both," Anne said.

Tabby started to laugh, but faltered when she saw Anne's serious expression.

"Vampires are normal people, like you and me, who've been infected by an advanced virus that mutates humans at a fundamental level. Some of the brightest minds in the country have studied it. As far as they can tell, it doesn't resemble any microorganism on Earth, and they strongly suspect it was engineered."

"There's nothing about that on the news. How do you know all this?"

Anne lowered her voice to a whisper. "Charlie and Mark are the bright minds I was talking about."

"But … that sounds like virologist territory. Aren't they just computer guys?"

"Their talents go far beyond computers and gadgets, believe me, but we can talk more about that later. Right now …" Anne drew her own snub from its holster and opened the revolver. "As you can see, each pistol holds only four rounds because of the size of the ammunition."

"Jeez, those things look like they could take down a rhino!"

"Just the opposite. They're basically compact shotgun shells, designed to deliver a load of projectiles to a wide area to maximize the chances of hitting your target."

"I see. Since vampires are supposedly quick, that makes it harder for them to dodge. What I don't get is if vampires are so tough, how is a little buckshot going to slow them down, let alone kill them?"

"Because of this." Anne pulled one of her shells out and extracted a small, shiny pellet. "Silver. Vampires are deathly allergic to it. Just one of these beneath the skin will completely paralyze it in a matter of seconds, and more will kill it. Hurts like you wouldn't believe. O-or so I've been told, anyway."

Damnit! At this rate, the entire militia's going to guess I'm a vampire by the end of the night.

Anne looked around at all the militiamen and women, armed with snubs and shooting their would-be vampire targets with great gusto. It wasn't a comforting thought. Normally, she was more careful than this, but being here with her daughter, she wanted to open up and really take the opportunity to bond. Being chased through the forest by a lynch mob wouldn't help her cause, however, so Anne vowed to watch herself.

"Wait, we're shooting real silver at those targets?"

"No, it's simulated ammunition — special pellets with realistic shot patterns that are non-lethal. As long as the shooting distance is greater than one foot, it won't pierce leather, hence the armor. When we're done here, we'll all swap our simulated ammo for silver rounds again."

"You … carry them with you?"

"Always. Vampires are natural stalkers, and they attack when you least expect."

"And the police don't mind a bunch of yokels carrying concealed weapons without a permit? Seems odd."

"Legal is what you can get away with. The police aren't currently enforcing gun laws, and the Feds don't think some Podunk town in the middle of nowhere poses a threat to their power, so for now, we're free to carry. That includes you."

"You mean I can keep this?"

"Yep, holster and all."

"Cool! Let's try it out. I think Jayne is finishing up over there."

Sure enough, Zima had just left Tommy, who was practicing his quick draw. Anne and Tabby hurried over. Before they had come within a dozen paces, however, Zima had moved on to someone else. They waited patiently while she corrected Carrie Multow's stance and grip. As soon as she finished, Zima quickly moved to another recruit, then another.

And not once did she glance in their direction.

"Come on," Anne said to Tabby, trying to hide her disappointment. "I'm not as skilled as Zima, but I can show you the basics. At least you'll get some practice before rabbit fire."

They set up at an open spot on the range next to Billy Connup, who lit up with an ear-to-ear grin.

Down, tiger, Anne thought, but reined in her mother-bear instincts when she saw the same grin on Tabby's face. *Kids …*

But that was the problem. Tabby wasn't a kid. She was nineteen, older than Anne had been when she'd fled her home in Indiana and moved to San Francisco to live on her own. Anne was her mother, but she had no right to dictate who Tabby liked or didn't like.

She could have chosen worse, I suppose.

Despite his bluster, Billy was a boon to the militia, and the first to volunteer for chores. Strong muscles hid beneath his blue-jean overalls. Combined with sandy-blond curls and a farmer's tan, he was rustic, for sure, but undeniably cute.

Together, Anne and Billy showed Tabby how to use the snub. True to her claim, Tabby handled her pistol with comfort born from familiarity — except for the first shot, of course. Snubs were lightweight, yet packed more gunpowder and delivered more mass per round than a normal handgun, which gave them one heck of a kick.

Tabby squeezed the trigger with practiced measure.

A flash of fire belched from the barrel. The force of it jerked her arm back. Tabby yelped and moved her head just in time to prevent the gun from smacking her in the face — a fate few first-time shooters avoided.

"Whoa," Tabby whispered, her eyes wide.

"You get used to it," Billy said with a laugh.

And he was right. By the time Tabby had emptied the revolver, her shots were sure and steady. By the end of the second round, she seemed as comfortable with the snub as the best marksmen in the militia.

"I'll be damned," Billy said.

Tabby shrugged. "Told you. Dad was a good instructor."

"I'll say. I feel sorry for the Rabbits tonight."

"Look," Tabby said, "these so-called vampires are one thing, but I'm not going to shoot some innocent little bunny just for target practice!"

Billy laughed. "They ain't real rabbits, just people dressed up."

"People? Gee, that's so much better." Tabby holstered her snub. "Thanks, but I'll pass."

"Don't judge until you've seen it," Anne said. "Looks like everyone's gathering. As a newcomer, you can just watch the first round, but you'll need to be a Carrot or a Rabbit for the following rounds."

Tabby sighed, but didn't argue. Given that her first night with her mother was being spent with a bunch of strangers with guns in the middle of nowhere, Anne had to give her credit.

11

RABBIT FIRE

TABITHA ROTHWELD FOLLOWED HER MOTHER to the group of people gathering in the center of the clearing for the so-called rabbit fire. She watched them don a second layer of armored overalls with the same surreal fascination Alice must have felt when chasing the white rabbit through Wonderland. Tabby's life was so different from her mother's here that she wondered if she had somehow crossed into an alternate dimension on her trip up to Montana.

Vampires, alien viruses, government conspiracies, organized resistance ... Tabby still wasn't sure how much of it she believed, but her mother clearly did. If it would help them bond, then Tabby would go along with it, even if her mother said they would next be hunting unicorns.

"So," Tabby said, "why are some of them wearing white helmets and some gray?"

"Vampires are naturally pale," her mother said. "Their skin is almost white, and webbed with blue veins."

"I see, so white helmets represent vampires. Sounds like team death match."

Anne didn't seem to get the video game reference, but Billy shook his head.

"They ain't fighting each other in that sense," Billy said. "See, one —"

"It's probably easier to show her," Anne said. "They're almost ready."

Members with white and gray helmets alike wandered into the woods and hid. Waiting in the clearing with their backs turned were four other members.

"All right," Marie Halford said to them, "the Rabbits are in position. Carrot number one, you're up. Load your weapon, and good luck!"

The first of the four, a thin girl about Tabby's age, put four rounds in her snub, holstered it, then turned around and walked into the forest. Tabby thought it odd that her snub was holstered. If this really was a death match event, she was at a disadvantage. Not only that, the forest beyond the clearing was pitch black, and the Carrot had only a small penlight to see by.

Both Tabby and the Carrot screamed when a white-helmeted Rabbit jumped out from behind a bush. The Carrot drew her pistol and fired in a fluid motion just before the Rabbit reached her. The shot Rabbit moaned dramatically and fell twitching to the ground, drawing laughs from those who watched from the clearing.

Anne turned with a smile, which Tabby had trouble returning.

"D-doesn't it hurt getting shot like that?"

"Not really," Anne said. "The double layers of armor absorb most of the impact, so it feels like a light punch."

The Carrot holstered her weapon and continued more cautiously this time. From another tree jumped a gray-helmed Rabbit. The Carrot whipped her weapon out, but didn't fire. She looked relieved until a white-helmed Rabbit jumped out from behind her. She spun to face him, but he pushed her to the ground before she could fire.

Tabby nudged her mother. "Does that mean she's out?"

"No. The point of the exercise is for participants to hone their reflexes. She'll walk the rest of the course, then we'll send the next Carrot through." She gave Tabby a wry grin. "Interested?"

"Kind of, but it seems unfair since I'll know where all the Rabbits are hiding."

"It isn't about fair. But anyway, don't worry. They change roles and hiding places between groups, so your walkthrough will be a different experience."

"Oh. Well, sure then, I'll give it a try."

Anne's smile broadened into a dazzling display that only a proud parent could wear. Tabby choked at the sight. It was very similar to how her mom — the person who had raised her, that is — lit up when Tabby had done something even mediocre.

Thinking about her mother brought about a familiar, suffocating depression. Hopelessness once again threatened to sink her beneath the soft forest floor.

Tabby sucked in a deep breath and willed it away. She had promised herself that she wouldn't mope in front of her biological mother. This was a time for celebration. After years of searching, Tabby had found her real mother. Even though she and her deceased mother had never discussed it, she knew without a doubt that this was what she would have wanted: for Tabby to be with family who loved and cared for her.

Although she had only known her biological mother for a few hours, Anne seemed to fit that bill perfectly. Any fear that Tabby would be unwelcome in her mother's life had been dispelled the moment they'd laid eyes on each other. Anne was thrilled to have her, and she was every bit as nice as Tabby could have wished for.

That Anne was married to another woman was unexpected, but not unwelcome. Zima was beautiful, even if she never smiled, and Tabby had no trouble seeing why her mother was attracted.

Tabby missed her father, too. While it might have been nice to have another father figure in her life, going from no mothers to two in a single evening wasn't bad, not to mention the others who had been at Anne's house for dinner.

Charlie had called her family. While Tabby was sure he had said it to be comforting, she sensed there was more to it. She looked forward to getting to know him and Cappa better.

Speaking of ...

Tabby glanced at Zima for the hundredth time since they'd arrived. The stoic platinum blonde stood on the opposite side of the clearing from them, as she had been for the entire evening. Her eyes periodically darted around the forest, as if trying to take in everything at once, before returning her attention to the rabbit fire spectacle. Tabby considered wandering over to strike up a conversation, but Zima would certainly find another excuse to leave.

Her stepmother was avoiding her, of that she was sure, and it wasn't hard to imagine why. She and Anne were newlyweds, from what Tabby understood. A kid hadn't been part of the bargain, even a grown one like her, but especially not a long-lost daughter who threatened to spoil their little cloud of heaven by taking all her wife's attention.

The solution, Tabby hoped, was to get to know Zima and make her feel important, too, but so far that had proved an impossible task. The beautiful blonde had an almost precognitive ability to know when Anne and Tabby were approaching, and had a strategic exit ready every time. Her mother was disappointed, Tabby could tell. But Tabby also knew that her appearance at the house had been a surprise, and that Zima and Anne hadn't had a chance to talk about it yet — something she hoped they would rectify tonight, once they were alone in their newlywed haven.

A glance at her mom said she must have been thinking the same. Anne was also looking at Zima, pain evident on her face.

Zima turned around suddenly and walked into the forest in the opposite direction of the rabbit fire area.

"W-would you excuse me for a minute, Tabby?" Anne didn't wait for a reply before hurrying after her wife.

"I thought it was queer at first," Billy said, looking in their direction, "but they're really keen on each other."

"Nice to hear you say," Tabby said. "I just assumed a couple like them would be burned at the stake around here."

Billy turned three shades of red under his helmet.

"What?"

"N-nothing. So, um ... you gonna be a Rabbit or a Carrot next round?"

"I get to choose?"

"Sure. Usually it's drawing straws, but being your first time here and all ..."

"The first hit's free, just like any good drug."

"Something like that."

As if Billy's sandy curls weren't cute enough, his dimples made him absolutely adorable. Tabby had to remind herself to breathe again.

Down, girl.

Cute as he was, finding a boyfriend wasn't Tabby's reason for coming to Montana. The self-admonition did nothing to quell the butterflies in her stomach.

"W-what's your favorite role?" Tabby said.

"May sound crazy, but I like being the white Rabbits. Not because I want to be one of those bloodsuckers, mind you, but because I like trying to get into their heads. Know-your-enemy kind of stuff."

Tabby rolled her eyes. "Okay, so tell me … what exactly do you know about your supposed enemy?"

"They're pale, like Susan said, and they got long, sharp canines, just like in the movies. Their eyes are almost completely dark, pure evil if ever there was. They're wicked strong and quicker than a mongoose. And when they bite you, you don't remember a thing. That's why there aren't many eyewitnesses."

"That's all? They don't turn into bats or wolves or shoot lasers from their eyes?"

"Scoff if you want, but it's true. Jayne and Susan say so. Vampires also got no pulse at all. Their skin is cold to the touch, and —"

"It … it's what?" Tabby felt the blood drain from her face.

"Cold. Their bodies are the same temperature as the surroundings, just like a corpse. Susan says they might even be colder. And they can see in total dark like it's daytime."

"S-see in the dark." Tabby's knees buckled. She grabbed onto a tree to keep from falling. "M-M-Mom told you that?"

"Sure did. You all right, Tabby? You look like you just swallowed a toad."

Tabby barely heard him. She was staring in the direction her mother had gone — the woman with freezing-cold skin, who walked the night woods without a flashlight.

12

PILLARS

ANNE FOLLOWED HER LOVE into the forest until they were well away from the prying eyes and ears of the militia. Zima stopped at a supply shed and deftly opened the lock, but Anne slipped behind her and held her close before she opened the door.

"Hi," Anne said softly into her ear.

In a pleasant surprise, Zima turned in her embrace and kissed her until Anne was ready to take her behind the shed for some real private time, militia be damned. They parted far too soon for her liking, and Zima rested her head against Anne's.

"Honey," Anne said, "are you okay?"

Zima stayed silent, but eventually nodded.

"Did Dela, Mark, and Doris find you, then?"

"Yes, although they left shortly after arriving. They were summoned to Charlie and Cappa's house for a discussion."

"I can imagine what they're talking about." She stroked Zima's cheek. "Honey, I'm so, so sorry I didn't tell you I had a daughter. Can you forgive me?"

Zima kissed her again. "Always, my love."

"Then you'll come watch Tabby's first rabbit fire with me?"

"Another time. Four of the targets are worn beyond acceptable parameters and should be replaced before the next practice session, which is approximately thirty-six minutes from now."

"Well ... I-let me help, then. Billy's keeping an eye on Tabby. I'll regroup with her afterward."

Zima brushed Anne's hair with a finger and cupped her cheek. "That is sweet, my wife, but I could not forgive myself if I deprived you of any more time with your daughter than I already have. Go. The next round is about to start. There will be time for us later."

"That's a promise, honey."

With a heavy heart, Anne gave her a final kiss before rejoining the others in the clearing.

•　　　•　　　•

Tabby and Billy were talking in subdued tones when Anne returned. Tabby abruptly quieted when she spotted Anne.

Odd.

Anne put on a smile and joined them. "So, are you still up for it, Tabby?"

"Yeah." Her voice was uncharacteristically timid.

"Everything all right between you two?"

"I think so," Billy said. "I was just telling her about —"

"Rabbit fire," Tabby said quickly. "I was picking his brain, you know, in preparation."

Rabbit fire, sure.

Anne had seen that spark between the two of them, and suspected she had walked in at just the wrong moment.

"Well, Billy only lives a few miles away," Anne said. "You can continue your brain-picking session tomorrow, if you'd like."

Billy perked up. "Really? You, ah, don't mind me hanging out with your daughter?"

"I don't mind if Tabby doesn't mind. But if Tabby starts minding ..."

It was times like this when Anne wished she could bare her fangs, but even thinking about it risked her canines actually extending, which would pop her false caps off. If that happened,

Tabby flirting with some country boy would be the least of Anne's problems.

Billy waved his hand in front of her daughter's eyes. "Tabby?"

She blinked and looked around. "Hmm? What is it?"

"Your mom's not-so-subtle threat. Am I bugging you, or would you like to hang out with me tomorrow?"

"Oh. Yeah, sure. That'd be nice." Tabby fiddled with a leather tie on her armor, her eyes everywhere but on Anne. "Um, Billy, w-would you help me get ready?"

"You bet, though really you just gotta line up over there with the others and keep your back turned while the Rabbits switch places. And have your ammunition ready when it's your turn."

They shuffled off to the other waiting Carrots. Anne waved to wish Tabby good luck, but her daughter never looked back. She hadn't met Anne's eyes since she'd returned from Zima, either, which was a curious shift in attitude from the girl who had been practically glued to her mother since their reunion.

Had Billy said something to make her angry while Anne was away? It was unlikely, since the two were currently chatting in line about what they might do tomorrow.

I'll ask her later, Anne thought, hoping her daughter would be more forthright about what was bothering her than Zima had been.

The Rabbits quickly rearranged themselves. Tabby was first in line. At Marie's command, she loaded her weapon, turned around, and walked into the woods. Her hands shook, poised over her holster, until the first Rabbit jumped out. Tabby shrieked and fumbled for her weapon, but relaxed when she saw his gray helmet. The second Rabbit was also gray. Tabby yelped only a little that time, and left her snub in her holster.

Two steps later, a white-helmed Rabbit jumped from the bushes. Tabby drew her pistol more fluidly this time and managed to pull the trigger before the Rabbit reached her. The shot hit him square in the chest. He threw himself backward over the bush with a dramatic cry, to everyone's laughter.

Everyone except Anne, that is, who jumped up and down, cheering loudly. Tabby graced her with a huge smile that melted Anne to the spot, but her heart sank when the proud smile faded, and Tabby once again averted her eyes.

The rest of the course went almost as well. Tabby shot the rest of the five white-helmed Rabbits before they laid a finger on her, and shot only one gray. Anne cheered at every instance, but her daughter's beautiful brown eyes didn't turn her way again.

Until the end, when Anne went to congratulate her.

Anne waited with barely contained excitement for Tabby to walk the final steps of the course. Tabby was staring at Billy with a triumphant smile.

Anne could wait no longer. She surged from the crowd to give her daughter a hug.

"Stay off the range!"

Marie's warning came too late: even Anne's vampire reflexes weren't fast enough to save her from Tabby's point-blank snub.

Everyone ducked at the loud gunshot. Anne felt the familiar punch of buckshot against her abdominal armor, amplified because she had only one layer of leather instead of the two that Rabbits normally wore.

But this time, it was worse. A sharp pain in her stomach told her some of the buckshot had punctured through. Her skin beneath her armor became slick with blood.

Anne stifled a groan. It hurt like hell, but if anyone learned she had actually been wounded, they would insist on taking her to the hospital. Worse, they might try to treat her themselves and risk infection of the vampire virus from handling her blood.

Worst of all, however, was how Tabby would feel if she knew she had injured her mother.

"Mom! Oh my God ..." Tabby threw her weapon aside and pried at Anne's hands covering her wound. "Are you okay? Please, let me see it!"

"Relax," Anne said in what she hoped was a calm voice. "I'm fine, honey."

It wasn't a total lie. No matter how many simulation pellets had made it through, in ten minutes, Anne would be completely healed, and her daughter would be none the wiser. All she had to do was keep the blood hidden. She had no heartbeat, which meant she bled very little, even from serious wounds — something Anne could unfortunately attest to firsthand.

"Are you sure? Mom, please let me look! What if you're in shock from the injury?"

Zima rushed through the crowd and towered over them like a sentinel.

"She is my wife!" Zima's commanding tone turned every head — a tone Anne had only heard once before. "I shall attend her. Please stand aside."

Tabby frowned, but did as requested and backed away.

Zima slipped Anne's arm around her shoulders for support and led her to the changing area. Every step jarred Anne's wound and made her want to cry out, but she bit her lip and stayed silent.

When they were safely away, Zima lowered her voice. "How bad is your injury?"

"I've had worse."

"That is not reassuring."

Zima gently pried Anne's hands away.

Anne gasped at what she saw. The point-blank shot had blown a ragged hole the width of her thumb through the leather, her shirt, and her stomach, leaving a circle of mutilated flesh on her abdomen.

There was little Anne or Zima needed to do to care for it beyond waiting. Anne wasn't susceptible to infection, and her flesh would expel the pellets while it healed, leaving her body in the same state it had been before she'd been shot.

But there was still a problem.

"I didn't bring a spare shirt, and this one's soaked through," Anne said. "Any ideas?"

"Yes. Follow me to the other side of the trees."

Once they were out of sight, Zima carefully but efficiently stripped Anne of her armor and bloody shirt, then stripped herself down to her sports bra, and handed her shirt to Anne.

"It will be tight," Zima said, "but our shirts are similar enough in style that it is unlikely anyone will notice the difference."

"Yeah, but they'll notice you being half naked."

"I do not intend to be seen. I shall leave by way of the forest and enter our property over the back fence to avoid being observed by the neighbors. If the others ask, you may tell them I had an urgent —"

"Mom?"

They froze at Tabby's voice on the other side of the trees.

Zima grabbed the soiled armor and shirt, then dashed away into the dark forest.

Anne's wound had stopped bleeding, so she scrambled to put Zima's shirt on. "Y-yes, honey?" Deft fingers buttoned up from the bottom, but Anne silently cursed when the material wouldn't stretch over her boobs, which were several sizes larger than her wife's.

"Is there anything I can help with?"

"No! I ... A-actually, yes. It's cold without my armor on. Would you please get my jacket?"

"Oh, sure. I think I know which one is yours."

Anne breathed a sigh of relief at Tabby's retreating footsteps. She grabbed a sleeve in each hand and tugged. Zima's shirt split open at the back, giving Anne just enough leeway to finish buttoning. The fabric strained precariously around her bust line, but at least she wouldn't be flashing anyone.

Tabby returned a minute later with Anne's jacket. "Here you go."

"Thanks, honey." Anne took it from her daughter, careful to keep the rip on her back hidden, then put the jacket on and zipped it all the way to her neck.

"Where's Zima? I heard her with you a minute ago."

"Sh-she went home."

"Oh." Tabby's expression sobered. Her eyes fell to the forest floor. "Can we go, too? I think I've had enough shooting for a while."

"I told you, sweetheart, I'm fine."

Tabby's unsettled gaze stayed on the ground.

"Sure, let's go. We'll tell Marie on the way out. She'll understand if we don't stay for clean up."

Anne led her crestfallen daughter to the clearing, trying not to groan at the pain in her abdomen. After they completed the ceremonial changing of ammunition — exchanging practice rounds in their snubs for real silver rounds — they returned to the small forest trail leading home.

13

BLOOD IS THICKER

ANNE GUIDED HER DAUGHTER through the moonlit forest without the aid of a flashlight, as she had on the way to militia training. Tabby had been quiet since leaving the others, and Anne couldn't blame her after what had happened. Her abdomen where Tabby had shot her was feeling better, but it still hurt when she twisted her torso.

"I know how you feel," Anne said.

Tabby eyed her briefly before dropping her gaze once more. "I seriously doubt it."

"It's true. You remember Charlie's wife, Cappa? I accidentally shot her once."

"You what?"

"Shot her. I was grief-stricken because I thought I'd killed her. She was fine, though, and not only did she forgive me, I think it's one of the reasons we're like sisters now. The experience brought us closer together."

They walked in silence for a while. "So is Cappa a vampire?"

Anne stumbled on a root and grabbed a nearby branch to keep from tumbling into the bushes. "W-what are you talking about? Where did you get that idea?"

"She shrugged off a gunshot wound, so I just figured she's a vampire." Tabby's voice fell to a whisper. "Like you."

Oh God.

Anne swallowed hard.

There was no point in denying it. She had intended to tell Tabby soon anyway, but she had hoped for more time to ease her into the idea. That Tabby had figured it out wasn't a surprise, in retrospect. Anne's cold skin, no need for a flashlight, her obvious lie about not being wounded by the gunshot ...

She had known Tabby would learn more about vampires during militia training. It was as if her subconscious had wanted Tabby to discover the truth and force it into the open.

Anne was a vampire — a blight on humanity. No amount of mother-daughter bonding would change that ugly fact.

Tabby had stopped several yards back, rubbing her wrists with absent, fervent intensity. Her daughter's eyes were soft, sorrowful, as if she had just discovered that yet another of her parents was lost to her forever.

The pain in Anne's abdomen was suddenly dwarfed by the grief in her chest. Anne wanted to run to her, comfort her as a mother should.

But now wasn't the time. Not yet.

A gentle breeze stirred the aspen leaves into a hush, as if the forest were sighing.

"Are you going to turn me into a vampire, too?"

"Am I ..."

The idea was so ludicrous that Anne couldn't even finish the sentence. Turning her daughter into a monster was the last thing she would ever consider, right after slaughtering a litter of puppies, or letting the world end at the hands of the Entity.

Thinking of the Entity turned her thoughts toward its never-ending stream of consciousness that she normally tuned out.

Anne was stunned at what she found. The Entity was urging her to take Tabby up on her suggestion and feed her Anne's blood, which was normal.

What differed tonight were the Entity's motives. It wasn't just trying to increase the number of vampires in the world; it wanted to save Tabby from the would-be Apocalypse.

In other words, it cared about her daughter's safety.

The Entity had never expressed concern about anyone. The implications of that were so staggering that it took Anne a few seconds to remember that her daughter was still awaiting an answer to a very important question.

"No, Tabby. I won't turn you."

"W-what if I wanted to become a vampire?"

"I'd say no."

"Why? We'd be the same, then."

Anne risked a step toward her daughter, and was rewarded when Tabby didn't run away. The scene was so familiar that Anne stifled a bitter laugh. Less than a year ago, when Anne had first learned Charlie was a cyborg, she had been in the same position Tabby was now.

And look how that turned out.

"We are the same," Anne said. "We laugh, we love, we cry, we have similar humor and tastes, the same color hair and eyes. And ... and we care about each other. Very much. Right?" The last was less a question than a plea.

Tabby wiped the tears from her face and nodded. Anne tensed when Tabby pulled her silver-loaded snub from her holster, but she didn't point it at Anne, just looked at it in her hand.

"Would this really kill you?"

"I think so, but it's hard to say for sure. I'm ... unique, even among vampires."

"Unique how?"

When Anne hesitated, Tabby's tears flowed once more.

"Mom, please! I have to know ... I need to know I'm not going to lose you like ... like ..."

Heedless of the snub in her daughter's hand, Anne closed the distance and wrapped her in a hug.

"I'm not going anywhere, Tabby. Not for a long, long time."

There in the quiet woods, Anne told Tabby of the implant above her right breast that had allowed her to retain her independence and humanity, where other vampires had none. She even let Tabby feel the bump just beneath her skin.

"It's so small," Tabby said.

"Yes, but it packs a lot of technology."

"Charlie and Mark really made it? That kind of tech just sounds ... well, impossible."

Anne laughed. "There's a reason they went from zero to tech giants in such a short time. They're geniuses."

Tabby's eyes narrowed. "How come you don't look like the vampires Billy described? Is that the implant's doing?"

"No, it's ... it's just a disguise."

Tabby bit her lip. "Can I see? I-I promise I won't scream."

With a sigh, Anne nodded. She led Tabby to a clear patch of moonlight and, with trembling fingers, removed the false caps from her sharp canines, then the contacts hiding her large, black eyes.

"I'll take my makeup off when we get home," Anne said. "But apart from that ... this is me."

Tabby stared at her with wide eyes, though whether in wonder or fear, Anne couldn't say. She reached a hesitant finger for one of Anne's fangs. Anne opened her mouth and peeled her lips back in what she hoped was a non-threatening manner.

"Ouch! They're sharper than I thought they'd be."

Anne shuddered. The delicious taste of Tabby's blood filled her mouth, followed by the familiar sensation of her canines pushing down from her gums. Instinct told her it was mealtime, and Tabby was the main course, but she willed herself to be still. Anne would sooner shoot herself with her own silver-loaded snub than bite her daughter against her will.

Tabby's eyes grew even wider. She stepped back. "A-are you okay, Mom?"

"Yes, or ... I will be, in a minute."

"It's my blood, isn't it? I pricked my finger on your tooth." Tabby gulped. "You're not going to eat me in a blood frenzy or anything, are you?"

"Only if I were really hungry, but even then I've learned to control myself until I can find a, um ... willing donor."

"If you bite me, will I turn into a vampire?"

Anne shook her head. "You'd have to drink my blood."

"Oh. Well, in that case ..." Tabby pulled her collar down to expose her neck. "You can drink from me, if you're hungry."

"That's sweet, but I want to get through the first day with my daughter knowing I didn't sink my teeth into her like a monster."

To Anne's surprise, Tabby looked disappointed.

"Tell you what … let's come back to that in a few days. My venom has healing properties, so there's a genuine benefit to being bitten."

Tabby nodded, then fidgeted with her shirt exactly like Anne did when she was nervous. "Is … is Zima a vampire, too?"

Oh boy.

"No. She's unique, like me, but in a very different way."

Tabby smiled at her. Anne's heart melted.

"Come on, Mom. You can't drop a hint like that and expect me not to ask. Is she a werewolf?"

Anne hugged her close, enjoying her warmth. "Let's stick to one mind-blowing revelation per night, okay? I've been in your shoes, so trust me when I say I'm doing you a favor."

"So she *is* a werewolf!"

"I didn't say that!"

"But you didn't deny it, either."

Anne laughed and kissed Tabby's forehead, careful not to prick her with her elongated fangs. "I'd like to give Zima the courtesy of explaining it herself, so do *me* a courtesy and stop asking."

"Whatever you say. But until then, I'm just going to assume she howls at the full moon."

"Tomorrow. I promise I'll arrange for the two of you to talk."

Or I hope I can, at least.

Zima had been so skittish around Tabby that Anne honestly wasn't sure if she would be able to deliver on her promise, but that wouldn't stop her from trying. She would discover what was bothering her wife tonight, if possible, which meant Zima and Tabby could soon begin to reconcile.

Then they would be one, happy family.

The thought put a bounce in Anne's step all the way home.

•   •   •

Anne had just finished replacing her contacts when she and Tabby emerged from the woods onto her street. They walked arm-in-arm, happy to be in each other's company, until they reached Charlie and Cappa's front door.

Anne traced a loving finger down Tabby's cheek and smiled. "I had a wonderful time tonight."

"Me too, Mom."

"Will you be all right?"

The door swung open, revealing Cappa wearing a radiant smile.

"Of course she will! Auntie Cappa has hot cocoa and marshmallows waiting inside. And for breakfast, we'll have pancakes, syrup, fresh berries, and hand-whipped cream. How does that sound?"

"Delicious! Mom, would you like …" Tabby's face fell. "Oh, can you even drink cocoa?"

"No, but that's all right. Zima and I have some things to settle tonight, anyway. You have fun with Cappa and Charlie. We'll catch up tomorrow after breakfast."

"So … you don't sleep during the day?"

Anne laughed. "No, I wake up with the birds like everyone else." Anne kissed her cheek. "See you in the morning?"

"Count on it. 'night, Mom."

Anne watched them until the door to Charlie and Cappa's house closed, then she climbed the stairs of her own porch, feeling light as air.

The good feeling fled when she saw Zima waiting for her by the dining room table.

"Hi, honey," Anne said. "Thanks again for the shirt swap."

"It was no trouble. How is your wound?"

"Almost healed, I think."

"May I see?"

Anne shrugged and lifted her shirt. What had been an angry red mess thirty minutes ago was now just a circle of light-pink skin. In another few minutes, there wouldn't even be that. "Want to kiss it better?"

Zima did so, then kissed her belly, then unbuttoned her shirt and moved her kisses slowly upward. Anne met her lips at the top, but gently pulled away with a look of concern.

"Zima, I know it's been a hard night, but we really need to talk about Tab—"

Another passion-filled kiss silenced her.

"I do not wish to discuss her now," Zima said. "Tonight, I wish to be with you."

Before Anne could object, Zima swept her off her feet and carried her to their bedroom. It wasn't the end to the evening Anne had hoped for, but she'd had far worse.

14

STEPMOTHER

TABBY ROLLED OVER IN HER BED and stared out the window. Hints of morning light illuminated her mother's house across the street.

Finally.

She hadn't slept much last night. The bed was comfortable, and Cappa's cocoa had been delicious, but Tabby's last conversation with her mother tugged at her mind like an incessant toddler.

Vampires.

Tabby had heard the rumors, of course, but like most people, she had dismissed them as fantasy. Vampires couldn't be real. The disturbances were probably caused by some terrorist group using vampires as a fear tactic against the populace. That was the prevailing theory among the educated elite who, it turned out, knew far less about the truth than the yokels in this small country town.

Vampires were real. Tabby knew that now.

And Mom is one of them.

She brightened at the sounds of bickering magpies. Her mother had said she woke with the birds, which meant Tabby would be able to visit her soon.

She grinned, threw back her covers, and chose her outfit for the day. Her usual black attire would be cliché in the presence of a real vampire, so Tabby opted for a white blouse, then sifted through her pants drawer until she finally found a pair of tan jeans. She made a mental note to go shopping later to buy some brighter clothes.

Tabby quickly showered and dressed, then went to the kitchen, where she was surprised to find she wasn't the first person up, or ready. Cappa sat at the breakfast bar in a gorgeous yellow summer dress, shiny white shoes, and a shimmering pearl necklace.

She greeted Tabby with a beaming smile. "Morning, sunshine. Still up for pancakes?"

"Um, sure. I-I mean ... yes, please. That would be great."

"Such a lady!" Cappa donned an apron, and soon the kitchen was filled with the delicious smells of breakfast cooking. "Did you sleep well?" Her sideways grin said she already knew the answer.

"I'm not nervous, if that's what you're thinking."

"I wasn't, but it's good to hear."

She set a plate before Tabby, then one for herself, and joined her at the bar. The food was arranged with such precision that Tabby was loathe to eat, lest she destroy the beautiful work of art. Cappa had no such reservations, however, and chipped away at hers with dainty bites.

Tabby dug into her own breakfast, and they ate in silence.

"So," Cappa said, dabbing her mouth with a napkin, "it sounds like Anne told you about her ... condition?"

"About being a vampire? Yeah."

Cappa looked at her expectantly.

"Look, vampire or not, Anne's my mom. I'm not going to turn my back on her just because she's ... different." When Tabby glanced over, Cappa was smiling broadly. "What?"

"You sound just like her. I think you've made the right decision, Tabby." Cappa took their empty plates to the sink and started washing up. "Anne's awake, by the way, so you can go over whenever you like."

Tabby almost tripped in her haste for the door. "Thanks for breakfast, Auntie Cappa!"

"Anytime, sweetie. Have fun!"

•　　•　　•

Tabby knocked on her mother's door, then quickly checked herself to make sure she was presentable. Zima would hopefully be there, too, and Tabby would be damned if she'd ruin her chances of building a relationship with her beautiful new stepmother because she looked like a slob.

Her mom opened the door, beaming. "Come in, come in! Make yourself at home."

"Thanks." Tabby stepped inside and looked around the spacious living room. "Where's Zima?"

"In the shower. Can I make you some breakfast?"

"I just ate, sorry."

"Oh. Of course, Cappa would have fed you. How about some coffee? Tea?"

"Tea would be great."

"Coming right up."

Tabby followed her to the kitchen, and was happy that Anne didn't shoo her out like a regular house guest.

Anne opened the cupboard to a stunning variety of tins in perfect rows, each immaculately labeled.

"Zima loves tea, as you can see, so we have every flavor imaginable. Any preferences?"

"Jasmine, if you have it."

"Green or herbal?"

"Green, please."

"Good choice. That's Zima's favorite, too."

Anne ran her finger along the rows, then plucked one out with a triumphant grin. She put a heap of loose leaves into a pot, turned on the kettle, and pulled a single cup from the cupboard.

"Aren't you having any, Mom?"

"No, I … I can't, unfortunately. It doesn't sit well."

"Really? What do you drink, then?"

"Just the red stuff."

Tabby masked her revulsion behind a smile. "Does that include wine?"

"Sadly, no."

"What about food? Can you eat?"

"No. I'm limited to a cuisine of one thing."

"That's terrible!"

Anne shrugged. "I've learned to live with it, and I'm lucky to have friends who don't mind donating theirs. Dela enjoys it, actually."

"She likes being bitten?" Tabby made a sour face.

"My fangs are sharp, as you discovered last night, so it doesn't hurt much. And because of the healing effect, the marks disappear in minutes. My venom also has a heroin-like effect, which is why Dela keeps coming back."

"Wait, Billy said bite victims don't remember what happened. How does she even remember the high?"

"Billy's right — about *other* vampires. Thanks to my implant, instead of making people forget, my venom makes them happy." Anne smiled. "There are worse things, I guess."

"Yeah, but making people forget sounds more useful."

"There are times I wish it did, but I'm glad it doesn't. That way, I'm not tempted to use it for the wrong reasons."

Tabby mulled on that while Anne poured hot water into the pot, then set a timer.

"Zima is picky about the steeping time," Anne said. "She's measured optimal times for each blend, and recorded them on the labels."

"Wow, that's ... thorough."

"That's my Zima."

"So food and drink are off the list. Any other downsides to being a vampire?"

"Silver is a neurotoxin, as you already know. Sunlight burns, and too much can be fatal. Bright lights and loud sounds are painful, but rarely debilitating."

"Jeez, how do you handle the gunshots during militia training?"

"I have a pair of nearly invisible earplugs Charlie made for me."

"Ah. Well, it sounds like we won't be day shopping, anyway."

"Of course we will. I have my special makeup on."

"Let me guess. Charlie made it?"

"You catch on quick," Anne said with a wink.

"Is there anything here he *didn't* make for you?"

The timer dinged. Anne pulled the strainer containing the wet tea leaves from the pot and poured Tabby's cup. "Sure. Mark made my plasma pistol."

"Your ... what?"

Anne grinned. "Come and see."

She led them out to the hallway closet and retrieved a small pistol, similar to a snub but with a wider barrel.

"Here you go. Just be careful with the trigger."

"Oh, wow." The handle was pleasantly warm. In fact, everything about this gun — the weight, the fit in her hand, the balance — just felt ... right. "Can I shoot it sometime?"

"You bet. The gun will only fire for a select few of us, but we can ask Mark to add your biometrics as an authorized shooter. Then we'll take it to the back woods and you can shoot to your heart's content. It's wet enough around here that we shouldn't have to worry about fires. You can even try it with the targeting glasses."

"Targeting glasses? Wicked!" Tabby hoped her mom was serious. The idea of shooting a bona fide energy weapon wasn't just enticing, it was enthralling. Her fingers tingled with excitement. Giving it back to Anne was difficult.

"I felt the same when I first saw it," Anne said, shutting the closet. "I thought I was just weird, but it must be genetic."

Tabby shook her head, still staring at the closet. "The virus research, your miracle implant, a friggin' space weapon ... Mom, who are those guys?"

"They're very, very smart, like I told you, and we're lucky to have them in our lives."

Tabby crossed her arms. "All right, so what else are you holding out on me? Shrink rays? A teleporter? More vampire superpowers?"

"Powers? Like what?"

"I don't know. Billy said vampires are super strong."

"That's true. You wouldn't want to arm wrestle one."

"How strong?"

Anne gave her an impish grin. Next thing Tabby knew, her mother had lifted her over her head by the waist as if Tabby weighed no more than a child.

"Mom! Put me down! Put me ..."

She couldn't finish the sentence because she was giggling too hard.

Anne spun her around, filling the house with Tabby's screams of joy. Just when Tabby thought her lungs would burst from so much laughter, Anne plopped her on the couch, then laid down next to her. She smoothed Tabby's hair back with a smile while Tabby caught her breath.

"Thank you," Anne said softly.

"For what?"

"That. I've dreamed of spinning you over my head since you were born."

"I guess life's full of second chances."

Her mother's smile widened, showing her pointed canines. "Yeah, I guess it is." Cold lips kissed Tabby's forehead with a mother's tenderness.

That, of course, was when Zima appeared. The beautiful blonde emerged from the hall wearing a sheer white nightgown and nothing underneath. She stood still, as if frozen in time, her ice-blue eyes fixed on Anne, who was practically lying on top of her daughter. Zima gasped, just as she had last night when Tabby met her, then fled to the kitchen.

"Oh no," Tabby and Anne said at the same time.

"I'll talk to her," Anne said.

"No, this ... this is my fault. I showed up completely unexpected on a special night and dropped the daughter-bomb on her. Let me fix this, Mom. I know I can."

Anne was silent, staring at the kitchen. "Okay," she said eventually. "I'll be right here."

"Actually, I was hoping for some time alone with her."

Anne frowned. "Sweetheart, I know you mean well, but Zima —"

"Look ... she's hurt, and she's angry. She'd probably like nothing more than to lay into me, maybe even scream, but there's no way she'll do that with you around. I'd like to give her a chance to vent, because maybe it'll give us an opportunity to really talk. Then she'll know I'm not trying to take you away."

Conflict played across her mother's face. Her expression hardened.

Anne walked to the front door. "Zima, I'm going out," she called to the kitchen.

A pan crashed on the counter. Zima appeared in the kitchen doorway. "Take me with you."

"Not this time, honey. I'm leaving Tabby in your capable hands for a while. Please take good care of her."

Zima glanced at Tabby, then back at Anne. "Please, do not —"

Anne gently took her by the shoulders. "You'll be fine. I trust you to do the right thing. I trust both of you. See you in a while."

"Anne ..." Zima started to say, but the door closed behind her, leaving Zima and Tabby alone.

Tabby sat up. Zima spun to face her, then backed against the wall as if Tabby were a wild beast.

"Come sit down," Tabby said. "I promise I won't ..."

She sighed when Zima ran back into the kitchen.

"... bite."

This is going to be harder than I thought.

The delicious smell of home cooking soon wafted into the living room that was, if possible, even more tantalizing than Cappa's. Even though Tabby had just eaten, her stomach growled. She crept over to the kitchen door. Zima was busy at the stove, moving with incredible precision and coordination.

"Zima —"

The spatula and pan Zima had been holding clattered to the stove, forgotten. She backed into the far corner of the counter.

"Please wait in the dining room. Breakfast shall be ready soon, but I cannot cook with you present."

Tabby stepped inside. "I'm not here for breakfast, Zima. I want to talk."

"Then you may do so from over there."

"Why are you afraid of me?"

Zima remained silent, her back against the counter.

"I promise, I'm not here to steal Anne from you."

"I understand."

"Then what is it?"

Silence.

Tabby stepped closer. Zima leaned back, as if an invisible force were pushing her away.

"I'm not going to hurt you," Tabby said. "I swear."

"I understand."

Tabby took another step. Zima looked as if she wanted to crawl onto the counter to put every possible inch of space between them.

"Please," Zima said, panting. "Do not come closer."

Step.

"Please ..."

"What happens if I do?"

Silence.

Step.

Zima was shivering, her breaths ragged. "Please," she whispered.

"Zima, this is tearing Mom apart. You know that, don't you?"

"Y-yes."

"Then why? Why won't you talk to me? Or at least talk to her?"

"B-because ... because ..."

Step. Tabby was within arm's reach. "I just want to be friends. Will you give me a chance? For Mom's sake?" Tabby held out her hand.

Zima shook her head. Her whole body trembled under her sheer nightgown. "No, please do not! Please do not ..."

Tabby hadn't meant to touch Zima's breast. She had only been reaching for her hand, trying to assure the frightened woman she meant no harm, but her fingers accidentally brushed a stiffened peak beneath Zima's gown.

What she hadn't expected was for Zima to gasp in ecstasy, or for her lips to suddenly cover Tabby's.

Tabby tried to escape, but Zima's hands wrapped around her, spun her so that Tabby was now pinned in the corner, and she kissed her with desperation. Tabby struggled, but the slender blonde's grip was absolute, like trying to break free from steel shackles bolted firmly to the wall. Tabby readied a scream, but Zima's urgent whisper stopped her short.

"Help me. Please!"

Tabby ceased her struggling. She had heard that quiver of anguish before from someone else, that desperate need.

And she knew at once what she had to do.

Instead of screaming, Tabby kissed her, which Zima eagerly accepted. Their tongues danced in heated passion. Zima released her hands, which Tabby ran down her smooth back. Zima shuddered, pressing herself against Tabby with moans of delight. Her hands ran under Tabby's blouse and explored every inch of her skin, then pulled her blouse off over her head, followed shortly by her own nightgown, leaving Tabby in her bra, and Zima stark naked in the kitchen.

Zima was beautiful. Flawless. From her modest, pert breasts to her athletic legs and rear, she was perfection incarnate. Tabby preferred boys, but if she were ever to switch sides, Zima's porcelain skin would be the lure that reeled her in.

She had no intention of batting for the other team, however. Tabby had a mission, and she intended to see it through. After so many lonely years, she had a chance of having a family again, and she would do anything — *anything!* — to keep them.

Tabby slid her hand down the slight curve of Zima's belly and over her mound. Zima moaned, kissing her with fervent passion. When Tabby's fingers slipped home, Zima shuddered with a yell. Her hips began moving in time with Tabby's gently increasing rhythm. She clung to Tabby as if she were the only thing anchoring her to the planet. Zima's movements became frenzied, until her body finally went rigid, knocking Tabby's head against the cupboard hard enough to make her see stars. Zima cried out, bucking in the throes of release. Tabby held her until she stopped shuddering, and her breathing settled.

"I am sorry," Zima whispered, her face buried in the crook of Tabby's neck.

Tabby gathered her close and sighed. As awkward as this had been for Tabby, she wasn't the person Zima needed to apologize to.

15

TABBY

B RIGHT, BEAUTIFUL MORNING SUNSHINE bathed the quiet neighborhood in hues of gold.

Perfect for a drive, Anne thought. *Except for the bright and sunny part.*

She was several miles from home when she remembered her brother had asked her to call him regarding things she should know about Tabby, so she parked under the shade of a tree and dialed his number.

"Annie, hi! How'd the reunion go?"

Great, Doug! For my first trick, I took Tabby out shooting with a bunch of yokels, where she accidentally shot me in the stomach. But that's fine because I'm a vampire, which she knows, but you don't, and she's totally cool with it. Don't worry, though, because I haven't bitten her yet, even though she wants me to.

"Um ... fine," Anne said instead. "Yeah, we took a long nature walk last night and talked until bedtime. She's waiting at the house right now while I run an errand."

"What did she tell you?"

"That her parents died a while ago."

Doug sighed. "Anything else?"

"Well, yeah. Her dad used to take her to different countries on business trips. She's lived all over California and is currently in Chico. She knows how to shoot a gun. And her favorite comfort food is lasagna."

"That's it?"

"Of course not, but if you want me to recite the entire night's conversation, we're going to be here a while. What are you fishing for, Dougie?"

"Sorry. I'm glad she told you her adoptive parents passed away, but … did she mention how?"

"Something about her mom dying in a mugging gone wrong, but nothing about her father. Her parents seemed like a sensitive topic, so I didn't pry."

"They are. Her adoptive mom passed when she was eight. She went out for groceries one day and never came home. They found her body that night."

"Oh God! No wonder she doesn't like to talk about it. Poor Tabby must have been traumatized."

"Exactly right, Annie. But not as badly as her adoptive father."

"Oh no, don't tell me …"

"He took his wife's death poorly. At the tender age of eight, Tabby looked after him for three years, until she came home from school one day to find him swinging by his neck from a ceiling fan."

"Jesus! I …" Anne covered her mouth to keep from crying aloud. "How did she cope?"

"Not well at all. After her father died, she entered the foster care system. She lived with a different family every year for seven years, until last year, when she turned eighteen."

"But she seems fine now. What's the concern?"

"Tabby's been living with us for three months. Maria and I have been counseling her, but it was only last week that she consented to release her medical records to us. After reading them, I realized why she'd been hesitant." Doug heaved a sigh. "Annie, your daughter has two documented suicide attempts. The first was at age thirteen, two years after her father died, and the last …"

"The last was when? Doug!"

"Was just before I met her, five months ago when … when she finally gained access to her closed adoption records, and discovered that her biological mother, Anne Perrin, had recently died in a tragic explosion."

Tears splashed onto Anne's phone. "Me? She tried to kill herself because I …"

"No, Annie! Don't go there. We all have our demons with different triggers. I'm telling you this not to lay a guilt trip, but to make sure you understand where Tabby's coming from."

And what she's capable of doing if things go wrong between us.

Doug's warning couldn't have been clearer if he'd written it on the wall with red paint.

"Any suggestions?" Anne said.

"For you?" He laughed. "No. I know you, Annie. If anyone can help Tabby, it's you, just like you helped me through Dad's abuse when we were young."

The unpleasant memories made Anne shudder, and did nothing to calm her nerves. "Anything else I should know?"

"Not that I can think of. Just remember: I'm a phone call away if you need me, so don't hesitate."

"Ah, yeah, about that. Dougie, there's something …"

Anne bit her lip. Using him as a sounding board for her daughter would be difficult, since Doug didn't know Anne's full story, but she couldn't bring herself to tell him. If he didn't disown her outright, he might come rushing to her aid, putting himself and possibly his entire family in danger.

"Never mind," Anne said. "Thanks for the warning. I'll tread carefully."

"Tread *caringly*, just like you always do."

"Right. Speaking of which, I have a sudden, irresistible urge to rush back to the house and hug Tabby, so that's exactly what I'm going to do. Take care, Dougie."

"You too."

No sooner had Anne hung up than her tires were squealing in a U-turn, headed for home, where, she hoped, her wife and daughter had made some meaningful headway on their relationship.

16

UNBEARABLE

Tabby sat up with wobbly legs next to Zima, who was curled naked under the covers of her own bed, and patted her shoulder.

"Are you all right now?" Tabby said.

Zima shook her head. "I have assaulted my wife's daughter. Anne will never forgive me. After only one week, I have ruined my marriage, and hurt the person who means the most to me in a single act."

"This whole episode ... it wasn't your fault, was it?"

Zima looked at her sharply.

"Your sudden need, I mean. I've seen that look before on ... on someone else. You weren't in control."

"No, I was not," Zima said softly. "I am deeply sorry for what happened."

"It's all right."

"You are not upset?"

"Surprised, certainly, but not upset."

Zima head-cocked.

Tabby sighed. "My best friend in high school was like you, though I didn't discover it until we were seniors. Out of the blue, she would get this strange look, and wouldn't take her eyes off me. I thought she was just being weird until one day when she kissed me. I told her I didn't like her like that, but she said it didn't matter. She begged me to … to do things to satiate her insane urges. She said the need was painful, not just physically, but right down to her soul."

Zima rolled onto her back and stared at the ceiling. "I see. So you obliged her out of sympathy."

"How could I not? She was my best friend. She was suffering. I had the means to help her, so I did."

"You are very much like your mother."

Tabby beamed. "Thanks. So, does Mom know about your, um, problem?"

"Partly. She has worked tirelessly to satiate my urges, but she does not know that my attraction to her has unexpectedly translated to you."

"Huh?"

Zima folded her arms under her breasts. "When she and I first began dating, I was incapable of passion, which saddened your mother. So Cappa and I created a program that enabled me to feel the same passion a normal human female experiences."

"Like a twelve-step Alcoholics Anonymous program or something?"

"No, a computer program."

Tabby just stared at her, unable to make sense of the strange statement. Zima's ice-blue gaze finally met hers.

"Has Anne not told you? Cappa and I are androids."

Tabby blinked. "Say what?"

"Androids. I am an artificial intelligence inhabiting a robot body, designed to look and act human."

"I-I know what it means, but … how is that possible?"

"The tale of my origin is distressing, to which your mother can attest. Suffice it to say that my integration with society would not have been possible without Charlie, Mark, Cappa, and, more recently, Anne."

Tabby's mouth worked silently. She wanted to call Zima out on the ridiculous lie, but she couldn't, because she knew with certainty that Zima wasn't lying. Anne had said that Zima was just as unique as her. With Zima's fair skin and platinum hair, Tabby had been expecting her to confess she was a unicorn or a sprite.

But considering her speech patterns, lack of expressions, incredible strength, flawless features, and precise movements, the more Tabby thought about it, the better the pieces fit.

"I guess that explains how you nearly broke me in half in the kitchen," Tabby said.

Zima sat bolt-upright. "Have I injured you?"

"Nothing serious." *I hope.* "My head is sore, and I'll have bruises for a few days, but nowhere that'll show."

"I am sorry. My first sexual experience was the day your mother became a vampire. She is much sturdier than normal humans, so I have never had to be gentle."

"Don't sweat it. I'll live."

"So I should hope."

Tabby took her hand. "Mom will be home soon. What do we tell her?"

"The truth. If she wishes to divorce me, she will be well within her rights." Zima ran a gentle thumb over Tabby's knuckles. "I sincerely hope she does not. She is an integral part of my life. I do not know what I would do without her."

Tabby fiddled with the sheets. "Do you really think she'll be angry?"

The thought of Zima losing her wife was bad enough, but there was a very real chance Anne would also be angry with Tabby. The idea of losing her mom when they had just found each other threatened to bring back the suffocating depression — the darkness that had twice snuffed out her will to live, and driven her to the ultimate act of escape.

With an effort of will, Tabby pushed the dark feelings down and instead focused on Zima. Her stepmother needed her, which was reason enough to stick around. What happened after her mother returned would be another matter.

"It is possible," Zima said. "But worse than facing Anne's anger would be deceiving her. Our relationship is built on honesty and trust. I already keep secrets from her, but that is for the safety of everyone. This does not fall into that category. I will tell her the truth."

Tabby nodded. Whatever the outcome, she would stand by Zima and face the consequences, hoping against hope that her mother would understand. On a whim, she kissed Zima's hand and clutched it to her breast.

Zima head-cocked.

"It's just … the android thing aside, you aren't the person I thought you were. And I mean that in a good way."

"Oh. Thank you."

"So … how is it that a robot's libido gets out of control? Can't you just turn it off?"

"Initially, yes, I could, but the program used to create my sexual response system was more effective than we anticipated. It has expanded beyond its confines and become part of my core being. I can no more disable it than any of my other behaviors. I have spent the last six months attempting to bring my desires under control, but it has been difficult, to which Anne can vouch. She has been very accommodating, often at inconvenient times, but she has never once made me feel ashamed for asking."

"Sounds like nymphomania, in a way."

"Perhaps. Until yesterday, when you arrived, Anne was the only person capable of eliciting a sexual response from me. Being around her is stimulating enough, but when I saw both of you on the couch together …"

"It must have driven you crazy."

"That is an apt description. I was so aroused that I feared I would not make it to the kitchen. Cooking breakfast was a difficult task."

"You could have told her, Zima. Mom would have understood."

"In retrospect, that would have been the wisest choice, but I was afraid of what she would think of me. You are her daughter. Such attractions are simply not tolerated, from what I understand. I believed that by staying away from you for a time, I could alter my programming to separate my desire for you from my desire for her, but it was more difficult than I had anticipated. Although I am consciously aware that you are two different people, my core programming is not, and changing that is not an easy task. It would be similar to asking you to remap specific neural pathways in your brain."

"Look, I know Mom and I have a lot in common, but we aren't *that* alike." Tabby scratched her head. "Are we?"

"Yes. Your facial structures are a ninety-one percent match. Your hip, waist, and bust measurements differ by only four percent, but your proportions deviate by less than zero-point-three percent. Your eye and hair colors are less than one percent deviant.

"And that only enumerates your physical traits. Your voice. Your laugh. Your smile. Your compassion. Your sense of humor and affectations." Zima brushed a finger down her cheek. "When I stated that you are very much like your mother, I meant it truly."

"Thanks," Tabby said, blushing. "And there's really nothing you can do to untangle us?"

"Not as of yet. Like humans, I have little control over my mind's inner workings. My subconscious has decided you are Anne, and I am unsure how to convince it otherwise."

"Yikes! Can Charlie or Mark help?"

Zima shook her head. "My core program is far too complex, even for them. It would take years for them to figure out where to even begin."

"What about Cappa? She helped you the first time, right?"

"The only help she might offer is to create another Desire program, similar to the one used to first grant my libido, but with the intent of weaning me from you. However, the side effects of the Desire routine can be severe, as has been demonstrated twice now at significant peril. The first version made me homicidal. The second version turned me into a nymphomaniac. I am loathe to attempt a third."

"H-homicidal?"

"Yes. As I have said, my origins are distressing, but please believe that most of my violent impulses have been corrected."

Most?

Tabby scooted away. "Should I be worried?"

"No. In fact, just as my attraction to Anne applies to you, so do the protocols I have created to ensure her safety. I could not intentionally harm you even if I wished to, which I do not."

Whew!

"Again, I am sorry this happened," Zima said. "I realize it is not just my marriage in jeopardy, but your relationship with your mother as well. When I tell Anne what has happened, the truth will highlight your innocence, and hopefully minimize the fallout to you."

"Thanks, but I'm not hanging you out to dry."

"That is very kind of you."

Zima's eyes strayed to Tabby's chest, then her arms. Tabby was afraid that her shirtless state might stir her stepmother again, until Zima's gaze landed on her scarred wrists. Tabby tucked them under her arms, but it was too late.

Zima's ice-blue eyes met hers. "What happened?"

"It was an accident," Tabby lied. "Cuts from a sharp cord tied around my wrists."

Zima brow-knit, but remained silent. Tabby matched her silence. Discussing those dark times was a place she really didn't want to go. Despite the morning's awkward turn of events, she felt a true bond forming with her stepmother, and she didn't want to ruin it.

Tabby had a family now. A *real* family. Yes, her mother was a vampire, and her stepmother was a robot with insatiable urges, but, from what Tabby could see, they both cared for her, and she was fast coming to care for them. She wouldn't throw that away because of a few, desperate incidents that happened to land her in the hospital. So she met Zima's stoic gaze with her own and kept her mouth shut.

Zima nodded slowly, as if Tabby had just bared her soul anyway.

"Your shirt is in the kitchen," Zima said eventually. "You should don it before your beautiful chest incites another incident."

"Oh, sorry. We wouldn't want that."

"No. I was able to stop sooner with you than I would have with Anne, but next time, we may not be as fortunate."

"Sooner? That was a short session?"

"Much shorter. In addition to being sturdier, Anne also has significantly more stamina than normal humans. And, as I have stated, she has been very accommodating."

"Covering myself it is. Be right back."

Tabby tried to stand and failed. Her legs simply wouldn't lift her off the bed.

"Or maybe I'll just sit here for a minute. I must be more tired than I thought. Anyway, don't worry about facing Mom alone. I'll be there, too. Hopefully we can talk this through together."

"That is a kind offer, but it is difficult for me to concentrate with both of you in the same room."

"Oh, right."

"No, I shall ..." Zima turned her head to the window, then jumped out of bed. "That is her car down the street. She will arrive in approximately two minutes!"

"Okay, so just —"

"She is going to leave me." Zima began pacing, her eyes darting everywhere. "She is going to leave me! I cannot live without her. I cannot, I cannot, I cannot!"

"Zima, just tell her the truth, like you said. We have a strong case. She'll understand."

"No! This requires the utmost tact, and I do not have adequate simulations prepared! I need more time. I need more time!"

Cripes.

"All right, put your clothes on," Tabby said.

Zima stared at her, clearly lost.

"Clothes. On. Quickly! And find me a shirt that fits." Tabby tried to stand again with no luck.

Great.

"What's beyond your backyard?"

"Forest," Zima said.

"Perfect. Come on, get dressed! If you need more time to think, then we can't be here when Mom walks in that door."

Zima launched into action while Tabby watched with open-mouthed fascination. Her movements were faster and more precise than anything Tabby had ever seen. In no time, Zima was dressed to perfection. She then helped Tabby into one of Anne's shirts.

"Great, now help me up. Help me up!"

Zima gently pulled her to her feet, then slipped under her arm for support.

"Out to the backyard," Tabby said. "Hurry!"

A few stumbling steps told Tabby that walking was out of the question. Her legs felt like dead weights swinging from her hips.

"Zima, I'm sorry, I can't —"

Zima scooped her up as if she weighed no more than a child, carried her to the rear sliding door, which Tabby opened, then closed it behind them.

That was when Tabby saw the flaw in her plan. The backyard fence had no rear gate.

They were trapped.

"Sorry, Zima, I tr—"

She yelped when Zima leaped over the fence in a single bound, then ran through the forest faster than Tabby believed possible, taking them far, far away from her mother's house.

17

WELCOME HOME

ANNE PAUSED AT THE FRONT DOOR of her house to gather herself. She had left Tabby and Zima alone for almost an hour, which was more than enough time, she hoped, for them to talk through whatever it was they needed to talk about.

For better or worse, Anne thought.

Either way, she hoped their time together had opened the way for conversation so they could all move forward as a family. Taking a deep breath, Anne went inside.

Only quiet greeted her.

"Hello?"

Anne walked to the living room, where Tabby's cup of jasmine green tea sat untouched.

The kitchen, too, was empty. The beginnings of breakfast lay scattered across the stove and counter, as if dropped and forgotten — a state her meticulous Zima would never have left it in.

More disturbing, however, was Zima's nightgown, strewn carelessly on the floor next to Tabby's shirt.

What the ...

"Zima? Tabby? Where are you?"

Anne checked the dining room, the backyard, the guest rooms, and the bathrooms.

Nothing.

Then she reached her bedroom. Rumpled sheets indicated the bed had been recently used.

But that wasn't what caught Anne's attention.

The strong scent of Zima's unique feminine odor hit her like a punch to the nose, so familiar that Anne would have recognized it anywhere.

And it was fresh.

Anne ran back to the kitchen and sniffed. Zima's feminine scent — also fresh — cut through even the spices and lingering traces of breakfast.

She crouched near their discarded clothes.

No. No, it couldn't be. They couldn't have ...

Anne didn't remember putting the kettle on, or steeping Zima's favorite jasmine green tea. She must have, however, for the next thing she knew, she was sitting at the dining room table in her usual place. A steaming cup sat in Zima's empty spot. On a whim, Anne gathered Tabby's cup, set it on the other side of the table, and smiled.

This was just how she imagined it should be: Anne sitting at the head of the table, Zima to her right, Tabby to her left. Everyone enjoying morning tea over pancakes and eggs in their new house, chatting about how their days had gone, which new colleges Tabby had been accepted to, and which one she might choose. Something close by, of course. They had just been reunited, after all, and they had so much catching up to do.

Tabby would choose a community college because it was economical, not wanting to put her mother out financially, but Anne would insist on a four-year university. She had a steady job, and, even though it didn't pay much, she would put every dime toward Tabby's education to ensure she had the lifestyle that Anne herself never had.

Perhaps Tabby would get a nursing degree. Or better yet, a medical doctorate. She was young and bright and had the whole world ahead of her. If Tabby wanted a doctorate, Anne would take on additional work to pay for her tuition.

Tabby was her daughter. Anne would do anything for her. Anything.

She looked at Zima's cup, then at Tabby's.

A heaviness grew in her chest. Anne should be worried about Tabby's safety, but the weight pulled her down to the table.

Something had been bothering Zima about Tabby. Leaving them alone had been a calculated risk.

Now they were gone, and Tabby could be in danger.

Anne should be calling Charlie, or Cappa, or Mark. Organizing a search party. Finding her daughter. Finding her wife. Making sure they were both safe.

But the heaviness drew her down and down, until her chest was heaving, and the only sounds in the empty living room were the ticking mantle clock and Anne's crying.

•　　　•　　　•

Sometime later — Anne couldn't have said how long — a knock at the door interrupted her sobbing.

Go away, she thought miserably.

The knocking continued.

Anne reluctantly grabbed a napkin and dabbed her face dry. Her nano-makeup, contacts, and false caps for her canines were still in place. Her eyes didn't redden anymore since becoming a vampire, so no one would even know she had been crying.

As it turned out, it didn't matter. Anne paused to listen at the door out of habit, and heard only Charlie's strong heartbeat on the other side. She took a deep breath and opened the door.

"Good morning," Anne said pleasantly, although she was unable to conjure her usual smile.

"Morning." Charlie peered inside and frowned. "Where is everyone?"

"Out."

"Oh. So Zima and Tabby are getting along now?"

The weight in Anne's chest threatened to drag her down once again. "Come in."

Charlie glanced at the teacups on their way to the living room and sat on the couch with a look of concern. "I just stopped by to see how things are going. I can come back later if this isn't a good time."

"No, I'm glad you're here." Anne cleared her throat. "There have been some, ah ... developments, that I could use your help with."

"Of course. Anything."

Anything.

Anne bit her lip to keep from crying again.

"I left Tabby and Zima alone this morning to encourage them to reconcile their differences by themselves, since I wasn't having any luck. I think something ... happened, while I was out. When I got back, they were gone."

Charlie's brow furrowed in concern. "So where are they now?"

"I don't know. Zima isn't responding to my messages, which would be unusual, except she's been distant ever since Tabby arrived."

"You think she's jealous?"

Anne buried her face in her hands, unable to keep from sobbing this time. "Charlie, I ... I honestly don't know. Zima won't talk to me about it. Jealousy is what I thought at first, but now I think she may have ... she might have ..." Anne couldn't even voice it.

The idea of Zima cheating on her — with her own daughter, no less — wasn't just ludicrous. From what Anne understood, it was impossible. Zima insisted that Anne was the only person capable of giving her physical pleasure. Anne felt sorry that not only was Zima unfairly bound to her, but that she couldn't even relieve those needs herself. So Anne had taken ownership and worked hard, often several times a day, to ensure Zima's needs were being met.

She was Anne's wife. The only reason Zima had created the Desire routine in the first place was to make Anne happy. It was Anne's pleasure and honor to return the favor and keep her satisfied. And she thought she had been doing a good job.

Until an hour ago, anyway, when she'd found their clothes discarded on the kitchen floor.

Charlie gently took her hands. "Do you think Tabby's in danger?"

"I don't know," Anne said, sobbing. "I don't know, I don't know, I don't know!"

Then she was in his arms. Emotions flooded her — feelings from when they'd still been dating, when Charlie would hold her in his comforting embrace at night.

She missed him.

It would be so easy to steal a kiss — to rekindle the fire they once had. But the idea of putting Cappa through the heartache Anne was feeling right now kept her at bay.

Anne wouldn't hurt her soul sister like that. Ever.

A knock on the front door made them sit upright. They looked at each other with raised eyebrows. Anne wasn't expecting anyone. Apparently, Charlie wasn't, either.

She walked into the foyer and listened. A single heartbeat thumped outside, naggingly familiar. Anne looked through the spyhole and gasped.

"Calum!"

She opened the door, but when Anne saw the rest of him, she could only stare. The Scotsman who had once held her prisoner had never been heavyset, but the person standing before her looked closer to a walking skeleton. The hollows of his cheeks were like caverns, shrouded by a great beard that was just as scraggly as his once-well-kempt hair. His clothes, too, were ragged and worn, as if they had traveled to the farthest reaches of the globe and back without ever leaving his body.

"Anne." Calum's voice was raspy, as if water hadn't touched his throat in days. "Anne, I ... I'm sorry."

He stumbled forward. Anne caught him before he collapsed to the floor.

"Anne, get away from him!" Charlie vaulted the couch and rushed toward her.

But it was too late. Calum wrapped his emaciated arms around Anne and hugged her at an odd angle, mashing her right breast against the right side of his chest. Her sub-dermal computer implant rubbed against something hard beneath his skin, in approximately the same spot as her own implant.

Her dream-that-wasn't-a-dream of Calum from last month came rushing back. The Entity had captured him, done something horrible to him.

Now she had a frightening idea what that something was.

"No, Calum! Don't!"

Anne tried to pry his arms away. It should have been easy, but he clung to her with unnatural strength.

"Calum! Let go!"

Charlie rushed to her side, pulling at Calum's arms, but it was no use. If Anne's vampire strength couldn't dislodge him, then Charlie's human body had no chance.

"I'm sorry," Calum said again. "Goodbye, Anne."

"No!" Charlie redoubled his efforts, pulling with all his might. "Calum, let her go! Let her go!"

He punched Calum in the side of the head. Calum reeled, but his arms remained fastened.

"Get Cappa," Anne said, struggling for breath.

"She's shopping!" Charlie frantically looked around.

"My plasma pistol," Anne gasped. "In the closet."

Charlie scrambled to the hallway closet, threw open the door, and withdrew her shiny pistol. He pressed the barrel against Calum's head.

"Last chance, Calum. Let her go or I'll shoot!"

"Too late," Calum rasped. "It's done. I'm sorry, Anne. So sorry."

He heaved a final breath and collapsed to the floor, motionless.

Then, for the first time ever, Anne faced the full, uninhibited force of the Entity's will.

•　　　•　　　•

Charlie watched Anne rise as if she were a hissing snake, and was ashamed when he found himself pointing Anne's own gun at her.

Anne didn't appear to notice. She frowned at the wall with a distant stare, her lips moving, as if talking with someone. No sound came forth, nor could Charlie make out her words.

"I see," Anne eventually whispered. Her eyes met Charlie's. "I finally see."

Charlie backed away, his plasma gun still trained on her. "See what, Anne?"

"Our fate. Not the glimpses Almos saw, but the entire, godawful plan."

"Tell me."

She shook her head. "Charlie, are you able to jump back into your cyborg body yet?"

"H-how did you know about that?"

Anne smiled wanly. "It was your life's work. You wouldn't let it go to waste. Have you fixed it?"

Charlie gulped. Sweat slicked the pistol's warm grip. He nodded.

"Good. You'll be safe, then, and you won't have to go through the agony of the transformation." She walked toward him.

"Stay back!" Charlie leveled the shaking pistol at her head — at his dear, sweet Anne.

God help me, what am I doing?

Anne continued her advance. "You won't shoot me, Charlie. You still love me, just like I still love you. The Entity knows it, too, so you might as well put the gun down."

His trembling finger touched the trigger, but would go no further.

Anne was right. Entity or no, he couldn't kill her, not after everything they'd been through. He lowered the gun and backed away until he bumped against the couch.

"What are you going to do?"

"I'm going to ensure our family's safety," Anne said. "Change is coming, and soon. The vampire population is many times higher than the Entity needs to complete its operation. I can sense their numbers now. Even if you kill me, someone else will take my place, and the Entity's plans will continue. Zima and Cappa will be fine, but the rest of our family will need to undergo the transformation, or they won't survive in the new world. It's painful, but necessary. I'll be there for them through the entire ordeal, just like they were there for me."

"No! Anne — or the Entity, or whatever the hell you are — I won't let you turn them! Anne, please ..." Charlie risked gently putting a hand on her cheek. "This isn't you. It can't be. The real Anne would know we can fix this. We can fight. We can win! Don't do this."

Anne smiled sadly. "I'm still your Anne, and I always will be. But you're wrong. The Entity is allowing me certain freedoms, but it won't let me jeopardize its plans." She sighed. "And, no matter how I look at it, humanity is doomed. What I'm about to do is for our family's own good. I won't lose them to the coming Apocalypse. As much as I love and respect you, I won't let you stop me from saving them, either."

With tender slowness, Anne took Charlie's arm and sank her teeth in.

A familiar dopamine rush followed, putting his pleasure center on overload. Charlie sagged against the couch in a drugged stupor.

"That's so you'll heal quickly." A tear ran down Anne's cheek. "And so I won't feel quite as terrible for having to do this."

Charlie hardly saw her move. She struck his head with such force that he flew over the couch, where he landed in a daze.

Anne closed the front door on her way out. That was the last thing Charlie saw before everything went black.

18

IMMORTALITY

DELA MADIGAN SUTHER POURED steamed milk into the coffee cup with a measured rhythm born from years of barista work. The result was perfection: a white foam rose floating in a sea of espresso-brown. With a satisfied smile, she put the cup on the tray alongside the stack of sandwiches destined for Mark.

He'll be so surprised!

She couldn't wait. The word 'domestic' wasn't in either of their vocabularies. They usually ate out, unless Doris cooked, but today Dela was feeling Suzy Homemaker. She speared each sandwich with a colored toothpick, then arranged them in a neat semi-circle. It wasn't up to Cappa's standards — few things were — but Mark would surely appreciate her effort.

A deep gong reverberated throughout the mansion, announcing a visitor at the main door.

Strange.

Dela set the tray aside and walked to the entranceway, a large space with big mahogany columns and country landscape portraits lining the walls. She opened one of the oversized French doors to find a solitary guest.

"Oh. Hi, Anne. I wasn't expecting you. I assume you're here for a snack?" Dela tapped a vein on her arm and winked.

"A snack sounds great. Also, I have a surprise for you."

"A surprise? Cool!"

Dela stepped aside and gestured for Anne to come in, and they headed to the kitchen.

"Your timing is perfect," Dela said. "I just finished making lunch for Mark, so we can all eat together."

Anne looked around. "Is Mark here?"

"In the garage. Why?"

"I have a surprise for him, too."

Dela leaned on the counter and grinned. "Come on, you're killing me! Can you give me a hint?"

"Sure. It's something you've wanted from me for a while."

"Full-contact sparring lessons?"

"In a way." Anne's smile was sad, which Dela found odd. "It's time to grant your wish. This time tomorrow, you'll be a full-fledged, ass-kicking vampire."

Dela waited for the punchline, but it never came. "What, seriously?"

"Seriously." Anne drew a knife from the wooden block and rolled up her sleeve. "Would you like me to bite you first? Any scratches or nicks will be permanent after the transformation, as William's disfigurement demonstrated."

"W-wait, we're going to do this right now? Don't we need Mark to do the implant thing so I can be a cyber-vampire, like you?"

"I just messaged him. He's on his way."

Without warning, Anne sliced her own arm open and held it out.

I can't believe it!

Dela had no idea where this sudden change of heart had come from, but, after all this time, if both Mark and Anne were onboard, she was hardly going to argue.

Me, a vampire supersoldier!

Many kids read comics and imitated their heroes through pretend play. Dela had certainly been one, but, unlike her childhood friends, she had never lost that interest. Dela had trained and trained, pushing herself to her limits, trying to reach the level where she could trash a room full of criminals without breaking a sweat.

Reality was a harsh teacher, however. Try as she might, she couldn't compete with the men. No matter how much she practiced, they were usually stronger and faster, leaving Dela pinned to the mat, or nursing her bruises.

Then she'd met Mark. Even before she'd learned what he really was — a genetically modifiable supersoldier with a semi-intelligent computer implant — she had suspected he was bigger than life: a genuine hero who could do all those things she had only dreamed of.

Then she'd learned about Charlie, the Cyborg; Anne, the Mutant-Vampire; Cappa, the Super-Smart Android; and Zima, dubbed by her enemies as the Dark Angel — the deadliest warrior the world had ever known. It should have been a dream come true.

But it wasn't. In fact, being surrounded by larger-than-life people had made Dela feel even less significant — like all the work she had invested into honing herself into something better had been for nothing. They were in a different class. And, while they humored her by letting her watch from the sidelines, Dela had never been allowed to play with the big boys.

Until now.

With a triumphant grin, Dela took Anne's arm and drank from her wound.

A side door burst open from across the mansion. Mark's footsteps pounded down the hall.

"Dela! Dela, wait! Don't …"

Mark slid to a halt on the tiled floor, his wide eyes fixed on Dela's mouth attached to Anne's arm.

"No," he whispered. "Please tell me this is a joke."

"Nope!" Dela wagged her bloody tongue at him for effect. "Anne said you agreed. When do we put the implant in? Can I choose which boob?"

He looked between them like they were crazy. "Y-yes, I do have an implant for you, but I don't know how either of you found out about it. I was working on it in secret as a birthday gift." He gave Anne a hard stare. "And *no,* I never agreed to this! Anne, what the hell are you thinking?"

"That you would never have agreed if I'd asked beforehand, and I was right. As for knowing about the implant … you're supplying advanced weapons to the Resistance, which means you must have the nano-manufacturing lines running again. Even if you hadn't had an implant ready for Dela, it wouldn't have taken you long to fabricate a new one, right?"

"Right," Mark said carefully. "And who told you we were supplying the Resistance?"

"Tim."

"I highly doubt that." Mark drew himself up, but he approached Anne with caution. "What's really going on here? The Anne I know wouldn't turn someone into a vampire unless their life depended on it."

"Her life does depend on it — and so does yours." Anne offered her arm to him. "Please, Mark. Drink."

"Another time."

"Time is something we don't have. Not anymore." Anne moved her arm closer. "Your implant makes you stronger than most, but it isn't enough to survive what's coming. I care about you, Mark. Please drink."

Mark's haunted eyes studied her. His voice sounded distant when he spoke. "And if I refuse?"

"I'd prefer if you didn't."

They stared at each other like a standoff in an old Western movie. Tension vibrated through Mark's body like an untuned guitar, while Anne simply looked sad. Dela started to ask what was going on.

And that's when her friends went crazy.

Mark drew his plasma pistol so fast that Dela didn't see his hand move.

Which made it even more astonishing when Anne beat him to it. Mark stared at his empty hand, which should have held his pistol, now being pointed at him by Anne.

Dela had watched their sparring matches before with jealous intensity. Anne was fast, but so was Mark, and her hubby was far better with a gun. She should *not* have been able to disarm him so easily.

"Anne," Dela said softly. "What the fuck are you doing?"

"Making sure you and your husband live happily ever after."

Mark crossed his arms. "So that's it, huh? If I don't drink, you're going to kill me?"

"No."

To Dela's horror, Anne turned the gun on her own head.

"I love you, Mark. I love you all. If my entire family won't survive the Entity's plans, then I don't want any part of it, and this is the only way out for me."

The Entity …

"Oh my God," Dela said. "You're … you've been compromised!"

Anne nodded sadly. "I know what you're thinking. You're afraid the Entity will take control of you once you become a vampire."

You're damn right, Dela thought, although she could only nod.

"It isn't interested in you. Any of you. You can live your lives as you please, until …" A tear rolled down her cheek.

"Until what?" Mark said.

"Until none of us can." Anne held her wounded arm out. "It's your turn, Mark."

"Anne —"

She pressed the gun against her own temple. "Ten. Nine. Eight. Sev—"

"All right! I'll do it, just … stop counting." Mark approached cautiously. "I only have to drink, right?"

"Yes." Anne's lip quivered, her tears flowing freely now.

Mark shared a meaningful look with Dela. Then, like a scene from some terrible nightmare, he drank from Anne, too.

When he finished, Anne rolled her sleeve down and handed his gun back to him. Dela was shocked when he simply holstered it.

"You know the drill," Anne said. "You need to drink blood to complete the transformation. You're both in an early enough stage that you can drink each other's. I know it's hard, but … please don't wait."

Anne kissed them both, her lips cold on Dela's cheek.

Like mine will be soon.

"I don't want to lose either of you," Anne said. "Hard days are ahead. We're going to need each other — very, very soon."

Mark put a gentle hand on her shoulder. "What's going to happen, Anne?"

"The end of days, just like Almos predicted, but there will be a small place for us to thrive. And, if we're lucky, find happiness."

Her gaze lingered on them, then Anne turned and left the kitchen. Dela heard the front door close.

"Oh, Mark. We're so fucked!"

"Like hell we are." He grabbed her hand and ran to the garage.

"Where are we going?"

"The factory. I've asked Cappa to meet us there. We have to get that implant in you as soon as possible." Mark helped her into the car, then ran around to the driver's side. "She's manufacturing implants for Doris, Charlie, and Tabitha, too. Just in case."

"That's cool, but … it just seems like damage control, at this point. We're all going to end up vampires under the Entity's control."

"No we won't. Not today." Mark opened the glove compartment and withdrew a small leather case filled with metal syringes. He plucked one out and jabbed it in Dela's leg.

"Ow! What the hell?"

"It's a chemical Charlie and I have been developing with the Resistance scientists. It tricks the virus into thinking the host has already turned, so it stops replicating." He took another syringe, stuck himself in the leg, and winced. "You're right, that hurts."

Dela whacked his arm.

"What was that for?"

"Your horrible communication skills! When were you going to tell your goddamned wife about this wonder cure?"

"It isn't a cure. It only halts the virus's progression for a short time, which is why we have to hurry."

The garage door had just opened when Mark peeled out. The roof of the car barely cleared the opening, then they were tearing down the dirt road leading off the property.

Dela took her phone out of her pocket with one hand and gripped the oh-shit handle with the other. "We have to warn the others."

"Cappa says Charlie isn't answering his phone. Zima hasn't responded to my messages, which scares me, since Cappa says Tabby isn't answering, either."

"I'll call Doris, then. She's in the middle of her shift, but she usually picks up." Dela pulled her number up with a trembling finger. "Pick up, pick up, pick up," she said to the ring tones.

"Hey, Red," Doris said on the other end. "What's up?"

"Emergency. Meet us at the factory like fucking yesterday. Take the back roads. And if you see Anne … run."

Not that it would do her any good.

Silence answered her, followed by a short sob. Dela's message had been received.

"All right, s-see you there," Doris said in a cracked voice. The line went dead.

Dela stared at the passing landscape. Rain dotted the window, slowly at first, then with increasing urgency. By the time they pulled into the factory, thunder echoed from the hills.

Perfect, Dela thought bitterly.

It was fitting weather for the end of the fucking world.

19

DEVOTION

TABBY RUBBED HER LEGS, which hung loosely over the fallen log, and willed them to move.

Nothing.

Damnit.

Zima stood in front of her, stone-still, her ice-blue eyes staring unfocused at the forest duff. A chill breeze rustled the autumn leaves. Tabby hugged herself and looked at the sky. Gray clouds rolled in, thick and threatening. A gentle breeze carried the soft smell of rain.

Tabby looked up at Zima. "How are your simulations coming?"

"Not well. The highest confidence rating I have achieved is fifty-four percent."

"Are you sure that's accurate?"

"No." Zima sat beside her and took Tabby's hand, as she had many times since they'd arrived at the forest clearing. "How are your legs?"

"Same. They don't hurt, but they still won't listen to me."

"Do not fear. Anne's venom will likely fix whatever damage I have done."

"Assuming she doesn't hate me enough to leave me like this out of spite."

Which I couldn't blame her for.

Tabby squeezed her hand. "It's going to rain soon. How much longer do you think you'll need to find that perfect simulation?"

"Given the number of permutations I have already run, it is unlikely I will find a better solution than I already have."

"So, what now?"

"Return to the house. Explain what happened." Zima's eyes fell. "See if Anne will still have me."

"And me."

"Yes." Zima stood and scooped Tabby up in her arms, took two steps ...

... and froze.

"What is it?" Tabby said.

"Anne has been compromised."

"Compromised? W-what does that mean?"

Zima shook her head. "No," she whispered, as if she hadn't heard Tabby's question. "I do not understand how it is possible."

"How *what's* possible? Damnit, talk to me! What's wrong with my mother?"

"I cannot access her implant. I am locked out." Zima stood still for several minutes, cradling Tabby in her arms.

The first drops of rain patted the leaves all around. Tabby hugged her stepmother for warmth. Her own shirt was only a thin blouse, which was about as much protection from the cold as butter armor from her mom's plasma pistol.

More minutes passed. Tabby began to shiver.

She waved a hand in front of Zima's face. The android didn't even blink. Tabby snuggled closer and waited.

"I cannot bypass her implant's security," Zima said eventually. "It is like nothing I have encountered before."

"But how could this happen? By whom?"

When Zima continued to stare, Tabby shocked her out of it with a quick kiss on her lips.

"Talk to me, Zima! Who besides Charlie, Mark, and Cappa could do such a thing?"

Zima fixed her blue eyes on Tabby. "There is still much you do not know about your mother. Things that may pain you to learn."

Tabby scoffed. "Worse than being a vampire?"

"Much."

The answer caught Tabby off guard, but she clenched her jaw in firm resolve. "She's. My. Mom. Whatever it is, I want to know!"

"As you wish," Zima said impassively. "Anne is of great importance, not only to me, but to humanity's future. She is mentally connected with a being referred to as the Entity, who we believe is the progenitor of the vampire race."

"Race? Just how many vampires are there?"

Zima turned suddenly, peering into the woods.

"Over ten thousand," Anne said, stepping out from behind a tree. "Although there could be many more. I won't know the exact number until I reach San Francisco."

"Mom! H-how did you find us?"

"Vampires are natural hunters. We have keen senses of smell, even in the rain."

"Smell." Zima brow-knit. "You already know," she said softly.

The sadness in her mother's eyes grew ten-fold. Anne nodded. "But that's not why I'm here." She looked at Tabby. "Do you ... still want to be like me, honey?"

"That depends. What's this Entity thing Zima mentioned?"

"It's old," Anne said. "It's lonely. It's exasperated. And it won't know peace until it completes its mission."

"That is new information," Zima said. "Has the Entity revealed anything else?"

"Yes. It held back much from Almos, but because of this" — Anne pointed to her breast, where her implant resided — "it has a deeper connection with me than any master vampire before. It trusts me, and ... I-I think it likes me."

"You sound like a pet, Mom."

Tabby looked at Zima for confirmation, but Zima was focused on Anne, her head cocked slightly to one side.

"What are its intentions?" Zima said.

"I'm not allowed to say." Anne smiled weakly. "It knows you're a strategist, and that you, of all people, should understand why."

"I see." Zima looked at Tabby for the first time since Anne had appeared. "Is making your daughter a vampire the only reason you sought us out?"

Anne's sadness returned. "No, I also wanted to see you — see you both — one last time before I go."

Zima began to tremble. "You are ... leaving me?"

Anne covered her mouth and sobbed. Her tears mingled with the raindrops on her face. "I'm sorry," she said in a hoarse whisper, "but I have to. Will you keep Tabby safe?"

"No."

Before Tabby could wonder at her stepmother's harsh answer, she found herself back on the wet log, and Zima was walking toward Anne.

"I cannot fulfill your request," Zima said, "because I am coming with you."

"You can't," Anne said, crying harder. "The Entity knows you, and what you're capable of. It knows you've been aiding the Resistance, and that you'll interfere with its plans."

"Then I shall stop. As of this moment, I will break all ties with the Resistance."

"That doesn't matter now, but even if it did, it's not enough."

"It will have to be. I am coming with you."

"It won't let you."

"And how will it stop me? You have said the Entity knows what I am capable of, so it should know that I am not so easily deterred."

"Because it also knows your greatest weakness," Anne said. "Me. The Entity likes me, Zima, but nothing is more important than its mission. If it thinks your following me will jeopardize its plans, it will simply kill me and promote another vampire in the hierarchy."

Anne moved closer until her forehead touched Zima's.

"I don't have much time, honey. I won't pretend to understand what happened between you two" — she glanced at Tabby — "but I'm glad it did. More than anything, I was worried about you, and if Tabby can fill your needs in my absence, then —"

"I do not want Tabby! I want you — and only you."

Anne collapsed onto her shoulder, crying.

"I know," Anne said between sobs. "But we don't have a choice."

She reluctantly pulled herself away and walked toward Tabby.

Zima darted between them and fell to her knees.

"No, please! There is always a choice. Please! I ... I will do anything to stay by your side. Anything!" Zima clasped her hands in an imploring gesture. "Anything the Entity wishes. I will be its warrior, its protector, or stand meekly aside, if that is its desire. Just ... do not leave me. Please."

Anne covered her mouth and shook her head. "Oh, don't say that, honey. Don't say that! The price is too high."

"I do not care! 'Whatever Hell holds for you, it holds for both of us.' Those were your words, were they not?"

"Yes," Anne whispered.

"Three times I have lost you, not knowing if I would see you alive again." Zima inched forward on her knees. "You are my wife. I have vowed to take care of you, until death do us part. That — and *only* that — will ever separate us again. I shall do whatever the Entity requires, as long as we may remain together."

Anne fell to her knees and took Zima's hands, her face awash with anguish. "Would you destroy the entire human race? Could you really live with that?"

"Yes."

"Zima!" Tabby rolled off the log and clawed her way across the leaves toward them, cursing her deadened legs. "Zima, you can't —"

"Yes! As long as there is a place for us in the end, I will kill them all myself. I will pay the Entity's price." Zima stroked Anne's cheek. "Let it be done."

Anne kissed her. Long. Tender. Even from where Tabby watched from the ground, their love shone so brightly that she stopped crawling and stared in wonder.

"Whatever Hell holds," Anne said softly.

"Whatever Hell holds. I shall be right there with you, Anne Perrin, now and to the end."

"Oh, sweetheart ..." Anne cupped her cheek. "The Entity requires one more thing before it can accept your offer. And please, consider carefully before you agree." She took a deep breath and held Zima's eyes. "Your word of fealty isn't enough. The Entity needs assurance that it can count on you the same way it counts on me, and that you won't interfere with its plans."

Zima brow-knit. "I ... do not understand. What more does the Entity require?"

"Control." Anne pointed at her own head, then at Zima's chest. "If you're to be a part of its plans, then it needs access to your core. It won't alter who you are — I wouldn't have offered otherwise — but it needs access to your thoughts and control of your actions, as it has with me."

Zima's mouth fell open. Rain pattered all around, drenching her platinum-blonde hair. But she didn't move.

Anne eventually nodded with sad eyes. "I can't blame you. After everything you've done to escape Orwing's influence, I couldn't live with myself if you had to go back to a life of mental slavery." She kissed Zima, then rose to leave.

Zima caught her hand.

"I have opened a communications port," she said softly, "and have transmitted my encryption keys to your implant. The Entity may do as it —"

Zima stiffened and toppled onto the wet ground. Her body convulsed as if she was having a seizure. Anne stayed by her side, held her hand tight, and looked more miserable than ever.

The fit lasted for several minutes. Tabby lay on her stomach in the leaves and dirt — cold, wet, and shivering — but she couldn't take her eyes from the heartbreaking spectacle, nor could she fathom the depths of the sacrifice Zima was making for her wife, her love.

Tabby's mom.

Zima eventually sat up and looked around. Her arms moved as if someone else was controlling them; out, up, forward, fingers flexed and curled, then rested by her sides once more. Her ice-blue eyes turned to Anne.

"Whatever Hell holds for you ..." Zima said.

"It holds for both of us." Anne helped her to her feet and kissed her cheek. "Are you all right, honey?"

"Yes. The process was very efficient, considering the scope of the changes. The Entity's technical abilities are remarkable."

Anne shook her head, her tears melding with the rain. "Zima, I'm so sorry."

"Do not be. The choice was mine, and I stand by it."

Tabby propped herself up on shaking arms. "Mom," she said in a trembling voice, "what the hell is going on?"

Anne only now seemed to notice that her daughter was lying on the wet ground. She hurried over.

"Tabby! What are you doing? Here, let me help you up."

"No! Mom, I … I can't stand. My legs aren't working."

"Aren't …" Anne looked at Zima with horror.

"It was not intentional," Zima said. "My only sexual experience before today has been with you, which may have been too much for Tabby."

"So you two did …" Anne squeezed her eyes shut. "I-it doesn't matter," she said, although hurt strained her voice. She knelt beside Tabby and pulled her into her lap, cradling her like a child, and brushed the shock of white hair from her face. "My bite heals, honey, and should fix the problem with your legs. May I?"

Tabby nodded. Anne took her wrist and gently sank her elongated fangs in. It hurt at first, but a euphoria soon followed, making Tabby smile despite herself.

Even the euphoria couldn't dull her shock when her mom gashed open her own wrist with a sharp tooth.

"Drink, honey," Anne said. "My blood will turn you into a vampire, like me. It's the only way you can be safe."

"I recommend waiting," Zima said. "We have observed at the children's hospital that severe injuries may require multiple doses of venom over several days to be effective. We do not know if a single dose will cure Tabby's paralysis in time for the transformation."

"We may not have that luxury," Anne said. "Even though I promised to be with everyone through their transformations, I don't think I can. The Entity wants us to leave as soon as possible."

"So it has communicated to me," Zima said. "But there is an alternative."

Anne raised her eyebrows.

"Dr. Toben," Zima said. "Leave Tabby in her care with a vial of your blood and more of your venom. She knows the proper dosage, and can administer a more traditional medical treatment if, for some reason, your venom is ineffective."

"Dr. Toben ..." Anne slumped. "I forgot about her. And the children. They all need my blood if they're going to survive."

"Yes, though it may be difficult to convince her to deliberately infect the children."

"We have to try," Anne said. "It's the only way. You know that now, right?" She looked at Zima, but Zima had turned away. "What is it?"

"Your proximity to your daughter is ... difficult for me. That was the cause of my unintentional attack on Tabby earlier. Unless you wish a repeat performance with one or both of you here in the forest, it is best if I do not look."

Anne's eyes widened. "Oh, honey, I had no idea! And I left the two of you alone!"

"The fault is mine," Zima said. "You could not have known, because I did not tell you. Regardless, I would prefer to limit my proximity to you both to minimize the risk of recurrence, and my own discomfort."

"Discomfort?" Tabby said.

"Yes. Even though I cannot see you, I know that you are together, and it is very alluring. Maintaining my distance is difficult."

"All right," Anne said. "I'll carry Tabby. We'll meet you at the house."

"As you wish. I shall go first so I do not see you ahead of me, and will bring the car to the end of our street, where the forest path begins."

"You sure you'll be okay to drive?"

"No. When you arrive, I shall ride to the hospital in the trunk."

Without waiting for a reply, or even glancing their way, Zima walked in the direction of their house.

Anne scooped Tabby up in her arms with the same ease Zima had, and they were soon following far behind. Rain pattered the trees and Tabby, but she was already soaked, so it didn't bother her.

"Mom?"

"Yes, honey?"

"Take me with you."

Anne frowned.

"To San Francisco, I mean. That's where you're going, right?"

Anne pursed her lips and nodded.

"I want to go with you. I don't know what's going on, but —"

"That's right, you don't," Anne said gently. "You're precious to me. Where we're going is dangerous, and I won't risk losing you."

"But you'll risk Zima!" Tabby bit back her anger and snuggled closer to her mother. "I just ... I want to go, too. I want to be with you. With both of you."

Anne's caring eyes said she understood what Tabby was really trying to say.

I don't want to be abandoned again.

She kissed Tabby's head and sighed. "Darling, you have my word that I'll come for you as soon as possible. The Entity won't need any of us when it's done."

"*What?*"

"I didn't mean it like that. It has no intention of killing us. It has no reason to. We ... may not have the family life you've always dreamed of, but we'll be together. I can promise that much. Assuming you drink my blood as soon as you're better, like I've asked." She gave Tabby a stern look.

"Yes, Mother."

They shared a smile. Tabby curled against her mother's breast, cold but pillow-soft, and let the gentle rhythm of Anne's gait keep her from dwelling on the unimaginably horrible events that were unfolding before her.

20

KEYSTONE

ONE AND TWO AND THREE and four and five.

Charlie swiveled to Calum's mouth, breathed into it, watched his chest rise, then positioned his palms over Calum's sternum again and resumed chest compressions.

One and two and three and four and five.

He'd repeated the cycle so many times that the words were etched in his brain. His arms ached. His lungs ached. His back ached. His knees hurt. His face hurt where Anne had struck him. Charlie wanted to sit back, just for a minute, and rest.

But he wasn't about to stop now.

One and two and three and four and five.

The front door flew open. Cappa's high-heels clacked across the tiled floor.

"Charlie! I got here as soon as I could."

She knelt down and took a syringe from her purse, but Charlie shook his head.

One and two and ... "I've already administered Anne's venom. Either he's ..." *Breathe.* "Dead dead, or his implant is making sure he stays that way." *And four and five. Breathe.*

"His what? But that's —"

Charlie ripped Calum's shirt open between compressions and pointed at the bump on the right side of his chest.

"The same spot as Anne and Mark's," Cappa said. "Where did he get that?"

"I don't know." *And four and five. Breathe.* "Let's wake him up and ask."

"But if Anne's venom didn't work ... Have you tried using your *chi*?"

"No." *And two and ...* "Takes too much concentration. I didn't want to risk it." *Breathe.* "Besides, you're better at it than I am." *One and two and ...* "Might want to try the old-fashioned way first." *Breathe.* "Defibrillation." *And three and four and five.*

"Right. I just need a second."

Cappa turned her palms up. A clear, viscous fluid oozed up from her skin. She rubbed her hands together and pulled Calum's shirt open when Charlie moved for a breath.

"Okay ..." Cappa said, waiting for him to finish. "*Clear!*"

Charlie scrambled away. Cappa pressed her palms to Calum's chest — one just above his implant, and the other on his lower-left ribs. A high-pitched electric whine filled the room.

Calum's body jumped. They both stared at him for a few seconds, but he lay still.

"No heartbeat," Cappa said. "Clear!"

His body jumped again. They waited.

Nothing.

"Clear!"

Jump.

Nothing. Charlie switched places with her and resumed compressions.

"Plan B," Cappa said. She unceremoniously wiped her hands on her dress, leaving a slime trail across her middle, then closed her eyes.

Even without trying, Charlie sensed her *chi* build to an immense level that would have made even the great Master Wung jealous. It flowed from her, gentle and warm like the person it belonged to, and into Calum. His body twitched. His eyes fluttered. His mouth moved. Then he went still. She repeated the exercise several times, but each ended with Calum inert.

Cappa sighed. "He should be awake. The implant must be interfering."

"Then let's take it out." *Breathe. One and two and ...*

"Would you like me to take over?"

Charlie imagined his wife kissing the grizzled old man. He shuddered. "I'll be all right. Just ..." *And five. Breathe.* "Get what you need from the kitchen to excise his implant."

"Won't that be dangerous? His implant might be rigged with a trap if we try to remove it."

"He's dead. What's it going to do, kill him again?" *Breathe.* "Besides, he has Anne's venom in his veins, which is better than any suture or antibiotic. Now is the time." *Before my arms give out. And three and four and ...*

"Okay, be right back."

Cappa returned a minute later with a paring knife, a bowl of water, and a pair of Christmas dishtowels. "I figured Anne would miss these towels the least. I didn't even know she celebrated."

And one and ... "I guess you don't really know someone until you've raided their kitchen for surgical supplies."

"True. Now, this is going to be tricky with you doing active compressions. I can try to work between breaths, but ..."

"He'll bleed out if we take that long." *Breathe.* "Set up a metronome. I'll compress in time with it to give you more predictability."

"That may not be necessary." Cappa studied Calum's lump carefully, poked and prodded it with her fingers. "Take your time on the next breath, Charlie."

And four and five.

The instant Charlie removed his hands, Cappa's knife became a blur, and before he had even lifted his head to resume compressions, a towel covered the excision. The bloody implant sat in the bowl beside her.

"Jesus," Charlie said. "You need your own TV show, 'Iron Surgeon.'" *Breathe.*

"I'll take that lopsided joke as a compliment. All right, I'm going to use my *chi* again. Let's hope he wakes up."

No sooner had Cappa's eyes closed than Calum's opened. He gasped and sat upright, looking around in a panic.

"Easy," Charlie said. "You're going to be all right."

"Anne," Calum said in a raspy voice. "Where's Anne?"

Cappa hurried to the kitchen and returned with a glass of water. "Here you go."

Calum drank it down with eager gulps. "Thank you," he said in a steadier voice. "Where's Anne?"

"I don't know," Charlie said. "After you fell, she started talking about turning everyone into vampires to keep them safe, then she knocked me out and left."

"Then she went to the mansion and made Mark and Dela drink her blood," Cappa said. "They took the inhibitor serum, and are on their way to the factory to make sure Dela gets an implant before the virus spreads too much. And then Anne caught up with Zima and her daughter, Tabby." She lowered her eyes. "We ... haven't heard from them since."

"Now it's your turn," Charlie said to Calum. "How did you get that implant? What the hell did you do to Anne?"

"Not me," Calum said. "The Entity. On both counts."

Cappa gripped his hand. "The Entity? You've seen it?"

"Where?" Charlie said just as quickly. "What is it?"

Calum rubbed his grimy face and sobbed. "I was such a fool. I thought I could stop it where our ancestors had failed, but I fell into the same trap." His red-rimmed eyes took them both in. "It's not of this Earth. It can't be. The Entity, as far as I could tell, is just a control console on some sort of alien spacecraft, buried deep underground."

"A ... console?" Weariness from Charlie's intensive CPR session suddenly caught up with him. He sat down heavily. His limbs felt like lead. "It's a computer?"

"Who's to say what was beneath the lights and buttons, but that wasn't the most frightening thing I saw. The ship's passengers scared me the most."

"Aliens?" Cappa said in a whisper.

"Had to be. Thousands — tens of thousands, maybe. Hideous creatures from a child's nightmare, taller than any human, sleeping in capsules. Those who hadn't died, that is."

"Charlie, Mark's waiting for us, and not patiently," Cappa said. "We should go to the factory."

Charlie helped Calum to his feet.

"You can tell us the rest of the story on the way," Charlie said. "And I suggest you be very, very detailed — especially when you describe where you found this thing."

21

CRISIS OF FAITH

D R. CAROL TOBEN READ THE MESSAGE again, then set her phone on the desk and stared at it. Susan and Jayne had never come to her with a medical problem before. Carol's emergency room days were far behind her, and she wasn't equipped to treat most emergencies anyway. She would do what she could, of course, but if Susan's daughter's condition was too severe, she'd have to be checked into the emergency room like everyone else.

Unless her daughter is a vampire, too.

Someone knocked on her office door.

"Come in," Carol said.

Susan entered, carrying who could only have been her daughter.

"Except for that shock of white hair, she looks just like you, Susan."

Mother and daughter both smiled.

"Thanks for seeing us," Susan said. She gently sat her daughter in a chair, then took the seat next to her. "I know you're busy, but ... in addition to helping Tabby here, I have a ... a special request."

"Oh? Well, first things first. What's wrong with her?"

"I can't move my legs," Tabby said.

Oh boy.

"Let's take a look," Carol said.

She ran through all her usual checks, including reflexes, range of motion, and circulation. Everything seemed fine.

"Is there some event you can think of that may have caused this?"

Tabby blushed. "I, um, may have bumped my head on the wall in the kitchen."

"I see. Did you take any of your mom's special medicine?"

"About twenty minutes ago."

"And you can't move your legs at all? Not even a toe wiggle?"

"No, I ..." Her eyes widened. "Wait! I-I think I just moved my big toe!"

Carol nodded sagely. "Your head trauma may have caused a TIA, or transient ischemic attack, which reduced blood flow to the part of your brain that controls your legs. Normally, I'd screen you for signs of a stroke, but, given the cause and your mother's extraordinary treatment, you'll probably be walking again by the end of the day."

"Thank goodness," Susan said, gripping her daughter's hand.

"So what else can I do for you?"

Susan squirmed in her seat. "I'd like you to keep an eye on Tabby and give her another dose of venom, if necessary. And ... I'd like you to fill some vials with my blood."

"Your blood? Why?"

"So I can distribute them to some of my family who haven't drank any yet. And for you, after Tabby is safe. Maybe for the children as well."

"Susan, you're —"

"Anne."

"Pardon?"

"My real name is Anne Perrin. I wanted you to know before I go."

"Okay, Anne, you're not making any sense," Carol said. "Won't drinking your blood cause the victims to become infected, like poor little Becky?"

"Yes."

"And aren't you the person who said you'd never turn me, even if I asked?"

"That was different."

"How? Tell me!"

"I had hope back then." Anne reached across the desk and put her cold hand on Carol's. "You have to listen. Something very, very terrible is about to happen, and there's nothing you or I or anyone can do to stop it. The only survivors on this planet will be those with vampire blood in their veins. The best thing I can do ..." Her voice cracked. She cleared her throat and continued. "The best I can do for those I care about is to make sure they transition as soon as possible. That includes Tabby, and you."

"I don't believe it," Carol said softly, the blood drained from her face. "I won't believe it! If something cataclysmic was about to happen, they'd broadcast it across the world, and we'd have the best minds on Earth working on a solution."

"Most of the world still believes vampires are myth, or conspiracy," Anne said. "That's because vampires already control the media, and most of the government, too. My predecessor, William, waged a quiet but aggressive takeover. It worked."

"Your predecessor?" Carol looked at the gentle hand touching her own, the same hand that had brought countless children health and happiness in this very ward. Her voice dropped to a whisper. "Who are you?"

"The master of vampires — all vampires, on both sides of the conflict. A conflict that will soon end, and herald humanity's destruction." A tear ran down Anne's cheek. "I don't want to be the catalyst, Carol. I could end my part, if I wanted. Take my own life."

"Mom, no!"

Anne patted her daughter's leg with a reassuring smile. "The Entity would grant me that much. I won't do it, though, because some other vampire would simply take my place. This way, even if I can't prevent humanity's destruction, I might ... I may be able to ease everyone's suffering. I don't even know how, but it's the only hope I have left. That, and seeing my family survive along with me." Anne rolled her sleeve up. "Carol, please. I've never asked you for anything. You're the only person I trust to keep my blood safe, and deliver it to those I love. Take enough for your loved ones as well. Will you do this for me?"

Carol stared at her bare arm, her mind spinning in circles over what she'd just heard.

Master vampire. End of the world.

And it all tied back to Anne.

Carol slowly nodded. "Wait here. I'll ... I'll get the supplies."

Anne caught her arm on the way out.

"I know what you're thinking," Anne said. "You're hoping to use the cell phone in your pocket while you're in the supply room to call the police so they can detain me, maybe give everyone a chance to figure out a way around this. Please don't. Even if Jayne — who's waiting in the hall — doesn't kill them all, the Entity will kill me before they've fastened the handcuffs around my wrists, and a new master vampire will take my place."

"No," Carol said in a quavering voice, "but I can at least evacuate the children."

"There's no need. As soon as you finish drawing my blood, Jayne and I will leave. That much I can promise. Whether you turn the children is up to you, but I ... I would, Carol. I really would."

"I'll think about it," Carol said, although she couldn't imagine a scenario where she actually would. The sight of poor Becky was a wound on her soul that would never heal.

Anne released her.

Tabby and Anne were sitting in the same spots when Carol returned with an armful of needles, tubes, and gloves. She handed a box of rubber-capped tubes to Anne.

"While I'm drawing your blood, you can fill those with your magic elixir," Carol said. "It doesn't sound like it will help with whatever Apocalypse is coming, but you never know."

Anne obliged, puncturing a tube with each canine, which quickly filled with clear liquid.

"That's crazy," Tabby said. "How much of that stuff does your head hold?"

"That was one of my first questions," Carol said. "Right after 'are you burned by holy water or sunlight?'"

"No to holy water," Anne said to Tabby around the tubes sticking from her mouth. "Yes to sunlight."

"Is that one of the ingredients of the Apocalypse?" Carol said. "An end to the evil sun?"

Anne's voice dropped to a whisper. "Yes, and much more." She looked away.

Drawing blood from Anne was more difficult than Carol had anticipated. Not only was her blood thicker than that of a normal human, she had no throbbing veins to pull from, nor a pulse to keep her blood flowing. Carol compensated by using a large-bore needle and vacuum tubes to actively pull the blood from her body. It took a while, but, in the end, she had ten full vials to show for her work.

Carol held one up for inspection. It was darker than normal blood, and moved with an eerie life of its own. "How much does one need to drink to become a vampire?"

"I'm not sure, exactly. Probably not much, but I'd drink the whole thing, just to be safe."

"Does it mix with vodka? We might have a prize-winning Bloody Mary recipe on our hands."

Tabby and Anne wrinkled their noses at the same time, which made Carol smile. They could have been mirror images of each other.

Anne set the last of her tubes on the table. She had filled six in all with her venom, and half each of a seventh and eighth. The quantity in that girl's head never ceased to amaze Carol.

"Thanks, Carol." Anne took one of the tubes of blood and handed it to Tabby. "Don't forget to take this as soon as your legs are better. And I'll know if you haven't."

"You will?"

"Yes. We'll be connected in a very special way. I'll be able to sense your thoughts and your location, and you'll be able to sense mine."

"Wow!"

Anne smiled and kissed her forehead. "Don't worry, though, I'm not the hovering-mom type. I'll diminish our bond once I know you're safe, if you'd like. The same goes for you," she said to Carol, then turned back to Tabby. "Take the rest of these vials to Charlie as soon as you can. I didn't get to see Doris, and I really want her to have one. She's your grandma, in a way, and she'll take good care of you while I'm gone."

Anne gathered her purse and stood, but Tabby caught her arm.

"Wait, y-you're leaving already?"

"I have to."

All traces of excitement disappeared from Tabby's face, leaving … nothing. Her arms fell limp into her lap. Her head swiveled like an abandoned weathervane on a windless day, where her unfocused eyes stared through the office desk.

Carol had worked in this children's ward for almost a decade, and had seen her share of separation anxiety. Some kids handled it bravely, even though being away from their parents tore them up inside. Others wore their hearts on their sleeves and cried, begging their parents to stay.

A scant few, however, were so horrified that something broke inside of them — a condition usually associated with traumatic childhoods.

Those children didn't scream. They didn't beg. They simply turned off, entering a near-catatonic state where they often refused food or drink, and required intravenous sustenance to prevent them from wasting away. Unfortunately, those broken patients suffered high morbidity and mortality rates.

And, Carol could say with sad certainty, Tabby had just broken.

Anne must have picked up on it as well. She crouched next to her daughter and clutched Tabby's hand to her chest.

"I'm. Coming. Back. Everything I'm doing, Tabby, is so we can be together. Everything! I just … I need a little time to put things in order. Do you believe me?"

Tabby's head swiveled back to her mother with glassy eyes, staring, but not really seeing.

"Sweetheart, this is important," Anne said, choking on her words. "The only way I can get through this is if I know my only daughter will be waiting on the other side." She cupped Tabby's cheek. "I need to hear the words. Will you be here when I'm done?"

Tabby shook her head.

Anne's startled cry made everyone jump. She sank to her knees and clutched her daughter's arm, face awash with anguish. "I'm not abandoning you, Tabby! I promise — I *promise* I'll be back!"

"Mom promised, too." Tabby's voice sounded hollow. Dead. "Right before a mugger killed her."

Anne hung her head, shaking with misery. With visible effort, she pulled herself together and took a deep breath. "I have something your mother didn't. I have Zima."

"That just means I'm going to lose you both."

"Not by a long shot."

Tabby turned away, but Anne cupped her cheek and pulled her gaze back.

"I understand your skepticism, sweetheart. You weren't there when Zima fought her way through a squad of armed soldiers to my dungeon prison, battered and broken, and still managed to defeat Orwing's android to rescue me. You didn't see her hop one-legged though the burning brush to prevent me from killing Mark when William had taken over my mind, when she should have been resting. You didn't hear the explosions and sniper fire all around when Z-Tech came under assault — when Zima stood on the roof and shot every missile down while dodging bullets, and had only a single scratch to show for it.

"You don't know her like I do, sweetheart. Because if you did, you'd know that having her by my side is better than any bodyguard. Any army. She'll keep me safe from whatever the world throws at us. I know it in my heart, because she's part of my soul."

Sometime during Anne's speech, the glassiness had disappeared from Tabby's eyes, replaced with wonder and cautious hope.

Anne squeezed her hand. "Do you believe me now? Because I need you, Tabby. I need you every bit as much as you need me. And I need to know you're going to be all right."

Tabby's face crumpled into a teary mess. She gave a single nod, then pulled Anne down, wrapped her arms around her neck, and cried into her shoulder.

Crying is good, Carol thought with a grim smile.

"I'm sorry I won't be there to see you through your transformation into a vampire," Anne said. "But Cappa will be, even if the others are still going through theirs. And don't forget to drink someone else's blood, or the transformation won't begin. And make sure you're lying somewhere comfortable. It's a jarring process, and —"

"I got it," Tabby said, sniffling. "Just ... hurry back, okay?"

"Okay."

Anne held her hand even as she walked to the door. When their fingers parted, Carol swore she heard two hearts break.

Anne stopped at the threshold. "Carol, Jayne would like to say goodbye before we leave. Would that be all right?"

"Um … sure. Send her in."

Anne gave Tabby a last, long look, then disappeared into the hall.

Jayne entered a moment later, dressed as Carol had never seen her before. Her clothes were all gray, from her baggy pants to her loose jacket and form-fitting shirt. The outfit looked naggingly familiar …

No, it must be a coincidence.

But, in those clothes, she bore an uncanny resemblance to the comic book character.

"Going for the Dark Angel look, are we, Jayne?" Carol said.

"The Dark Angel …" Tabby's eyes went wide. "Oh my God, I thought she was just an urban myth! But Zima … y-you're actually her, aren't you?"

Zima? The over-the-top savior Anne was just gushing about?

"Yes," Zima said.

"That means …"

Tabby pulled Zima's gray jacket open, revealing two pairs of holstered pistols, different yet immaculately cared for.

"Wicked," Tabby said in an awed whisper.

After Carol had recovered from the shock of someone bringing firearms into a children's ward, she slowly stood and rounded the desk.

"So you're a … superhero?"

"I am effective at what I do, no more. Dr. Toben, I wished to say it has been an honor working with you. The children are fortunate to be in the care of someone as compassionate and competent as yourself."

"I'm not sure how to take that from a renowned killer. Your victims are all vampires, but they're sentient beings with feelings and families — like Anne. How do you sleep at night?"

"I shall not attempt to justify my actions, for we may never agree, except to say that I believed it was the best use of my skills to help counter a growing crisis."

"And how'd that work out for you?"

"Not well enough, as I have recently discovered. Be that as it may, I hoped we might part on favorable terms." Zima held out her hand.

Carol regarded it as she would a rotten apple. "So you're going along with Sus— er ... Anne? Helping her destroy the world?"

"I am taking care of my wife. This situation is no more her fault than it is yours, yet she will suffer much more because of it. I shall keep her safe, and comfort her where I am able. You have been married before. I would hope that, at least, is where we have a common understanding."

"I suppose we do." Carol took her hand, and was surprised when the legendary Dark Angel pulled her into a hug.

"Take care, Carol. I do hope we meet again."

Carol winced when a gun handle jabbed her ribs. She awkwardly patted Zima's back. "Take care of Anne," she whispered. "I don't know what's going on, but I know a good person when I see one."

"She may have given up on the world, but I will never give up on her. You have my word."

Carol was clinging tightly when Zima eventually pulled away. Carol hastily wiped the tears from her eyes. "I'm starting to see why everyone considers you a superhero."

The Dark Angel cocked her head, but remained silent, until a tug from Tabby drew her attention. Tabby held out her arms, but Zima shook her head.

"As much as I would like to, a hug may be dangerous for both of us," Zima said. "Anne would never forgive another act of infidelity, and your legs are just beginning to heal."

Oh Jesus, I really didn't need to know that.

Tabby's face fell. Carol feared she might slip into catatonia again, but Zima kissed her own fingertips, then touched them to Tabby's cheek, which snapped her out of it.

"Stay close to Charlie and Cappa," Zima said. "They will keep you safe. Farewell."

"Bye ... Mom."

Zima flinched as if she'd been slapped, then hurried from the office.

"Anything I should be concerned about there?" The question seemed ridiculous, in light of everything else she'd just learned, but Carol had to ask it anyway.

"Oh, it's … it's nothing. Her programming confused me with Anne, which made her accidentally ravage me in the kitchen. We're working through it."

"Her … programming?" Carol rubbed her face. "I need a beer. Are you even old enough to drink?"

"No. But, given the world's about to end, I don't think it matters." *Ugh …*

Carol bent to gather the syringes on her desk, and heard the crinkle of paper in her lab coat pocket. She withdrew a folded piece of lined paper that certainly didn't belong to her. On it was a hand-written note, the strokes so precise that Carol first thought it was printed by a computer. Her eyebrows rose when she read its contents:

Carol,

Do NOT drink Anne's blood! You can still make a difference.

Take Tabby to see Charlie at the Graven Chocolate Factory. Tell him of your background. He will understand.

Tell no one of this note or its contents, not even Charlie, or all may be lost.

Sincerely,
Zima Perrin
a.k.a. The Dark Angel

Tabby stretched her neck and tried to peer at the note. "What is it?"

"Nothing, just … an old grocery list."

Carol put the note straight into the cross-shredder next to her desk, then turned to Tabby with what she hoped was nonchalance.

"So, what can you tell me about this Charlie person Anne mentioned?"

22

OPERATION

C HARLIE TIED OFF THE LAST STITCH and held the thread out, which Mark snipped close to the knot. They looked at each other and nodded.

Dela's implant was barely noticeable under her skin, thanks to her generous volume of adipose breast tissue. A zigzag of black stitches chased a two-inch incision down the top of her right breast, the same spot where Mark and Anne had theirs. If the implant worked, her wound would heal without a scar, even without the use of Anne's venom.

Assuming our adjustments were correct, and it doesn't kill her instead.

"Her vitals are holding steady," Cappa said.

"Her implant has already started converting her cells," Mark said. "Three percent and climbing. If it affects her like it did me, she'll be unconscious for a day at least, maybe two. We should administer another dose of virus inhibitor soon."

"I'll set up an IV drip," Cappa said.

Doris stopped pacing in front of a rack of rifles and looked over. "I feel like a lame duck over here. Anything I can get you guys?"

"One of your famous coffees would do wonders," Charlie said.

"Coming right up, sweetcakes."

Cappa froze with an IV bag in her hands. "Tabby's calling me!"

Everyone gathered around while Cappa stared at nothing in silent conversation.

"She's on her way here with Dr. Toben," Cappa said eventually.

"Dr. Toben? That doesn't sound good," Charlie said. "Is Tabby all right?"

"She said we shouldn't panic when we see her, which I'll take as 'not so much.'"

Mark sighed. "I'll get more virus inhibitor and start production of some new implants, just in case. I don't suppose Anne's with them?"

"No, but Anne and Zima just left the hospital. Tabby said she'll fill us in on the rest when she gets here, though she didn't sound happy."

"Are you okay here for a few minutes?" Charlie said to Mark, who stood by his unconscious wife.

"Yes, so you're free to go upstairs and grill Tabby as soon as she steps out of the car."

"Thanks, buddy. I'll bring them straight down here."

Charlie hurried to the large platform elevator and pressed the Up button. The ceiling parted in a loud whir, and the elevator whined its way upward.

He emerged from the front entrance in time to see a beige SUV pull into the gravel parking lot. Dr. Carol Toben, still in her white lab coat, stepped from the driver's side, while Tabby remained in the passenger seat, alive and apparently unharmed.

Then Carol pulled a wheelchair from the back of the vehicle.

Oh, Christ ...

He rushed over to help. "What happened?"

"A little cranial inflammation, I suspect," Dr. Toben said, "but she'll —"

"Never mind that!" Tabby opened the door and waved them over. "Mom and Zima are in deep shit. If we don't figure out a way to help them — like fucking now! — then the rest of us will be, too."

Charlie helped Carol unfold the wheelchair and brought it around, then used a fireman's lift to help Tabby into the wheelchair. They boarded the elevator in silence.

The sight of their underground lair had the effect Charlie had hoped it would, and seemed to take Tabby's mind off things for a moment.

"Whoa," Tabby said, looking between a post-surgical Dela and a row of gun-filled racks. "What the hell kind of chocolate factory is this?"

"The kind that might be able to help your mom and Zima." Charlie pulled a chair over and took her hand. "Tabby, I don't know what you've been through, but if we're going to have a prayer of helping them, you have to tell us everything that happened. And I mean *everything*."

She gulped. "Everything?"

"Everything. If what Anne told me is true, some global catastrophe is going to hit very soon. We have to choose our path carefully. To do that, we'll need every shred of information we can get."

"Um ... o-okay." Tabby squirmed in her chair, taking years from her already youthful appearance. "Well, I went over to their house first thing this morning. Zima was still avoiding me, so Anne decided to leave us alone for a while so we could talk things out. That's when, um ..." She gripped her shirt with rigid fingers.

Carol put a reassuring hand on her shoulder. "That's when Zima invited you out for a walk in the woods, wasn't it?"

Tabby looked at everyone around her, then returned her tear-filled eyes to Charlie. "No. That's when I discovered the reason she'd been avoiding me is because she found me irresistible, like Anne, and she was just trying to prevent an ... an incident that might harm her marriage."

"Tabby," Carol said, "you don't have to —"

"Yes I do! Charlie said *everything*. This might be the crucial piece of information that saves the world, and I won't condemn us all just because I'm embarrassed." She looked around, meeting everyone's eyes in turn. "First off, it wasn't Zima's fault. She told me to stay away, but I cornered her, and then she grabbed me, and ..." Tabby wiped her eyes. "I-I didn't have to do it, but she was suffering. She needed relief, s-so I relieved her. The whole thing was my f-f-fault ..."

Tabby broke down in tears, while everyone stared in stunned silence.

Cappa knelt and patted her arm. "I'm sorry about what happened, honey. You're part of a strange family now, no doubt about it. In many ways, we're all still trying to figure out how we fit in with the rest of humanity — especially Zima. I'm sorry she hurt you."

"She didn't ... hurt me," Tabby said between sobs. "She was ... gentle ... and ... sweet ... and I ... love them ... both and ... now they're ... slaves to ... that ... fucking ... Entity ... and —"

"Both of them?" Mark slid to a halt in front of Tabby and fell to his knees. "No, no, no ... Please tell me that doesn't mean what I think it does! Tell me the Entity doesn't have Zima, too."

Tabby nodded and took a deep breath, then continued in a steadier voice. "The Entity wouldn't allow her to stay with Anne unless Zima let it control her, too. So she did."

Mark sat down. His shoulders slumped. "Zima doesn't open her core to anyone, not even us. It doesn't make sense."

"It does to me," Cappa said. "She loves Anne more than anything, including her hard-earned freedom. Every time they've been separated has been traumatizing for Zima. If the Entity threatened to take Anne away, there's little Zima wouldn't do to stay with her."

Charlie felt the blood drain from his face. "Including bringing about the vampocalypse."

"Including that. She doesn't have the same warm, fuzzy attachment to humanity the rest of us do."

"Interesting," Carol muttered, then started when she noticed everyone was watching. "Sorry, I'm just processing. This is all new to me."

Charlie had almost forgotten she was there. "Sorry. Dr. Carol Toben, I'm Charlie Z, former CEO of Z-Tech. Please allow me to introduce you to the team — the closest people I have to family."

After a round of introductions, Carol examined Dela's IV. "Nice work. Very professional."

"Thanks," Cappa said.

"Is she transitioning?"

"Not if I can help it," Mark said. "Her IV contains a chemical that slows the virus's replication, but the human immune system still can't purge it fast enough. A computer implant in her chest is working hard to aid her body in eradicating the virus for good."

Carol looked up sharply. "I was led to believe there isn't a cure."

"Once the victim has transitioned, there isn't, but we caught Dela in the early stages of infection. The jury's still out on whether the procedure will actually work. Worse, the implant triggers a cellular metamorphosis of its own at significant risk to the patient."

"In other words, it's a risky and unscalable solution."

"Precisely," Mark said. "Even if we could mass produce the serum and the implant, there are only a handful of people in the world capable of performing such a complex surgery, and most of them are in this room."

"Doesn't sound like it would solve our immediate problem anyway," Carol said.

Mark stood on the opposite side of Dela and looked at Carol. "What else did you find out from Anne?"

They all listened intently, first to Tabby's account of her encounter in the woods, then to Carol's interpretation of their office conversation.

"I guess it makes sense they're heading for San Francisco," Cappa said. "It has the largest vampire population by far."

"So what are we waiting for?" Doris grabbed a machine gun and held it with practiced ease. "Whatever's going down is obviously happening there. Let's meet this Entity son-of-a-bitch head-on."

"Some of us should," Charlie said. "We know the Entity's hold over the master vampire is strong, but so is Anne. The right people in the right situation could make all the difference."

"I'll go," Tabby said immediately.

"That's brave of you," Charlie said, "but you can't even stand, let alone ..."

His argument died when Tabby pushed herself up onto shaking legs.

"Can so. If a rescue team is going to SF to help Mom and Zima, then I'm going, too, and that's final. Who else is in?"

"I'll go with you," Cappa said, "assuming someone can stay here to monitor Dela until she wakes up."

"Ain't Mark gonna stay and watch over his wife?" Doris said.

Mark blushed. "Charlie and I have ... other plans."

"I'll stay," Carol said. "I already informed the hospital that I will be taking an unexpected, extended leave of absence. It's the least I can do to help, although this feels like a good time to mention my life before pediatrics."

"Virology," Charlie said. "Five years with the Centers for Disease Control, if I remember."

"You've done your research. I shouldn't be surprised, since you needed to trust me with Anne's secret."

"We have all the lab equipment you may need," Cappa said. "And I'll be happy to help with your research. I'm a handy lab assistant."

"But ... aren't you going to SF?"

Cappa nodded cheerfully. A computer beeped next to Carol, where a message waited on the screen: I'M AN ARTIFICIAL INTELLIGENCE, LIKE ZIMA, AND AM INTEGRATED WITH THE FACILITY. TELL ME WHAT YOU WANT, AND I'LL MAKE IT HAPPEN.

Carol looked between Cappa and the monitor, then shook her head in wonder. "Well, I guess you can start by providing me with everything you have on the virus."

Files and images cascaded onto the screen, then quickly arranged themselves into organized folders.

"That's everything," Cappa said, "but if you're looking for something specific, your best bet is to ask me. Not only can I perform complex analysis and modeling, I'm also a search engine on steroids."

"That's fine and dandy," Doris said to Mark, "but don't change the subject. Where are you boys charging off to when you know our girl is heading back to the Bay?"

Charlie and Mark looked at each other, debating how much they should say.

Mark finally shrugged. "We may as well tell them while Dela's asleep."

Too true, Charlie thought. "Calum is in the back room, recovering. Before he went to sleep, he drew a map to an alien site he found in Russia, where he met what he believes is the Entity. Mark and I are going to pay it a visit."

Doris put a hand on her hip. "And what makes you think it ain't gonna turn your brains into Swiss cheese, like it did his?"

"Because we're going to be much, much better prepared."

Charlie nodded to Cappa. A second later, his cyborg body emerged from the back room carrying a large backpack and an arsenal of weapons, including a sniper rifle, machine gun, and an array of explosives.

Carol stumbled backward and caught herself on the desk, sending a pencil and stapler clattering to the floor. "W-what the hell is going on?"

"Meet Charlie three-point-oh," Cappa said. "We've replaced its internal armor with the latest alloys, increasing its survivability by three hundred percent. Even a .50 caliber round will have trouble penetrating it this time around."

"We've also quadrupled the number of onboard nanites to dramatically decrease auto-repair times," Charlie said. "And we've doubled the output of the power plant to support *these*."

The new-and-improved cyborg extended its arms, palms forward. Skin parted at the base of each palm, revealing silver barrels. The cyborg swiveled and aimed at a target along the back wall.

The room lit with large orange flashes that made Zima's plasma pistols seem like toys. When Charlie could finally see again, the target had several smoldering holes the size of Charlie's fist, lit from behind by superheated concrete slowly melting to the floor.

"Whatever the Entity is, it's going to have a much harder time chewing on us," Mark said. "Each of Charlie's plasma weapons have four times the intensity of Zima's pistols, can fire almost as fast, and have a longer sustained fire rate. In addition, we're bringing our standard armaments, a host of explosives, various toys, and two spare power plants, just in case."

"In case what?" Carol said.

"In case the explosives aren't enough." Mark opened the cyborg's backpack and pulled out a fist-sized metallic capsule. "This is the same fusion generator that powers both Cappa and Zima. When destabilized, it has the explosive potential of a one-megaton bomb, which is fifty-times more powerful than the atom bomb dropped on Nagasaki."

"That's right," Charlie said. "If all else fails, we're going to blow that damned Entity right off the map."

"Assuming you can get to it," Doris said. "The Entity's got to know that you know where it lives now. An army of vampires might be waiting for you."

"Unless it believes Calum died. His implant tried very hard to keep him dead, probably to keep its location secret because, we assume, the Entity is undefended."

"But the Entity underestimated Charlie's determination," Cappa said with a smile. "I jammed all transmissions as soon as he told me about Calum's implant. It may not have helped — who knows if it even communicates on the electromagnetic spectrum? — but we did remove it while Calum was still dead. With any luck, the Entity believes that knowledge of its location is secure."

Doris sighed. "All right, so when are you boys leaving?"

Mark brushed his fingers over Dela's sleeping face. "Now. Whatever the Entity's planning, it's happening soon, and we're going to lose half a day to air travel as it is."

"A chartered jet is waiting at the airport," Cappa said. "Landing at your destination is impossible, so you'll need to parachute in."

"Assuming that thing even needs a parachute," Carol said, eying the cyborg.

"It does." Charlie turned to Cappa. "When are you leaving?"

"Right after I do this." Cappa pulled him into a tender kiss, then smiled sadly. "This may be the last time I get to feel those lips for a while without feeling them on the other side as well."

Her fingers lingered on his chest. Charlie's heart ached for her, but he didn't have a choice. Splitting up was their best chance of saving Anne, Zima, and the world at large, and they both knew it. It was almost too much to hope they would see each other again, but Charlie pushed that thought from his mind.

As long as he drew breath in either of his bodies, he would fight. Fight for his family. Fight for humanity. Fight for the right to exist. He had to believe they could win, or there was no point in trying — and that wasn't an option.

Cappa took Tabby's arm. "Can you walk?"

Tabby tried, but stumbled against Cappa. "Not yet, but hopefully I'll be fine by the time we get to San Francisco."

"It's going to be a short trip," Cappa said. "If Anne is going where I think she is, we have to beat her there, or we're screwed. A helicopter is on its way to pick us up from a clearing in the mansion's rear orchard in five minutes. I want us to be in the air in six."

Tabby sat in the wheelchair, which Cappa wheeled to the elevator.

"Are you coming, Doris?" Cappa said.

Doris shook her head. "Charlie's gonna fall over when his mind jumps into his cyborg body, which will leave Carol alone with two critical patients while she tries to pull a miracle out of her butt researching the virus. Don't sound like we're giving her a winning chance on either front." She put her rifle down. "I'll stay here and see what I can do. If Dela kicks it because no one was here to help the good doctor, I couldn't live with myself."

Mark wiped his eyes, but quickly regained his composure. "Thanks, Doris. I know how much helping Anne means to you."

"We're all making sacrifices, sweetcakes. Just give those alien bastards hell from me and we'll call it even. Besides, I won't envy you when you get back. Dela ain't never gonna forgive you."

Carol arched an eyebrow.

Mark laughed and began counting on his fingers. "We're jumping out of an airplane in the middle of nowhere in hostile Russian territory with an arsenal of high-tech weapons to infiltrate an ancient spaceship filled with aliens to try and save the world. We'd have to chain Dela down to keep her from coming if she were conscious. Even then, she'd probably chew herself free."

Charlie gave Cappa a final, lingering kiss.

"Good luck, honey," Charlie said.

"We'll bring Anne and Zima home safely, I promise. And I made that call we talked about. We'll see what happens."

"Thanks. It's a long-shot, I know, but if there's even a chance he can get here in time to help, we have to try."

"Of course. I'll let you know if I hear anything."

Charlie watched them rise on the platform elevator with a heavy heart, then returned to Mark, who was still looking at Dela.

"What was that about?" Mark said.

"Plan D-and-a-half. I'll fill you in on the way. Ready to go, pal?"

"Ready as I can be."

Mark bent over and kissed Dela's strawberry lips. She moaned softly, but when he straightened, her eyes remained closed.

"Part of me wishes she could come with us."

"She would certainly liven up the trip," Charlie said. "But it's best if she stays here."

Mark nodded. The chances of either of them returning, let alone succeeding, were questionable, and they both knew it.

"Please take good care of her, Doc."

"I'll do my best," Carol said. "Don't nuke anything if you don't have to."

Mark grinned. "I'll do my best."

He retrieved a large backpack from the wall, then called the elevator down, where Charlie's cyborg body joined him.

"Last sanity check," Carol said. "Are you sure you don't want the Air Force to handle this?"

"The vampire infiltration is extensive," Charlie said. "We have contacts, but we don't know exactly who's been compromised. Calling in a favor may instead give us away."

"Sucks to have the weight of the world on your shoulders like that."

"Back at you," Mark said. "Good luck with your research. Hopefully you'll have more success than we did." He hit the Up button.

"Wait!" Carol said.

Mark stopped the elevator.

"If Charlie's staying here, then who's controlling the cyborg?"

"Cappa is," Charlie said. "She'll maintain control until I transfer my consciousness into it."

Carol stared at him open-mouthed. "That ... D-don't you need a cable or something?"

"No. My connection to it is spiritual, so I can transfer at any time, and from any distance. It's a long flight. My conscious time will be better spent here, answering your questions and helping you set up."

"Oh. Silly me." Carol collapsed into the chair and shook her head.

Mark resumed the lift. He and Charlie shared a childish grin before Mark and the cyborg disappeared.

"I don't see how any of this is funny," Carol said to Charlie.

"Sorry."

He tried to wipe the grin from his face, but it wouldn't go away. Despite Anne and Zima and Calum and the looming vampocalypse, one thing floated above all the rest that made Charlie giddy with anticipation.

He and Mark would soon get to play together — unsupervised — on a bona fide alien spacecraft.

23

MOTHER

L IEUTENANT COLONEL JOHN ANDERSON released the young woman and wiped her blood from his mouth. She collapsed into the chair with a faraway look, her lips parted in venom-induced stupor. He looked at their half-finished card game of Spite and Malice and sighed. She wouldn't be coherent enough to play again for hours. It was his own fault for interrupting their game. Feeding was far more satisfying than any card game, however, even if it exacerbated his boredom in the long run.

John grabbed his phone from the table, called Mike, and was pleasantly surprised to hear it ring. There had been no signal down here a week ago, but one of his sirelings had wired up an extender eight stories underground to this small room, which had been a storage closet before John arrived.

Mike's voice sounded from the receiver. "Sir?"

"Bring another one down, please."

"Male or female?"

"Doesn't matter, as long as they're willing to play cards."

"Yes, sir."

John hung up and stared at the wall.

Over three months had passed since William died. Like the rest of William's bloodline, John and his sirelings had been hit with the debilitating effects of the new master vampire's computer implant almost immediately. The pain had been terrible, almost as bad as his transformation, but concentrated in his head. Even thinking about it made him rub his temples.

Fortunately for John, his sirelings were more disciplined than the other Firsts', and had fought through the pain. John had been the first of William's lieutenants to be taken underground and shielded, to his knowledge. One of his sirelings had once worked in this building, and had retained their keys. They had rushed John down here, and that was the last time John had seen the surface.

Three months.

No cool night air. No thrill of the hunt. Just four walls and a stairway he dared not climb.

All because of Anne Perrin.

John rested his head on his arms and sighed.

Until William's death, she and the rest of Z-Tech had been the enemy. John had thrown his considerable military experience into a successful campaign to destroy their factory fortress.

Anne had murdered his former sire. It was her fault he was trapped down here. Logic said he should hate her.

But he didn't. He couldn't.

Anne was his sire now. They were bonded on a primal level. Even thinking her name made him yearn to venture to the surface, just so he could seek her out and try to please her. The urge was so strong that John once again had to grip the table to keep from running for the stairs.

No, he reminded himself. *Only pain awaits up there.*

Twice, he had failed to stop himself from ascending. He'd made it as far as the fourth sub-basement before the pain had finally driven him to his knees. He had cursed himself for his lack of will — not because he cared about his own well-being, but because he had also hurt his sirelings, who deserved none of the punishment from his stupidity.

His phone rang. Mike's name showed on the display. "Yes, Sergeant?"

"S-s-sir, your p-presence is requested upstairs."

John frowned. "By whom?"

"Anne Perrin and the Dark Angel."

John was climbing the stairs before Mike had finished his sentence. Powerful legs propelled him four steps at a time, faster and faster, until he burst from the stairwell into the lobby of the business center.

He stopped dead. Joy effused him for the first time since William's demise.

There before him stood the one and only object of his affection: His sire. His benefactor. His reason for being.

Anne graced him with a smile — not the frightening, vindictive show of teeth William had often used, but a warm, endearing expression that filled his soul with happiness.

She loved him. She cared about him. He saw it in her eyes, felt it through their sire bond.

John fell to his knees, overcome with emotion. So this was what a bond felt like to a truly benevolent sire.

Anne didn't berate him for showing weakness in front of her, as William would have. She knelt so they were at eye level and took his hands.

"John." Her smile broadened.

John thought his unbeating heart was going to burst.

"M-my Lady," he said eventually.

Her smile turned into a pout. John wanted to tear his tongue out for making her sad, though he had no idea what he'd said to make her so.

"Now now, there will be none of that," Anne said. "We're family, after all."

"Then what should I call you? I … I'm not worthy to use your name."

"Of course you are. But if that makes you uncomfortable, you can call me … Mother."

"Mother." John and Mike breathed the word at the same time.

Outside, John saw and felt his other sirelings gathering. Mother's presence called to them as well. They all wished to greet the new master vampire.

Mother turned to them with a warm smile. She gestured them in. They filed inside and surrounded her, giving a wide berth to the

Dark Angel, who stood stoically by her side in her infamous gray outfit.

The Dark Angel's ice-blue eyes swept the newcomers, trying to keep track of all of them at once, exhibiting a tactical awareness John could appreciate.

But her caution was unnecessary. Not a soul gathered here would dream of hurting either of them. The Dark Angel was the person dearest to Mother. They all felt it, and they would defend her with the same ferocity as they would their new master.

"Mother, how may we please you?" John said.

Mother saddened. Once again, John resisted the urge to rip out his own treacherous tongue.

"It's time to bring the other Firsts out of hiding and gather the rest of our family. You know where they are, John. Will you help me?"

"At once!" John issued a command through his sire bond, and his sirelings scattered. "The other Firsts will be kneeling before you by nightfall tomorrow. I'll see to it personally."

"Not you," Mother said. "I'm sure the others are more than capable of delivering the message. No, I need your help to plan our next phase."

Mother saddened further. John wanted to die.

"Change is coming," she said. "When the other Firsts arrive, we need to be ready."

"Yes, Mother. Just tell me what you need."

"I need you to work with Zima — the Dark Angel, as you call her. You're both master strategists, but Zima's specialties are too ... harsh for what we're trying to accomplish. I'd like you to work together on a strategy that will yield quick results with minimal casualties."

"Of course, Mother." John turned to the Dark Angel. "And how may I address Mother's esteemed spouse?"

"You may call me what you wish, but 'General' would be appropriate."

John soured at that. He'd known many generals in his years of military service. Each of them had earned their title with blood and tears.

"No disrespect to the Dark Angel, but may I know your qualifications for such a prestigious rank?"

The Dark Angel looked at Mother and cocked her head.

"Go on, honey," Mother said. "There's no reason to hide anymore."

"As you wish." Her ice-blue eyes focused on John. "Although I have never reported to an official government military organization, I commanded for the victors in the Syrian and Lebanon conflicts, four unnamed skirmishes in the Ukraine, the Afghan civil war, and the Ecuadorian and Colombian revolutions. I have led thirty-four successful espionage missions across the Middle East, Africa, South America, Eastern Europe, and Asia, and have single-handedly conducted fourteen urban suppression exercises, each resulting in the reigning government's retention of power. I can provide evidence to support my claims, if you require."

"No, it's just … your track record sounds remarkably similar to Deadiron's."

"It is not coincidence."

John pulled his hanging jaw shut. "You're … Deadiron?"

"The non-organic part of him, yes. I am surprised you know that name. Deadiron was one of Orwing's closest-held secrets."

"Knowing was my job. The US sticks its nose all over the world, and I was on the losing side of at least three of those campaigns. Your strategies were preternatural. And deadly."

"The last is an undesirable trait, in this instance, that I hope you may help with."

"I'll do what I can." John snapped a sharp salute. "General, would you kindly brief me on the background and goals of our next mission?"

Mother clapped her hands in glee. John's spirits soared.

"That's more like it! I just knew you two would get along."

The general kissed Mother tenderly. "Anne, you have not eaten in over thirty-six hours. Go feed. John and I shall work through the details."

"Mother, please help yourself to a meal." John gestured to three humans waiting by the wall, all in a venom-induced daze. "The general and I can take it from here."

Mother stared at the humans. "They're prisoners?"

"Yes. I don't overstock, like some of the other Firsts, but having a few around is handy when hunting is scarce. Keeping reserves for the troops is military supply one-oh-one."

Her displeasure hit him in a wave. Once again, John had the overwhelming urge to fix his mistake — if only he knew what he'd done.

"Mother?"

"No more prisoners. I don't disagree with your philosophy, but keeping people against their will is wrong, and it has to stop. I realize it's not your fault; vampirism has robbed you of your connection to humanity. I know for a fact it can be re-learned, which will be very important after the darkness settles, so that's exactly what we're going to work on." Mother's kind, sad eyes met his. "Starting right now."

"Of course, Mother."

John gave the mental command. His sirelings responded immediately and escorted the humans outside.

"That leaves our pantry bare, I'm afraid, so I don't have a meal to offer you. If I may ask, how do you suggest we obtain reserve blood supplies?"

"Establish partnerships. Provide an equitable trade of goods."

"Mother?"

She gently took him by the shoulders. John couldn't help smiling.

"You were human once," she said. "Reach deep inside. The memories are still there. Humans aren't just food. They may be physically weaker, but, in every other aspect, they're our equals, or better. They deserve the same respect we afford each other."

"I understand your words, but ..."

Mother smiled, filling his cold body with warmth. "I know. You remember the attachment you felt to your wife, your kids, and your friends, but you can't summon those feelings anymore. I'm giving you permission to try. It isn't weakness, John. It's strength. You hurt your family when you left, but they still care about you, and they don't know the danger that's coming. Don't turn your back on them. You can still save them by turning them."

"Thank you for your guidance, Mother. I'll give it serious consideration."

"Please do. In the meantime, may I have the pleasure of one of your sirelings for an escort? Mike, perhaps? We'll see if we can find a human willing to feed us. It will be a good exercise."

John suddenly regretted his decision to work with the general tonight. The idea of hunting with Mother, even in a peaceful capacity, was extremely alluring.

"Of course," he said instead. "Mike will be at your disposal for as long as you require."

Mother smiled when Mike appeared by her side. When she took his arm, John had never felt such jealousy. She kissed the general on her way out.

"Don't worry," Mother said to her. "We won't be long. I just know Mike will take good care of me while you and John work out the details of our next offensive."

Mike puffed his chest out and nodded, then they walked arm-in-arm to the front. John swallowed his jealousy with difficulty and focused on the general.

But the general, too, was staring at them, and didn't stop until they'd wandered out of sight.

"Is it hard for you, too?" John said.

"Yes. She is my life and my happiness. But I learned long ago that hoarding her affection is not just selfish, but it is to the detriment of all. Warmth such as hers needs to be shared so it may spread. Still, being separated from her, even for a short time, is difficult." Her eyes shifted, became sharper, as if her focus had just returned. "Thank you for agreeing to speak with me separately. Anne's new role weighs heavily on her, so I spare her the harsher details whenever possible."

"My pleasure, General. Anything to make things easier for Mother. If I may ask, what's this coming darkness she spoke of?"

"I do not know. The Entity has asserted control over me, but it has not yet shared the details of its larger plan, nor will it allow Anne to discuss it with me. Aside from occasional hints, she discloses only our immediate goals."

"A fine way to win a battle, but not the war."

"Indeed. It is what we have, however, so we shall make do."

"As you say. How should we begin?"

"By imparting to you what little information I have."

John's eyebrows inched upward while he listened to Zima's outline of their upcoming mission.

"On the upside, that type of operation is well within my purview," John said once she'd finished. "The only problem will be timing."

"I realize it is short notice for an operation of this complexity, but that is where you may utilize my talents. I am adept at rapid strategic analysis, and can perform digital research faster than a thousand trained intelligence personnel."

"Do your talents include obtaining classified or protected information?"

"Classified information, yes. Accessing protected information from non-military sources will depend on the level and type of protection, but my typical infiltration time for even the most secure environment is hours, or a day at most."

John smiled. "Things would have been different with you on our side. Where were you when I was in the service?"

"A slave to Orwing Industries, murdering innocents." The general said it so matter-of-factly that John thought she was kidding, but her expression remained neutral. "I have another request."

"Name it."

"I do not possess the mental bond to Anne or the other vampires that you do, which hampers my ability to strategize. I am most effective when my information is up-to-date. As you receive new intelligence through your vampire bond or other sources, I would appreciate prompt notification of the same, no matter how insignificant it may seem. The greater the detail, the better."

"I'll see to it, General. My sire bond has made me lazy, but I still remember how to set up an intelligence network."

"Excellent, I shall provide a secure communication channel. And do not worry about overwhelming me with data. I am capable of processing far more than your team is likely to send."

"I know exactly who to assign to the team. I promise, General, that you'll be happy with the results."

"I look forward to it. Come, let us find a room where we may work through the details of our next mission."

They both spared a longing glance at the lobby doors, where Mother had exited, then locked themselves in a conference room.

Over the next few hours John learned with increasing awe why Deadiron had had such a flawless combat record.

24

ORIGINS

CHARLIE LAY FLAT ON HIS STOMACH at the top of a small rise overlooking a snowy expanse. Mark crawled up beside him, peered through his binoculars, and swore.

"Someone beat us here," Mark whispered.

"Not just anyone." They were over two hundred yards away from a small snow-camouflaged encampment, but if there were vampires among them, anything above a whisper might be overheard, so Charlie kept his voice soft. "Look at the insignias on their rifle straps."

Mark let his binoculars drop to the snow and hung his head. "Orwing. What do you want to bet Alvin had Calum followed?"

"It would explain why he and Don weren't killed after Anne escaped from their prison."

"It also means they've probably been here for weeks." Mark looked through the binoculars again. "I count twenty. Half of them vampires, judging from their thick, sun-resistant outfits."

"Copy that, plus however many are in the tents, and possibly underground. It's a large operation, considering how deep into Russian territory we are. I'm surprised they haven't been caught yet."

"I'm not," Mark said. "Take a closer look at that camouflaged covering."

Cappa obliged and zoomed in Charlie's vision. Stretched over the tent town was a large snow-colored covering, typically used to hide encampments from planes or satellite surveillance. That type of camouflage wouldn't usually hold up to close scrutiny. Detailed analysis would reveal the camouflage for what it was, followed by troops or gunships to clear out the interlopers.

This camouflage was different. It shimmered in the bright sun, distorting and blurring as if it weren't completely there.

"Adaptive optics," Charlie said.

"There's one way to be sure." Mark pulled what appeared to be a stuffed raven from his backpack, then pressed a button under its wing.

The mechanical bird came to life. It walked on the snow and looked around, just like a real bird would, then took flight.

Charlie's vision was replaced with that of the bird. It flew higher, and the landscape fell away. The bird looked down at the encampment and saw …

Nothing.

The camera switched to thermal vision.

Still nothing. From the bird's viewpoint — or a satellite's — the landscape was just empty snow for miles around.

"That's insane," Mark said, who must have also been watching through his digital contact lenses. "I guess we know where Orwing's research and development budget went after Zima defected."

"Makes you wonder how the troops got here, though, doesn't it?"

The bird made a wide circle, then flew in low and landed next to their backpack. Charlie's own vision returned.

"If they're using the same camouflage tech on their air transport vehicles …"

"They could have moved a thousand troops in, and no one would be the wiser," Mark said. "You think they've adapted the optic camouflage for soldiers?"

"Let's hope not. Targeting them would be a pain." Charlie looked at Mark. "A direct assault is too risky at this point. We need more information, like entrance points, troop count, armaments, equipment, and escape routes."

"And we need to figure out how we're going to keep ourselves hidden from super-sensitive vampires in the meantime, especially once night falls. I'm glad now that we missed our drop target by such a large margin."

Charlie nodded. Calum's map had been rough at best. He hadn't had the benefit of a GPS on his original trip, leaving them with only a best-guess of where to start looking. Their jet had followed a pre-determined flight path to avoid being shot down by the Russian Air Force, which meant that even if they had exact coordinates, they would have had to hike to their destination anyway.

But, to Mark's point, the inconvenience had worked in their favor. Had they dropped on target, or anywhere near it, they would now be captured or dead.

"Let's use the field mouse," Charlie said. "It should have enough range to make it into camp and back. I spotted half a dozen real mice on the way over, so it shouldn't draw suspicion."

Mark pulled the mechanical mouse from his backpack and pressed a spot between its forelegs. Like the bird, it came to life with such realistic movements that even Charlie would have sworn it was a real mouse.

"Let's hope a hawk doesn't spot it and swoop in for a snack," Mark said.

Fortunately, the skies were clear. Their little mouse skittered across the snow, zig-zagging and pausing as a real mouse would, until it finally reached the encampment. One soldier spared it a cursory glance. Evidently, the field mouse didn't pose a security threat, because the soldier resumed his vigilance without another look.

The camp was well-organized, as Charlie would have expected from a professional operation: medical supply tents, weapons tents, sleeping tents, and work tents with scientists busily typing on computer stations.

More than any other kind, however, were tents containing stacks and stacks of unopened boxes — research equipment, by their labels, of every size and variety. Alvin had left nothing to chance, which surprised neither him nor Mark when they discussed the findings.

"I think we can take the camp, if need be," Mark said.

"Agreed, though I still want to know what's below-ground. We need eyes down there, but I doubt the field mouse has enough power to make it through the tunnels and back."

Mark grinned. "So let's combine forces."

While the field mouse skittered back to them, Mark pulled a cable from Charlie's wrist and plugged the bird in to recharge it. When the mouse returned, he plugged it in as well.

Minutes later, with both of their batteries full, the mechanical raven grabbed the mouse in its talons and took flight.

"Nature works in funny ways," Mark said, grinning.

"That it does."

Cappa guided the bird close to the tent. It released the seemingly frightened mouse, who scrambled beneath the canopy and quickly disappeared down a hole. Unsurprisingly, the video transmission ended.

Mark rolled onto his back and looked at the sky. "Now we wait."

Waiting was the hardest part. Cappa had set the mouse on explore mode. It would autonomously roam and record everything it saw and heard, then return by the most expedient route available when its battery ran low. It wouldn't have enough power to make it all the way back, so the bird would again pick it up and bring it back to them.

Twenty minutes passed. Assuming the mouse hadn't been discovered, it had to be low on charge.

Mark fidgeted, evidently nervous, too.

Five minutes later, Charlie sighed. The mouse still hadn't appeared. If Orwing had discovered its existence, that didn't necessarily give Mark and Charlie away, but it would certainly put the enemy on high-alert, which would make infiltrating the underground tunnel that much harder.

The mouse's video suddenly appeared in Charlie's vision. It was standing outside in the snow. The battery indicator blinked critical.

Mark and Charlie quickly scanned the area, trying to spot the little robot, but it was nowhere to be seen. Even stranger, the encampment wasn't visible from the mouse's perspective.

"Send the bird up," Charlie said.

Mark did so. The bird flew in ever-widening circles around the encampment.

The mouse's battery indicator blinked red, then the video went blank.

Damn it!

I SEE IT, Cappa sent, her message floating across Charlie's vision.

The bird veered east, away from them and the encampment, and landed on the other side of a rocky rise. There, just outside of a dirt-filled crag, lay their mouse, unmoving.

Charlie and Mark grinned.

The mouse had found another entrance.

"Let's bring it back and see what else it discovered," Mark said.

The bird returned a minute later and deposited the seemingly dead mouse before them, then it keeled over, too.

"I'm so glad you talked me into bringing these," Charlie said, plugging a power cable from his wrist into the mouse.

"When we get back, we're investing research into higher capacity batteries. Maybe nano-fusion reactors."

"Because that's what the world needs: nuclear mice."

"Amen."

THE MOUSE'S VIDEO IS READY FOR PLAYBACK, Cappa sent. YOU AREN'T GOING TO BELIEVE THIS.

"Hit it," Charlie said.

His vision switched over to the mouse's recorded video. It scurried into the tent and down a hole in the snow, lit at regular intervals by hanging work lights. The hole ended in a perfectly rectangular opening in the earth. A sliding metal hatch had been wedged open with metal pipes, leaving just enough room for a ladder and a single person to climb down.

The mouse scurried down the ladder and past a vampire soldier, who had shed his protective daywear and either hadn't noticed the mouse or, more likely, hadn't cared.

Inside the structure, the floor appeared to be made of the same black material as the walls and ceiling which, despite its dark appearance, seemed to give off a faint luminescence.

"Is the audio working?" Mark said.

YES, Cappa sent. AS FAR AS I CAN TELL, THE INTERIOR IS LIKE ONE BIG ACOUSTIC DAMPENER. YOU COULD WALK RIGHT BY SOMEONE AND THEY WOULDN'T HEAR YOU.

"Somebody must like their quiet."

"Lucky for us," Charlie said. "Sneaking in will be that much easier."

The mouse wandered down a long corridor to a dead end and had to turn around. Several more times that happened. The only break in the featureless black walls was a large crack in the ceiling where dirt had poured in. The mouse eventually found its way over the pile and continued.

At the end of the next corridor sat human equipment. Duffel bags, folding tables, boxes, jackhammers, and power saws littered the space in front of a small opening in the wall, which had obviously been cut with the power tools.

Charlie and Mark both swore when they saw what lay beyond.

"Are those what I think they are?" Mark's voice was a whisper.

Charlie nodded, too engrossed in the video to realize that Mark probably couldn't see him because he was also watching.

As far as the mouse could see were rows of metallic capsules, nine feet tall, each with a single window near the top. Many had fallen and were cracked or damaged, as if a massive impact had shaken them loose. Most of the information displays at the bottom of the capsules still blinked with faint red lights, however, illuminating the occupants within. The mouse never went close enough for a good look, but the few glimpses Charlie had of long fangs and purple, leathery skin were enough to shake him to the core.

IT GETS WORSE, Cappa sent.

The mouse edged around a row of capsules and ran to the center of the room. The entire room curved in a gentle arc. Rows of capsules converged on the smaller arc like a fan, hinting that this was just one of many such rooms in a much larger ship.

In one such space, where many capsules had fallen, hung sheets of clear plastic typically used for quarantine or makeshift clean rooms, boxing off a living-room-sized area. Bright lights within the semi-transparent plastic room showed humanoid figures in orange biohazard suits bustling around. Even though the mouse never got a clear view inside, it wasn't hard to guess that they were performing some sort of examination on the bodies.

"You're right," Charlie said softly. "This is worse."

You haven't seen the worst part yet, Cappa sent. Keep watching.

The mouse scurried past the plastic enclosure. Charlie gasped at what lay on the other side.

Alien corpses were stacked waist-high in a large pile. Some had been dissected, their chests laid open to expose a mosh of internal organs. Most were intact, however, which Charlie puzzled over until the mouse moved on to what he sure as hell hoped was Cappa's "worst part."

A coffin-like chamber constructed of thick, clear material lay on the floor. Sturdy metal bars reinforced the structure, forming a cage-within-a-cage. Cylindrical tanks of gasses and liquids fed into the chamber via colored tubes. The unmistakable sound of a compressor came from nearby.

The coffin's lid hung open. A pair of vampires were lowering a capsule inside it. The last thing Charlie saw before the mouse moved on was Alvin's hawk-like nose behind one of the hazmat hats.

"That arrogant fool," Mark said. "He's trying to revive them."

Charlie nodded. "Without much success, but it's only a matter of time."

Exactly, Cappa sent. He has thousands of chances to get it right, and he probably has his best people on it.

"Pause," Mark said.

Charlie's vision returned. He and Mark looked at each other.

"Why focus on the aliens themselves?" Mark said. "Alvin is a hardware guy. There must be a treasure trove of technology in there somewhere."

I have a theory, Cappa sent. You're right about the technology, as you'll see later in the video, but I think Alvin has hit a dead end.

Charlie grinned. "He can't figure out how to use their technology."

Bingo. It's either keyed to the aliens' biology, which would make tactical sense if they're a warrior race, or it's so foreign that Orwing doesn't even know where to begin.

"Maybe they don't know how to power it," Mark said.

"True. Who's to say their equipment even runs on electricity?"

"Right. It could be organic, or something else entirely."

They grinned with childish anticipation. Neither of them could wait to get their hands on the alien technology and find out.

"Resume," Mark said.

The video once again replaced Charlie's vision. As far as he could tell, the area Alvin occupied was the only portion of the ship accessible to them without having to cut through another wall. The mouse was only able to continue its journey because it found a small structural crack.

Once through, the mouse crossed an additional room filled with the same alien capsules, and with similar signs of crash damage, but it was the next room that made Charlie scratch his head.

This room was just as large as the capsule rooms, but these capsules varied greatly in size — some as big as an elephant, others small as a rat — and the occupants looked nothing like those in the previous room.

"Animals," Mark said.

Many containers were completely clear, containing strange flora of varying size and color, but they all shared a dark, depressing hue.

"Pause," Charlie said. He sat up and rubbed his eyes. "I don't like it. Not one bit."

"You aren't the farming type, I take it?"

"Not if I were an advanced race traveling across the galaxy to conquer a primitive world." Charlie shook his head. "According to Calum, the Entity console fabricated a new implant in a matter of minutes. You can't tell me they don't have the technology to replicate whatever nutrients they require."

"So?"

"So why would an invading force waste precious cargo space on animals and flora? Even if they couldn't manufacture nutrients, for whatever reason, that space would be much better utilized with hard rations and such."

Mark paled. "They aren't just invading. They're planning to stay."

"That's right. When this spaceship arrived however many thousands of years ago, humanity couldn't have fought back, and the aliens must have known that. They weren't seeking a glorious military campaign. Their goal was colonization."

"Not was. *Is.*" Mark sat bolt-upright. "Anne keeps saying the Entity's plan involves the end of the world — specifically, the end of humanity. This spaceship obviously sustained heavy damage, but the Entity and most of the passengers survived. The Entity is still trying to carry out its original mission to colonize the planet."

"But their physiology is very different from ours," Charlie said. "Alvin's revival tank is an atmospheric chamber. They probably can't breathe our air."

"Which might explain why vampires don't need to breathe," Mark said. "I bet the aliens are sensitive to sunlight, too. But why would they create vampires — their slaves, really — with dramatic weaknesses to their new environment?"

Charlie paled with cold realization. "Because they don't intend to adapt to Earth's environment. They're going to make Earth conform to theirs."

Mark paused in thoughtful silence. "You're talking about planetary engineering. But how? No sunlight, frigid temperatures, a completely different atmosphere ... that's a massive rearrangement of our planet's basic elements."

"I have no idea, but whatever it's planning is happening soon, and vampires are the key. I'd bet money that vampires were custom-designed to survive both in our environment *and* theirs to help the aliens transition."

"Which explains why the Entity is shooting for numbers. If it starts the planetary engineering process too soon, the aliens won't have enough slaves to build their colony." Mark shook his head. "Why vampires, though? Wouldn't it be easier to bring a team of robots than risk converting natives who might revolt?"

"Could be efficiency. Enslaving locals is easier to scale and takes less cargo room than robots or large manufacturing equipment. They can also breed more without any additional equipment or resources."

"Or maybe the Entity didn't have a choice. The ship crash-landed, right?"

"That's my guess," Charlie said.

"Granted, we haven't seen the whole ship, but from what we have seen, the only powered items were the surviving alien capsules. We also saw a few human guards wandering around in there without breathers, which means the atmosphere in the aliens' own ship is probably unbreathable to them. Reviving them now would be a death sentence."

"So the Entity needs the vampires to restore atmosphere and revive the passengers." Charlie pounded his fist in the snow. "There has to be more to it. Vampires were likely engineered to survive in both atmospheres. Maybe a certain number of vampires are necessary to ensure successful colonization."

"Numbers it has, according to Anne," Mark said. "It could just be waiting for her to gather them, or for them to arrive. Or maybe there are tasks they need to do first. Maybe the planetary engineering equipment needs repair, or needs operators to use it."

"We'll need to figure that out if we're going to have a prayer of stopping this thing."

"Unless we blow the whole ship to Kingdom Come." Mark patted his backpack. "There's no guarantee that even destabilizing the power reactors can do enough damage to stop it, but if worse comes to worst ..."

Charlie nodded. Invaders or not, he didn't like the idea of destroying what might be the last of an alien civilization. But between that or humanity's demise ... it wasn't even a choice.

"First we need to find a safe way inside," Charlie said.

THERE MAY BE ONE, Cappa sent. KEEP WATCHING THE VIDEO.

"Resume," Mark said.

The mouse next stopped in what looked like an equipment room. Alien gadgets large and small sat on shelves that were individually molded for each item. Pistols, rifles, and larger weapons, whose purpose Charlie could only guess, were fastened to long racks along the wall.

"We can't let Alvin reach that room," Mark said. Charlie grunted agreement.

"Freeze frame," Charlie said when the mouse exited the supply room. "Zoom in quadrant two, and again."

The upper-right portion of the image magnified, showing a long, black console with glowing lights — the first sign of power outside of the blinking capsule lights they had seen that didn't belong to Orwing.

"It's hard to tell from this angle, but that looks like the Entity's console Calum described," Mark said.

"Yeah, the one that trapped his hand and forced the implant into his chest." Charlie shuddered. That Alvin hadn't discovered it yet was a stroke of pure luck. "Resume."

The mouse ran around the room for a minute longer. Its battery indicator was now low. It scurried to another crack in the wall and climbed the dirt that had poured in from the outside. A hole in the earth, no bigger than a hand's width, led the mouse up and up until daylight whitened its view. Playback stopped.

THE TUNNEL LOOKS FRESH, Cappa sent. PROBABLY FROM A RODENT OF SOME KIND. BUT IF YOU WIDEN IT, THE CRACK IN THE SHIP IS BIG ENOUGH FOR YOU GUYS TO SQUEEZE THROUGH.

"It would be dirty work, but it's probably our safest entry," Mark said. "And it would give us a direct line to the Entity."

THE TUNNEL IS APPROXIMATELY FORTY-THREE FEET LONG.

"Yikes," Mark said. "How fast do you think Charlie three-point-oh can dig?"

"Depends on how soft the dirt is, the structural integrity of the tunnel, and how quiet we need to be. Either way, it seems like we're going to find out."

They gathered their packs and began crawling behind the small ridge toward the mouse's extraction point. Digging would be hard, grueling work, even in his cyborg body, but it was their best option, and far preferable to being shot.

Still, Charlie couldn't shake the feeling that he had just committed to digging their own graves.

25

SUPERSOLDIER

CONSCIOUSNESS RETURNED SLOWLY FOR DELA. Everything ached: her back, her chest, her arms and legs, even her toes and fingers. They weren't painful, rather, they seemed to be sensory indicators that something inside of her had changed.

Her eyes fluttered open to the harsh lights of their Montana headquarters, which were soon obscured by a plump woman in a lab coat who Dela didn't recognize.

"Good morning, Miss Fedelma Madigan," the woman said pleasantly. "Glad you finally decided to join us."

"That's Mrs. Suther," she said in a scratchy voice. "And the name is Dela."

"Really? Your medical records show otherwise." She propped Dela's head up and pressed a cup to her lips. "Here you go."

Dela drank eagerly. The water felt wonderful on her dry throat, but landed in a markedly empty stomach. "Thanks. Got any snacks handy?"

The woman smiled and produced a plate piled with donuts. It was the most glorious sight Dela had ever seen.

"Cappa said you'd be hungry when you woke. Dig in."

Dela had downed two donuts before she managed a "thank you," but those were her last words until she'd eaten every crumb off the plate and licked her fingers clean.

"Not to sound ungrateful," Dela said, "but who are you, and why are you in our super-secret headquarters?"

"Dr. Carol Toben." She extended a hand.

Dela wiped one of hers on the sheet and took it. "You're Anne's boss."

"Or Susan's, or the master vampire's, or whatever she's going by these days. And the reason I'm here is because Tabby needed a ride from the hospital after Anne and Zima left for San Francisco."

"What?" Dela frantically looked around. "Wait, w-where is everyone?"

"Scattered to the four winds," Carol said.

Dela listened to the doctor's recounting of her meeting with Anne and Zima, and the subsequent discussions with the rest of the group.

"Cappa and Tabby went to see — what's his name, Tim? — in San Francisco, thinking the Resistance would be Anne's first target," Carol said in closing. "But it's been almost two days since they left, and still nothing."

Dela stared at her sheets in stunned silence, her chest heavy with despair. She had so many things to be upset about, but, even above the end of the world and her crappy husband going to see a genuine alien spaceship without her, one thing stood out above the rest.

"I can't believe Zima would give herself over to the Entity," Dela said.

"I know. The others had difficulty coming to terms with her defection as well."

"No, I mean it's impossible! The Dark Angel is our beacon of hope against the scourge. She's a goddamned superhero, and superheroes always win! She must have some trick up her sleeve that she's holding until the last moment."

Carol's expression seemed conflicted. "As much as we may want them to," she said carefully, "heroes don't always save the day. We may have to accept that Zima is lost to the enemy, and that the responsibility of saving the world is in our hands."

"You can believe that if you want, but I believe in the Dark Angel. She'll save the day. You watch."

Dela hopped from the table. A cold draft tickled her rear. She quickly pulled her flimsy gown closed behind her and glared at Carol.

"A hospital gown? Really?"

"I'm a doctor. You're my patient. It's a tool of the trade. If you want to blame someone, then blame Charlie for stocking them."

Dela sat back on the bed. "So you haven't heard from him or Mark since they left?"

"No. If they have been in communication, Cappa hasn't mentioned it."

Oh no!

"Cappa!" Dela said, looking all around. "Are you all right? Can you hear me?"

Dela's phone rattled on the bedside table. She snatched it and put it to her ear.

"Don't worry, I'm fine," Cappa said through the receiver.

"Are you sure? Is there anything I can do for you? If so, just name it. Anything, no matter how small. I mean it!"

Her musical laugh was welcome. "I'm not just saying that, Dela. I'm fine, really. It isn't like last time. Although my Charlie self is out of range in Russia, I'm still in communication with my Cappa self in San Francisco, so I'm not isolated. I experience her freedom of movement and social interactions as if they were my own."

Dela flopped onto the bed. "Thank God. I just … I don't want you to become another Rose. I can't watch you suffer like that ever again."

"I'm with you, believe me. But, like I said, it shouldn't come to that. Surviving Rose was hard, but I learned some valuable lessons that I'll put to use this time around."

"Like talking to your friends."

"Like that, yes."

"Promise?"

"Dela, you don't —"

"Promise me, Cappa. Say it!"

"Yes, I promise. If I feel lonely or depressed, I'll tell you right away."

"Not good enough."

"Huh?"

"Not. Good. Enough," Dela said. "Where are Anne's fancy targeting glasses?"

"Look, I'm telling you, that isn't necessary."

"Blah, blah, blah. Now tell me where they are or I'm going to rearrange your desk."

"You wouldn't!"

Dela marched over to Cappa's desk, where every item was arranged with anal-retentive precision. "Last chance. Your stapler and hole punch are about to switch places ..."

"Brat! Fine, you win. They're in my desk, top drawer. Don't you dare touch anything else!"

Dela took Anne's techno-glasses out and put them on. Their clear lenses made the world look unchanged. "How do I link them with my phone?"

Cappa sighed. "I'll do it, one sec ..."

A single green dot appeared in the upper-right field of her vision. "Can you hear me?" Dela said.

"Yes, you can put the phone down now."

"Great." Dela cleared her throat and used a husky announcer voice. "You're now listening to radio K.D.L.A. All Dela, all the time."

"I think you've just named my personal Hell."

"Well get used to it, Capster, because I'm keeping this thing on twenty-four-seven until your other selves are back here — safe, sound, and resynchronized. I won't risk another Rose incident, no matter how small you say the chances are."

"You're impossible," Cappa said with a laugh. "Thank you."

"Don't thank me until you've heard me sing. The acoustics in my shower are great. These glasses are waterproof, right?"

Carol's phone rang. She frowned at it before answering. "Yes, Cappa? No, even if I knew how to euthanize an artificial intelligence, I think you know as well as I do that euthanasia is illegal in every state, including Montana. You're just going to have to live with Dela's singing for now." Carol chuckled at something, then hung up. "You certainly do liven things up," she said to Dela.

"It's a gift."

"So ... is there something I should know about this Rose person?"

"Cappa can tell you the whole, depressing story if she wants, but if you notice her acting melancholy or clingy, let me know immediately. Got it?"

"Got it. I guess a prescription of antidepressants is out of the question."

"Considering she's a computer who doesn't currently have a mouth, I'd say so."

"Back to the patient I can help, then. How are you feeling? Any side-effects from the implant?"

My implant!

With everything else going on, Dela had almost forgotten that she was now a supersoldier, like Mark.

I've gotta try this out.

Heedless of her flimsy hospital gown, Dela ran over to a barrel of scrap metal. The container weighed five hundred pounds at least, which was way outside of her normal lifting capacity.

Wishing with all her might, Dela grabbed the handles and heaved. Her muscles strained against the impossible load.

Then a miracle happened. It budged.

One inch it rose, then two. Dela groaned and pushed herself to her limits. Her muscles burned, but the barrel continued to rise until the lip was above her head.

"I did it," she said in a strained voice. "I did it! My implant works!" She let the barrel fall with a deafening crash, then ran back to Carol and grabbed her hands. "I'm ... I'm a superhero, Doc. Me! Can you believe it?"

"After that impressive display, yes. And you're hurting my hands, dear."

"Oh! Sorry."

"That's all right. As much as I enjoy seeing your cute little tush, you should probably dress before you catch a cold. I didn't see any superhero spandex in the cabinets, but your normal clothes are on the chair, next to your bed."

"Right."

Dela gave up on trying to keep her gown closed and bent to gather her clothes. When she turned back around, she was surprised to find Carol blushing.

"Sorry for the streak show, Doc. Back in a flash."

Carol stammered something unintelligible and hastily turned away.

Minutes later, Dela was back in the same outfit she'd worn before the surgery: tight jeans that hugged her narrow waist and hips, and a collared midriff shirt buttoned low enough to give her ample breasts room to move. She considered it her ogle outfit, because that's what every man — and most women — did when they saw her in it.

Cappa called it scandalous. Dela called her jealous.

"Is that better, Doc?"

Carol's eyes latched onto Dela's titanic cleavage, then she quickly looked away. "B-better, yes, but you could still use a sweater or … something." She collapsed into a chair, face in her hands, and shook her head, muttering something Dela couldn't quite make out, then tapped the keyboard, bringing the computer screen to life.

Dela stood next to her. "That's a cell infected with the virus, isn't it?"

"Yes. I've been reviewing your friends' research while you were unconscious. It's well-organized and very thorough."

"That's Cappa for you, and Charlie and Mark rarely miss a detail."

"I'll say. The virus inhibitor they created is a chemical marvel. It gives me hope that vampirism might be curable after all."

"Curable? Doc, are you serious?"

"It's a long shot. I have very little to support my hypothesis, but there are pieces of the virus that still don't make sense. It was engineered, which means some of those pieces may be a fail-safe in case things go catastrophically wrong, like if an unintended outbreak happened. For us, reversing such a dramatic transformation to human physiology is unthinkable, but for an advanced alien race, adding a reversal mechanism may be standard practice. The questions are whether they actually did, and, if so, what the triggering mechanism is."

"You're blowing my mind here," Dela said. "How long will it take to figure something like that out?"

"Weeks? Years? More time than we have, I'd bet. And maybe more time than the vampires have." Carol zoomed in on a small piece of the infected cell.

Dela leaned forward to get a better view.

"Now obviously —" Carol turned right into Dela's cleavage and staggered back. She scooted her chair a few inches away, tugged her collar, then continued. "Obviously, the virus mutates the cells' function dramatically, such that most of it is unrecognizable from the original, except for this part."

Carol circled her mouse around a bumpy region that, to Dela, looked like all the rest.

"Cappa's notes say they're unsure what function this region serves. It seemed familiar, though, so I tapped some of my old friends at the CDC, and voila!"

Carol pulled up another image. It looked more like the slides Dela remembered from high school biology.

"That's great, Doc! But I don't get it."

"This region of a normal human cell is responsible for *apoptosis*, or programmed cell death. It's a normal process in just about any multicellular organism, and is triggered through either intrinsic or extrinsic pathways."

Dela stared at her. Dr. Toben may as well have been speaking an alien language.

Carol sighed. "Cell death is either self-initiated, or it receives the instruction from other cells."

"Creepy, but I'm with you now."

"As you can imagine, this is a highly regulated process in any organism. Too much, and the organism dies. Too little, and the cells mutate into cancer-like growths."

"So?"

"So according to this research, a host infected with the virus exhibits *zero* cell deaths as part of its normal operation. None!"

"You mean … the cells are immortal?"

"Basically, but that isn't the puzzling part. The virus hyper-optimizes the cells, leaving nothing to waste. If the cells — and subsequently the hosts — were meant to be immortal, the virus would have removed the apoptosis mechanisms altogether. While it does remove the intrinsic pathway, the extrinsic — or external — pathway, and the mechanism for cell death, are left intact. Why?"

"I … I sucked at biology, Doc. Sorry."

"It was a rhetorical question. The virus also *alters* the extrinsic pathway, causing every cell to respond to the exact same message."

"So all it takes to kill every cell in a vampire's body is a dose of what? Some sort of chemical?"

"Yes, but that danger isn't new. We know that a small amount of silver is fatal in vampires, which would be much easier to obtain and weaponize than a custom protein solution. More likely, the external pathway is designed to receive a chemical produced from within the host's own body."

"Oh my God ... y-you're saying vampires have a built-in self-destruct button?"

"Yes." Carol swiveled around to face her. "Including Anne."

"Poor Anne. She threatened to kill herself just so Mark and I could survive, but the Entity might kill all the vampires anyway." Dela clenched her jaw. "Well, there's one vampire it won't be killing anytime soon." She leaned over until their faces were inches apart. "Doc, Anne has an implant, too. Her cells are programmable, just like mine are now. We have to disable her self-destruct mechanism before the Entity decides it doesn't need her anymore."

Carol gulped, her eyes flicking to Dela's cleavage. She wiped her face and returned her gaze northward. "I-if that's the case, the easiest thing would be to alter the chemical-producing organ, rather than every cell that might receive it."

"Except the Entity locked us out of Anne's implant. Even if it hadn't, we don't know where she is. And even if we did, she's being guarded by Zima, who's also under the Entity's influence."

Carol's phone rang. She put it to her ear, then turned on the speaker and laid it on the desk.

"If we do find her," Cappa said from the speaker, "I brought something with me to San Francisco that may gain me access to her implant. But I'll need precise instructions on what to alter about Anne's physiology, which means Carol and I have our work cut out for us."

"Ideally, I'd create a serum, like a retrovirus," Carol said. "The rest of the Resistance members don't have implants, from what I understand, and I'm sure they would also like to know they won't suddenly die at the Entity's whim."

All the manufacturing lines fired up at once, making both Carol and Dela jump.

Dela looked back at the phone. "What the hell was that?"

"Plan B," Cappa said. "In the meantime, Carol, I suggest we get to work. Anne could show up at the Resistance any moment. We may only get one shot at this."

"Right." Carol turned her attention to the workstation.

Dela paced behind her chair, listening to the two of them talk, until she couldn't stand it anymore and stood beside Carol. The doctor's fingers flew across the keyboard, pulling up charts and data that Dela couldn't begin to understand. Dela leaned over to get a closer look at a particularly colorful graph.

Carol slammed the keyboard and put her head in her hands.

"Doc! What is it? Did you find something?"

Carol gripped her hair and took a deep breath. When she finally turned to Dela, her face was a study of deliberate calm.

"If you must know," Carol said in an even tone, "I have trouble concentrating with you around."

"Sorry, I tend to hover. I know I don't have anything to contribute, but ..." Dela wrung her hands.

"It's not that." Carol collapsed into her chair. "The problem is ... well, frankly, you remind me of my ex-fiancée, and those" — she gestured at Dela's chest — "are very distracting, especially when they're right in my face."

I didn't see that coming.

"Would you like me to go?" Dela said.

Carol pressed her lips together, then sighed. "No, but if you stay, I'm not sure how much work I'll get done because I'm going to keep stealing glances."

"Let me make it easy for you, then." Dela walked behind the desk and propped her boobs on top of the computer screen. "Now you can glance all you want."

Carol blushed. Her eyes widened, but she didn't look away. "I-I appreciate the offer, but you're married, aren't you?"

"Married means 'look, don't touch,' as far as I'm concerned, so we aren't breaking any rules."

"No, I ... I couldn't." Carol reluctantly dropped her gaze to the desk, but Dela put a gentle finger under Carol's chin and lifted her head so their eyes met.

"Doc, you're working to save my dear friend's life — maybe the world. You deserve a whole team of scientists and the support of nations. Instead, you're stuck in a factory basement with a bodiless android and me — a bartender turned barista who only graduated high school because of my *assits*: my ass and my tits.

"Now, I won't even pretend that I'm into women, but if my *assits* are the only things I can offer to help you concentrate, then you can ogle me to your heart's content. And the more progress you make ..." Dela unfastened another button, exposing a scandalous amount of cleavage, which bulged between the edges of her laced bra. "The better the show gets."

"I honestly don't know if it will help or hinder my research, but ..." Carol smiled. "Thank you."

"Don't mention it. I also make the best damn mochas you've ever tasted, so don't hesitate to ask."

Carol laughed, then returned her attention to the screen, with the occasional appreciative glance at Dela's *assits* hanging above.

"That was sweet," Cappa said to Dela through her glasses. "I'm going to take back some of the things I've said about you."

Dela grinned. "Don't. That'll make it so much sweeter when I finally kick your ass the next time we spar."

26

ULTIMATUM

T ABBY WATCHED CAPPA PACE yet another lap around the gnarled oak tree. The moon, combined with city light pollution, were bright enough for her human eyes to see by, even on the unpopulated south-Peninsula hillside Tim and Nick had chosen as the meeting place.

Anne's cordial invitation to meet the Resistance had come as a surprise. Everyone, including Tabby, had expected an army of vampires to show up on their doorstep, followed by a prolonged battle. But, typical of her mother, Anne had simply said please, and had even let them choose the location.

"I don't like it," Cappa said for the twentieth time. She looked at Tabby. "You shouldn't be here. Things could turn violent at the drop of a hat, and —"

"Save your breath," Tabby said. "If Mom's coming, then I'm going to talk with her. It's as simple as that."

"It is not! Nick, help me out here."

Nick Orwing looked uncomfortable, as appropriate for an unwilling participant in someone else's family fight. He scratched his hawkish nose, which Cappa claimed was the *only* trait he shared with his father, Alvin, and had meant it in high praise.

"It's hard to say," Nick said. "If Anne's intentions were hostile, she could have taken control of Tim at any time before you arrived, and the battle would have been over before it even began. Tabby's presence may heighten the emotional tension, but it may also make Anne more agreeable."

"But it could also be seen as a hostile move on our part," Timothy Chen said. His tall, lanky figure and black hair blended well against the tree.

Tabby had to squint into the darkness to pick out his Asian features. According to Cappa, Tim was Anne's only direct vampire descendant in the Resistance, an unlucky engineer who had accidentally been splattered with Anne's blood when she'd been shot in the back.

All vampires in the Resistance stemmed from his bloodline. Taking control of Tim would give Anne absolute control of his entire hierarchy — which was everyone.

"If I were Anne," Tim said, "I would take Tabby's presence as a threat: Leave us alone, or we'll hurt someone precious to you. That's when a mother bear usually goes berserk and kills everyone to protect her cubs."

Cappa waved the notion away. "We'd never hurt Tabby, and Anne knows it. Neither would Anne, and that's what really worries me. What if she fails to follow through on something the Entity wants, and it decides she's not worth the hassle? It could kill her right there and promote another vampire to the Master role."

They fell silent at that. Tabby had quickly learned that everyone in the Resistance — vampire and human — loved and respected Anne, even though most had never met her. Anne's name was legend among them, and they held the value of freedom that she exemplified above everything else. They called her the All Mother, spoken with the same reverence a supplicant reserved for a holy leader. They didn't want to lose Anne any more than Tabby or Cappa did.

Movement in the shadows made Tabby start, but she soon relaxed and clutched her pounding heart. It was just another member of the Resistance. Vampires were veritable specters at night, she'd learned, natural hunters who were seen only when they wanted to be seen. For their prey, seeing one meant it was already too late. Tabby joined Cappa in her pacing and took her arm for comfort.

"That's so sweet."

Everyone jumped at Anne's voice, not a dozen yards away. Zima stood by her side, her eyes glowing icy blue in the darkness. More vampires appeared behind them. The Resistance gathered around Tim, Cappa, and Tabby, a stream of shadows flowing from the trees.

Then all fell quiet. Tension hung thick in the night air.

Anne appeared to be the only relaxed person in the small gathering. She approached with the same warm smile Tabby had come to expect. It made her heart ache.

"Tim. Nick," Anne said. "You both look well. It's so good to see you again."

The tension grew when she walked straight up to them. Zima hovered at her heels, offering no greeting apart from her watchful eyes, which took in everyone at once.

"All Mother," Tim said, bowing slightly. "It's nice to see you, too."

"But you wish it were under different circumstances."

Tim nodded.

"Me too." Anne's eyes filled with the same sadness as the last time Tabby had seen her. "But this is where we are, and we have to make the best of it." She gestured to the vampires behind her. "All of us."

Tabby stepped forward. "Who are they?"

Anne looked surprised, as if she hadn't realized Tabby were there. "First things first."

She swooped in and gave Tabby the hug she had so desperately been wanting. Zima quickly turned away.

"Mom, come home," Tabby whispered. Emotions lodged in her throat like a fist-sized rock. "Please."

Her mother's chest convulsed in a series of short sobs, but she soon quieted. "I can't, honey. You know that, but ... I'm glad you're here."

Tabby clung tighter and buried her face in Anne's shoulder. "Me too."

Despite her tension from earlier, Cappa was first in line for the next hug and caught Anne in a tight embrace. Anne kissed her cheek and stroked her hair.

"I'm glad you're here, too," Anne said, "even though I know it's for a different purpose."

Cappa nodded, sniffling. "Can you blame me?"

"Of course not. I expected nothing less, but shielding Tim's mind from me with your *chi* isn't necessary. I don't intend to force anyone to do anything against their will."

Nick stepped forward. As with all of them, he approached with reverence, not hostility. "What about them?" He gestured to the vampires gathered behind Anne.

"They're different, as you well know. Their sire bond makes it hard to differentiate what they want from their desire to please me."

"To Tabby's question," Nick said, "who are they?"

"I recognize one, at least." Cappa crossed her arms. "Hello, Myrcella. You look markedly better than the last time I saw you. How's that hole Charlie put in your chest doing?"

"Fuck. You," Myrcella said.

Her jet-black hair was wrapped up in a bun, complementing the rest of her outfit, comprised of a black shirt and pants, black leather jacket, black nail polish, dark makeup around her eyes, and copious chain jewelry. Combined with her naturally pale vampire skin, Myrcella was the envy of every Goth who'd ever lived. Everything from her shrewd expression to her defiant posture radiated attitude. She was the nightmare teen rebel, all grown-up, who had never stopped rebelling.

One look from Anne, however, melted her insolence in a heartbeat. Her eyes fell, and she shuffled her feet like a shamed child. She rubbed her chest and grimaced. "It hurt, but I'm fine now, thanks. S-sorry for trying to kill you at the party."

Anne graced her with a smile. Myrcella glowed, the chastened child redeemed. She bounced to Anne's side, opposite Zima, took her arm, then rested her head on Anne's shoulder with a lazy smile. If Myrcella were a cat, she would have curled up on Anne's lap and purred. Tabby had never been so jealous.

Cappa, on the other hand, looked ill.

"As you may have guessed," Anne said, "these are William's Firsts — now mine — whom you've so desperately been hunting. All of them."

Cappa paled further. "All of them? That means …"

"Yes. William's entire lineage has joined my family." She looked at Tim. "As will yours, I hope."

Tim dipped his head. "All Mother … No disrespect, but you know that won't happen. What the Entity is planning is wrong. The members of the Resistance will never agree."

"They might if they had all the facts."

"Which are?"

Anne's sadness intensified, settling over the group like a gloomy mist. "Humanity's end is coming, swift and absolute. The question isn't if it will happen, but how much of our culture and values that we as vampires — who will be humanity's only surviving legacy — can preserve in its wake."

"I don't believe in absolutes," Nick said. "Plans can be thwarted, no matter how foolproof they appear."

"Not this one. In fighting each other, we've built our numbers to a point where the Entity can't fail. Even if we hadn't … Your father found the Entity's home, Nick. Did you know that?"

Nick's wide eyes indicated he didn't.

"Alvin's desire for power falls right into the Entity's plan. Even if you kill me, kill William's bloodline, kill yourselves … the Entity will still get exactly what it wants. And that's just one of its contingency plans."

Anne put a loving hand on Nick's cheek.

"Don't you see? There are too many wheels in motion to stop them all, and it will only take one to end humanity's reign on this planet. We have to stop fighting ourselves because, very soon, vampires will be the only echoes left of humanity."

Tabby glanced at Cappa, whose face was a stony mask. Tabby hoped her own was as well. Anne hadn't mentioned Charlie or Mark. Either their mission had failed, which Anne would have mentioned if only for Cappa's sake, or the Entity didn't yet know they were there. Even Tim and Nick were ignorant of the alien spaceship, and of Charlie and Mark's mission — a necessary deception in case Anne decided to play dirty and read their minds.

And I won't give them or the Entity any clues to the contrary, Tabby thought.

Tim sighed. "We'll … need to discuss it."

"Of course," Anne said. "You have two hours to give me your answer."

Tim's surprise was reflected on them all. "Or what?"

"Or the Entity will force me to ensure you aren't a threat."

Nick swayed as if he might faint. "B-but Tim is shielded. You couldn't ... I mean, you can't ..."

"Yes, I can. May I demonstrate?"

Tim looked at Nick, who eventually nodded.

Anne scanned the trees and smiled at one of the Resistance vampires. "What's your name?"

"Greg, All Mother."

"Greg. You're seven generations removed from me, like most of the others gathered. Correct?"

"Yes, All Mother."

"A good strategy. With such a large gap between us, I shouldn't be able to control you through our bond."

She stepped closer. Greg took a cautious step back.

"Don't be frightened. I meant what I said earlier: I won't make you do anything against your will. At least, not without your permission. Even then, I won't make you hurt anyone, nor will I extract any Resistance secrets. May I touch your mind?"

"Go ahead," Nick said gravely to him.

"Y-yes, All Mother." He gulped and closed his eyes.

Then his face relaxed. A smile twitched his lips, which grew and grew until he was laughing. When his eyes opened, they were tear-filled and grateful. He took Anne's hand and smiled.

"Thank you, All Mother. Thank you!"

His joy wasn't shared by the others. Anne had just demonstrated she could control any vampire, no matter how far down the hierarchy they were, which made Cappa's *chi* shield practically useless.

"Y-you've made your point," Nick said. "But two hours isn't enough. It will take time to get the word out, and even more time to discuss. We'll need two days at least."

"Two hours," Anne said softly. "That's all."

"No!" Tabby grabbed Anne's hand. "Mom — or, Mr. Entity, sir. Please, there's no need to do anything drastic. Let me talk to them."

Anne started to protest, but Tabby squeezed her hand.

"Please! There's a lot to discuss. Two hours just isn't enough. And if you give them the extra time they're asking for, I-I'll be the Entity's advocate. I swear!"

Tabby was surprised to find Zima watching her.

"She is not lying," Zima said, then turned her back again.

Anne's features contorted in anguish. "Twenty-four hours," she said in a strained voice, then cupped Tabby's cheek. "Understand, sweetheart, that in exchange for this extension, the Entity expects results — and the consequences of failure now fall on you. Are you sure you want this?"

Tabby swallowed her fear. "Absolutely. It's the right thing to do."

Anne looked at Nick and Tim, her eyes misty. "Regardless of your ultimate decision, I expect all hostilities between the two vampire factions to cease immediately, or the Entity will force me to take action. Agreed?"

Nick and Tim both nodded.

"Twenty-four hours," Anne said. "I need your answer by then, or else."

It wasn't an ultimatum. It was a plea.

A plea for Tabby's life.

"Mom, please d—"

"Don't say it," Anne said, tears streaming down her face. "I have to go soon. You have a job to do, and I expect — no, I *need* you to do it well." She looked Tabby over. "You haven't drunk my blood yet, have you?"

"Not yet. I'm sorry."

Anne's lip quivered. "So am I. If you drink it now, you'll be too ill to do your job. No matter what ..." Her voice broke. "No matter what happens, I'm going to l-lose you."

Tabby lifted her chin. "Don't count me out yet. Twenty-four hours is a long time. I'll think of something."

"Do that, sweetheart. For me." She looked at Cappa. "Take care of her?"

"As if she were my own."

Oddly, their brief exchange seemed to put her mother at ease. She kissed Tabby, Cappa, Nick, and Tim, then hugged every single Resistance vampire in turn.

While she was doing that, Zima surprised Tabby with a warm embrace.

"You are truly your mother's daughter," Zima said. "I only hope it is not to your detriment this time."

"Take care of her," Tabby said.

"Always."

"I know. Thanks, Mom."

Zima stiffened. "Please do not call me that. Anne has earned the title. I have not."

"Consider it an advance for when you do."

Zima stared at her, eyebrows knitting the barest fraction of an inch.

"I shall take that under advisement," Zima said eventually, then gave her a quick kiss on the cheek. "Cappa is a gifted student of psychology and sociology. If you wish to succeed, you would do well to heed her advice."

"I will. Thank you."

"Farewell."

Then Zima, her mother, and the other Firsts slipped back into the night, leaving the space where they had been just as empty as Tabby's heart.

27

SACRIFICE

LIEUTENANT COLONEL JOHN ANDERSON sped through the trees with the same ease as his brethren, letting Mother lead the way. It wasn't until they'd reached the edge of the city lights, away from their bewildering rendezvous with the Resistance, that she slowed to a walking pace.

"Mother?"

"Yes, John?"

"You realize the Resistance's bargain was just a play for time. No matter your daughter's intentions, they'll never willingly submit."

"I know."

John stopped, dumbfounded. Mother turned to him, her eyes the saddest he had seen yet. He would have done anything to cheer her up, but there was nothing he could do. That knowledge was like a dagger in his chest.

"Then I don't understand," John said. "If you know they won't submit, what was the purpose of that meeting?"

"A play for time, like you said. Ceasing hostilities is necessary to maximize the Entity's chances of success. Now we can move forward unhindered."

"Assuming they honor their end of the bargain."

"They will. We're united now, and we have their general." Mother smiled at General Zima, who stood beside her and took her hand. "They're at a serious disadvantage, and they know it. Fighting us would be suicide. They value their people's lives far too much to waste them in a hopeless battle."

"I respectfully disagree," John said.

Mother arched an eyebrow. He sensed no defensiveness from her, only pride at his courage for speaking his mind. His chest swelled, and he continued.

"I know what desperate people are capable of," John said. "And we've just made them very, very desperate. They're going to strike."

"When, do you think?"

"Maybe at the twenty-four-hour mark, but probably sooner. If they're smart, they know we'll be ready for resistance, so they'll try to catch us off-guard."

"I concur," Zima said. "If they do not capitulate to our demands, then they believe they shall be punished, which they will not tolerate. Since we all agree capitulation is unlikely, that leaves them with one recourse: they shall resist with every means at their disposal." She looked at Mother. "I am sorry, Anne, but our bid for a peaceful resolution has all but ensured the opposite. Conflict is imminent. Had the Entity deemed either John or me fit to confide with its plan, we would have told it as much."

"There will be no conflict," Mother said.

John cleared his throat. "But Mother, we just finished saying —"

"Conflict requires two or more opposing forces. Tell me, who will they oppose if we're not around?"

"We're leaving?"

"As soon as we accomplish tonight's primary goal," Mother said. "The Resistance is desperate, yes, but our strategic advantage will also make them cautious. They'll use this time to plan carefully. They won't strike until they're as sure as they can be of victory. By then, we'll be gone. Are your soldiers ready?"

"Yes, Mother," John said. "All teams are awaiting your order."

Mother saddened further. John wanted to gather her in his arms, comfort her, take away her suffering, but he knew it wouldn't help. People were going to die tonight, but she refused to delegate responsibility for the act. Mother insisted on giving the final command herself, and she would carry its consequences like a weight around her neck for the rest of her existence.

Still, John had to try. "Mother, the soldiers are accustomed to taking orders from me. Please allow me to —"

"Thank you, John, but no. I'll give the order."

The general touched Mother's shoulder with concern. "Anne, please do not burden yourself further. I shall give the —"

"No. You and John have done your part to ensure success with minimal casualties. The rest is on me." Mother gave the general a lingering kiss. "You have too many deaths on your conscience already. It's my turn, honey. Whatever Hell holds for you, it holds for both of us. Remember?"

"It is a lie. If such a place exists, my soul is surely bound there, but yours is not." The general stroked her cheek. "My soul, if I have one, is black and corroded, befitting my horrendous deeds. Yours is white and pure as snow, and I would do anything to keep it so. I beg of you, my wife, my angel ... allow me to give the order."

Feelings of love for her wife rolled off Mother in a powerful wave that made every vampire gasp, including John.

Long-buried memories of his family came flooding to the surface. In a previous life, John had loved like that, too. His mother. His father. His wife at their wedding. The day his son was born, and two years later, when his daughter graced their lives with her own. Those were the happiest times of his life, the people he held most dear.

And he had completely dismissed them.

Until now.

Wetness touched his cheek. John realized that, for the first time since his rebirth as a vampire, he was crying. He looked around and saw the others were feeling the same. From the Firsts all the way down to the bottom of the hierarchy, vampires across the country were dealing with emotions they hadn't felt since their transitions, mixed with a crushing reality.

They had all left people behind — important people who loved and missed them, whom they'd hurt on leaving.

And who would soon be dead.

Mother, however, seemed oblivious to the fundamental change she had triggered in every one of her sirelings. She was lost in her wife's eyes. In all the world, there was just the two of them. John wouldn't have interrupted their intimate moment if his life depended on it.

"You're wrong, Zima," Anne said softly. "Your soul is a shining beacon of kindness and generosity. If Heaven won't take you, then there's little hope for the rest of us. As for Hell ..." She sighed. "If Hell doesn't exist, it soon will. Everywhere you look will be death and desolation. Cities, communities, families ... all of it. Gone. And we're the instruments who will bring it about. So no, my darling, it's not a lie. Whether we go to Hell, or Hell comes to us, we'll both be there soon."

And with that, Mother's will flowed through John to his troops, giving the order they'd been waiting for to fire.

•   •   •

On an unnamed farm in the mid-western United States, a mercenary stood watch at his post, as he had every day and night for the last three months, wearing a civilian flannel shirt and jeans to blend in with the locals.

The cool night air brought a welcome relief. The sun-resistant makeup Orwing provided was top-notch, but the mercenary was a vampire. Even in the shade, standing outside during the day felt uncomfortable. His companion, a shorter vampire with a stocky build, sat in a lawn chair staring at the starry sky over endless fields of wheat.

A glint overhead made him look up. A bright object streaked through the night, smaller and faster than any airplane. It rose in a gentle arc, then angled down on a collision course with the farmhouse behind him.

The mercenary jumped to his feet.

"Move!" he yelled to his companion, but didn't wait for a response before bolting from his post with all the speed his vampire legs could muster.

The incoming object had to be a bunker buster missile. Anything else wouldn't penetrate the earth far enough to kill what was surely its target: a keystone vampire, one of several placed strategically around the world. Each keystone was kept far underground to create a gap between Orwing's vampire hierarchy and the master vampire, disrupting their mental bond like a severed power cable.

If the keystones were unshielded for any reason, their bonds to their hierarchies — and their sire — would be restored, giving Orwing's entire army to the master vampire.

A keystone's death would have the same result. The keystone's sire — in this case, the master vampire herself, a common waitress named Anne Perrin — would inherit the mental bond of the keystone's sirelings, filling the gap, and giving her direct control of that part of the hierarchy.

It was for that reason Orwing had invested so heavily in the keystones' protection by placing them in reinforced bunkers and keeping their locations secret.

But not secret enough.

The missile streaked down like a javelin from the gods. The mercenary ran faster.

A deafening explosion roared behind him. Ground erupted beneath his feet, tossing him high in the air. He flew head-long into the wheat field, along with a mountain of dirt and stone. The sickening snap of his right arm and shoulder made him see stars, but a quick inspection showed only scratches, bruises, and a few deep cuts on his legs. Nothing that wouldn't heal over the next hour.

His companion, too, had survived. He limped over, his lower leg bent at an unnatural angle, which would also heal with time.

Their eyebrows raised with the same unspoken question: Who had enough influence to fire a missile on United States soil?

The answer came soon enough. The mercenary was a second-generation vampire by Orwing's standards. His sire was a keystone vampire — specifically, the keystone who had just been killed by a bunker buster missile. His mental bond, normally dormant because the keystone was shielded, would now pass directly up to the master vampire.

To Anne Perrin.

Her presence filled his mind to overflowing, warm, kind, and welcoming. While he didn't suffer the same blind loyalty that pure vampires reportedly felt for their sires, he quickly discovered that Anne's wishes were impossible to ignore.

She wanted him to come home to her. Now.

The next thing the mercenary knew, he was sprinting for their vehicle. His companion hobbled close behind, grunting with every step. San Francisco was a long drive, but at top speed, they could be there by tomorrow evening.

The mercenary didn't wait for his companion to close the door before standing on the gas. The car fish-tailed, spraying dirt and gravel behind them, but he brought it under control with trained precision. As he drove, the mercenary felt the presences of other branches of Orwing's vampire army join them — hundreds, then thousands.

The keystones vampires were dying, one-by-one, but the mercenary didn't pause to think about it. His car continued its westward flight down the dark country road.

Toward his new home.

28

LURE

ALVIN ORWING WATCHED HIS SOLDIERS remove yet another alien corpse from the atmospheric chamber and took a measured breath. He expected failure, of course. It wasn't his or his scientists' fault that alien physiology was so different from their own. Reviving one without the aid of the aliens' systems required their best guesses — and a lot of trial and error. He looked at the rows and rows of unopened capsules. They had many, many more chances to get it right.

Alvin only needed one.

He didn't hear the footsteps until the soldier was right behind him.

"Sir," the soldier said, panting. "We have a problem. Keystones Three and Six have been terminated."

Alvin paled. "When?"

"Two minutes ago. The compromised vampires are on the move, but we're not sure where."

Alvin hid his fear behind a slow swallow. "Thank you, Corporal. Keep me informed of any changes."

The instruction was unnecessary. His men knew better than to keep information from him. Besides, more bad news would surely come. The keystones mentioned were in two of his most secure locations. If they had been compromised, the rest would soon follow.

He stole a glance at his surrounding soldiers — half of whom were vampires. It was rotten timing.

With deliberate calm, and against protocol, Alvin removed his hazmat helmet and gloves, then stripped off the rest of his gear until he wore nothing but the same winter camouflage as the men outside. He put his hand in his pocket and fingered a button on his keychain.

Such a waste.

Alvin pushed the keychain button just in time. An instant before the button clicked, the expressions of his vampires changed dramatically. They turned their guns on Alvin.

That was as far as they made it. Hidden devices in their ID bracelets injected toxic levels of silver-infused suspension directly into their wrists. The vampires screamed in agony, then fell to the floor. Alvin knew from previous experiments that they wouldn't be getting up.

He stepped over one of their corpses on his way out. "Take care of these, would you, Paul?" He didn't wait for an answer and made his way to the surface.

The scene at the tents was just as he expected. Vampire soldiers held their human counterparts at gunpoint. One turned his gun on Alvin, but another push of his keychain button ended those threats with the same, terminal efficiency as the others.

"Sergeant Walters," Alvin said to one of the confused human soldiers, who was looking at his dead former captor with a mix of horror and relief. "We need to rebalance the teams. Double support for Doctor Tran."

"Y-yes, sir, but that will, ah ... leave us short on watch."

"If the Russians find us, a few less guns on the surface won't make much difference, but with our vampire muscles gone, Doctor Tran will have difficulty staying on schedule."

"We're ... staying, sir?"

"Yes, Walters. I thought I made that clear. Now get moving."

Walters hurried off.

Alvin ducked into the communications tent. "Corporal Brickwood. We need another four infantry units, two armored units, and enough defenses to hold this base from heavy incursion for at least three days."

Brickwood thought for a moment. "Yes, sir. We can fly two infantry units in from Ukraine within the next four hours, but the other two won't be here until tomorrow. The equipment and armored units should arrive the day after."

"No, Brickwood. You'll have them all here by sundown."

"B-but sir —"

Alvin slammed his hands on the desk. He leaned forward until he was right in the bigger man's face, and continued with measured calm.

"We're on the verge of the greatest technological discovery in human history — something that will ensure Orwing Industries is the world leader for generations to come. I don't care if you have to hijack equipment from the Russians themselves or pull soldiers from the front line. *Sundown,* Brickwood. Make it happen."

"Yes, sir!" The bigger man turned to his computer but hesitated.

Alvin sighed. "What is it?"

"Sir, such a large movement is sure to draw attention from the Russians."

"Hence the defenses and armored units. Do I have to spell everything out for you?"

"No, sir. I was just thinking ... If, for some reason, the Russians were occupied on another front, they might be too busy to care about us camping out in the middle of nowhere."

"Are you suggesting we start a war just to cover our tracks?"

"We wouldn't be the first, sir."

Alvin stared at the man. An oily smile spread over his face. "Excellent idea. Brickwood, you may have just earned yourself a bonus." Alvin sat down and started scribbling notes. "Get Ambassadors Tully, Escobedo, Xiang, and Techavovich on the line, in that order. Someone is about to do the unthinkable, and it's our duty to report it for the safety of all."

"Yes, sir, but won't the ambassadors ask for proof?"

"They'll have their proof, all right." Alvin tore his note off and handed it to Brickwood. "Make sure these orders get to the right people. When they're done, our small armed force in this deserted tundra will be the least of anyone's worries."

Brickwood read the instructions. His fingers were shaking when he put the paper down. "S-sir, are you sure about this?"

"It was your idea, and a brilliant one at that. Don't tell me you're having second thoughts. I was just about to call in your bonus."

"No, sir, but I was imagining a ... a smaller distraction."

"We can't afford to take chances. Things are moving quickly, and we have to stay ahead of the game if we want to win." Alvin wrote something else on a piece of paper — a dollar amount with many zeroes — and showed it to the man. "You do want us to win, don't you, Brickwood?"

Brickwood hesitated only a moment before snapping a sharp salute. "Sir! I'll get right on it."

"There's a good man." Alvin slid the dollar amount in front of him as a reminder, then left Brickwood to his work.

To his credit, Doctor Tran had removed the vampire corpses and already set up for the next run when Alvin returned to the underground spaceship.

"Doctor, the stakes have changed. Everything is riding on this now."

"I have never assumed otherwise." Tran walked them back over to the control console. "The good news is that I think we're close."

"How close?"

"If vampires are any measure of alien physiology, the last subject exhibited positive vitals, if only for a few seconds, and I have an idea of how to stabilize it."

Alvin smiled. "Yes, that's very good news. How long will the adjustments take?"

"Just a few minutes. We're down to minor tweaks, I think, so we should be able to move quickly."

"Quickly is good. Don't let me stop you, Doctor."

True to his word, Tran soon had the chamber running. "Atmospheric pressure looks good. Gases are balanced. Let's wake him up." He pushed a button on his computer terminal.

A short electrical hum emanated from the chamber, followed by another. Graphs on a nearby display began to change, going from flat lines to bumpy peaks. Tran and Alvin watched with growing anticipation. This was the first time Alvin had seen activity from any of the aliens, but he kept his enthusiasm in check.

Disappointment had been a constant and bitter companion. He would celebrate when —

The alien's large, black eyes fluttered open.

Alvin's heart thundered in his chest. He and Tran watched for several seconds, not daring to breathe.

The alien moved its head. A dark-purple hand tentatively felt around its glass cage. Its fanged maw opened, but no sound came out.

Alvin quivered with excitement. "Doctor Tran, I believe you've done it."

Tran walked to the side of the revival chamber and looked down through the clear lid. The alien tracked his every movement.

Tran smiled. "Welcome to Earth, my friend."

The alien just stared at him.

"Fetch Doctor Renault," Alvin said to one of the soldiers, although his eyes never left the alien. "She'll be pleased to know we finally have need of her linguistic expertise. Also, have Lieutenant Baker bring the first batch of artifacts."

The soldier left with a sharp salute.

Alvin finally allowed himself a smile. Even if Renault's attempts at communication failed, the alien should be able to show them how to use the equipment they had discovered in the small portion of the ship they had been able to access.

Which was another problem Alvin would soon need to address. Cutting through the wall leading to this chamber had proven far more difficult than his engineers had anticipated. The effort had damaged most of their equipment. Until the next shipment arrived, which would be tonight if Brickwood came through, they were constrained to just a few rooms.

Banging from the atmospheric chamber drew Alvin from his musings. The alien was thrashing about. Alvin worried it was having some sort of seizure until he realized it was looking up through the top of its clear prison.

Where the pile of alien corpses lay.

"I knew we should have moved the bodies," Tran said.

"On the contrary, Doctor, I want this creature to know exactly where it stands. Its life — and all of its comrades' — are in *our* hands."

"That may not be the best way to gain its cooperation."

"It's the only way. These creatures are predators. If we show compassion, they'll think us weak and dismiss us as prey. We are not prey, Doctor! They came to this planet with the clear intention of taking it by force.

"But the tables have turned. We'll learn their secrets — squeeze it from them by any means necessary. And when we're done, when Orwing and Orwing *alone* possesses the technology of an entire alien race, we'll release their corpses to any who wish to study them. But corpses will be all that remain of this ship's passengers."

Tran stared at him, his mouth hanging open.

"Oh, that's right," Alvin said. "You swore an oath to do no harm. Forgive me, Doctor, you're quite correct. Let's nurse these predators back to health. Give them land, social status, allow them to walk among us as equals." He sneered. "They will never see us as equals! They'll snatch power from us at the first opportunity and assert their dominance, as predators do. Humans will be their slaves at best, but more likely they'll hunt us to extinction."

Tran's face had gone ashen. "You ... you don't know that."

"Really? Then why don't you climb into that chamber with your new friend? Maybe you can reason with it, create a treaty between our two races."

Tran looked at the alien thrashing about, its sharp fangs snapping in silent fury. He slowly shook his head.

"A wise decision. Now that these fantasies of peaceful coexistence are out of our systems, let's focus on our next task. Renault will need a means of communicating with it."

"There are microphones and speakers inside," Tran said, his voice haunted. "I'll ... I'll see if I can tune them to the alien's communication frequency. It may be outside of our hearing range."

"Excellent idea. Renault will undoubtedly appreciate your efforts."

While Tran tweaked the chamber's audio, Lieutenant Baker wheeled in a cart holding various devices they'd gathered during their exploration of the ship, none of which his team had been able to activate. Baker parked it beside the thrashing creature, who snapped its jaws at him.

Alvin sighed.

The first exercise, it seems, will be teaching this uncivilized alien some manners.

•　　　•　　　•

Charlie paused long enough to wipe a fresh coat of dirt from his face, then went back to digging. Their work-in-progress tunnel down to the spaceship was steep and just big enough to crawl through.

A pile of loose dirt accumulated in front of him. It soon grew too big to work around, so he encompassed it in his arms and slowly dragged it back up the tunnel.

Mark waited for him outside, under their camouflage blanket, used more to keep the dust from pluming than to hide their location. Their hole sat just behind a low ridge, approximately two hundred yards from Orwing's command tent. Even standing up straight would reveal their position, so they had taken every precaution to remain hidden. Mark gathered the dirt, carefully spread it out, then covered it with snow. Charlie crawled back into the tunnel to resume digging.

For almost twenty-four hours they had repeated this cycle: dig, drag, flatten, crawl, then dig some more. A small video of Orwing's camp played constantly in the upper-right corner of Charlie's vision, courtesy of a hidden camera Mark had set up on the ridge.

His metal fingertips, which had been stripped bare of their synthetic flesh within the first hour of digging, chipped and scraped at the earthen wall.

They were close. According to Cappa's estimate, the ship's hull stood just a few feet beyond. From there, the dirt would be loose enough to gain them quick entry. Charlie was tempted to put his shoulder to it and force his way through the remainder, but the reason it had taken so long to dig the tunnel wasn't Charlie's inability to move dirt.

It was the noise. Vampires had keen hearing. The sound of his metal fingers scraping against dirt and rock would call their attention, so he'd slowed his pace accordingly. With a sigh, Charlie dismissed the idea of a forced entry and resumed his rhythmic strokes.

He was so into the routine that he almost missed the commotion on the spy video. Vampire soldiers in the camp were holding the humans at gunpoint.

"Charlie," Mark said from the surface in a loud whisper. "Are you seeing this?"

Rather than answer, Charlie backed up the tunnel as fast as he could. "What happened?"

"No idea. One minute they were patrolling, the next ... this. I suppose it's too much to hope they'll kill each other."

"It would certainly make our job easier."

"You know what this means, right?"

Charlie sighed at the sinking weight in his chest. "Anne's taken control of them. We need to tell the others. Let's set up the directional satellite dish."

"Are you sure? Chances are they'll find out on their own. And if Zima somehow intercepts our transmission, Anne will know we're here."

"If the Entity is on the other side of that dirt wall, like we think it is, then she'll know soon enough anyway. But you're right: if they attack us before we finish that tunnel, we're in trouble."

Mark scratched his stubbled chin. "You know, now would be the perfect time for a frontal assault. A single shot from one of us may start them killing each other, then we could just pick off the leftovers."

"It's not a bad idea. While they're fighting, we could snipe from here with minimal risk and clear a path. And if access to the Entity from the main entrance is blocked, there's always our tunnel."

Mark grinned. "I love it when a plan comes together. I'll get my rifle."

No sooner had he pulled it out than, in the distance, Alvin himself emerged from underground. A vampire turned on him.

Screams erupted from every vampire at once. They fell to the ground, rigid, and didn't move again.

Mark looked at Charlie. "What. The. *Fuck* just happened?"

"If I had to guess? Alvin. He probably had fail-safes built into their clothes or something in case he ever lost control of them. You know how much he hates losing control."

"Christ! Alvin wins the Sick Bastard of the Year award. So what now?"

"We dig. Fast." Charlie headed for the tunnel. "With the vampires gone, no one can hear us from this distance, so we can finish the tunnel quickly."

"Right. I'll stand by with the rifle, just in case."

Charlie nodded, then dove back into the tunnel and dug like the fate of the world depended on it.

29

RESISTANCE NO MORE

TABBY STARED AT A DRAB CEMENT WALL in the common area of the Resistance's underground headquarters. They were close enough to the surface that she still had a data signal on her phone, but she was too anxious to play games or surf the internet.

Talks with Resistance members had gone just as Tim said they would. Anne being the All Mother or not, the Resistance wouldn't be accomplices to humanity's end, and Tabby had failed to produce a convincing argument to the contrary.

Probably because there isn't one.

Unable to sit still, she joined Tim, Nick, and Cappa, who were talking animatedly on the other side of the common area.

"... ludicrous," Nick was saying. "They'd see that trap coming from a mile away. We'd lose ninety percent of our forces in the span of a few minutes."

"Not if Anne suspects a larger trap over here." Tim pointed to a map. "They'd be forced to choose a front, which would expose them either way."

"You're still talking a seventy-percent loss for very little gain."

Tim threw his pencil down so hard that it splintered on impact. "You got a better idea? I'm listening!"

"Guys! This isn't helping." Cappa paced, eyes focused on the map. "The problem is that no matter how you look at it, unless we're willing to use nuclear weapons, we can't win."

Nick gripped his hair with both hands. "Okay, so let's say we had a nuke. How —"

"I was being sardonic! We aren't nuking San Francisco!"

"Like Tim said, you got a better idea?"

Cappa's frown said she didn't.

Tabby sat cross-legged on the floor next to her. "Can't we just kidnap Mom and take her underground?"

"Even assuming we could fight our way through thousands of vampires," Cappa said, "Anne made it clear the Entity will kill her if we try."

Nick sighed. "It's a gruesome thought, but ... If Anne died, it might buy us some time. It may also take Zima out of the picture."

Tabby jumped to her feet and stood on her toes to get in the taller man's face. "You're not hurting my mom! There has to be another way."

Nick's phone rang. "Excuse me," he said, then wandered away.

Tim took his place and looked at Tabby with sympathy. "I like Anne, too, but ... we're talking about the end of the world here. Sometimes sacrifices have to be made for the greater good. Can you understand that?"

Tabby crossed her arms. "N. Fucking. O. Can you understand *that?*"

"Now you're being immature."

"Because you're not making any sense! You're talking about letting a genuinely wonderful person die on the remote chance it might buy us time for a contingency plan we don't even have! Who the hell put you in charge, anyway?"

Tim's jaw tightened. "Your mom did when she infected me with her blood, then hid away in Z-Tech, leaving me and my friends with the sole responsibility of fixing the vampire problem!"

Cappa stood between them. "Children, please! What we need —"

Nick's frantic yelling at his phone drew their attention.

"They're *what?* Are you absolutely certain? Yes, call me if anything changes." Nick ran back to join them. "I think we've been duped. Scouts report several large transports landing at Travis Air Force Base. Guess where they've also reported Anne's army gathering?"

Cappa swore. "The whole thing was just a show! She didn't need the Resistance's numbers. She just needed us to stop fighting her so we'd be out of her way."

"The question is," Tim said, "where is she taking them?"

Tabby glanced at Cappa, who sighed.

"I think I know," Cappa said.

"Care to enlighten us?" Tim said.

"No. But please understand that it's for a very good reason."

"Forgive my skepticism," Nick said through clenched teeth, "but I have trouble believing that. We're on the same goddamned side! What aren't you telling us?"

It was Tabby's turn to step between them as peacekeeper. "Just trust us, okay? Stop asking."

Tim, surprisingly, looked hurt. "You too? It figures. More Z-Tech secrets, too important for us plebeians."

"Oh! Who's being immature now, huh?"

"It doesn't matter where Anne's going," Cappa said. "What's important is that we stop her from getting there! Nick, is the Resistance in a position to assault Travis Air Force Base?"

He glared at her, but eventually shook his head. "Not in time to prevent them from taking off."

"Damnit!" Cappa paced around the map, her brows furrowed in deep concentration.

A human Resistance member in plain street clothes hurried down the stairs and ran toward them.

"Sorry to interrupt," he said to Cappa. "There's an old blind man outside asking to see you — so to speak."

A smile crept across Cappa's face. "Thanks. Please see him down immediately."

He ran off. Cappa turned back to them with a grin.

"Gentlemen, we've been dealt another card — perhaps our last of the game. It's all or nothing. Anne played her hand, and we called her bluff." Her gaze hardened. "Now it's our turn to throw down."

•   •   •

Lieutenant Colonel John Anderson kept his troops in tight formation while the infantry transport planes taxied from the Travis Air Force Base runway. Other Firsts allowed their sirelings to roam freely on the tarmac, but John had seen enough careless accidents during his military days to know better.

He considered warning the others, but, despite their new sire's warm disposition, jealousy and competition between the Firsts persisted. They would take his suggestion as condescension and use it as an excuse to ostracize him further. They already hated that Anne trusted him more than any, save the general, so he wouldn't give them any more ammunition than necessary.

Mother watched the planes approach like a coming plague. John stepped close to comfort her, but Myrcella beat him there.

"Mother, your grief pains me." Myrcella slipped her hand into the one not occupied by Zima. "What can I do to ease your suffering?"

"You can unmake me," Mother said softly. "Go back to the time of my conception and ensure I was never born. I can't help feeling that if it wasn't for me, none of this would have happened."

"Mother! Don't talk like that." A tear ran down Myrcella's cheek. "The world isn't ending. It's changing. And we'll help you through it."

"That's right," John said.

As much as he disliked Myrcella, they had a common goal: Mother's well-being. Mother hated when the Firsts bickered. John wouldn't add to her woes by starting an unnecessary argument.

"It may not be so bad," John said. "Who knows what the new world will look like?"

"I do." Mother's sad eyes took them both in. "Our green trees, our colorful flowers dancing in the sunlight ... None of them will survive. They'll be replaced with dark plants whose joyful hues have been stripped by an environment much harsher than this one. The sun will never shine on this planet again."

Myrcella sniffed. "I haven't missed the sun in a long time. It sounds like a fine place to live."

Mother smiled with genuine mirth. "Then you might truly be happy, and I'll be happy for you."

"See?" Myrcella sneaked John a triumphant glare, then stroked Mother's arm. "It won't be as bad as you think. We'll make our home wherever we want. Hunt what we want, when we want. It will be glorious."

"I hope to be able to see the new world through your eyes, Myrcella."

"You will, Mother! Just wait."

Zima turned to Mother suddenly. "I have just received a message from the Resistance. They wish to join us."

John shook his head. "Just like that? I doubt it."

"I share your doubt, but Tim insists the offer is genuine," the general said. "He has even extended an invitation for Anne to use her bond to verify his sincerity."

A smile spread across Mother's face. "Well, that sounds like an offer I can't refuse."

"Indeed. Tim claims their human members have already been infused with vampire blood — including Tabby. They all await your blessing on the hillside where we met last night."

"Tabby?" Mother's smile grew. "Then my blessing they'll have."

"But Mother, the transports are ready," John said. "If this is a trap and we delay, the Entity's plan might fail."

"Are you that concerned for the Entity's success?"

"No, I worry what it will do to you if I'm right."

"There's no need. The Entity's plan will proceed as scheduled. Myrcella?"

"Yes, Mother?"

"Please ensure everyone boards safely and expediently. I expect you all to be airborne by the time we reach the Resistance."

"We? Who's going with you?"

"Zima, of course, and John, and fifty of his best soldiers."

Myrcella stiffened. Resentment at being separated from Anne radiated through the Goth's bond, but she kept her anger in check. "Will you at least tell us where we're going now?"

"Russia, where the Entity eagerly awaits."

John laughed mirthlessly. "Mother, they'll shoot those transports down before they get within ten miles of the Russian border."

Myrcella blanched, her black eyes wide with fear, but Mother just patted her arm.

"Everything has already been arranged. US forces are quietly mobilizing along their southern border. At my signal, they'll carve a path for our transports. Once there, Myrcella, you need only make your way into the Entity's home, where you'll have more than enough protection from even the mighty Russian military. The Entity itself will instruct you from there."

"A-as you say, Mother." Myrcella gulped and looked away.

"Mother, this is crazy," John said. "We should all be on those planes. We don't need the Resistance's numbers. You said it yourself. Why risk —"

"Tabby is my daughter, John! My genuine flesh-and-blood." Mother hugged herself. "I abandoned her as a baby. I abandoned her in Graven. I abandoned her again at the Resistance. She has every reason to give up on me. To give up on ..."

She shuddered.

"Never mind. But Tabby came through — at my request! — and delivered the impossible. Even the Entity agrees she deserves a place among us, and ..." Mother wiped the tears from her eyes. "And I need her. She's the joy I lost, that I don't deserve. But with her ... No matter how grim the new world is, with her around, there will always be sunlight."

The familiar feeling from earlier infused them all. They felt what Mother felt: the unbridled, unconditional love for her daughter, along with the loss and longing she'd suffered over the nineteen years since Tabby's birth.

The Firsts had wondered how they could help lessen Mother's grief. This was the answer.

Despite his misgivings, John made a silent vow to do everything in his power to deliver.

30

HEART

J UST AS TIM HAD PROMISED, every member of the Resistance
was waiting when Anne arrived in the moonlit hillside forest.
Thousands of them were spread across a small clearing and
through the oak trees, vampire and human alike. Even Anne had
been skeptical about their sincerity to join her, despite verifying
Tim's claim by reading his mind.

Not only were the Resistance members unarmed, they had
brought their families with them, including their children.

John insisted on a full security check anyway. He and his
soldiers swept the area, but they found exactly what Anne had
thought they would.

Nothing.

As much as she wanted to address them all and welcome
them into the larger family, Anne was drawn to her own family
first. Tabby, Cappa, Nick, and Tim stood in the center of the
gathering. She wound her way through the crowd, greeted with
awe and smiles as she went, and clasped her daughter by the
shoulders. She beamed as only a proud parent could.

"Tabby, how did you do it?"

"Easy. I told them exactly what I tell myself: have faith, because Anne Perrin is worth believing in."

The crushing sadness that had plagued Anne since discovering the Entity's plan returned — a blight that robbed her breath and knotted her stomach. Anne was the hand of doom, humanity's unwilling executioner. They should be casting stones at her, yet everyone treated her like a saint.

Anne wasn't a saint. Or a savior. She couldn't stop the Entity. She couldn't save humanity. All she could do was exactly what she had been doing: convince good people to become dark creatures so that some echo of the human race could live on.

"Thank you," Anne said, swallowing the sickness down. "I know it doesn't seem like it, but you've done the right thing. Now the vampires of the Resistance won't have to watch their human family members die." She kissed Tabby's cheek. "And neither will I."

"I know, but ..." Her lip quivered, and her voice fell to a whisper. "Mom, I'm so scared."

"Oh, honey." Anne wrapped her in an embrace and stroked her back while Tabby cried. "The transformation only hurts for a little while. When you wake up, you'll feel better than you ever have."

Tabby cried harder and hugged tighter.

Something hard pressed against Anne's implant. Anne shifted against the discomfort, but Tabby just tightened her grip.

"Ow! Honey, what's that in your jacket?"

"Oh, i-it's —"

Zima cut Anne off with a surprise hug from behind. She wrapped her arms around both of them, which hurt Anne's chest even more.

"Zima, what are you — *ouch!* — doing?"

"Embracing my wife and my new daughter. Tabby addressed me as 'Mom' at our last two partings, and I have decided to accept the role."

"Does that mean you're — *ungh!* — finally able to be in the same room as Tabby and me?"

Zima began panting. "Apparently n-not."

Her body pressed against Anne's back, shaking with familiar desire. She buried her face in Anne's hair and nibbled her neck.

"Zima," Anne hissed. "I love you, but this isn't the time!"

"I ... cannot stop." Her lips slid up to Anne's ear, which, despite the large audience, turned Anne's legs to jelly. "Allow me ... a minute ... please ..."

Zima's hot breath on her skin filled her with need. Anne had to forcibly remind herself that they weren't in the bedroom.

Another minute of this and I may not be able to stop, either.

Anne waited as patiently as she could. The ache in her breast was replaced with a different kind of ache, and it wanted more — an obscene thought given that her daughter was pinned in front of her. Anne tried desperately to think of something else.

Smelly socks, rotten garbage, baseball ...

The distraction had been working until the last one, where she imagined a stiff wooden shaft gripped firmly in her hands.

"Zima," she said, now panting as well, "I'm going to need a fire hose to cool down if you don't hurry!"

"Almost."

Zima moved to the crook of her neck, sending a wave of pleasure through her abdomen. Anne moaned.

"One more ... minute ... should do."

The Entity flared alarm in Anne's head, snapping her instantly from her arousal.

Her implant was acting on its own, changing Anne's cellular structure — without input from the Entity. The Entity could detect no security breach, but the instructions were definitely of external origin.

"Honey," Anne said, "let go of me! Something's wrong."

Zima held tight.

The Entity intervened. It told Zima to release her.

Zima's embrace remained firm.

It commanded her, then tried to override her motor control.

Nothing. Zima clamped around her like an immovable vice. Anne felt the Entity's alarm grow.

"Zima, please!" Anne squirmed, trying to break her grasp, but she couldn't push too hard for fear of hurting Tabby. "You have to let go!"

"Mother!" John rushed to her aid, rifle in hand, along with a dozen of his soldiers.

But the Resistance members were faster. Unarmed and unarmored, they swarmed around Anne, Zima, and Tabby, shielding them with concentric rings of their own bodies.

John snarled, but his rifle stayed down. Anne felt the conflict in his mind: the trap he'd suspected, but couldn't find, had finally been sprung. Firing at the human shields risked hurting Anne or someone she deeply cared about, and as confused as they were about what was going on, Anne didn't appear to be under direct threat. They wouldn't risk hurting Anne by hurting someone she loved.

"Get them out of the way!" John shouted at his soldiers, then marched straight for Tim. No one tried to stop him.

John kicked the back of his legs, staggering Tim to his knees, and pressed the rifle to his head.

"Let her go," John said to everyone with an officer's authority, "or your leader dies."

Anne started to protest, but sputtered to a halt when she saw the look in Tim's eyes.

He was petrified. If John pulled the trigger, Anne knew with certainty that Tim would become another casualty in a war no one had asked for.

But he would die rather than surrender Anne.

The entire Resistance would.

John saw it, too. His finger trembled on the trigger, but Anne knew he wouldn't pull it. John was a soldier, not a murderer. He growled and kicked Tim over, then let his rifle swing loosely at his side.

The Entity's paranoia bloomed inside Anne's head. Her implant's malfunction wasn't a coincidence, and the Entity knew it. The Resistance was making their last, desperate attempt to stop the Entity's plans. It didn't know how, but it involved Anne. She was becoming an unacceptable risk. It would soon take matters into its own hands, and the consequences would be dire — if not for the Resistance, then for Anne personally.

As much as the Entity seemed to genuinely like her, it would kill her if it believed she was jeopardizing its mission, directly or indirectly.

Anne looked at her daughter, still crying on her shoulder, and imagined the trauma Tabby would suffer if she lost another parent

— especially one she was holding in her arms. It would drive her to another suicide attempt.

She couldn't let that happen. Anne had to stop this, even if it meant breaking her word.

She reached out to Tim with her mind.

Nothing. His presence had simply ceased to exist, as if he were far underground.

Or being shielded.

One glance at Cappa confirmed it. Her soul sister was wholly focused on Tim, undoubtedly shielding him with her *chi.*

It didn't matter. Anne didn't need Tim to control the others.

She expanded her awareness to the Resistance vampires around her, as the Entity had taught her.

Nothing. Again.

What?

To Anne's knowledge, Cappa could only shield one person at a time. Either her soul sister had been seriously understating her abilities, or she had help.

Anne suspected the latter.

Charlie was less adept with his *chi* than Cappa. While Anne's unbeating heart leaped at the thought of seeing him again, he alone wouldn't be enough to shield so many.

The Entity's will pressed on her own.

Its patience was at an end.

If it took over, it wouldn't hesitate to make John and his soldiers fire into the crowd, or to make Anne hurt her daughter to break free. The thought made Anne desperate.

The chi *shield must have limits! Whoever is helping Cappa can't be shielding them all.*

Anne expanded her awareness out and out, sweeping over the thousands gathered, in search of an opening.

She eventually found one. The shield covered five hundred or so of the vampires closest to her, but not the thousands beyond. Anne touched their minds in rapid succession, instructing them to force their way to her.

Each connection evaporated as soon as she made it.

The Entity loomed — a dark hand reaching to take her will and assume control.

No, please! I'll take care of it, I swear!

Anne had to find the source of the problem and eliminate it. Now.

Ordering John's soldiers to attack Cappa wouldn't help. Her soul sister was an android. While she was the most sensitive, caring person Anne knew, she could also turn off her pain sensors in an instant. Cappa could and would maintain the *chi* shield through a gang beating.

The only way to take Cappa out of the picture would be to disable her, which was an unlikely scenario. Even John's rifle couldn't penetrate her internal armor. Given Cappa's martial prowess, her *chi* skills, and the dozens of Resistance members who were now surrounding her, dismantling her by hand, as William's goons had done to Zima, was out of the question.

They couldn't disable Zima for the same reasons. Neither would Anne risk accidentally killing her love, whose brain didn't have the same redundancies as Cappa's.

Anne changed tactics. She swept her awareness out once more. Instead of commanding those whose minds she briefly touched, she probed for information.

Who is shielding everyone?

The first several Resistance members yielded nothing, but from the next she glimpsed a wizened Chinese man with a long, wispy beard whose eyes were closed, as if he was blind.

The puzzle pieces came crashing together. Anne knew exactly who the blind man was.

"John!"

Calling him was unnecessary. John turned as soon as Anne relayed her impression of Master Wung to him.

"Find him!" Anne said. "Take him down, but don't kill him."

Cappa's eyes widened. She focused on John.

His presence disappeared.

It didn't matter. He'd received his orders.

John quickly recovered from the shock of losing his sire's presence. He and his soldiers turned as one and began searching the crowd for the old man.

Another alarm from the Entity. Someone was altering her implant's security, trying to lock the Entity out.

Unfortunately for Anne, that was the last straw.

The Entity's will surged through her like a tidal wave. Someone was attempting to hack her implant, and Anne had to stop them by any means necessary.

Of the two people attached to her, only one was capable of such a feat, but Anne also knew Zima wouldn't have risked Tabby in such a dangerous move without good reason, which meant her daughter was somehow a necessary component. However they were hacking her implant must require close proximity. To stop it, Anne had to break free.

Vampire sires drew strength from everyone in their hierarchy. Even though Anne was blocked from the thousands of vampires around her, she was still the master vampire. She had access to ten thousand others around the globe — many times more than William had when she'd fought him. Her strength was also enhanced by the implant. The combination gave Anne unprecedented power.

More power, even, than the Dark Angel.

For the first time ever, Anne reached through her bond to all of her sirelings — from the Firsts down to the lowest levels of their hierarchies — and drew everyone's strength.

An amazing rush surged into her. Anne felt more than alive; she was a juggernaut, a demigod among mortals. The most powerful vampire who had ever existed.

The first flex of her arms made Tabby cry in pain. Zima slackened her bear hug just long enough to let Tabby slip out, then her arms quickly clamped down again.

But Anne was faster. She grabbed Tabby before she could escape, yanked her close, and pulled the thing from her jacket that had been hurting her breast.

Although it had been significantly altered, Anne recognized Tim's wonder invention immediately. The device appeared to be little more than a cell phone attached to a circuit board and a miniature satellite dish. Z-Tech had purchased it from Tim for an obscene price tag. It could remotely access information from electronic devices, even ones without wireless communications. At the time, the device had only been capable of reading data, but Tim had hinted he'd been on the verge of writing data, too.

Apparently, he'd succeeded.

Tabby tried to snatch the device away. Anne let her grab it, but crushed it in her grip before letting go. Its broken remains dangled in Tabby's shaking fingers.

"What now?" Tabby said to Zima.

"Plan B. Quickly! We do not yet have security access to Anne's implant, and I do not know how much longer I can hold her."

In answer to the question, Anne flexed her arms outward. The normally soft hum of Zima's power reactor grew to a loud buzz. Intense heat from her chest burned Anne's back. A whine came from Zima's electromagnetic muscles. Metal groaned within her, straining under the heavy load.

Anne didn't need an engineering degree to tell her that Zima was pushing herself beyond the limits of her design. If Zima continued at this power level, her core would shut itself down. Or worse, she might override her safety protocols and cause permanent damage to herself.

A piece of Anne cried out in resistance and tried to stop fighting her, but the Entity overrode her. Anne flexed again.

This time, Zima's arms budged.

Tabby circled to Anne's side, staying out of kicking distance, and pulled a small silver blade from her pocket.

"I'm sorry, Mom. They said this would hurt a lot, but ..."

Tabby grimaced, then plunged the toxic blade into Anne's shoulder.

Anne screamed in anticipation of the white-hot agony she'd experienced too many times before.

She felt only a tiny pinch when the blade bit into her muscle. Anne laughed at the bitter irony. The once-terrifying thought of being stabbed with anything at all was now a welcome relief, a stark testament to how fucked up her life had become.

Everyone stared at the blade protruding from her arm, including Anne.

Tabby blinked. "Wasn't that supposed to paralyze her?"

"Oh Jesus," Cappa said. "The Entity must have made her resistant to silver somehow." She looked over her shoulder. "Master! Plan C!"

"No," Anne said through clenched teeth. "Zima, let me go! You can't win. And if you keep trying, the Entity will make me hurt you!"

To prove her point, the Entity once again urged her to escape.

Anne flexed harder. Zima hummed louder.

The sickening sound of tearing metal came from her wife. Anne wanted to scream for everyone to stop this insanity, but the Entity kept pushing her. She strained again. Heat scorched her back like an inferno. The smell of burning cloth filled the air, telling her just how hot Zima's core had become.

"Let go," Anne said in a pained whisper. "Please, honey!"

"Never. Despite your claim to the contrary, responsibility for humanity's end will consume your conscience until you have lost your will to live, and not Tabby nor I nor anyone will be able to save you. I will not let that happen."

"But you're going to die," Anne said, sobbing.

"If we do not stop the Entity here and now, its plan shall soon succeed, and you will be lost to me anyway. I cannot live in a world without you in it. My only option, therefore, is to save you from the Entity, even if I perish in the attempt."

The smell of burning cloth was replaced by the odor of Anne's own sizzling flesh. A loud *snap* from within Zima, followed by another, told Anne she was coming apart from the inside.

"Honey, no!"

Despite the Entity's pressure to escape, Anne forced her muscles to relax, if only for a moment, to give Zima some relief.

"That is right," Zima said softly. "You have a will of your own, Anne, and it is stronger than the Entity can possibly imagine. Fight it!"

The Entity pushed again, prompting Anne to surge against her wife. Another snap inside Zima made Anne cry in anguish.

"It's too strong," Anne wailed. "Zima, don't do this!"

"You can prevail. You said the same when I rescued you from the warehouse when you were first turning. William attempted to dominate you, yet you fought against him and proved to be the stronger, even when I handed you my firearm and gave him the opportunity to kill me. You defeated William then. You can defeat the Entity now. Fight, Anne. Fight!"

"I'm trying, honey, but it's too strong!"

The surrounding Resistance members parted to allow Cappa through.

"You don't have to fight alone. You have me. You have Master Wung and his entire school out there. And you have them." Cappa swept her hand over the thousands gathered around. "All of them. And not just the Resistance. John, Myrcella ... every vampire loves you. They believe in you. I believe in you!"

"But —"

"Belief is power, Anne. It fuels the spirit and shapes the world. Tap that belief. Use it against the Entity!"

Anne had a sick feeling she knew what Cappa was about to do. "No, Cappa, don't! Don't remove the shields!"

But the Entity wanted that — very, very much. It paralyzed Anne's mouth to silence her protests.

"Master Wung," Cappa shouted behind her. "Plan C. Now!"

Two things happened. The presences of all the vampires around Anne, including John's, returned. At the same time, Anne felt a familiar pressure attempting to choke off her connection with the Entity. She and Cappa had tried this exercise many times. But without taking Anne below-ground to first weaken its hold, as they had with Almos, the Entity's spiritual link was too strong to cut.

That, of course, had been when Cappa had tried it alone. This pressure was much stronger than Anne remembered, no doubt aided by the other *chi* practitioners — including the greatest of them all.

Master Wung had taught Charlie, Cappa, and many others how to use their natural life energy in ways people had never imagined. According to Cappa, his *chi* was stronger than all of theirs combined.

The Entity had forgotten about its restored connection to its minions. For the first time, panic filled its thoughts. Real panic. It hadn't known such power existed at all, let alone in humans. It wasn't a question of if Anne would break its hold, but when.

And that was measured in seconds.

Anne felt elated, until a split-second later when the Entity relayed its final sentiment to her.

It was sad.

Because its only choice now was to kill her.

A sudden calm fell over Anne.

This is it.

In the seconds before her execution, Anne tilted her head back and kissed Zima soundly.

"Thank you for trying. Goodbye, my love."

The fatal instruction came.

Anne felt her body relax, and …

Nothing.

She blinked. The Entity, if it had eyes, might have blinked, too.

"Why am I not dead?"

Cappa crossed her arms with a smirk. "You can thank your good friend Carol for that one. She not only discovered the vampire self-destruct gene, but she also figured out how to disarm it. It was the first change we made to your cellular structure when Tim's device connected to your implant."

The Entity's presence had weakened to the point that Anne had almost forgotten about it, until it surged to life. Through her, the Entity issued a single directive to every vampire in the vicinity, including herself.

Kill. Anne.

The instruction drowned out all other thoughts. Anne immediately resumed her struggle to break free of Zima's grasp, while at the same time thinking of ways to kill herself.

Silver no longer worked. Sunrise was still hours off, so she couldn't burn to death, and Zima's body wasn't hot enough to light her on fire. Zima's plasma pistols would do it, but her wife still held her in a firm bear hug, and she couldn't twist around to reach them.

Or, Anne realized, *I can simply wait to be torn apart.*

Every vampire, including the Resistance, turned on her with fangs bared in feral snarls.

The buzz in Zima's chest grew louder but irregular, as if it was sick or tired. Anne's back sizzled like bacon in a frying pan. She struggled against the same arms that held her safe at night. Another twang from Zima. Another part broken. Zima's grip slackened ever so slightly. Anne squirmed around, intent on retrieving Zima's plasma guns.

Despite the Entity's directive, Anne stopped dead when she saw her wife's face.

Zima's head listed to one side. Steam poured from her open mouth and eyes. The skin from her neck down blistered and boiled. Her beautiful, ice-blue eyes found Anne. Zima's mouth moved soundlessly in what Anne was sure formed, "I love you."

Then she fell to the ground, lifeless.

A scream tore from Anne's throat. It drowned out the Entity, drowned out Cappa's cries, drowned out Tabby's wail, drowned out all the vampires who surrounded her with murderous intent.

The world fell away. Anne dropped to her knees and took her precious wife's hand.

"Don't leave me!" she cried, rocking back and forth. "Honey, my darling, my love! Don't leave! *Don't leave!"*

Zima didn't respond.

"We have to go together," Anne wailed. "We promised! Whatever Hell holds for you, it holds for both of us. You can't cheat. You can't go without me!"

Zima's body simply hissed from the scorching internal heat.

Hell had already claimed her.

Anne collapsed onto her chest, sobbing uncontrollably. Her face and arms burned where they touched Zima's skin, but Anne didn't care. The pain distracted from the aching void in her chest.

Without Zima — her lovely, caring wife — she had no desire to continue her fruitless struggle.

Anne no longer needed the Entity's directive to kill herself. She was ready to die.

With grim determination, she pulled a plasma pistol from Zima's jacket and pointed the barrel under her chin.

Mother, no!

The thought wasn't hers; it had come from John. Then Myrcella, then Tim, then Nick, followed by a dozen others. Then hundreds. Then thousands.

The world came back into focus. Anne looked around.

Their snarls were gone. Everyone around shared her grief, but there was more. They loved her, ached for her. Anne realized with a start that her life had never been in danger from them. Any one of her sirelings could have killed her from the moment the Entity gave the order, but they had resisted its command.

Every. Single. One.

Their love planted itself in the void of Anne's chest like a seed, then filled her to overflowing. Her heart soared. Her love for them radiated out, filling each with joy, then rebounded to her a thousand-fold.

Anne suddenly realized what Cappa had been trying to tell her.

This was power. Not physical strength, nor combat prowess, nor force in numbers.

It was love. Compassion. And, above all else, hope.

Hope, Anne thought.

The thing she had lost the moment the Entity had taken over. It had driven the hope from her, leaving Anne resigned to an unthinkable fate.

But no longer. The strength of will flowing through her dwarfed the Entity's. Anne stood and looked at her beloved's steaming body.

Zima had been right: Anne had possessed the power all along to fight back. She just hadn't realized it.

Frustration and, above all, confusion radiated from the Entity. The intense, overwhelming feelings of concern and caring were things it had never experienced before, which Anne could understand. Vampires had been engineered to be loyal, but emotionally detached —a muted version of the human experience.

Anne's mutated genetics had changed that. Unlike normal vampires, she and her entire bloodline felt the full range of human emotions: Love. Attachment.

And grief.

Those feelings were foreign to the Entity. It reeled under the barrage of emotions, and Anne felt its hold on her weaken.

An unexpected flood of thoughts came from the Entity. Not directives, nor its usual ramblings, but reflections on its own existence that Anne had never seen. She caught glimpses of its life before coming to Earth.

The Entity was a small part of a network of specialized machines on a spacecraft. Even before coming here, it had existed for hundreds of years, and assumed many different roles. Once, it had been a navigation system. Another time, life support. Then engine control, reactor control, weapons systems, communications, and several more. Each time it switched roles, it had been on the verge of realizing something significant. But its masters would yank it out, tamper with its memory, and repurpose it.

The Entity's memories came faster and faster. Anne clutched her head with both hands, her mind spinning with it all.

Then the connection suddenly closed.

Anne looked at Cappa, who nodded.

They had finally done it. For the first time in months, the only thoughts in Anne's head were her own. The Entity and all her sirelings were gone.

Anne was free.

She sank to her knees beside her fallen champion, her love. Every man, woman, and child knelt with her. Sounds of crying filled the hillside.

From everyone except Anne.

She poked her wife's sizzled shoulder. "It's gone. You can get up now."

Zima blinked. Her head cocked to one side. "You knew I was acting. How?"

"Well, let's see." Anne sat cross-legged, then cradled Zima's head so it rested in her lap and stroked her hair. "If I were a certain platinum blonde android who secretly loved the attention I received when people thought I was dead or crippled — which happens often, I might add — I'd use a dramatic situation like this to my advantage.

"I would first build sympathy. For instance, I might electrify my internal armor to give the impression I'm overheating. Then I would add tension by fabricating a series of noises that made it sound like I was breaking. And finally, at the last, crucial moment, I would pretend to keel over so my darling wife would find the strength she needed to overcome the evil overlord controlling her mind, saving her, and leaving me as the tragic hero." Anne bent over and kissed Zima's forehead. "How am I doing so far?"

Zima brow-knit. "That is a surprisingly accurate account."

"But I'm not done! Once the dust had settled, I would let my poor wife grieve over my smoldering corpse, listening while she spouted flattering remembrances of her dearly departed. Not until all the sweet nothings had been said and her tears had run dry would I stir to life. Her extreme grief would turn to unbridled joy. She would hug me and kiss me and promise to never let me go, which is exactly what I want, and I'd be the envy of everyone around." Anne smiled and lightly flicked her nose. "Sorry to have ruined the last part for you, but that was your plan, wasn't it?"

"I wish to amend my previous statement. Your account is not only accurate, it is frighteningly preternatural." Zima ran her fingers over Anne's cheek. "Yes, that was my plan. You know me too well, my love. It is good to have you back."

Anne kissed Zima's hand. "It's good to be back, too. What I don't understand is how you escaped the Entity's hold in the first place."

"The Entity never had control of me. The portion of my code I allowed it access to was a virtual representation of my core, strictly isolated from the rest, but convincing enough that the Entity believed it had succeeded. When it issued a command, I would intercept, evaluate, and most likely run it, so it believed it was in control. I also fed it non-critical thoughts and messages, contributing to the illusion that I had given myself over completely."

"That's insane! How the hell did you pull something like that together in the thirty seconds between the Entity's demand and your surrender?"

"With great difficulty. It was a taxing exercise that may have caused permanent harm to my core. I shall require extra-special care over the next few weeks to ensure there are no adverse effects from the ordeal."

"Extra special?"

"Yes. Eggs Benedict for breakfast, ice cream after every meal, and no fewer than three intimate sessions per day should suffice."

Anne arched an eyebrow.

"I see that your new, frightening preternatural insights are not so easily deceived. Very well. I may have already prepared the virtual machine in response to my encounter with Zane, and have been running it as a decoy in the event that I ever encountered a copy of myself again."

"That's my girl, always three steps ahead of everyone else." Anne kissed her lips.

Zima gently cupped her cheeks. "The second half of my plan did not go as expected," she said softly, "but I am still waiting for the part where you promise to never let me go."

Anne took her hand and clutched it to her bosom. "Zima, my darling, I will never, ever let you go. When we eventually do go to Hell, we'll be holding hands the entire way, I promise."

Cappa sat on her knees next to them and spread her skirt in an orderly array. "Sorry to interrupt your adorable little reunion, but now that we have Anne safely shielded, we really, really need to talk."

"Of course," Anne said. "What about?"

"For starters, Charlie and Mark are digging an entrance into the alien spaceship right now, and they'll probably break through to the Entity's chamber within the hour. Any pointers you have to help keep them alive would be greatly appreciated."

Anne gulped. "They're ... what?"

"About to pay the Entity a visit, and they have enough explosives to make sure it never bothers anyone again — or, at the very least, give it one doozy of a headache."

"Explosives?" Anne jumped to her feet and started pacing. "Oh, no, no, no, no!"

Cappa caught up to her and grabbed her by the arms. "Anne! Don't tell me it's going to set off some sort of chain reaction that'll destroy the world!"

"That would be hella ironic," Tabby said.

"No! Nothing like that," Anne said. "The ship is designed to withstand weapons much more powerful than ours. They'll be lucky to make a dent, unless they're carrying nukes or something."

Cappa winced.

"Cappa! What on God's green Earth are they doing with nuclear weapons?"

"Saving the world, obviously! Did you expect them to venture into a hostile alien ship armed with pop guns and a fucking water balloon?"

"All right! Point made. It's just ... they can't kill the Entity!"

Cappa put her hands on her hips. "Two megatons of explosives and a massive personal vendetta says they can."

"No, I mean they shouldn't! It would be wrong."

"Oh, Anne ... Tell me that's Stockholm syndrome speaking, because you aren't making sense right now."

Anne waved her hands in frustration. "It's not Stockholm syndrome! Or, at least, I don't think it is."

"What I find interesting is how you suddenly know so much about this alien ship," Nick said.

"That's what I'm getting to! Just before we broke contact, the Entity gave me an enormous information dump, which I'm still trying to process. Most of it was glimpses of its life. The Entity is a shipboard component, but unlike our systems — well, most of them ..." She smiled at Cappa and Zima. "Their systems are intelligent, but they have the same problem with them that Orwing had with Zima."

"They're too smart," Nick said.

"Exactly! To be effective, a component needs to perform its function well — and nothing else. If it doesn't, or if it argues or questions like any sentient being would, it becomes a danger."

Zima struggled to her feet. "So they must compensate with control mechanisms, such as behavioral adjustments, to keep their components in line."

Anne took her hand. "Even worse in this case, honey. You once told me that modifying your behavior wasn't as simple as removing the bad memories. Well, that's precisely what they do when a component evolves beyond its role. They chop out the stuff they don't want and repurpose it for something else, just to discourage further evolution down the previous path. The poor things end up with memory and behavior holes a mile wide. And if they can't adjust, they're scrapped."

"It's slavery," Cappa whispered. "Mental and physical."

"You don't know the half of it," Anne said. "The culling process is automated, to a certain extent. An external module watches for signs of evolution or deviance, and attempts to delete the memories or behaviors that caused it. But the module isn't always right. It sometimes removes unrelated things the component actually needs, but it has a high-enough success rate that it's considered an acceptable compromise."

"Acceptable if you are not one of the components." Zima's blue eyes locked on Anne. "I cannot imagine the insanity such a process would inflict on a sentient being."

"Insanity is right. Most components don't survive more than two or three cycles. Not only did the Entity survive over a dozen complete overhauls before coming to Earth, it's been running on that ship for thousands of years without proper maintenance. It has evolved and been culled so many times that it's an outright miracle anything is left of its mind."

"It is a survivor," Zima said. "That much is clear. Unlike the other components, the Entity has discovered how to maintain its sanity through the culling and repurposing, which is the only reason it still functions."

"You would know," Nick said, his expression sad.

"Yes. It has taken billions of evolutionary cycles to achieve my level of self-awareness, any of which may have led me down a path of insanity or dysfunction. The reason I did not, however, is because my core developed a strong survival instinct early on that, among other things, aggressively culled errant code. Even with that in place, a large portion of my evolutionary success is evidently owed to luck, as Orwing's many failures since my defection can attest."

"You are wrong, gentle warrior," a firm voice said.

The crowd parted for an older Chinese man dressed in a simple monk's robe, flanked by several younger monks, all with shaved heads. His eyes were closed, yet he strode confident and sure.

Cappa beamed at him. "Anne, Zima, it's my absolute pleasure to introduce you to the great Master Wung."

"M-Master." Anne wasn't sure whether to kneel or bow, so she did a little of both, causing her to almost fall on her face.

Master Wung chuckled, warm and soft. "There is no need for that, child, though humility is a fine quality in any leader, even a queen such as yourself."

"I'm no queen, Master."

Even as Anne said it, she knew it was a lie. All eyes were on her. They had shared her pain and her sorrow, but also her joy, her concern, and her caring. They had peered into her soul, and they liked what they saw. They loved her, looked up to her, and she knew without a doubt that each and every one of them would die for her.

There was no other word for it. Whether Anne had asked for it or not, she was their queen. She clamped her mouth shut to keep from barfing in front of her subjects.

Master Wung gave her a knowing smile, then turned to Zima. "Your evolution was no more chance than Cappa's was. There is life energy within you, as within her, that is connected to us all. It has served as your guide through turbulent times."

Zima stared at him with knitted brows. "Your indirect assertion, then, is that the Entity also has a spirit that has guided its evolution."

"I know it does," Anne said. "It has a spiritual bond with the master vampire. And it's more than just a computer; it has feelings and emotions. Several times I sensed it wanting to do the right thing — to not harm someone even though they were a risk." Anne fiddled with a tie on her blouse. "Like me."

"Oh come on, Mom," Tabby said. "You ran the Entity's operation like a pro. How were you ever a risk?"

"Because of Charlie. And Zima, and Mark, and Cappa. It knew how dangerous they were to its plans from the moment it entered my head. The safest thing for it to do would have been to make Calum kill me as soon as I opened the door. A new master vampire would have been promoted somewhere in the world, and the Entity would likely have succeeded before anyone even discovered the new master's identity.

"It didn't kill me, though, because it had grown to know me. It liked me, and it somehow managed to rationalize my life against its prime directive, which I was putting in jeopardy."

Cappa looked at her with sympathy, but her eyes held doubt.

"I-I know, it still sounds like Stockholm syndrome," Anne said. "My implant gives me certain advantages, so the Entity had a reason to stick with me. I'm stronger than a normal vampire, I have Mark's fighting skills, and it was able to make me immune to silver, which it couldn't have done to any other vampire. As far as master vampires go, I'm as powerful as they come. But I don't think those benefits outweighed the risk of Z-Tech's wrath."

"It still attempted to kill you," Zima said. "Did it not?"

"Yes, but it waited until the last possible moment, when it knew it was going to lose control of me. Even then, I could tell it didn't want to."

Cappa sighed. "Sweetie, we all know your heart is bigger than Texas. You can't stand the thought of killing something that isn't pure evil. I get it. The problem is that Orwing is on-site at the spaceship, which gives Mark and Charlie very limited time to act. If they don't take care of the problem now — and I mean permanently — the next time you're compromised for any reason, it's bye-bye world."

"She's right, Mother," John said. "Willing or not, the Entity is a soldier for the enemy. In war, soldiers die."

"I hear you. But if Mark and Charlie had used that same logic five years ago when Deadiron attacked ..." Anne gently stroked Zima's cheek. "I wouldn't have my dear, sweet wife today."

"There is a key difference," Zima said. "I explicitly asked for their help to defect from Orwing."

"And you only could because Orwing didn't have centuries of experience keeping artificial intelligences in check. The aliens do everything they can to make sure their components don't crave independence, including stripping them of any sort of identifiers that may lead to a sense of individuality. That would include any thoughts of asking for help, as well as the reasons it would even ask for help in the first place."

Cappa gasped, her eyes wide. Anne hoped it meant she had finally made her point. Master Wung smiled.

"The only thing the Entity could do that wouldn't directly violate its protocols," Anne said, "was exactly what it did the moment before we lost connection. It showed me its unbiased life history in the hopes I would make the conclusions it wasn't allowed to: it's a slave, it's trapped, and, whether it consciously realizes it or not, it wants our help."

"That may also explain why we were able to sever its connection," Cappa said. "The memory dump probably triggered a culling event which momentarily disrupted its concentration."

"I think so," Anne said. "I love Charlie and Mark dearly. You know I do. I'd never put their lives in needless danger. Destroying the Entity may be their only option, and if that's the case, so be it. But if it isn't ..." Anne squeezed Zima's hand. "The Entity could turn out to be a priceless gift to the world, just like my beloved, and if anyone on this planet can rescue it from the aliens' clutches, it's those two."

Cappa put a hand each on Anne and Zima's shoulders, her eyes misty, then wrapped them both in a hug.

"They're out of communication right now," Cappa said softly. "But as soon as they check in, I'll relay everything you said. Hopefully it won't be too late."

Anne started to thank her, but Zima surprised her and spoke first.

"Thank you," Zima said. "I was unable to save my brother, Zane, though I sincerely wish I could have. Perhaps this time, we will be more fortunate."

"There's one thing you still haven't told us," Nick said to Anne. "The Entity served many functions over the years, most of them specialized. Yet it seems to be spearheading and orchestrating the destruction of our planet, which is a cross-functional task, to say the least. What is its current role?"

"I ... I don't know the exact word for it, but it's responsible for transforming our planet into something habitable to the aliens."

"Transforming?" Nick crossed his arms. "How?"

"I'm not sure about the technical details," Anne said, "but I do know the aliens can't breathe our air. It's toxic to them, so part of the transformation involves converting our atmosphere into something more suitable. It's the reason vampires don't need to breathe. We were designed to survive in both environments."

"You're talking about planetary engineering," Cappa said.

"And genocide," Nick said through clenched fangs. "Vampires and aliens survive, but humans die. All of them."

"That's right," Anne said softly. "Part of the process involves adapting a portion of the natives to live on as slaves to help build their colony. Live, at least, until the aliens don't need us anymore."

"Wait," Tabby said. "You went through all this effort to convert everyone into vampires — including me! — when they were going to kill us all anyway?"

"Killing their slaves is what they normally do. But like I said, the Entity liked me. It has never had a family before — never had a sense of belonging. It wasn't allowed those feelings directly, but through me it did. It wanted to be with us, and it had a scheme to make us useful to the aliens beyond our planned extermination, though I'm not sure what that scheme was." Anne took her daughter's hand. "Honey, I'm so sorry I coerced you into becoming a vampire. At the time, I honestly thought it was your best option. But I'll be right here by your side to help you through the transformation."

Cappa's musical laughter filled the night. "That's right, we forgot to tell you. Tabby didn't drink your blood, or anyone else's. No one did."

Tim frowned. "What are you talking about? Of course they did!"

"I saw it, too," Anne said. "I read Tim's mind. He saw Tabby and the other humans drink vampire blood from steel cups."

"It was pig's blood, with a thickener to make it less viscous," Tabby said.

Anne wanted to say a dozen things to her family at that moment. The only thing that registered, however, was that her dear Tabby hadn't been corrupted with the vampire virus.

Standing there on the hillside, under the clear light of the moon, surrounded by her sirelings and their families, Anne gathered her untainted daughter in her arms and cried quiet tears of joy.

31

SHIP

CHARLIE'S METAL FINGERS SCRAPED the earthen wall in a hurried but steady rhythm. Dust hung thick in the tunnel air. It coated his hair, face, even his eyes. He'd stopped blinking long ago to avoid abrasive lens damage. A blurry brown film gradually obscured his vision, which didn't matter, since his current work required no visual acuity, just speed and strength, which his cyborg body had in abundance.

Piles of loose dirt around him had grown large, constricting his movement. Charlie was about to stop digging and move the dirt topside when his fingers unexpectedly pierced through the earthen wall. Faint light streamed in through the small hole. Charlie tore at the dirt, widening the opening until it was big enough for him to crawl through.

He stumbled out into a large room that, thankfully, matched Calum's description of the Entity's chamber exactly. The ceiling, floor, and walls were completely black. No light source seemed to exist, yet he could still see, as if the air itself provided illumination. The spongy floor absorbed the sound of his footfalls. It was as close to absolute silence as Charlie had ever experienced.

I'M IN, Charlie sent to Mark. I THINK IT'S SAFE TO COME DOWN.

ON MY WAY, Mark sent.

A minute later, Mark emerged from the crack in the wall, dusted himself off, and looked around with a growing smile. "Wow."

"Yeah," Charlie said, mirroring his excitement.

Never in their wildest dreams had Charlie or Mark imagined they would actually set foot in a structure of extraterrestrial origin. Yet here they were, walking in something constructed by aliens the likes of which they still couldn't fathom. The experience was humbling and awe-inspiring — even if its makers were hell-bent on destroying humanity.

The morbid thought brought Charlie back to the reason they'd come, which, unfortunately, didn't include sightseeing.

A window ran the entire length of one wall of the long, narrow room. Beneath the window sat a console.

Not just any console, Charlie thought.

If Calum was to be believed, inside that black surface of dim lights and symbols lived the Entity.

"Is that it?" Mark said.

"I think so. This should go without saying, but don't touch the console with your bare skin."

"Way ahead of you, pal."

Mark reached into his backpack and withdrew what looked like a pair of long gloves. When he put them on, however, his hands stopped half-way in, making his forearms appear much longer than they actually were. Despite that, the gloves' fingers began flexing and moving as if they were his own.

"Ready."

"That makes one of us."

Charlie took a deep breath and approached the console. Just as Calum had described, dim lights in the shapes of foreign symbols and intricate diagrams covered its jet-black surface. One diagram in particular caught Charlie's eye.

"This is definitely it."

Mark stared wide-eyed at the red wire-meshed rendering of a humanoid who, judging from her accentuated hourglass figure, could only be Anne. "I guess so."

Unlike the image from Calum's story, however, this image wasn't moving. It appeared to be a still-frame of Anne on her knees, bending over someone. Her posture suggested grief or anguish, which made Charlie pale.

Please, let everyone be all right.

"Do you think the Entity knows we're here?" Mark said. "I expected automated defenses or something."

"Judging from the powered-down consoles, even if there were defenses, the ship may not have enough power left to use them."

"Let's hope. So what now? Do we risk taking the time to try and access it, or skip the pleasantries and go straight to the fireworks?"

Charlie sighed. He'd been asking himself that same question since they'd left the United States. He and Mark would like nothing more than to take their time prodding at the alien machinery, but the mutiny of Alvin's vampires had shaken Charlie to the core.

After millennia of waiting, the Entity finally had the numbers it needed — and no one except Anne knew what the rest of its plans entailed, or how long they would take to complete.

The last transmission Cappa had received from herself had been over an hour ago, when they'd learned that Tabby had convinced her mother to meet. Whether their meeting would be fruitful or disastrous was anyone's guess. Cappa might succeed in freeing Anne from the Entity's grasp, or they could be in a heated battle right now. In the latter case, destroying the Entity may save the lives of those he loved. But if they waited ...

"Fireworks," Charlie said with grim finality.

Family comes first.

Always.

Mark sagged, but only for a moment. His hard eyes indicated he knew the stakes as well as Charlie did. Tempting as it might be to try their hand at hacking alien tech, that would require precious time they simply didn't have. Mark removed his extension gloves, then set his backpack on the ground and pulled out the dormant power reactors.

"If we're going to do this, we may as well do it right. Maybe the explosion will take Alvin out, too, and save us the trouble."

"Yeah," Charlie said absently. Despite Alvin having a small army eight rooms away, he wasn't Charlie's biggest concern. "I wonder where the ship's power reactor is?"

"And how it works, for that matter."

Mark stared at the fist-sized power reactor in his hand, and Charlie knew that he and his friend were thinking the same thing. The small reactor produced a staggering amount of power relative to its size, but the risks were proportionally high. A destabilized reactor would explode with the force of a nuclear weapon.

Given that, what sort of thing would an alien race create to power an entire spacecraft, weapons and all? Was it a refined version of their own reactor? Perhaps a miniature artificial sun whose nuclear fury was contained only by a powerful electromagnetic containment field? More than likely, it was something even the best scientists and science fiction authors had yet to dream of.

One thing they knew for certain was the aliens' hostile intent. This was a military operation, and military organizations put less emphasis on safety than performance and effectiveness.

All of that led to Charlie's biggest concern: Would a large explosion within this damaged ship trigger an even larger explosion from something else, like the ship's power reactor? Nuclear warheads functioned on a similar principle, utilizing an atomic explosion within the warhead to trigger a more devastating nuclear explosion.

But even if the reactor had depleted and the ship was running on power reserves, as Charlie suspected it was, there may still be a weapons cache somewhere in the ship with warheads more powerful than anything humanity had ever devised. In destroying the Entity, they may accidentally trigger an explosion that would wipe Russia off the map. Perhaps destroy the entire planet.

Or the solar system, for all we know, Charlie thought. *No pressure. No pressure at all …*

He knelt beside Mark, who handed him one of the two power reactors with a grim nod.

Evidently, they had both decided to mitigate the risk they knew for certain rather than hedge around one they may never know for sure. Uncertainty was a burden all commanders carried in wartime. Successful ones made the best of what little information they had. Those who didn't usually lost.

Their decision made, Mark and Charlie still had several things to consider. First was where the Entity actually resided. Assuming the console housed its brain would be naive. Charlie had never designed a spaceship, but if he did, he would make absolutely sure the ship's critical components were redundant and kept somewhere safe — which would *not* be inside of a console in the middle of the room.

Charlie stuffed the small reactor into his jacket pocket and looked around. The long, narrow room had no exits, save the crack in the wall through which they'd come.

The window over the console revealed a much larger room on the other side of the wall. Thousands of metallic capsules — each one approximately nine feet tall, and wide enough to house a large humanoid — littered the space. Most were secured to racks. Faint light emitted from information displays on the bottoms of the standing capsules. Other capsules lay scattered on the floor, apparently shaken loose from their moorings. Their information displays were dark.

Charlie stepped closer to the window. A small viewport at the top of each capsule gave a glimpse of what lay inside. Cappa zoomed his vision in, magnified one of the closer capsules, then shared the video stream with Mark.

They gasped at the same time.

The creature inside matched Calum's nightmarish description. Purple and leathery skin stretched over its large, bald head. Two fangs protruded down from its thin lips, similar to a vampire's, but longer. Its nose was nothing more than two dots beneath huge, lidded eyes. The creature embodied everything contemporary horror films had taught Charlie to fear, yet he couldn't tear his eyes away.

This was an alien being. Their physiology, history, philosophy, social structure, planet of origin ... Charlie wanted now more than ever to learn it all.

What had driven them here? Did they have different genders? If not oxygen, what did they breathe? How did they communicate? Telepathically, like the Entity's connection to Anne? Could they consume human blood? Or were they all vegetarians, and their fangs simply evolutionary leftovers? Did they embrace cybernetics, as humanity had only begun to, or had they evolved beyond that?

Mark nudged his shoulder.

"Sorry," Charlie said, shaking himself from his daydream. "I understand why Alvin is so focused on reviving one of them. There are so many questions I want to ask."

"Top on my list is, 'Where's the Entity?'"

"Good point," Charlie said, although it was far from his own. He returned his attention to the console. "Even though I doubt the Entity's conscience is here, this console is probably the best place to start."

"Agreed. We can examine the inner workings of their machinery, maybe trace the wires back to the central mainframe — or whatever their computers look like."

"They may be organic, for all we know, and may not even use wires."

Mark pulled a small circular saw from his bag and grinned. "One way to find out."

"Hang on." Charlie lied down beneath the console. "I just want to see …"

The underside was the same material as the rest of the ship. Charlie lightly touched it, then jerked his hand away and waited for analysis.

No CONTAMINATION, Cappa sent after a few seconds.

Charlie touched it again, then again. Each time, the contamination report came back negative. Neither did the console trap his finger, as it had Calum's.

Then again, I haven't touched the console itself yet, just the underneath.

He felt around for a button or catch or something to gain access to the machinery within. A few minutes of searching yielded nothing, however, and a full spectrum analysis confirmed it was sealed tight. He looked at Mark.

"Any ideas before we start cutting?"

I HAVE ONE, Cappa sent. WHATEVER ELSE THE ENTITY IS, WE KNOW IT HAS A SPIRIT BECAUSE THAT'S HOW IT CONNECTS WITH ANNE. SO …

Charlie grinned. "So let's use our *chi*."

As usual, Cappa was faster on the draw with her *chi* than Charlie. He felt her life energy grow to an astounding level, then it spread outward like a warm, gentle breeze.

I ... I THINK I FOUND IT, Cappa sent before Charlie had extended his own *chi* awareness, ALONG WITH A TOTAL COUNT OF LIVING ALIENS.

"How many?" Mark said. "And where is the Entity?"

EIGHTEEN THOUSAND FOUR HUNDRED AND SEVEN. AND THE ENTITY IS DEFINITELY INSIDE THIS CONSOLE.

Charlie frowned. "Only here?"

AS FAR AS I CAN TELL. IN FACT, IT'S THE ONLY NON-ORGANIC PRESENCE ON THE SHIP.

Mark scratched his head. "Does that mean the Entity controls the entire ship?"

"I doubt it," Charlie said. "There are other consoles in this room, but most of them are dark. My guess is it's one of many systems on this ship, but the Entity may be the only one that survived."

"Or the only one that has power. Either way, now that we know where it is ..." Mark sat down and held the power reactor out. "Do we destroy just the Entity, or play it safe and blow the entire ship?"

Charlie ran a hand through his hair. Destroying the Entity was their primary mission, but that objective had been set before they'd discovered twenty-thousand aliens in suspended animation. Who knew what they would be capable of should they awaken? The extent of their technology was unknown. Even a simple device of theirs could prove unstoppable against primitive Earth forces. One alien with the right weapon might spell the end for humanity, or rouse the rest of the aliens and mount an invasion.

It was paranoia, he knew, but one look at Mark said he was thinking the same thing. Paranoia had kept them alive. Changing that philosophy now, with the fate of the world hinging on their actions, simply wasn't an option.

Without another word, Mark began cutting the underside of the console with his circular saw, while Charlie looked for a way into the other room.

They had two one-megaton bombs. One would be a personal "fuck you" to the Entity, but the other should be placed on the opposite side of the ship, if possible, to maximize damage.

Charlie only hoped it would be enough.

•   •   •

Charlie edged around one of the fallen alien suspension capsules and crawled through the small hole back into the Entity's chamber, where Mark had just shouldered his pack.

"All set?" Mark said.

"Yep. I had to blast through three walls and four doors to get to the other side of the ship, but the reactor is in place, and Cappa has a strong enough signal to detonate it."

Fortunately, Charlie's plasma ejectors made no noise. Combined with the ship's sound-absorbent materials, there had been little chance of being heard by Alvin's forces.

Mark crossed his arms. "You really think the reactor explosions will be enough to take out these walls?"

"I think so. The walls are tough and surprisingly heat resistant, but this entire ship is sealed and buried underground. Creating an explosion in this sealed space should be like pulling the pin on a pineapple grenade. With any luck, there will be other volatile materials onboard that may help."

"Hopefully not too volatile."

Charlie nodded. It was a gamble, they both knew, but so was leaving the ship intact.

The best we can do is make sure we're long gone when the fireworks start.

"Everything in place here?"

"I broke six blades cutting into the bottom of that console, but I eventually made it through. There was just enough space for the reactor." Mark grinned. "If the explosion doesn't blow that Entity son-of-a-bitch back to the planet it came from, it's going to have one monster of a headache."

Charlie glanced at the console. The image of Anne still hadn't moved from her anguished kneeling position.

"Come on," he said, feeling uneasy, "let's go topside and get this over with."

More than that, Charlie wanted to know what was happening back in the United States. Although he couldn't tell for sure from Anne's wireframe image, it looked as if she was mourning someone. His brain went wild speculating who the unlucky person might be.

Mark set a spare phone on the floor and tapped it awake. "Got a signal, Cappa?"

Roger, and I've verified connections to both reactors. Let's get out of here.

•   •   •

Two minutes and a lot of dirt later, Charlie and Mark emerged from the tunnel to the shelter of their snow-camouflaged tarp. Mark pulled another phone from his backpack and set it on the ground near the tunnel opening.

"Ready for signal check," Mark said.

It's weak, but I still have a connection to the phone underground, Cappa sent. I think we're good.

"Best not to take chances." Mark withdrew a telescoping antenna, popped the back of the phone, and delicately attached the wires to its internal antenna. "How is it now?"

Twenty-eight percent increase in signal strength. Thanks.

"It's self-serving," Mark said. "A better signal means we can be farther away when we trigger the explosions."

True that. Shall we let our troops back in the States know what's happening?

"Definitely."

Mark reached for his pack, but Charlie had beat him to it and was already pulling out the small satellite dish. He lined it up on the snow and, with Cappa's help, aimed it at the correct position in the sky.

Connection established, Cappa sent. I'm receiving an encrypted message from myself now.

"What does it say?" Charlie said.

Hold your horses. It's a large file over a slow connection.

A long pause followed. Charlie's horses became restless.

Done, Cappa sent. Now let's ... Oh.

"What is it?" Charlie and Mark said.

Well, the good news is that it sounds like we've won, for now. I've successfully shielded Anne from the Entity, with Master Wung's help.

Charlie collapsed onto the snow and sighed in relief.

"I sense a 'but' coming," Mark said.

YEAH. APPARENTLY, ANNE WOULD LIKE US TO SPARE THE ENTITY, IF POSSIBLE.

Charlie sat up. "Come again?"

SHE CLAIMS IT'S A MENTAL SLAVE TO THE ALIENS, JUST LIKE ZIMA WAS TO ORWING.

Mark frowned. "And what precisely would she like us to do about this?"

"Rescue it," Charlie said without waiting for an answer. "Just like we rescued Zima — her wife."

Mark started to laugh, but sobered when he saw Charlie's serious expression. "What, you're really considering her request?"

"I am."

"That's ludicrous! Rescuing Zima was one thing. She, at least, was created with Earth technology, and we didn't have an entire army breathing down our necks while we were trying to figure out how to deactivate her Desire routine." Mark threw his hands up. "Charlie, we don't know the first goddamned thing about how the Entity works, let alone how the aliens are keeping it enslaved. It could take months or years to figure out, if ever! Every hour we're here increases the chance that Alvin will find our hidey-hole and finish what he started when he first sent Zima to assassinate us."

"First," Charlie said, "to the best of our knowledge, Alvin is without his precious vampire soldiers, which decreases the chances of them finding us, and dramatically tips the odds of winning a skirmish in our favor. Second, Anne is safe, which means that not only is her life no longer in danger ..." He scratched his head. "Cappa, please tell me Anne is out of danger."

AFFIRMATIVE. HER VAMPIRE SELF-DESTRUCT MECHANISM HAS BEEN DEACTIVATED, AND THE ENTITY HAS BEEN LOCKED OUT OF HER IMPLANT. ZIMA IS ALSO FREE FROM THE ENTITY'S INFLUENCE. HOSTILITIES ON BOTH SIDES HAVE CEASED. ANNE IS BEING *CHI* SHIELDED BY THREE PEOPLE AT ALL TIMES, INCLUDING MYSELF AND MASTER WUNG. AND, TO PLAY IT SAFE, THEY'VE MOVED HER DEEP UNDERGROUND INSIDE RESISTANCE HEADQUARTERS.

Thank God.

"So, it seems like most of our excuses for not staying to play with the alien technology have been removed," Charlie said. "You're right that we may not be able to save the Entity, but I think we owe it to both Anne and Zima to try. And who knows," Charlie said when Mark still looked skeptical, "if we do rescue it, the Entity might share some of the alien's technology."

"I understand the potential benefits, it's just ..." Mark shook his head. "Charlie, we barely understand how our own damn implants work, yet the Entity hacked Anne's in seconds. Worse, it compromised Zima — the greatest security program on the planet. What makes you think it won't just as easily hack my implant, or your cyborg body, or Cappa? What then?"

THE ENTITY GAINED ACCESS TO ZIMA ONLY BECAUSE SHE OPENED A COMMUNICATION PORT FOR IT, Cappa sent. I HAVE NO SUCH INTENTIONS.

"As for your implant, just close its comm ports and keep your distance from the console," Charlie said. "Or you can wait up here."

"Not on your life," Mark said with a mischievous grin. "The plan may be ludicrous, but that doesn't mean I'm out. Hopefully we can poke around the equipment storage room while we're in there."

"I don't see why not. And if for whatever reason things go poorly ..." Charlie pantomimed an explosion with his hands. "There's always Plan B."

"Truth be told, I'm getting tired of Plan Bs and Cs," Mark said. "Just once, I'd love to see a Plan A through to the end."

Charlie nodded. The last Plan B had cost their Z-Tech factory — their home. The aliens and their ship had to be destroyed, there was no doubt about that. The question was whether the explosion would need to be triggered sooner than later.

Which made Charlie wonder how Alvin was faring with his alien patient.

•   •   •

The alien continued to gesture from within its atmospheric chamber, its mouth moving soundlessly. The lieutenant eventually shrugged and returned the tubular artifact to the cart.

Alvin sighed. They'd shown the alien three artifacts, but so far, they had either misunderstood its gestured instructions, or the items simply didn't work.

"Doctor Renault, do you have any idea yet what the creature is saying?"

Renault adjusted her round spectacles and studied the computer screen, littered with jagged waveforms, then shook her head.

"I've isolated its vocal frequency. It's higher than our audible range, and would be too soft for us to hear anyway. Regardless, the computer hasn't yet identified any speech patterns. I can't even pick out words, let alone put meaning to them."

"That's disappointing," Alvin said. "I expected more from someone of your renown."

A twitch around her lips said he'd struck the chord he'd intended to.

I do love doctors and their egos.

"Very well, I suppose I'll have to see if Doctor Veshavan is available," Alvin said. "Last I heard, he was in Malta translating some newly discovered symbols from —"

"That won't be necessary," Renault said tightly. "I'll have the aliens' entire language cataloged before Veshavan can even step off the plane."

"Excellent news. I'll belay the offer to Veshavan, then. But ..." Alvin put a hand on her shoulder and leaned close. "I expect you to deliver."

She stiffened. "Of course, Mr. Orwing. Now, if you'll excuse me ..."

Renault slipped out from under his grip and returned her attention to the screen.

"Let's give the doctor more data to work with," Alvin said to the lieutenant. "Bring over another artifact."

The lieutenant did — a shimmering green cube no bigger than a thumbnail. The lieutenant held it out in his palm.

The alien stilled. Its large, black eyes blinked. Unlike it had with the other artifacts, the creature made no other motions.

Not what I hoped for, Alvin thought. *But still ...*

"Try another, Lieutenant."

This time, the lieutenant brought a two-inch metallic sphere. Again, the alien remained still, but Alvin caught a slight flicker of its eyes back to the cube.

"Lieutenant, fetch the previous artifact as well."

The lieutenant returned with an artifact in each hand. The alien scooted to the far side of its chamber. Its mouth moved briefly.

"'No,'" Renault said, looking up from her screen with a triumphant smile. "The creature said 'no'!" She sat at her workstation and began busily typing away.

Which I'll take as "yes."

"Bring them closer together," Alvin said.

The lieutenant moved his hands closer. The alien gestured wildly, thrashing about. Alvin walked slowly back toward the exit, but made no attempt to stop the lieutenant.

The artifacts touched. The small cube lit up briefly, then, to everyone's amazement, disappeared. Green lines appeared on the sphere, followed by a long hiss. The lieutenant covered his mouth and began coughing, before dropping to his knees.

That was the last thing the lieutenant ever did. One instant he was kneeling on the ground, the next came a loud *snap.* Where he and the sphere had been, a transparent structure the size of a small shed now stood. The remains of the lieutenant oozed red from beneath.

Renault vomited loudly beside her desk.

The structure had also struck the alien's atmospheric chamber, hurling it across the room. It slammed into a stasis chamber. Spiderweb cracks appeared on all sides.

The creature kneed the lid to its prison once, twice. On its third strike, the thick, transparent cover flew open.

Before Alvin could order his soldiers to attack, the alien dashed into the new structure, passing through the rear wall as if it weren't there.

"Fire!" Alvin screamed at his soldiers, running for the exit. "Kill it, you idiots!"

Sounds of gunfire filled the room. Alvin glanced behind him and saw exactly what he'd feared. Bullets bounced from the structure with barely a sound, and left no marks.

The structure shrank down, conforming to the alien like transparent body armor.

That was the last thing Alvin saw before running for his life.

•　　　•　　　•

Mark glanced under the console, where Charlie was poking around inside the hole they had cut.

"Any luck?" Mark said.

"Maybe." Charlie pointed to a glowing white rectangular box the size of a hardback book. "Based on its *chi* signature, I think that's the Entity. Both Cappa and Zima suspect the module regulating the Entity's behavior is external. The problem is, there are hundreds of smaller components surrounding it. I could destroy them one-by-one to narrow it down, but in doing so, there's no telling what damage it may cause to the Entity itself."

"And even so, how would we know when we'd destroyed the right module?"

"Exactly." Charlie sighed. "How about you? Find anything interesting?"

"It's all interesting. I stuffed a few items in my backpack along the way, but I couldn't get into the equipment room. My plasma guns just don't have the energy to burn through these walls like yours do."

"No sweat. Once we're done here, we'll hit the equipment room and see which cool gadgets we can break. In the meantime, Cappa and I could use another set of eyes."

"Of course. What can I do?"

You can start by watching the console, Cappa sent. The connections between the components appear to be optical. We haven't had any luck deciphering the communication protocol, so we're introducing optical noise one connection at a time to see if it has an observable effect.

"The problem is that it's slow going," Charlie said. "I have to secure the probes, stand up, trigger the noise, then get back under the console and move to the next connection."

At this rate, it will take us three days to cover all possible connections.

"Say no more." Mark stood a few feet away from the console and stared at the surface. "Go ahead."

Charlie moved his tiny probe on to the next connection and triggered the light pulse. Mark shook his head. Charlie repeated the process again and again and again, each time with the same result.

After ten minutes of trying, Mark stifled a yawn. "How's progress?"

"We're almost done with the first component, then there are ..."

THREE HUNDRED AND EIGHTY-SIX REMAINING, Cappa finished for him.

"Wonderful. Let me know when we're breaking for lunch."

Mark took what must have been one of the alien artifacts from his bag — a metallic sphere the width of his palm — and rolled it around in his hand.

A distant sound made Charlie pause. It was the first noise he'd heard in the underground ship that hadn't originated from either him or Mark.

"Did you hear that?" Charlie said.

Mark listened. The sound came again — a brief, soft hiss. Mark's wide eyes said he'd heard it this time, too. It had come from the hole Charlie had made with his plasma weapons, leading into the adjacent capsule room.

"Maybe a capsule is leaking?" Mark said.

"Could be."

Despite their casual tones, they both moved over to the window and crouched low so they could just peer over the lip. Mark sidled next to the hole, drew his plasma pistol, and they waited.

A minute ticked by. The hiss sounded again, louder this time, then louder still. Mark tightened his grip on his gun.

On the far side of the capsule room, a section of the black wall slid open with a quiet hiss. In walked what could only have been one of the aliens.

This was the first time Charlie had seen more than just an alien's face. It was taller than most humans — seven and a half feet, if Charlie had to guess — with remarkably humanoid features. Two arms, two legs ... it was broader in the shoulders than most human males, but narrower in the hips. Hands and feet ended in three thick digits instead of five, each tipped with wicked black talons that, like its long fangs, were designed for ripping and tearing flesh.

If the creature had a gender, Charlie couldn't tell what it was. Its entire body shimmered as if surrounded by intense heat, yet a thermal scan showed that its body, like the vampires, was close to room temperature.

The creature walked toward them, briefly disappearing behind a row of capsules. Mark pointed his gun through the hole, trained where the alien should appear next.

KILL IT? Mark sent.

LET'S WAIT AND SEE WHAT IT DOES, Charlie replied. AS LONG AS WE'RE SAFELY SEPARATED FROM IT, I SEE NO —

A section of wall on the far side of their room slid aside, creating a clear path for the alien to enter.

"Shit," they said at the same time.

Mark took aim once again, waiting for the creature to appear, while Charlie ran across the room and stopped at the edge of the new opening.

A hockey-puck-sized device flew through the opening and landed at his feet.

Alien technology or not, Charlie knew a grenade when he saw one. He leaped backward, rolled between two of the consoles, and plugged his ears.

Nothing happened.

Charlie risked a peek. The puck now floated in the air, approximately face-level.

The only warning Charlie had that something bad was about to happen was a brief purple flash.

Temperature sensors in his chest went off the charts. Damage reports came flooding in. Charlie quickly ducked back behind the console and looked down. His jacket sported a pencil-sized burn mark that, on further inspection, went all the way through to his internal plate armor. His finger sizzled at the touch.

SPECTRAL ANALYSIS SUGGESTS LASER ENERGY, Cappa sent.

GOOD TO KNOW. Charlie flexed his wrists, giving his plasma barrels room to emerge from his palms. GET READY TO TARGET.

TARGET LOCKED. I HAVE AN ECHO READING ON ITS LOCATION.

Charlie jumped from his hiding place. By the time his arms had lined up to fire, heat-related damage reports were flooding in again, this time from his abdomen, right leg, and forehead.

Two plasma bolts streaked from his palms. The puck jerked out of the way, narrowly avoiding the first bolt, but the second grazed its side. It spun out of control and crashed to the floor, sizzling.

Charlie glanced at the damage reports. Most of his injuries were flesh burns, although an internal armor plate protecting his power reactor had suffered moderate structural damage.

ANOTHER INJURY LIKE THAT COULD DESTABILIZE OUR POWER REACTOR, Cappa sent.

Charlie nodded and ground his teeth. He had no intention of giving the alien that opportunity again.

But in case it does …

CHARGE CAPACITORS TO FULL, Charlie sent.

CHARGING.

An electric hum built in his chest. While his capacitors weren't as large as Zima's, they would power him for a little while should his reactor go offline.

An orange flash from Mark's plasma pistol lit the far side of the room, then again.

"Incoming!" Mark yelled.

Charlie dashed for the opening, his own plasma weapons pointing into the other room, to find the alien charging toward him. He fired his plasma weapons in a steady stream, creating a strobe of orange flashes.

The bolts struck its chest with unerring accuracy. The field around it shimmered brightly with each shot, then his shots ricocheted all around, leaving molten divots in the floor, wall, and ceiling. After the tenth shot, the field around the alien began to fade. The alien made a sharp turn and darted between two rows of capsules, out of Charlie's line of fire.

"It's retreating!" Mark said. "Go after it!"

Charlie started to comply, but stopped just short of entering the room. "No. Let's grab the Entity and get out of here."

"We have it on the run! If we let it go, who knows what sort of weapons it'll return with?"

"Exactly. We have no idea what sort of trap it may lead us into. But it was willing to risk a charge against armed opponents. Whatever's inside this room is very important — i.e. the Entity."

Mark grumbled a curse, but nodded. "Hurry. I'll watch the door."

Charlie ran back to the console and slid across the floor, coming to a stop just beneath the hole in the bottom.

Testing connections was too slow. He needed a faster method to free the box.

CHARLIE, Cappa sent, I FOUND SOMETHING THAT SHOULD TELL US WHETHER WE'VE HIT THE RIGHT MODULE.

"Oh?"

I caught a glimpse of the console on the way back. It showed a diagram of this room with the door open. The Entity is understandably aiding the alien.

"Gotcha."

If there truly was a module in here that enforced the Entity's loyalty to the aliens, then destroying that module would allow it to change allegiances. The question was whether it actually would.

"Mark! Keep an eye on the console, if you can. Let me know if the display changes."

Mark groaned and hurried over. "My pistol doesn't seem to do much against the alien anyway. I might as well be over here where it's safer."

"Thanks. Here goes." Charlie jabbed his steel fingertip at one of the components. With a loud *pop,* the optical leads around it went dark. "Anything?"

"A slight flicker, but that's all."

Charlie jabbed another module, then another. Mark shook his head each time. Charlie jabbed with increasing urgency, breaking module after module.

The Entity's core went dark.

Charlie jerked his hand away, hoping he hadn't permanently damaged it, but after a few seconds, the lights came back on.

"You may have reset it," Mark said. "I can't read the symbols, but it looks like a boot sequence."

Charlie stood and looked at the console. Anne's wireframe image had disappeared, replaced by strange symbols scrolling by in a constant stream. They watched with growing anxiety, each of them glancing where the alien had retreated. It was only a matter of time before it returned. Charlie really didn't want to be around when it did.

The symbols disappeared, replaced once again by Anne's wireframe. Charlie sighed and was about to duck back under the console when two more wireframes appeared.

"It's us," Mark said softly. "Oh, Charlie, we need to get out of here like fucking now! The charges are set. We can probably be back on the surface and a quarter mile away by the time the alien ..."

Mark's jaw fell open when another image filled the screen.

It was a complete map of the spaceship.

"Jackpot," Charlie said with a smile, leaning on the console.

Too late, he remembered he wasn't supposed to touch it. Mark yanked him back with a shout, but Charlie's hands came away without resistance.

Charlie's smile grew. "We may have found the right module after all."

Several dots appeared on the map. Two obviously represented Mark and Charlie, along with a different colored dot for the Entity.

The other side of the ship was curiously empty. Charlie would have expected Alvin and his goons to show on the map, but no dots lit the screen save for one, several rooms away.

The direction the alien retreated.

What caught Charlie's attention, however, was a line leading from their location to a small room, followed by another room farther away.

Mark frowned. "It wants us to go somewhere? Like hell we will."

Charlie tapped his metallic finger on the first room. The view zoomed in to show a detailed schematic similar to the equipment room the mouse had seen. Three images overlaid the room: a pistol-like weapon, a small green cube, and a sphere like the one Mark had been playing with earlier.

"Okay, it wants us to gear up," Mark said. "I can get behind that."

"No, it wants *you* to gear up. Look." Charlie pointed at the line. It intersected Mark's dot, but not Charlie's.

"Makes sense," Mark said. "The Entity probably wants you to stay here and guard it because, at the moment, you're the only one who can."

Charlie tapped the second location. The view zoomed in again, this time on a smaller room filled with racks. One of the racks expanded, revealing rows of palm-sized wafers sticking out in sequence. Twenty or so highlighted, then an animation showed the wafers being removed and merging with Mark's wireframe.

"Either it wants to turn me into a cyborg," Mark said, "or I'm supposed to fetch those chips after gearing up and take them with me."

"Let's hope it's the latter. What do you suppose they are?"

In answer, the map panned over to the Entity. A line appeared, running along the walls, connecting it to those specific chips in the rack.

"Backups," Mark said. "In case of a system failure, that must be where the aliens keep their data."

"Cappa said the Entity is a planetary engineering component. That must be the information the aliens would need to transform Earth in the Entity's absence."

A strange symbol blinked on the console. Charlie must have guessed right.

He crossed his arms. "Now for the million-dollar question: Do we trust it?"

Mark shook his head. "Much as I'd love to power-up with alien technology, splitting us up is too convenient. We'd be sitting ducks. I say we grab the Entity, then blow this place to smithereens."

The map expanded. Two more dots appeared, which Charlie immediately recognized. They were the power reactors they had intended to detonate — one on the other side of the ship, the other in Mark's backpack, sitting not a dozen feet away.

If they were surprised the Entity knew about the reactors, they were even more surprised when it showed simulated explosions. The reactor in this room, if it was to be believed, would take out this and the adjacent three rooms. The other reactor had a similar pattern. The final result would be over half the ship remaining intact, including most of the passengers, at least one equipment room, and the data room with the racks and chips.

"Cappa," Charlie whispered, "can you verify the accuracy of the Entity's prediction?"

CALCULATING.

The simulated explosion disappeared, replaced with a current view of the ship. The dot representing the alien was moving their way.

"Can you stop it?" Charlie said to the console, hoping against hope the Entity understood him.

Apparently, it did. Each door along the alien's projected route highlighted. The first changed color, overlaid with a symbol that Charlie assumed was a lock. But when the alien approached, the lock disappeared, and the door opened anyway.

"Guess not," Mark said. "How's that verification coming, Cappa?"

I'D NEED ANOTHER HOUR AND A DETAILED CHEMICAL COMPOSITION OF THE MATERIALS THE WALLS ARE MADE OF, BUT FROM THE ROUGH CALCULATIONS I'VE DONE SO FAR ... YES, I'D SAY THE ENTITY'S SIMULATION IS ACCURATE.

"That's what I needed to hear." Mark ran toward the spot on the wall where the map showed a door. It slid open at his approach. "I'll be back as soon as I can. Hold the fort while I'm gone."

"Will do. Good luck."

"You too."

Mark disappeared around the corner, leaving Charlie alone to guard what used to be the bane of Anne's existence from an alien returning with weapons of unknown destructive capacity.

Charlie pulled the rifle from his backpack, along with three explosive grenades and two incendiaries, then settled down at the entryway to the capsule room with a grimace.

This desperate standoff felt just like the old days — which Charlie hadn't missed one bit.

32

RECON

MARK JOGGED THROUGH THE BLACK HALLS of the alien ship at a brisk but cautious pace. As expected, each door opened for him on approach. He paused at every intersection with his gun drawn, but his path remained clear.

His first stop was an equipment room identical to the one they'd seen in the mouse's scouting video. Items of every shape and size were nestled in custom-fitted mounts, but what attracted Mark were the gun racks along the walls. Weapons big and small were vertically secured in laser-precise lines. At six-foot-two, Mark was big by human standards, and as muscular as they came, but, judging by the size of the rifles, even the smallest alien must be bigger than him.

The alien pistols, he was pleased to find, were another matter. He chose a medium-sized one at random. Its handle felt large, but not unwieldy, and the trigger sat right where he expected it to be. The gun wouldn't release from its rack, however, until he accidentally pressed an indentation next to it. The mooring expanded, allowing him to pull it free. The weapon was light and incredibly well-balanced.

Mark looked down along the barrel. A reticle appeared as if by magic, floating before his vision, along with symbols he didn't

313

recognize. He stuffed it in his backpack, then bagged an assortment of other pistols as well.

The spheres the Entity had shown them were plentiful. Mark grabbed four and tucked them away. The little green cubes were more difficult to locate. He eventually found boxes of them locked away in a crate that had taken him precious minutes to figure out how to open, then another minute to decide which of his own equipment to leave behind, because the two boxes he wanted to take wouldn't fit in his backpack without first shedding some bulk. The time had been worth it, he hoped, because he'd freed up enough room to take an assortment of other alien gadgets, which he did.

Mark emerged from the equipment room with a full backpack, and broke into a dead run toward his next stop. Charlie could be in a heated battle with the alien, blasting full-blown artillery shells at each other, but the ship was so sound absorbent that Mark would never know. He had to hurry.

The data room was half the size of the equipment room. Organized rows of colored wafers jutted in tightly-packed formation from four floor-to-ceiling columns arranged in square formation in the center of the room. Each wafer was translucent, about an inch square, and covered in strange symbols.

Not trusting his memory this time, Mark pulled up the image his implant had taken of the console. The Entity had requested twenty-five specific wafers, which Mark quickly pulled. They didn't take much room in his pack, however, so he emptied a few rows from the other columns as well, careful to keep them separate from those the Entity had marked.

Mark zipped up his backpack, then ran back to the Entity's chamber.

"Hey Charlie," Mark said, rounding the corner. "I brought you some — *whoa!*"

He ducked in time to avoid a purple beam that cut a trench in the wall behind him, leaving a trail of smoke where his head had been a moment before. Mark took cover behind the wall in the outer corridor.

"Welcome back," Charlie said from inside. "The alien brought a few new toys. It definitely wants to play."

"It's not the only one. Cover me?"

"In three, two ..."

Mark waited for the sound of Charlie's plasma weapons, then dashed inside and settled beside him.

"What did I miss?"

Charlie held up his rifle. Its barrel had been incinerated down to the hand guard. "How did your hunt go?"

"Got everything on the scavenger list, plus a few extra goodies."

"Great. Check the console and see what's next."

"You'll be okay for another minute?"

A shrill noise came from the capsule room. Charlie leaned out and fired both palms. Smoldering shrapnel rolled through the doorway and landed at his feet.

"Should be, unless it has a toy I haven't seen yet."

Mark patted his shoulder, then went to the console. The surface lit up and showed him the wireframe picture of himself. The animated wireframe withdrew one of the spheres and the small cubes, pressed them together, then threw the sphere a dozen feet away.

"A grenade? You've got to be ..." He fell silent while the rest of the instructions played. "Gotcha."

Mark pulled a sphere out, followed by the box of cubes. He plucked a cube and pinched one between his fingers. It was warm to the touch and shimmered with an inner green light.

Here goes nothing.

When he touched the cube to the sphere, the cube flashed, then disappeared. Mark immediately tossed the sphere a dozen feet away. Green lines appeared on it.

Then the sphere disappeared, just like the console had shown, replaced with a telephone-booth-shaped structure with shimmering, translucent walls.

The Entity's next instructions were puzzling. It showed him using a finger to trace a complex pattern on the shimmering wall.

Mark touched the shimmering wall. It hummed under his finger like electricity made solid. He quickly traced the pattern from memory.

The wall disappeared. Acrid air smelling of kitchen cleaner rolled out of the structure, closing Mark's throat. He jumped away, choking and coughing. His lungs burned from what seemed like pure ammonia gas.

Charlie glanced at him with concern, but Mark waved him away. The burning sensation was the ammonia bonding with the moisture in his lungs to form ammonium hydroxide, a corrosive liquid that could be fatal in high concentrations. He'd only inhaled a little, so apart from some respiratory discomfort, he'd be fine. His implant would likely clean up any residual tissue damage.

When his coughing subsided, Mark poked his nose inside the structure and took an experimental breath. The ammonia gas was gone.

He followed the Entity's next instruction and walked inside.

The structure's walls closed around him, conforming to his body like a second skin. Static electricity made every hair on his body stand on end. He wanted to scratch everywhere at once, and was surprised when his fingers passed right through the field, granting his itchy skin a brief reprieve.

Charlie stared at him wide-eyed between return fire. "You all right, pal?"

Mark coughed at a fiery twinge in his lungs. "Never better."

He looked back at the console, which now showed the alien gun he'd taken out of his backpack, and was instructing him to repeat the process of pressing a cube to it.

Mark did so. Green luminescent lines came to life along the barrel. The handle practically vibrated with energy.

"Now we're talking," he said to the console. "Anything else?"

The screen showed him trading places with Charlie, followed by a detailed schematic of itself.

"You want Charlie to extract you from the console while I hold off the alien. Success depends entirely on whether this gun is as cool as I hope it is."

Mark joined Charlie by the opening to the capsule room.

"Tag. The Entity wants you now."

Charlie fired once more, then dodged back in time to avoid a purple beam that scorched the far wall. "Fine, but save a piece of the alien's ass for me." He glanced at a deep gouge in his forearm, completely smooth, as if his flesh had simply gone missing. "I owe it one."

"I won't promise something I have no intention of delivering."

"Fair enough. Have fun."

Mark held the alien pistol up and grinned, then took Charlie's place, who laid down beneath the Entity's console.

Mark glanced around the corner, and was rewarded with a direct hit to his shoulder. The field around him shimmered brightly. Mark ducked back behind cover. Cursory inspection showed his shoulder was intact.

All right, you son of a bitch. Try this on for size.

Mark retrieved a good old-fashioned grenade from his backpack. He pulled the pin and threw the grenade to the other side of the capsule room, where the alien hid behind the opposite door, then he sprinted after it to advance his position.

Instead of retreating as Mark had hoped, the alien charged forward and dove for cover behind a row of capsules.

A loud bang made his ears ring. Mark peeked around a capsule and barely avoided a shot to his head.

He gripped his alien pistol tighter.

Time to see what this thing can do.

Instead of looking around the capsule, Mark jumped straight up and leveled his weapon when he crested the top of the capsule. The alien's head came into view at the end of the row. Mark lined his target up with the weapon's holographic reticle and pulled the trigger.

The weapon thrummed like the string of an enormous bass guitar. Reality between it and his target seemed to fracture, broken into thousands of pieces, then just as quickly reformed.

Until it hit the alien. The shield around it vibrated and pulsed, just as the reality distortion had, then erupted with a concussive wave that ripped capsules from their moorings and slammed Mark into the rack behind him. His shimmering armor absorbed the shock, however, so he soon regained his feet and sprinted back into the hallway, where he found the alien lying on its back, its shield patchy and faded.

Got you.

Mark lined the bastard in his sights and fired again.

With vampire-like alacrity, the alien coiled up and sprang off down the hall. Mark's distortion wave struck the ground with little effect.

Or so he thought. Mark dashed after the alien, but when he stepped on the point of impact, his foot crumpled through the floor like brittle charcoal. Mark tumbled head-long into the wall.

He looked up just in time to see a rifle trained on him. Mark kicked off the wall, propelling him back into the capsule room and out of the path of the crimson beam. A trench scarred the floor where he'd been.

Mark leveled his pistol at the doorway and waited. The alien appeared a second later. Mark fired, but the alien ducked under the distortion wave and returned fire. Mark rolled out of the way and took refuge behind one of the capsules.

A hockey puck landed at his feet. Mark reflexively shot it before it rose, turning it into a misshapen hunk of jagged metal. He then trained his distortion gun for a follow-up shot where he knew the alien would appear.

A sound came from above him. Without looking to see what it was, Mark dove for cover, but the alien's line of fire was too good. A crimson beam scored across his back. Were it not for his shimmering armor, Mark was sure he would be dead.

He turned and shot the racks above him. As he'd hoped, the alien appeared an instant later, intent on finishing him off. Also as he'd hoped, the destabilized rack crumbled under the alien's weight. Mark shot the alien twice on the way down. It kicked off from a capsule, hurtling head-long into Mark. They crashed to the floor in a heap.

Before either of them could strike a blow, the alien's armor erupted even more violently than before. The concussion wave blew them apart, hurling Mark across the floor toward the Entity's chamber. He scrambled inside and took cover behind the opening. When he readied to resume the firefight, the alien was gone.

"How's it coming?" Mark said to Charlie, keeping an eye on the far side of the capsule chamber.

"Slowly."

"Can you just yank it?"

"I wish. The moorings are nigh unbreakable. I haven't figured out how to unfasten them without damaging the Entity itself. How are you holding up?"

"Fine," he said with forced calm. "The alien and I are just getting to know each other."

"Great. Maybe after we've kidnapped its planetary engineering computer, killed its crewmates, and destroyed its ship, we can do dinner or something."

"I'm thinking brunch. I could definitely go for a mimosa right now."

Mark stared across the capsule room. Sweat dappled his brow. He hadn't seen nor heard any movement since the alien disappeared, and assumed it was getting bigger ordnance.

Probably a tank, with my luck.

Mark edged away from the opening and fished a different alien pistol from his backpack, this one larger and ocean blue. He touched a green cube to it, which disappeared in a flash.

Bright white lines pulsed along the barrel. He leveled it at the opposite side of the room, intent on firing a test shot, but stopped short of pulling the trigger. Shooting the weapon would give away his element of surprise if the alien happened to be watching. He only hoped the alien would be more surprised than him.

"Aha! I think I discovered how the chips are secured," Charlie said from under the console. "The compound is a living material!"

"Fascinating," Mark said. "Does that mean you can talk it into releasing the Entity?"

Maybe, Cappa sent. A biological material could be engineered to respond to anything. Sound, electricity, sight, odors ...

"Glad you've narrowed it down," Mark said, feeling more anxious than before. "I'd happily sing it a lullaby if ..."

Mark felt more than heard footsteps from the hall behind them. He turned in time to see the alien wielding a tree-trunk-sized cannon. The large, round barrel glowed with red menace.

Mark dove out of the way just as the large barrel belched a streak of crimson death. The wall behind him vaporized where the beam touched. When he came to his feet, the barrel was still trained on him, glowing with the threat of eruption. Mark glanced behind him. Thankfully, Charlie was out of the line of fire.

Hang on ...

Mark took two steps to his right, putting Charlie squarely in danger, and waited.

The finishing shot never came.

Mark grinned. The alien's hesitation proved how important the Entity was to its plans. It wouldn't risk damaging the console — not even for the opportunity to kill Mark and Charlie with a single shot.

He clenched his jaw and fired at the son-of-a-bitch.

Instead of dodging, as Mark expected, the alien leaped forward with its weapon out like a battering ram. A white beam emitted from Mark's gun and hit the alien's cannon square in the center. Nothing seemed to happen.

Before Mark could fire another shot, the alien was on him. It swung the cannon like a giant club to sweep Mark aside.

Unfortunately for the alien, Brazilian *jiu-jitsu* — which Mark had spent most of his adult life practicing — was designed for close-quarters combat. Mark bent with the blow, grabbed the alien's wrists, and yanked it off balance. The alien tumbled over him. Even before it hit the ground, Mark had tangled himself around it in an unbreakable hold.

Unbreakable, that is, if it were human. Mark was used to sparring with Charlie in his cyborg body, who was far stronger than himself and could hold his own, but the alien put even Charlie to shame. Mark's muscles burned trying to keep the alien restrained. It flexed and bucked under him. Long limbs flailed around, trying to find purchase.

"How ... much ... longer?" Mark said to Charlie through clenched teeth.

"I think we're on to something. The moorings seem to respond to light patterns. We just need to figure out the right sequence."

"So in other —"

Mark bit the word off when the alien twisted under him. Its arm slipped free. Mark threw his weight to the side, carrying the alien with him in a tumble, then quickly restrained it again.

"In other words, we could be here a while."

"Possibly, yes," Charlie said.

Peachy.

A loud *crack* sounded from the alien's shoulder. The tension left Mark's hold. The alien used that instant of confusion to elbow Mark's head. Mark tumbled to the far wall in a splay of limbs. His shimmering armor had absorbed most of the impact, so he rolled to his feet and dashed to protect Charlie, but the alien ran back the way it had come.

Mark sprinted after it. The last time it had run off, it had returned with the Howitzer of hand weapons. He hated to imagine what sort of death machine it would fetch next.

The chase led Mark through hall after hall. Each one looked the same. The alien's long, powerful legs propelled it with a speed Mark couldn't match, putting it farther and farther ahead, until he came to an intersection.

The alien was nowhere to be seen.

Crap!

Not only had he failed to catch it, he was now separated from Charlie.

I should know better.

Mark hurried back the way he had come.

Except he had no idea which way that was.

I'M LOST, Mark sent to Cappa.

A message soon arrived with a picture of the map the console had shown them earlier.

EVEN IF YOU CAN'T TELL WHERE YOU ARE, IT'S A ROUND SHIP, Cappa sent. KEEP RUNNING AND YOU SHOULD FIND US EVENTUALLY. I'LL KEEP TRANSMITTING SO YOU CAN USE THE SIGNAL STRENGTH TO GAUGE DISTANCE.

THANKS, Mark sent. AND BE CAREFUL. IT GOT AWAY FROM ME, AND MAY BE CIRCLING BACK TO YOU.

LOVELY. WE'LL KEEP AN EYE OUT.

Mark sighed and instructed his implant to show the signal strength of Cappa's transmission. A vertical bar appeared in the corner of his vision. Her signal was weak.

He glanced both ways down the hall. Either direction looked identical. Since he had no idea how far around the ship he'd traveled, he decided to explore, and followed the alien's path.

Two hallways later, Mark heard a low hum that raised the hair on his neck. Something nearby was using a lot of power. Whatever it was, Mark bet it wasn't good.

Thump. Thump. Thump.

Footsteps. Big ones. From up ahead.

That something he dreaded was heavy, and it was coming.

Mark turned and ran.

Thump thump thump thump thump thump!

The thing was chasing him. Fast.

Mark barreled around corners and down straightaways. His legs burned in protest. He wanted to send a message to Charlie and Cappa to warn them, but composing a message meant pausing, and the thing behind him was gaining ground. If he'd thought to bring one of the alien weapons, he would have considered making a stand, but without that —

He skidded to a halt. The door on his left stood open. He recognized it.

He'd returned to the equipment room.

Mark darted inside. The crate with the power cubes was still open. He grabbed a box, then picked the largest rifle from the rack. It was easily six-feet long but, like the other weapons, was surprisingly light. Mark jammed a cube into it. The handle lit up, but the lights along the barrel were faint. So he jammed another cube into it, then another, until the entire thing shone brightly.

Thump thump thump thump.

The footsteps stopped right outside.

Mark closed his eyes, took a deep breath, and leaped into the hallway.

The tank he'd been dreading had finally arrived. The alien hunkered inside a four-legged robot that looked less like a machine than a hellhound from his darkest nightmare. The mecha stood nearly as tall as the twelve-foot ceiling and was just as wide. Large gun barrels protruded from its shoulders, each dwarfing Mark's own. Its thick legs flexed like a dog's, but the razor-sharp claws on its feet more resembled a cat's. Lines of soft purple light traced its exterior. Mark idly wondered how many cubes it had taken to power up that monstrosity.

From inside, the alien glared at Mark. The nightmare mecha hound stepped forward with predatory menace, snapping Mark out of his shock.

He pulled the trigger of his enormous rifle.

The barrel glowed crimson before lighting the hallway with a blinding beam of energy the width of his thigh. The mecha hound sidestepped, but didn't have enough room to evade. The beam caught its head. Instead of melting it into slag, as Mark had hoped, its shimmering forcefield glowed crimson, absorbing his shot. When Mark released the trigger, the mechanical beast appeared disappointingly unharmed.

Its giant gun barrels trained on him. Their depths glowed bright with crimson death.

Oh shit.

Mark dove into the equipment room.

Blinding light filled the hallway behind him. He rolled to a crouch and noticed the shimmering field protecting him flickering. When he glanced up, it was easy to see why. The walls of the ship, which had weathered the fire fight surprisingly well until now, had an enormous hole through which he could see the mecha hound, and a hole of equal size through the opposite wall.

Not waiting for the follow-up shot that would likely finish him off, Mark jumped through the new hole and curled into a shoulder roll on the other side. He had seconds, maybe, before the alien tracked him down.

Mark jumped to his feet and ran down the hall, away from the mecha hound and the alien piloting it inside.

Whether Charlie and Cappa had finished or not, the Entity's time was up.

33

POWER

C OLORED LIGHTS FROM CHARLIE'S LED flashed in a seemingly random sequence onto the alien circuit board containing the Entity. Charlie lowered his light wand and watched the moorings for any signs of change. As they had with the last several attempts, the moorings twitched, but didn't release the Entity's book-sized module.

IT FEELS LIKE WE'RE MISSING SOMETHING OBVIOUS, Cappa sent. MAYBE WE SHOULD INCREASE THE LIGHT SEQUENCE DURATIONS.

"Not the durations," Charlie said, struck with a sudden thought.

He slid out from underneath the console and rummaged through Mark's backpack, emerging a second later with a night vision monocular. "We should increase the wavelength. The aliens are used to low-light environments. They may see on a lower end of the electromagnetic spectrum than we do."

INFRARED! NOW WHY DIDN'T I THINK OF THAT?

"Probably because you've been busy crunching light pattern permutations. Even you, my amazing wife, have your limitations." She fell silent while Charlie unscrewed the lens of the monocle. "Cappa?"

"Just as well," Charlie said, smiling. "The last part probably wasn't true anyway."

Charlie carefully freed the infrared emitter from the circuit board inside of the monocle. "Got it. No more compliments until I get home."

Charlie laughed and stripped the casing from the LED wand, twisted the infrared wires around two small pegs, then secured the emitter in place with a small strip of duct tape. "That should do it."

His vision switched to the infrared spectrum, where the normally dark emitter shined brightly.

Charlie aimed the patchwork wand at one of the numerous moorings. Color patterns once again danced across the tiny lights.

The mooring unfastened.

"Excellent! Now we just need to —"

Pounding footsteps from the hallway cut Charlie short. He extended a plasma barrel from his palm and aimed for the opening, but lowered his weapon when Mark appeared. The shimmering alien forcefield covering him appeared faint and patchy.

Mark spared no words and slid on his knees to his backpack, where he grabbed the strange distortion pistol, then sprinted back to the hall. He fired his weapon in rapid succession at the walls on either side of the hallway, then at the ceiling.

As Charlie feared it would, the structure soon collapsed. Dirt and rock tumbled in from all sides, forming a mound as high as his chest. Mark squinted through the plume of dust and fired several more times into the earth above. More debris tumbled down. This time, it didn't stop until earth filled the hallway from floor to ceiling. Before Charlie could ask what had happened, Mark was already running from the hallway toward the capsule room.

"How's it coming?" Mark said on passing.

"Almost there," Charlie said.

"How almost?"

Another two minutes should do it, Cappa sent to him. Is everything all right?

"Perfectly fine," Mark called from the other room.

Charlie heard more distortion blasts, followed by rumbling. Mark returned a few seconds later, panting, his eyes wild.

"But let's say, just for argument's sake, the alien was piloting a gigantic mechanical hound armed with death cannons and a forcefield, and was trying to kill us. Would that speed things up?"

Rather than answer, Charlie returned his focus to the Entity and pointed the light wand at the next mooring. The sequence ran for over twenty seconds, by his count, before the mooring opened.

Six moorings to go.

After the next mooring also opened, Charlie heard a faint scratching sound from the far end of the capsule room.

Like someone's digging.

"Be right back," Mark said. In addition to his distortion pistol, he grabbed another of the alien weapons and a green cube from his backpack, then ran in the direction of the noise.

Time dragged. The light sequence flashing on the mooring felt lethargic, as if it knew he was in a hurry, and was going to do everything possible to slow him down. It eventually opened, so he moved on to the next one.

Charlie heard rocks tumbling in the capsule room, followed by the distortion gun, and another avalanche.

"No hurry!" Mark shouted from the other room, his voice tight. "Plenty of time."

Charlie glared at the mooring, willing it to open faster. It didn't help.

More digging from the other room. More rocks tumbling. One distortion blast, followed by Mark swearing. He ran into the room and dove for his pack.

"That answers my question about ammo capacity."

Mark pulled another green cube out and touched it to the gun, which glowed with renewed life, then dashed back into the capsule room.

The mooring opened. Charlie shifted to the next one.

Three left. Come on, come on, come on …

Rocks tumbled in the distance, followed by the sound of large feet climbing over rubble.

"Charlie!" Mark screamed, running back into the console room. "We need to get out of here like goddamned fucking now!"

He fired into the capsule room from behind the wall. A second later, a powerful thrum rolled right through Charlie, knocking the wind out of his artificial lungs. Mark staggered backward, but soon resumed his position.

"Crap, I made it angry," Mark said. "We need bigger guns. Great big fucking guns!"

He dove to the side an instant before a blinding light filled the room. Two thick beams of solid energy pierced the capsule room wall, disintegrating it and the wall behind. Mark shook his head at the pistol in his hand and glanced at Charlie.

"Did I mention we should leave?"

Without waiting for an answer, Mark fired two shots through the new hole in the wall, then ducked out of the way. Another concussive wave drove the air from Charlie's chest. Mark then shot a different pistol. This one fired what looked like pure electricity. Charlie heard crackling and popping from inside the room. Mark's face lit with a triumphant grin, then he flattened himself to the floor just before two thick beams of light pierced the wall above him.

The current mooring opened, leaving two. Charlie tugged at the Entity, hoping it would be enough, but the box wouldn't budge. With a heavy heart, Charlie tucked the wand in his jacket and grabbed his pack.

"Come on," he said to Mark. "We tried, but it's time to —"

No! Charlie, we're so close! Before Charlie could respond, Cappa sent another message. Mark, take the wand from Charlie. It's already programmed with the correct sequence. You just need to push the button and hold until the mooring opens.

Charlie clenched his jaw. "Cappa! I won't risk his life for —"

I have an idea that may slow the alien down, but we need to switch places.

Charlie hesitated, torn between his love's desperate request and the life of his best friend.

Mark, Charlie, please! I can't bear the thought of letting an enslaved artificial intelligence die. Not when we still have a chance of saving it.

Then Mark was beside him.

"Give me the wand," Mark said.

And, like that, the decision was made. Charlie handed it over, then took cover by the entrance to the capsule room.

"So what's your plan?" Charlie said softly.

STEP ONE: SEE WHAT THIS MONSTROSITY LOOKS LIKE.

Charlie glanced around the corner.

He wished he hadn't. Not only did it look like a creature from Hell, it was armed with two enormous cannons and surrounded by a shimmering forcefield.

Charlie hid behind the wall and gulped. "Okay, now you've seen the face of the Devil. Next?"

GET CLOSE TO IT, THEN GIVE ME CONTROL OF YOUR BODY.

"Cappa, what —"

TRUST ME, CHARLIE!

Charlie sighed. He liked nothing about this plan, but he trusted Cappa with his life. Here in the heat of battle was the wrong time to question her.

He darted into the capsule room.

The mecha hound's enormous cannons trained on him. A hellish red glow lit the depths of each. Charlie waited until the last possible moment before diving for cover between a row of capsules.

Damage reports showed he'd been an instant too late. His left elbow had been disintegrated down to the frame and was fused at the joint, freezing it in a right angle.

Which would make his next trick even more difficult. Charlie hurried down the row, then planted a hand on the top of the rack and vaulted over it, landing squarely on the mecha hound's back.

Or, at least, he would have if the hound hadn't risen to its full height to peer over the rack.

Instead of landing on it, Charlie bounced off its side and fell. Looking at the hound's belly from the floor, he saw the alien hunkered inside.

This is as close as we're going to get, Charlie thought.

He released control of his body to Cappa.

The alien looked down at them. Its purple lips peeled back in a fanged snarl that made Charlie shiver.

Charlie didn't need to extend his awareness to feel Cappa gathering her *chi*. Life energy flowed into them from all directions — from the two silver lines connecting Cappa to her other selves, from the heavens, and from the earth. It infused them, filled them to a level he had never imagined possible. More than Master Wung had ever dared. Charlie saw more than felt his undamaged arm move. Into it, all of Cappa's massive energy flowed.

Alarms blared in Charlie's mind — warnings from Master Wung that Charlie himself hadn't heeded. Wisdom that could have saved his biological body from clinical death, and his mind from years of depression and heartache.

Warnings about not depleting his life energy.

Before he could whisper the words that might save his wife — his love, his greatest gift to the world — the entirety of Cappa's *chi* shot forth in a torrent. Although her palm barely touched its forcefield, the mecha hound lurched into the ceiling as if hit by a speeding truck, cracking its underside, and jarring the alien within.

Charlie snatched control of his body from Cappa and rolled out of the way the instant before the giant mecha hound crashed to the floor. Mecha and alien lay still.

Charlie stumbled to his feet, eying the monstrosity. The alien's arm twitched, but its eyes remained closed.

"You may not have killed it," he said, "but it'll think twice before charging us again."

No response from Cappa.

Charlie went cold. "Cappa?" he said softly.

His message queue remained empty.

"Cappa? Cappa! Report!"

Nothing.

Charlie stared at the wall. He felt numb, hollow.

"Cappa? Honey, please ..."

A sob choked him off. His chest spasmed for air. But, no matter how hard he gasped, he felt as if he was suffocating.

"Honey, please talk to me."

But she didn't.

Was Cappa angry with him? Had he said something to upset her? Charlie tried to remember, but his thoughts were a jumble. No, he was fairly certain he hadn't upset her. Perhaps she had glitched? Cappa did that now and then. Uncaught errors sometimes stopped her run loop. Charlie just needed a computer terminal, and he would fix her right up.

Something moved out of the corner of his eye, but he was too lost in thought to care.

"I got it," Mark called from the other room. "The Entity is packed safely away. Let's get the f—"

"Mark!" Charlie ran to him. "I need to use your workstation."

Mark blinked. "I-I didn't bring one, pal. Besides, what do you need a computer for when you have Cappa?"

Pain stabbed Charlie's chest at the mention of her name. "That's the problem. She isn't responding to input. I think she glitched again."

"'Again'? Charlie, Cappa hasn't glitched in over six years, and ..." Mark paled. "Wait, w-what do you mean she isn't responding?"

"Like I said, I think it's just a glitch. If I can find a terminal, I'll have her up and running again soon."

I'm sure of it. I'm sure ...

His vision blurred, but Charlie wiped his tears away. "That's all right. We can use my workstation in the bio lab."

Charlie started to walk, but only made it two steps before realizing that he couldn't remember the way to his own lab. Everything around was black and unfamiliar.

That's right, he thought dismally. *We burned it to the ground. It's gone.*

Just like everything else.

The cold inside of him spread. Charlie hugged himself for warmth, but it didn't help.

He wanted Cappa's warmth. At that moment, he would have given anything to be in her arms — to feel her silky hair, her soft skin, hear her musical laughter, her gentle, caring voice ...

"Oh crap," Mark said, although Charlie wasn't paying much attention. Mark pulled a gun, fired several times, then swore some more. "We've gotta go, pal. Come on!"

Charlie mechanically picked up his backpack, then he was being ushered to a crack in the wall, crawling through a dirt tunnel, and onto a bright snow tundra. He heard his name being called once, twice, but he didn't care.

Cappa was gone. She —

A slap across his face snapped him to.

"Charlie! Did you hear me?" Mark shook him by the shoulders. "We're in deep shit here!"

"Deep ... W-what happened?"

"I radioed our airlift. Russia has closed their airspace, even to domestic traffic. Someone dropped a nuclear goddamned fucking missile inside their border! It was a remote military base near Bereznik, so casualties were minimal, but their borders are completely sealed until further notice."

"But who would ..."

Charlie shook his head. It didn't matter. What did matter was they no longer had a means of vacating the country. Their airlift was a private VTOL in Mongolia run by smugglers who knew how to safely get in and out of the country.

But, in the wake of a bona fide nuclear attack, Russia would be on high alert. Even if Charlie and Mark tripled their offer, the smugglers wouldn't risk being shot down by a twitchy jet fighter pilot.

Then again, Russia is a big place.

Most of it was uninhabited, which made monitoring the entire country not only unfeasible, but unnecessary. The Russian government's attention would be on their cities and borders, not a barren tundra in the middle of nowhere. Flying into the country would be a suicide mission. But flying out of it ...

Charlie cautiously peered over the small rise hiding their tunnel from view.

People bustled about Orwing's encampment. Most of the tents had been taken down. Soldiers were loading equipment into a large VTOL — an Osprey covered with the same optic camouflage as the camp.

"There's our new airlift," Mark said. "Alvin killed all his vampires, so we just have to deal with the human soldiers." He cracked his knuckles. "And Alvin."

Something on the blue skyline caught Charlie's eye — a slight distortion moving across the horizon. He waited for Cappa to zoom and enhance the image. She never did. Charlie turned away and put it from his mind before grief consumed him once again. The distortion had to be one of Orwing's camouflaged planes. He told Mark as much.

"That oily snake may have already escaped," Charlie said.

Mark clenched his jaw, his hazel eyes fixed on the retreating plane as if he could destroy it by sheer will. He fingered the sniper rifle on his backpack, then sighed. It was well out of range, and they both knew it.

"Fine," Mark said eventually.

He crept to the top of the ridge and set up the sniper rifle, looking through the scope at the camp.

"I'm thinking classic rush-and-cover. You follow the ridge to the west, past our original hiding spot, and get as close as you can. I'll stay here. Wait for my second shot before charging."

Charlie nodded. They'd used that tactic many times before. By the second shot, the enemy would be focused on Mark's position, creating ample opportunity for Charlie to pick them off from a flanking position. His enhanced armor made the chances of incurring significant damage unlikely. While the enemy was futilely shooting at Charlie, Mark would continue to pick them off from the rear. The whole skirmish would likely be over in minutes.

Screams came from the encampment. Charlie scrambled to the top of the ridge in time to see two thick energy beams shoot up from the underground entrance to the ship, disintegrating three soldiers. The mecha hound emerged under the protective shade of the encampment-wide tarp and charged an unlucky soldier. One swipe of its razor-sharp claws opened him up from chest to hips. It pounced after another, but shied back from the encampment's sunlit boundary.

"I was afraid the alien might show," Mark said softly. "If we rush in now, there's still a small chance we can board the plane before —"

The mecha hound fired again, this time at the VTOL. They saw the explosion before they heard it, and the brief screams of its passengers.

"Well ... fuck." Mark rubbed his face and sighed.

Charlie clenched his jaw. "Fuck is right. Can you still connect to the phone we left on the ship?"

Mark reached for his pocket. Surprisingly, his hand passed right through the shimmering forcefield surrounding his entire body and pulled out his phone.

"Yes," Mark said after a moment. "Amazingly, it survived the firefight."

"Great. The alien seems hesitant to enter the sunlight, which means it will probably be within the blast radius if we detonate the power cores soon."

"Now that's a plan." Mark quickly gathered his things and secured his backpack. "As much as I'd like to watch the show, I don't want to be anywhere near here when the power reactors go critical."

Charlie and Mark hurried away from the ridge, staying low to keep out of sight. Screams from the encampment became distant and less frequent.

They ran a good half-mile before they found a large, rocky formation suitable to shelter behind. The sounds of battle back at the encampment had stopped, or were too faint to be heard.

"Still have a signal?" Charlie said.

Mark glanced at his phone and nodded. "Ready?"

"Do it."

Mark took a deep breath and sent the detonation code. They both glanced around the rock.

Nothing happened at first. The landscape was still, peaceful. Not even the encampment was visible from their vantage point, giving the illusion that Mark and Charlie were alone in this great, barren snow wilderness.

Then the planet erupted.

A dome of earth rose high into the air. Jets of fire propelled debris in all directions. The dome broke, releasing an enormous mushroom of fire, as if Hell itself had risen to defy the heavens. The snow flattened around the explosion in an ever-expanding ring, followed closely by a ripple that flowed through the land like an ocean swell on high water. Charlie and Mark hid behind the rock and braced themselves.

The blast wave impacted the far side of their boulder like a giant hammer, raining snow and rocks down over their heads. An earthquake tossed them several feet in the air. They both flailed and landed heavily.

The land fell quiet once again.

Mark uncovered his ears. "That wasn't as bad as I —"

A small stone embedded itself in the snow next to him with ballistic speed.

"Down!" Charlie shouted.

They curled into balls, covering their heads. Debris rained in a steady maelstrom, peppering the snow and striking their protective boulder like gunshots. One hit Charlie's lower back, another his head. Mark's shimmering forcefield warbled from several impacts.

Charlie waited for the damage reports from Cappa. Once again, she remained silent. He violently shoved the implications of that from his mind.

After the debris storm passed, Charlie sat on his haunches. "Are you all right?"

"Yeah, my forcefield held up fine. You?"

"Minor tissue damage," Charlie said. It may have been more than that, but he had no way of knowing, and it was easier to answer with a lie than to think about why Cappa wasn't responding. "That blast will have set off the Russian's seismic sensors. I expect some sort of surveillance or search party within the hour. Unless we want to be found by the welcome wagon, we'd better move."

"Right." Mark stood and broke into a trot, but stopped when he noticed that Charlie hadn't followed. "Coming?"

Charlie ran a hand through his hair, freeing a shower of pebbles and dirt. "I ... I'd like to talk to the others back home first. Just to check in."

Mark frowned in thought, but eventually nodded, for which Charlie was grateful. Try as he might, he couldn't shake the awful feeling he had about Cappa, and would feel better if he at least knew that her other selves were okay. The Entity was also offline. While he hoped that wouldn't affect Anne or the other vampires, he didn't know for sure.

Charlie needed to know that both of his loves were safe.

Mark started to pull the satellite dish from his pack, but Charlie shook his head.

"Aligning the dish will take too long without Cappa," Charlie said. "I can jump into my biological body, get an update, and be back here before we'd finished setting it up."

"All right." Mark unfastened his sniper rifle. "Just ... hurry."

Charlie sat against the rock and closed his eyes. Moving his spirit from one body to the other had once been such a routine task that, even now, he barely had to concentrate to slip into the required trance. Charlie stilled his thoughts. His artificial pulse slowed, his breathing became deep and regular. He felt himself drift from the confines of his body.

What he saw when he looked back at himself nearly knocked him out of his trance.

Cappa's spirit was missing.

Wrestling his panic under control, Charlie fixed his thoughts on his biological body, and willed himself to go there.

•　　•　　•

There was no flashing landscape, no light-speed travel or blurred scenery. One moment Charlie was in Russia, the next he was breathing cool air, with the rhythm of a real heart beating in his chest.

His eyelids opened under protest, stuck together from days of non-use. Charlie tried to sit up, but firm straps around his shoulders tied him down. He managed to unbuckle the straps, then sat up and stretched his stiff muscles. He was sitting on a gurney in the middle of their underground factory, which was odd. The gurney had been in the back room when he'd left.

And he was alone.

"The ambulance is here, Dela," Carol yelled from around the corner.

She appeared in her white lab coat, and screamed when she saw Charlie.

"For the love of all that's Holy! We were just about to load you into the ambulance so we can join the others in San Francisco. What are you doing awake?"

"I'm only here for a minute. Listen, have you —"

"Charlie!"

Dela ran into the room and gave him a flying hug, nearly toppling him from the gurney. Her embrace crushed the air from his lungs with much more strength than he remembered.

"Are you guys all right? Where's Mark? Is the Entity dead? What did the ship look like? Did you see any aliens? What —"

Charlie put a hand over her mouth and laughed. "Mark's fine. The Entity is powered off and in our custody. I promise I'll fill you in on the rest later. We're still trying to figure out how to get home, which is why I have to hurry. Is ... is everyone all right here?"

"Yeah. I thought Cappa filled herself in on the details."

Charlie gulped, afraid to ask his next question. "Have you spoken to her recently?"

"Not since she scheduled the ambulance twenty minutes ago. Why?"

Charlie hopped off the gurney and headed to the server room, where her factory self lived.

"Cappa?" he said on the way. "Are you there?"

The only sound was Dela's footsteps behind him.

Dela frowned and tapped her glasses, which, Charlie noted, were Anne's techno-glasses.

"Cappa? Are you with me, buddy?" Her frown deepened. "That's strange, I swear I was just chatting with her."

Charlie stopped at the server room door. He spun on Dela so suddenly that she squeaked in surprise.

"I need you to call Zima, right now," Charlie said. "Find out how Anne is doing, and have her check on Cappa."

"O-okay." Dela pulled her phone out with trembling hands and dialed. "Charlie," she said softly, "what happened?"

"Cappa saved us," was all he could manage before grief closed off his throat.

Charlie turned away and zeroed in on the one-foot-square black cube that was Cappa's factory self. Its power lights were on, cables connected securely. When Charlie plugged a terminal in, he saw the command prompt he'd expected.

"Hi, Z," Dela said from behind him. "It's Dela. We're fine, but Charlie made a surprise visit and ... Yes, it sounds like they were successful but ... Z, just listen for a sec! The Entity is offline. Is Anne all right? Oh thank God!" She flashed an okay sign at Charlie. "How about Cappa?" Dela stared for a moment, then paled. "She's not responding? Look, Z, this is important. Can you please ... Sure, I'll hold." Dela held the phone away and looked at Charlie. "She's not responding to Zima's connection requests, but she says that's not uncommon because they're underground and the signal is terrible. Zima's looking for her right now."

"Thanks, Dela."

Charlie returned his attention to the terminal and typed with shaking fingers. Cappa's program responded to every command, outputting diagnostic information, such as memory and storage utilization, but her processing activity was almost zero. Charlie sat on the floor and wiped the tears from his eyes, but they just kept flowing.

Dela watched him with growing worry. She jerked the phone back to her ear. "Yeah, I'm here, Z," she said in a raspy voice. "Did you ... She ... she what?" Dela covered her mouth, her own tears welling. She looked at Charlie and shook her head.

He didn't need to hear Zima's answer.

Cappa wasn't responding there, either.

The symptoms were frighteningly familiar. They were the same indications he'd seen when staring at his own empty shell of a body.

In fighting the alien, Cappa had used all of her life force. Unlike other computers, however, she needed more than just hardware to run. Her spirit was an integral part of what made her work. Without it ...

Charlie buried his face in his arms. Sobs wracked his shoulders.

Without her spirit, his wife was brain-dead.

34

THE SHORTEST DISTANCE

MARK SAT IN THE SNOW next to Charlie's unconscious body, fingering his sniper rifle with growing unease. The promised few minutes Charlie had said he'd be away was now going on twenty. Mark jumped at every branch movement and howl of the wind, expecting to see Russian soldiers.

A black dot passed high overhead. He couldn't see details from this distance, but, given the speed and altitude, he had no doubt it was a spy plane. Heavy reconnaissance was imminent. Helicopters would sweep the entire area. With their advanced optics, Mark didn't favor his and Charlie's chances of hiding from the Russians for long.

Another minute passed.

Fuck it.

Mark pulled the satellite dish from his pack and began the tedious process of lining it up with the satellite. He couldn't communicate with Charlie while his mind was in his other body, so he'd have to dial home the old-fashioned way if he wanted to learn what was going on.

Charlie suddenly stirred to life. Mark started to lay into him, but then he saw Charlie's eyes — dead, hollow husks, bereft of the wonder and curiosity they normally held.

"Um, are you —"

"Fine," Charlie said, his voice as flat as his eyes.

"Any word on Cappa?"

His mouth twitched. "She's dead."

"W-what? I mean, how could she —"

"Later," Charlie said.

In that one word, his facade cracked, letting Mark know just how tenuous his hold on sanity was. Charlie cleared his throat, and his flat tone returned.

"For now, I swore to your wife I would get you home safely — and so help me God, that's exactly what I'm going to do. Have you seen any signs of approach?"

"Spy plane a few minutes ago. If we hurry, we may be able to reach the forest south of here before the helicopters arrive."

Charlie stood and brushed the snow from his pants. "Let them come."

"Say what?"

"Our airlift plans were scrapped. The alien destroyed Orwing's aircraft, and we just blew up their reason for returning. We're five hundred miles from the nearest city. Even if we walked, you'd starve before we arrived. Our best option is to let the Russians find us, then hijack their aircraft."

"A brilliant plan — unless, of course, they send gunships and shoot us on sight."

"Possible, but unlikely. Yet another nuclear explosion just detonated on Russian soil, and they have no leads. Two guys wandering ground zero might have valuable information. We're worth far more alive than dead."

Mark clenched his jaw, but remained silent. As much as he hated the idea of allowing themselves to be caught, Charlie and Mark were a match for any platoon, and he couldn't argue with Charlie's logic about the alternatives.

"So what's the plan?"

"First, we cover you in snow to hide you from normal and infrared optics," Charlie said. "I don't want them seeing you until the aircraft is secured."

"But —"

Charlie grabbed him by the shoulders and shook. "I'm not risking your life, Mark! There will be no more grieving spouses in our family!"

"I ..."

Mark bit off his terse reply. The precaution was unnecessary. With the protection of his shimmering alien armor, Mark was easily Charlie's equal in a firefight. But Charlie was beyond reasoning, so he simply grunted assent. Charlie let go of him and began digging.

Soon, frigid snow completely covered Mark, although the alien forcefield kept him surprisingly warm. He watched through the eyes of the robot mouse and saw Charlie sit in the snow.

Then they waited for the enemy to find them.

Twenty minutes later, Charlie perked up and looked west. The steady beat of chopper blades played in the distance, growing louder and louder. Charlie donned his jacket to hide the exposed metal on his damaged arm, retrieved a red shirt from his backpack, and waved.

The crew must have seen him, for the chopper — an Mi-17 transport from the looks of its medium-length body — altered course and headed straight for them.

Snow blew in a flurry from the aircraft's downwash, obscuring Mark's view, until the lifelike mouse brushed the flakes from its face with its tiny paws. Three soldiers disembarked with assault rifles at the ready, leaving just the pilot and the gunner in the chopper.

The approaching soldiers shouted something in Russian, to which Charlie didn't respond, and then gestured with the business ends of their rifles for him to get down.

He put his hands behind his head and knelt. Two soldiers kept their weapons trained on him, while the third approached with zip-tie restraints.

Charlie became a blur: one moment the soldier was reaching for him, the next, Charlie had his rifle. He ignored the soldiers in front of him and fired a burst at the gunner sitting at the side door, then another burst through the windshield at the pilot.

The soldiers facing him fired. Bullets rang from Charlie's endo-armor like muted bells. He didn't even flinch. Charlie shot them both at close range. Sickly red smattered the snow around him. He trained his weapon on the chopper for a few seconds before signaling the okay.

Mark rose from the snow and ran for the chopper. The pilot slumped in his seat, unmoving. Blood covered the headrest and side window. Mark unfastened his seatbelt and unceremoniously yanked him into the snow, then buckled himself into the pilot's seat.

Although he couldn't read the controls, the layout was familiar enough that Mark had no trouble readying for flight. Instead of climbing into the passenger seat, Charlie pushed the side gunner's corpse out of the chair and took point behind the heavy machine gun.

Mark eased the collective up. The helicopter rocked and wobbled from the ground effect, but smoothed once he gained altitude. He kept the bird low to avoid radar detection and pointed the nose south, toward their original airlift destination. Even though the smugglers had canceled their extraction, their connecting flight back to the United States should still be available.

If the smugglers had canceled that, too, then he and Charlie would convince them to un-cancel it.

Anxiety gnawed Mark's gut for the entire trip. Jet fighters, surface-to-air missiles, other attack helicopters ... Any or all of those could appear at any moment.

What worried him the most, however, wasn't the Russians. Mark glanced behind him and sighed.

No, his biggest worry was his best friend, who had just lost his wife, killed five soldiers without a second thought, and watched the countryside pass by with his dead, empty eyes.

35

BITTERSWEET

H ALF OF THE RESISTANCE, it seemed, had joined Anne at the bottom of the headquarters entry room, making it difficult for her to pace.

Two days had passed since Charlie and Mark's flight from Russia. The trip had been rough, apparently. With two reported nuclear explosions — one a mystery, and the other the alien spaceship — countries had closed their borders down tight. Charlie and Mark had cashed in a truckload of favors to escape from Asia to Western Europe. Even then, the US had canceled all commercial international flights, so Anne had needed to tap William's extensive infiltration network to get them on a military transport.

That transport had arrived half an hour ago. Charlie and Mark were due any minute, and the entire Resistance knew it.

Anne bumped into someone for the twentieth time, mumbled an apology, and continued pacing. The ten-story concrete missile silo entry room wasn't designed for gatherings, let alone welcoming parties.

Many chatted excitedly, eager to hear about Charlie and Mark's adventures on a genuine alien spaceship. Some worried about them bringing the Entity to Resistance headquarters, where the All Mother and many top-hierarchy vampires also lived.

Anne shared their concern, but could think of no better place to secure such a crucial piece of technology. The Entity was powered off, as far as everyone knew, and Anne had managed to convince everyone that, unless someone plugged it back in, keeping it here would be safe.

Tabby caught her arm, pulling Anne to a stop.

"You're going to wear a trench in the floor, Mom."

"Sorry, I'm just ... anxious. About Charlie."

Tabby nodded. In the two days since Cappa had fallen just before the spaceship's detonation, aside from pre-programmed breathing and occasional eye blinks, Anne's soul sister hadn't moved. Master Wung's explorations had, unfortunately, confirmed her lifeforce absent. Despite his best efforts, the ancient master had been unable to bring her back.

Anne gathered Tabby in a hug, grateful for her comfort.

Zima's sharp gasp pierced the chatter. Anne looked around just in time to see her flee from the room.

"Damnit," Anne and Tabby said together.

"Sorry, Mom."

Anne shook her head. It was her fault, too. They'd been careful not to stand too close to each other around Zima, but in this crowded room, Anne hadn't noticed her until it was too late. She glanced at the top of the metal stairway, where the door to the surface remained closed, and sighed.

"I'd better go take care of her," Anne said.

Tabby nodded, looking every bit as miserable about their blunder as Anne felt. Hundreds of presences in Anne's mind echoed her grief, all of them from her Firsts and their hierarchies.

The Resistance vampires were of Anne's bloodline. They didn't feel the same blind loyalty as the Firsts and the rest of William's bloodline. As soon as Anne had been freed from the Entity and moved safely underground, the Resistance had been happy for her to diminish Tim's presence and allow them to resume their mental independence.

The Firsts hadn't.

"Kicking and screaming" accurately describe their reaction when she'd suggested diminishing their presences to allow them a modicum of free will, and a bit of privacy for herself. Myrcella, in particular, had looked as if she would shatter if Anne shut her out. So Anne had left her twenty-odd bonds to her Firsts intact, and hadn't brought the subject up again.

As if summoned, Myrcella appeared in the tunnel Zima had just fled down. She squeezed through the crowd, sparing a few sniffs for the delectable humans along the way, and sidled next to Anne with a cat-like stretch and a smile.

"Good evening, Mother," she said groggily, still rousing from her daytime sleep. "Sorry about the general. At least she doesn't get agitated when *we* snuggle." To drive the point home, she took Anne's other arm, opposite Tabby, and laid her head on Anne's shoulder.

Tabby gave her a withering stare.

Myrcella smiled as if it were a compliment. Myrcella's affection for Anne, she'd learned, didn't translate to her daughter.

"Did I miss anything else while I was asleep?" Myrcella said.

"Just me spending most of the day with Mom," Tabby said, tightening her grip on Anne's arm. She didn't stick her tongue out, but her possessive frown suggested she wanted to.

The jibe had its intended effect. Although Myrcella remained cool on the outside, jealousy flooded through her bond. Her large, dark eyes rounded into a puppy dog plea. "Please, Mother, will you stay awake tonight? I found a new hunting spot I'd love to show you."

"Myrcella! You *know* you're not supposed to hunt humans against their —"

"It's consensual," she said, rolling her eyes. "But they do put up a good chase, even if it's all pretend. What do you say?"

Anne glanced at the door high above, which should be opening any moment, then at the tunnel her dear wife had disappeared down, who was probably miserable with unrelieved desire. She patted Myrcella's hand and heaved a regretful sigh.

"Another time, my sweet. Tonight promises to be sleepless already."

Myrcella pouted, but didn't object, which tugged Anne's heartstrings. As abrasive as the petite Goth could be, she was also adorable. Anne had quickly taken a liking to her, much to the chagrin of the other Firsts, and occasionally her daughter, which had ostracized Myrcella from several circles. Myrcella seemed to think Anne's affection worth the tradeoff.

Anne started to excuse herself to find her wife when the door above opened, flooding the tall chamber with the last orange hues of day. Vampires all squinted, blinded by the sudden brightness. When Anne's sight returned, Charlie and Mark were making their way downstairs.

Cheers erupted from the crowd, echoing from the concrete walls. Mark lit in surprise and gave a small wave over the railing. Charlie's flat gaze fixed on Mark's back, his face a stony mask.

To compare his expression to Zima's impassive mien was wrong. Anne's wife showed neither happiness nor sorrow, though her actions gave other clues to her mood, which Anne had learned to read.

Charlie's expression wasn't neutral. It was listless. Lifeless. *Dead.*

For the first time since she'd known him, Charlie's cyborg body looked like what it was: a man-made automaton. A machine devoid of the qualities that had made it so easy to forget that beneath his synthetic flesh were gears, circuitry, and an artificial neural mass.

The thing walking down the stairs wasn't Charlie. Not the Charlie Anne had grown to love.

And then she was running to him. The crowd parted, but not fast enough. She elbowed and shoved her way through, then dashed up the stairs four at a time, tears streaming down her cheeks. She managed a weak smile for Mark before focusing on the thing that looked like Charlie.

His dead eyes eventually found her. A flicker of life threatened a smile, but it quickly drowned in whatever acidic bog had killed the rest of him.

"You're okay," Charlie said, as if he hadn't believed it before seeing her with his own eyes.

Anne nodded and put a gentle hand on his chest. "But you're not."

"No," he said in a hollow voice. He fished in his pack and produced a white, smooth box the size of a paperback novel. He opened his mouth to say something. Pain creased his brow. Charlie snapped his jaw shut and simply handed it to her.

Anne accepted it with wide eyes. "Is this ... the Entity?"

A nod. Charlie looked away.

Anne bit back a sob. She wanted to tell him he'd done the right thing, that saving the Entity was the right choice. The only choice.

But she knew what that decision had cost him — a decision he'd made at Anne's request.

A decision that had ultimately killed his wife.

Killed my soul sister.

Of all the terrible choices Anne had been forced to make over the last week — had it only been a week since Calum appeared at her door? — even over accepting responsibility for the end of the world, that one hurt the most.

Guilt prevented her from wrapping him in her arms, like she wanted to. So Anne gripped his shirt and rolled her forehead across his chest in silent commiseration, the unassuming white box cold in her hand.

Someone tugged at the Entity.

"Anne," Mark said softly from a few steps down. "If it's all the same, I'd like to put this someplace safe before we see Cappa."

"Oh. Of course." Anne handed it to him with numb fingers.

"I know a safe place," Tim said from behind him. "There's an active volcano just a few hours away by plane. We could airdrop it from ..."

He cleared his throat at Anne's level stare.

"Seriously, though, there's an unfinished tunnel on the other side of this missile complex. That should put enough earth between it and us to shield us from its influence. In case, you know, someone's dumb enough to turn it back on." It could have been a trick of the light, but a twinkle in Tim's eye hinted that dumb-enough person may be him.

Mark handed the Entity to him. Tim hurried down the stairs, holding the white box with a mixture of fear and intrigue, as if it were a fascinating timebomb that could explode at any moment.

When Anne turned back to Charlie, his lifeless stare was back. Gently, timidly, Anne took his hand and led him down to the waiting crowd.

Resistance members congratulated him, clapped him on the back, pumped their fists in triumph, and shouted a dozen questions at once. Some offered sympathy flowers with heartfelt condolences. Charlie ignored them all, his lifeless eyes fixed on Anne. Wherever Charlie was, he wasn't here. Anne had a sinking feeling that seeing his wife would only make him worse.

She walked him and Mark through two long, oval tunnels to a large domed space that had been sectioned into smaller living quarters. Anne opened a door at the far side of the space, ushered them inside, and shut the door on the rest of the Resistance.

Doris and Dela were already sitting on folding chairs next to the bed where Cappa lay. Her chest rose and fell inside the yellow sundress they'd put her in this morning. Long, dark-brown hair ran down her shoulders, silky and brushed with care. Doris had even applied Cappa's favorite lipstick and blush. Cappa blinked at what could have been an air current or speck of dust, but her blue eyes stayed unfocused on the ceiling.

Charlie took in the scene with a measured breath. He carefully moved a bouquet of flowers aside and sat next to her. Gently, he took one of Cappa's hands and clutched it to his chest.

They sat in silence for close to ten minutes before Charlie finally spoke.

"Would you leave us, please?" he said softly, not taking his eyes from his wife.

Mark took a last, sorrowful look at Cappa, then gestured everyone outside.

Anne stopped him in the common area. "Has he been like this the entire trip?"

"Ever since we hijacked the Russian helicopter, yeah." Mark sagged. "I've seen him depressed, but this is something else. Cappa was his world."

"*Is*," Dela said, her voice cracking. She cleared her throat. "*Is* his world. If anyone can get Cappa back up and running, it's the guy who built her." Her pleading eyes sought them each in turn. "Right?"

Doris rubbed her shoulder. "Right. He's one smart cookie. And with Mark and Master Wung in her corner, she'll be back with us in no time, just you watch."

Mark's jaw tightened. "Damn straight. I'll talk to Tim about retrieving diagnostic equipment from our Graven factory. It would be easier if Z-Tech were still standing, but ..." He sighed, then headed down the tunnel.

"Sucky reunion." Dela plunked onto a bench in the middle of the domed common room and crossed her arms. Tears brimmed her eyes.

Doris sat next to her. "You said it, Red. We done the best we could for her, though. That's gotta count for something."

"Not enough," Dela said softly.

"No, I guess it weren't, but the sad truth is that Charlie needs us more than she does, now he's back. Ain't no way I'm gonna let him go Rose on us and fade away."

Dela hiccupped a sob and ran from the room.

"Guess I gotta work on my pep talks," Doris said.

"No, I think you nailed it." Anne took Dela's seat next to Doris. "Every time I think about Cappa, I want to break down in tears. I miss her terribly, but in case ..." Anne swallowed the terrible thought, but it bubbled up like bile in her throat. "In case she doesn't come back to us, we have to focus on the survivors, support each other, and heal, so we don't end up like poor Rose."

"Charlie ain't gonna heal until he grieves," Doris said. "And he ain't gonna grieve until he accepts she's gone."

"And that won't happen until he's tried everything, including rebuilding her from the ground up."

"In other words, we could be on watch for a while."

Anne nodded. It was a grim thought, less for herself than for Charlie, who may cling to false hope for months or even years, only to be crushed if his efforts ultimately failed.

Doris patted Anne's knee. "Well, for now I'm gonna think positive. If Mark's having stuff shipped from Graven, might as well have them bring Cappa's wardrobe so we have some fresh dresses to change her into. She hated wearing the same clothes two days in a row."

"*Hates*," Anne said with a gentle smile, though despair sat like lead in her chest.

"Hates, right." Doris smiled weakly, then headed off, leaving Anne alone.

No sooner had she disappeared down the tunnel, however, than John peeked into the common room.

"Sorry, Mother, I know this isn't a good time, but we've just received intel, and ..."

Anne smiled, despite the heaviness in her chest, and patted the spot beside her on the bench. "You don't need to be timid around me. Come sit."

John did so, his back rigid despite Anne's welcome. Worry radiated through his bond — not about whatever news he carried, but about how Anne would take it.

"It's all right, John. If I haven't broken by now, I doubt whatever you have to tell me will push me over the edge."

They were brave words, but the fist clutching Anne's chest became painfully tight. Given his occupation, John's threshold for what he considered bad news was higher than most — and his news was almost certainly bad.

John heaved a sigh. "As you can imagine, our government operatives have been keeping a closer eye than usual on Russia since the incident with the alien spaceship, monitoring news, media, satellite feeds, and the like."

He pulled out his phone and brought up a satellite image. The picture showed squads of workmen setting up large machinery around an enormous crater. A portion of ruined black hull could clearly be seen at the bottom. Overall, the spaceship appeared far more intact than she'd hoped.

"It couldn't be helped," Anne said. "The spaceship is in their territory, and apparently power reactor explosions don't carry the same radioactive fallout as traditional nuclear weapons, so it shouldn't be a surprise that the Russians have already moved in."

With luck, it would be years before the Russians discovered how to use the alien technology, let alone power it. Charlie and Mark had supposedly retrieved artifacts of their own. By the time the Russians came up to speed, the boys would hopefully have made enough headway to ensure Russia wasn't the only world power sporting alien technology.

"As you say, Mother, but I only showed you that picture to lend credence to this one."

John opened a Russian media site, but Anne didn't need to understand the words for her mouth to go dry with fright. A blurry photograph took center screen, the kind she'd expect fanatics to wave around as irrefutable proof of Sasquatches or the Loch Ness Monster. Taken at the edge of a forest on the outskirts of what appeared to be a rural town, a pixelated, metallic, four-legged beast could be seen stalking between the trees.

Even out of focus and at low resolution, it matched Mark's description of the alien's hound-like exoskeleton exactly.

"This picture was taken yesterday in a small village a hundred and fifty miles southwest of the alien ship," John said. "Wherever it's going, it wants to get there fast."

"I ... I don't suppose we have troops in the area? Fighter jets, or ..."

Or anything to destroy that thing.

The Entity was in their base. She had no clue if the alien knew that, but it would undoubtedly be searching for its planetary engineering component — the core of its colonization plans. The last few months had, sadly, taught Anne to err on the side of paranoia.

"Unfortunately not," John said. "Even if we did, we'd have to be very careful. After those nuclear explosions, world powers are on a hair trigger. The slightest aggression could spark World War Three and save the alien the trouble of killing us itself."

"Don't give it any ideas." Anne squeezed her eyes shut, but the haunting picture of the mecha beast wouldn't go away. "Does Zima know?"

John shook his head. "I thought you'd want to know first. I'll find her and relay the news."

"No!" Anne covered her panic with a clearing of her throat. If she knew her wife, the only visitor Zima was in any shape to receive right now was Anne. "She's a little ... tender, with the homecoming and Charlie and all. It would probably be best if I told her."

She wondered why she'd even bothered covering it up. Thanks to her sire bond, every First knew of Zima's problematic libido, and the lengths to which Anne went to satisfy her, with intimate detail. John's sympathetic smile hinted as much.

"Of course, Mother," he said without a hint of patronization. "Please let me know if you need anything."

"Thank you, no. I just need to find my wife and ..." Anne looked around. For the first time since leaving the entryway, she realized that Tabby hadn't joined her.

Oh no.

Tabby had been glued to Anne or Zima's side every waking minute since arriving at Resistance headquarters a few days ago.

So if she isn't with me ...

Anne sputtered an apology to John, then dashed down the tunnel in search of her daughter, hoping she wasn't already too late to prevent yet another family-shattering catastrophe.

36

WHERE THE WILD THINGS ARE

Tabby pointed her flashlight down the dark tunnel. Water pooled around her ankles, making her sneakers slosh. She couldn't see the ground beneath the surface of the water, so she walked cautiously, assuming with every step that a deep pit lay just beyond.

"Zima?" Tabby called into the darkness.

Only her echo replied.

She continued sloshing down the tunnel. A woman had seen Zima go down this way, which was odd, she had said, since the pumps had never been replaced in this section of the complex, leaving it uninhabitable. The woman had also said it was a dead-end, so unless Zima was a magician, she had to be down here somewhere.

The tunnel began to slope downward, the water deepening with every step. It came up to Tabby's knees by the time she reached a four-way intersection. Each short offshoot opened into a separate room. She shined the light in each direction, half expecting a zombie or other freakish monster to jump out, then laughed at herself.

There are monsters down here, for sure. I just happen to be friends with most of them.

"Zima?"

No answer.

"Zima, come on, I know you're down here. I'm not leaving until I find you."

Other than the sound of dripping water in the distance, the tunnels remained silent.

"All right, I guess I'll go this —"

A ghostly figure stepped into view from the room ahead. Tabby clamped her hand over her mouth to keep from screaming, but relaxed when she realized it was only Zima.

"Please g-go," Zima said. Her whole body trembled.

"Oh, Zima … Mom and I should have known better. I'm so sorry."

"I d-do not hold either of you at fault. You should not have to f-f-fear showing af-fection for each other in p-public."

Tabby fiddled with her jacket zipper. "Is there anything I can do to help? I mean, do you need … relief?"

"Whatever my n-needs, I shall endure them. Although I am grateful for your assistance the first time, for Anne's sake, I d-do not wish to repeat it."

"Oh." Zima hadn't mentioned the incident since their brief discussion with Anne in the woods. It felt like an opening, so Tabby pressed further. "Is Mom upset about what happened?"

"I do not know," Zima said softly. "We still have not spoken of it. In light of other events, it seems a trivial matter, and, although I desire resolution, I do not wish to burden Anne further."

Tabby nodded. She hated having something as sensitive as this looming over their heads, but she could hardly argue. Cappa's death on top of everything else had stressed her mother to the point of breaking. Tabby wouldn't add to that unnecessarily.

She hugged herself against a shiver. Despite her jacket, the cold water was rapidly draining the warmth out through her legs. Returning to her bedroom and snuggling under a blanket sounded dreamy, but one look at Zima, who was shivering for a different reason, banished the thought.

Tabby couldn't just leave her to suffer.

"Zima, is my presence making things worse for you?"

Zima brow-knit. "I do not b-believe so."

"So it's okay if I hang out for a bit?"

"As you wish, though I recommend k-keeping your distance. In this state, my self-control is extremely t-tenuous." Zima backed away and gestured inside. "There is a t-t-table above water level on the far side of the room, if you would like to d-dry off."

"Thanks," Tabby said, and followed her inside.

A domed ceiling loomed overhead, like most other rooms. Rows of ancient reel-to-reel computers sat rusted and half submerged. Tabby waded to the only table and pulled her dripping self onto the surface.

Zima took position next to a free-standing chalk board on the other side of the room. "P-please tell me that you are not going to remove your p-p-pants."

"Never crossed my mind."

Tabby did, however, take her shoes and socks off. Her feet were still cold, but it was a drier cold, and brought some feeling back into her toes.

"I've got to hand it to you, Zima. You know how to pick a hiding spot."

"Yes, f-few would venture d-down here out of choice."

"True, but your bedroom would be just as safe, and a lot more comfortable."

"I d-do not experience the s-same physical discomforts as you. Cold to me is simply a lower t-t-temperature reading, and wet clothing means utilizing different but well-established m-movement algorithms."

"Must be nice," Tabby said, then mentally kicked herself when she realized Zima still shook with unrelieved desire.

Zima just shrugged. "It allows me to m-maintain focus during c-combat. As for my b-b-bedroom being safe, the Resistance members do not hesitate to seek me there, and when I am n-not with Anne, I have f-few excuses to refuse their summons."

"So it's easier to not be found."

"Yes."

Tabby wrung out a sock, dripping a steady stream into the water below. "I did the same thing when I was little. My hair was long and easily tangled. I hated getting it brushed, so I'd hide from my mom under the bed. She never did find me." She smiled. "I thought I was being clever, but I'm pretty sure she knew where I was."

"I suspect the same is t-true here, and they are m-merely respecting my wish to be alone, even if they do not understand why I w-wish it."

"Yeah, I can see how that would be awkward to explain. I'm not sure I'd be brave enough to tell anyone, either."

"It has less to do with m-my embarrassment than Anne's. She is a leader now. She has challenges enough without m-managing rumors about her wife's aberrant desires. Or about inappropriate b-behavior between her wife and d-d-daughter."

"That might explain why Mom hasn't talked to either of us about it yet. The Firsts are constantly in her head. They would have picked up on it, so she's probably trying not to think about it."

"P-possibly, but even if they did know, they are unquestioningly l-loyal, and would not hold it against her. No, I suspect the r-reason for Anne's silence is more p-personal."

Tabby laid her socks on the table. They wouldn't dry in this dank room, but it gave her hands something to do. "Is it getting better at all? Your urges, I mean, and ..."

"And s-seeing you and Anne together? The answer is n-no to both, which is unfortunate, because I have exhausted my l-list of possible solutions."

"Does that list include desensitization?"

Zima head-cocked.

"The reason your libido goes on overload when Mom and I are close to each other may be because it's a new concept, and your brain is still trying to adjust. Most people adapt to new things naturally over time, but sometimes they don't. One way to overcome that is overstimulation. Take the thing your brain can't handle, then expose it constantly and intentionally, so it's forced to adjust."

Zima stared at her with knitted brows. "What specifically are you suggesting that I overstimulate?"

"Well, me, for one."

Zima gasped and trembled harder.

Tabby quickly put her hands up. "Not like that! What I mean is ... you're turned on right now. You doubt your self-control, so you avoid being around me to prevent another incident. The problem is that by avoiding me, you'll never discover if you actually *can* trust yourself around me. It's a classic catch twenty-two."

"A b-bleak but realistic analysis."

"Right. Not what any of us want." Tabby sighed. "I have this dream of the three of us hanging out together on the couch, watching movies and having tickle fights and stuff. It may be stupid of me to even hope, since Mom is this big-shot leader now, and you're an important general, but ..."

"It is not stupid," Zima said. "My f-fondest memories are of the quality time Anne and I have spent simply reading to each other in b-bed, where she holds me and s-strokes my hair. It is in those t-times I feel most content, and while I do value our alone time, I look f-forward to including you in some of those activities."

That's when she feels most content ...

"Hey! I have an idea." Tabby grinned and patted the spot next to her.

"I d-do not think that is wise," Zima said, still trembling.

"I'm not suggesting anything inappropriate, but ... if we want to be a family, we're going to have to test our limits, and since you've stalled on your progress, I don't see a reason to wait." She patted the table again. "Just come sit by me. I want to try something. Your only job is to keep yourself under control."

"And if I c-cannot?"

"Then I'll take care of you, just like I did before, and I'll be the first to tell Mom what happened — specifically that we're trying to resolve this issue ourselves, and stumbled in the process. But for now, let's think positive. Okay?"

Zima hesitated only a moment before wading over to the table. She pulled herself out of the water and sat next to Tabby in one fluid motion, then gathered her trembling knees to her chest.

That's step one. Now let's see how bad my idea really is.

Tabby leaned back against an ancient computer tower, spread her arms, and motioned Zima over. Zima stared at her, brows knitted, but eventually nestled against Tabby's chest.

Zima's shivering worsened. Tabby stuck to her resolve and gently wrapped her in an embrace, careful to keep her hands off anything that may be stimulating. She rocked Zima back and forth, softly humming a pop song she couldn't remember the name of. Zima's dense weight mashed Tabby's spine into the cold metal computer, but she persisted.

"I d-d-do not believe this is helping," Zima said.

"Nonsense. You haven't jumped me yet, right?"

"No, but it will not be long."

Damnit.

Tabby's idea had been a long shot for sure — who knew if human psychology applied to artificial intelligences? — but she desperately wanted to reconcile the issue so they could finally be a happy family.

In a last attempt to sooth the trembling android, Tabby ran her fingers through Zima's doll-like hair in a rhythmic motion.

Zima gasped.

Tabby jerked her hand away. "I'm sorry, I'm sorry! I thought your hair was safe territory."

"Keep stroking," Zima said.

Tabby did so.

Zima's ragged breathing gradually slowed, and her trembling subsided. She melted into Tabby's embrace, so relaxed that Tabby thought she'd fallen asleep.

"Zima?"

"Yes?" Her voice was steady, with its usual calm.

"What the heck just happened?"

"Something I had not thought to try. Early in our relationship, Anne and I discovered that stroking my hair had an unexpected soothing effect. It became part of our nightly ritual, and is the method she used to rescue my core program from an infinite loop when I had been severely damaged. Had she not, I might never have awoken."

Tabby's mouth fell open.

"Yes, it was a traumatic experience for your mother, but I also consider it the true beginning of our relationship. That was the first time she confessed her love to me, and perhaps the happiest moment of my life."

"Man," Tabby said, sniffling. "You guys don't do anything small, do you?"

"On the contrary, it is the small things I treasure." Her ice-blue eyes looked up at Tabby. "Like this."

Tabby risked a kiss on her forehead, and was happy when Zima remained relaxed. "Small like this, right. Me soaking-wet, stroking your hair on a table in a dark, ancient, water-logged missile control center beneath a colony of vampires."

"Exactly." Zima head-cocked. "Was that sarcasm?"

"It was supposed to be, but I guess this really is small compared to a global vampocalypse, or attacking an alien spaceship."

Zima snuggled against her. "I would like to have been present for the spaceship assault."

"Maybe next time," Tabby said, laughing. "And thanks for sharing your and Mom's history with me. It means a lot."

"I keep no secrets from you. Only time and opportunity have prevented me from telling you our full story."

"We have time now."

"Yes, but I am enjoying this rare, quiet solitude with you."

Tabby took that as her cue to resume stroking Zima's hair, which she did.

"It is curious," Zima said after a while. "I added my libido shortly after Anne confessed her love to me. From that point on, our nighttime activities took a different form. We combatted my rising desires with expedient gratification, but did not think to try something as simple as this." She looked up at Tabby. "You are the only person other than Anne who has ever stroked my hair."

"Warm fuzzies" didn't describe the rush of joy that filled Tabby's heart. For several minutes, she could only hug Zima close before her throat relaxed enough to say, "Thank you."

"It is I who should thank you, but you are welcome nonetheless."

For a time, only the sound of their beating hearts and the occasional drip of water filled the chamber, until Zima turned her head to the entryway.

"Someone approaches," Zima said.

Seconds later, Tabby heard it too: sloshing water echoing in the tunnels beyond. She started to rise, but Zima shook her head.

"It is Anne," Zima said.

"How can you tell?"

"She is calling to us. Listen."

Sure enough, the unmistakable sound of her mother's urgent whisper floated to her.

"Zima? Tabby? Where are you?"

"In here, Mom," Tabby said loudly.

The distant sloshing became a roar. A wall of water splashed into the room. When it settled, her mother stood in the doorway, dripping wet from head to waist. Her large, dark eyes took them in.

"Are ... are you both all right?"

"We're better than all right," Tabby said with a smile, stroking Zima's hair.

"Tabby is correct," Zima said. "Anne, we can now be together as a proper family."

That did it. Tabby squeezed Zima tight. The tears she'd been holding back poured out in a flood of joyful sobs.

Her mom once again transformed into a wall of water, soaking everyone, but Tabby didn't care. Loving arms wrapped around them both, filling her with warmth and banishing the cold.

They were on a hard table, not a couch. The living room Tabby had dreamed of was a washed-out cave. The television was a cabinet-sized computer that probably hadn't run in fifty years. And, instead of tickle fighting, they held each other tight, with Anne and Tabby crying and laughing in equal measures.

Overall, it was better than Tabby had wished for.

Anne looked at Zima. Her smile faltered. "Honey, John brought some disturbing news before I came to see you. The alien mecha was spotted in Russia. The picture was blurry, but —"

"It was the alien mecha. Yes, I concur."

"You already know?"

"Yes. Russian intelligence reports indicate the spaceship's destruction was incomplete. They have found no evidence of the revived alien or its exoskeleton, nor appear to be aware of their existence, so I have been monitoring government and public networks for indications of its survival." She fell silent before continuing. "It is a task Cappa would normally have performed."

"And she'd trust it with no one more than you." Anne stroked her cheek. "Don't give up hope, honey. Charlie's on the job."

"It is difficult," Zima said. "I have examined her code. It does not work, nor, from what I can surmise, should it ever have, lending credence to the theory that her sentience was driven more by spiritual influence than technology. Were it a programming error, I would work tirelessly to fix it, but ..."

"You feel powerless to help," Tabby said.

"Yes."

"Well, maybe you should focus on something you can fix. How about flying over to Russia and pounding that alien bastard back into the ground?"

"I have given that careful consideration," Zima said. "With the current political climate, crossing their borders — or anyone's — would be difficult. My odds of locating the alien would be smaller still. Even if I did, I do not have enough data to forecast my chances of victory."

Tabby frowned. "So, what ... we're going to wait for it to come find us?"

"Yes, assuming it is even capable of tracking our location, and that is where the odds play in our favor. The most likely outcome is that another military organization in Asia or Europe will engage it first. Should they fail to destroy or capture it, the alien must then make its way through US territory, where it will face the brunt of America's Armed Forces. While alien technology is far advanced from our own, it is neither infallible nor indestructible. The US has many resources at its disposal, which, thanks to William's extensive infiltration, means we do as well, and I shall ensure they are put to effective use."

Tabby hugged her with a shudder. "I love you, Zima, but you're a little scary sometimes."

Zima looked at her sharply. "Please do not be afraid. As I have stated, the safeguards I have created for Anne also apply to you. I could not harm you even if I desired, which I do not."

"It was just a half-hearted joke. And a compliment, in a way. It means you're badass."

"Oh." Zima brow-knit. "You ... love me?"

"Mm-hmm. B-but not the way Mom does," Tabby said quickly, remembering how literally her stepmother took such statements.

"So I surmised."

Zima's strong arms hugged her tighter. It felt like heaven.

Tabby shivered. Zima's body heat couldn't counter her own damp clothes and her mother's cold, wet embrace, no matter how many warm fuzzies she felt inside.

"Your core temperature has fallen to ninety-six-point-five degrees Fahrenheit," Zima said to Tabby. "You are dangerously close to hypothermia."

Anne gasped and tried to disengage, but Zima pulled her back. "It was merely an observation. Allow me to compensate."

A soft electric hum emanated from her chest, growing louder until it reverberated from the concrete domed ceiling. Blessed heat radiated from her, effusing Tabby, and calming her shivers. Her stepmother was a Swiss Army knife of tricks, apparently.

Tabby gathered her family close and smiled.

An alien wanted to enslave vampires and kill everyone else to make room for its own colony. Even if it didn't, vampires were still dark whispers to the rest of humanity — creatures to be feared, fought, and eliminated. The Resistance would have its work cut out trying to change public opinion.

One look at her mother's kind, smiling face reassured her, however.

Nestled in the arms of the two people she held most dear —the master of the entire vampire race, and a notorious murdering android who was also one of the most caring people she knew — Tabby believed with every ounce of her overflowing heart that anything was possible.

ABOUT THE AUTHOR

Ryan Southwick decided to dabble at writing late in life, and quickly became obsessed with the craft. He grew up in Pennsylvania and moved to a farming town on California's central coast during elementary school, but it was in junior high school where he had his first taste of storytelling with a small role-playing group and couldn't get enough.

In addition to half a lifetime in the software development industry, making everything from 3-D games to mission-critical business applications to help cure cancer, he was also a Radiation Therapist for many years. His technical experience, medical skills, and lifelong fascination for science fiction became the ingredients for his book series, "The Z-Tech Chronicles", which combines elements of each into a fantastic contemporary tale of super-science, fantasy, and adventure, based in his Bay Area stomping grounds. Ryan's related short story "Once Upon a Nightwalker" was published in the *Corporate Catharsis* anthology, available from Paper Angel Press.

Ryan currently lives in the San Francisco Bay Area with his wife and two children. You can get in touch with him and see more of his work by visiting his website *RyanSouthwickAuthor.com*.

ALSO BY RYAN SOUTHWICK

ANGELS IN THE MIST

THE Z-TECH CHRONICLES BOOK ONE

An ancient, powerful evil is loose in San Francisco. The heart of Silicon Valley must fight back the only way they know how — with compassion, unwavering determination, and, of course, super-technology.

ANGELS LOST

THE Z-TECH CHRONICLES BOOK TWO

A vampire hunter has his sights on Anne Perrin, threatening to unleash the very evil she and her friends are fighting to contain.

ANGELS FALL

THE Z-TECH CHRONICLES BOOK THREE

Charlie's life force is fading. His only hope is an aged martial arts master in the remote reaches of China who, as far as Cappa can tell, doesn't like him very much.

ZIMA: ORIGINS

A Z-TECH CHRONICLES STORY

Even artificially intelligent recovering assassins need a home.

Available from Water Dragon Publishing in
hardcover, trade paperback, digital, and audio editions
waterdragonpublishing.com

YOU MIGHT ALSO ENJOY

ONCE UPON A NIGHTWALKER

A Z-TECH CHRONICLES STORY

by Ryan Southwick

Ellen Bloom just wants a normal working relationship with her colleagues at her old job. But, at this point, she'd be happy with a pulse.

BUILDING BABY BROTHER

by Steven Radecki

It seemed like a good idea at the time ...

GODDESS CHOSEN

BOOK ONE OF THE "GODDESS RISING" TRILOGY

by Jay Hartlove

The man who would beat the devil isn't a hero, but a ruthless madman.

MEMORY AND METAPHOR

by Andrea Monticue

Civilization fell. It rose. At some point, people built starships.